Twice Upon
a Time

Twice Upon a Time

Kent C. Griswold

PROLOGUE

This story could not have happened to anyone other than Steve Harris. No one else had lived his life, remembered his memories, knew his secrets, shared his parentage, or could have been in the same situation on that fateful day. People and their lives are in fact more unique than snowflakes, which, though each differs in size and appearance, are all generally some shade of white, composed primarily of water, and hexagonal in shape. Not illogically, though against all odds, it will happen again sometime.

This story is not just about Steve. It is also about Madaline. Madaline Wallace. So, why start with Steve? Madaline comes before Steve alphabetically. And let us not forget the fading cliché, "ladies first." Nevertheless, there is a method to my madness. Madness is, after all, a relative term. I have started with Steve because he is, as Madaline will not let him forget, six months and one day older than she. As we shall discover, moreover, it could be argued, as I am sure it will be, that God intended it to be this way. Back to Steve . . .

CHAPTER
ONE

On a cloudy evening when nightfall appeared to have come an hour or so too early, at a distance of half a football field—only three clean strokes in a rower's scull—Steve Harris could have passed for a handful of other members of the Harvard crew team pulling into Newell Boat House after a solo workout following the team's regular practice. As he drew closer to shore, a silent observer pulled on her sweatshirt to buffer her body from the growing chill lacing the late September air. Steve hauled his single scull from the murky waters of the Charles River and hoisted it overhead to carry it to its berth on one of the racks inside. As he came into the light, Madaline could see his nearly shoulder-length blond hair caked to his head with sweat and the spray from the river. Though Steve kept his hair long in the back as a half-hearted form of collegiate protest to parental control, his hair in front and on the sides was close-cropped because he grew tired of constantly flipping his head to get the hair out of his eyes while he was rowing. Madaline particularly liked his new style because Steve had let her cut it for him. She was quite proud because it was the first time she had cut anyone's hair. After she had shortened up the left side that was a bit longer than the right after the first round, it looked as good as any other cut she had seen on him.

It was not his golden hair, however, that first attracted Madaline to Steve. Rather, it was his eyes. Even when he was sad, his eyes still shined with a brilliance not unlike the bright blue screen of a computer's

Super VGA color monitor. She had to laugh at herself for thinking of that image after taking her first computer class, Natural Sciences 110, more commonly referred to as "Programming Bytes." One afternoon, Albert, the computer lab assistant, found her mumbling incoherently and blowing gentle air kisses to a blank computer screen. Albert did not get out of the lab much and found this highly amusing. Fortunately for her self-esteem, Madaline came out of her reverie before Albert was able to get his Camcorder battery attached. Though back in "real time"—in class that day, Madaline had learned that term for live concurrent time as opposed to "batch time" which could happen later—Madaline recognized the agonizing blend of pleasure and pain and knew that she was falling in love with Steve. Before diving into her homework assignment, she allowed herself to drift a moment longer imagining herself with her beloved for the rest of eternity. Little did she realize then what that could mean.

*   *   *

The latest shipment of plutonium had been divided into eight portions of various sizes. The two explosions scheduled for that day would help narrow the calibrations to within 50 microns. William Harris and his wife, Miriam, monitored the explosions via a lead and Plexiglas shielded video camera in their subterranean lab. William flipped the switch and watched the pencil on the launch pad in the lab. Miriam watched her husband; she would watch the video later. When the temporary burn on his retinas from the blue and white flash had cleared, William looked where the new #2 pencil had been. The eraser and metal band appeared to have melted into a pink and gold blob. The wood and lead of the pencil had largely disappeared leaving only charred remnants. The computers whirred as they registered and analyzed the latest data. William was pleased though he tried not to show it while he reported on the results to his wife. Miriam could hardly wait to write to Steve at college to share the good news. They were getting closer and closer to mastering the effects of atomic reactions on inanimate objects.

A short while later, the launch table had been cleared and the second, larger explosion was ready. This test was more risky and their nerves were taught. Miriam was at the helm this time. She activated the video and pressed her thumb down on the switch. A full floor away, through layers of concrete and metal, the sound of the explosion nearly deafened them. Miriam managed to close her eyes before she was blinded. The energy released from the matter in the second pencil and the plutonium exceeded their calculations. The damage to the lab would take days to repair. Miriam decided not to write to Steve about this. She did not want to worry her only son. They would certainly have better luck next time and she could write then.

*   *   *

Steve and Madaline did not meet until the second semester of their sophomore year. They had two classes together, though one was a lecture class in Economics with over 400 students so they rarely saw each other. The other class was philosophy of science that started the semester with 25 students, most of whom were seniors, but had dwindled to 14 by the final. Even though Steve was perpetually late to this class, Madaline generally sat near the back and Steve was usually able to find a seat next to her. They had sat next to each other the first day and Madaline had boldly, while trying to sound casual, said, "Hi!" Steve found her North Carolina accent beguiling. He mused to himself about how a "southern belle" could have gotten into Harvard with its competitive admissions process. He figured it must have had something to do with "regional diversity" which he had read about in one of the college catalogues. When she responded with poise and alacrity to Professor Brewster's first question about the assigned reading, Steve was impressed even though he knew her answer was wrong. When Professor Brewster congratulated her on her insightful and correct response, Steve's stereotype of southern women met the same fate as the earthworm he had placed in the microwave the previous summer. He had read about the consumer who had used her microwave to dry off her cat, Fluffy, after giving it a bath. She had sued the manufacturer for failing to put a warning label advising her against using her microwave for this purr-pose. Steve wanted to see if the earthworm would explode as the cat had purr-portedly done. It did.

Steve figured that a brainiac in such an eye-pleasing package could be beneficial to his grade in Phil-Sci. Besides, he was beginning to like her and the dulcet alto tones that enmeshed her lilting southern twang.

Over time, he would lose awareness of her accent, but he would almost always be comforted by the warmth of her voice.

Madaline got her long rich coffee colored hair and her hazel eyes from her mother who was born in Northern Ireland. Her high cheekbones and her height (nearly 5'9") came from her father who was born in the United States, but of Polish and Danish ancestry. Her great grandfather, Pietr Waloczasiewicz, had been renamed Peter Wallace when he had passed through Ellis Island many years ago. Both of her parents were heavy set, so Madaline was extra proud of her narrow waist which she figured was her own doing, not the result of thin genes. Her hair was very full and poured down over her chest and her back like lava straining to reach the inward curves of her waist. Madaline usually wore her hair down and let it stay loose instead of in a ponytail or tied with a ribbon. She had started this in seventh grade when she became aware that her breasts were not growing as quickly as those of her friends. She used her hair as a shield from the probing glances of the pubescent boys in her class who were now far too aware of these female appendages. Because of this one self-perceived shortcoming, Madaline never realized the totality of her beauty. She adopted the mannerisms of a wallflower, focusing on her books and declining any male advances that she believed were out of pity or in jest. She could not imagine that a guy could actually think she was pretty.

In Madaline's hometown of Durham, boys and girls were rarely friends. Guys might date a girl on the weekend, but the rest of the time, they spent with their buddies. Somehow, Steve seemed different. Madaline was not sure where their relationship was going. Steve and Madaline started studying together, but only in the afternoons and only in the library or coffee shop, never in either one's room. Unbeknownst to Madaline, Steve already had a girlfriend, Catherine, a sophomore at Wellesley College who had gone to Steve's high school in Pennsylvania. When Madaline asked Steve if he wanted to join her and some of her girlfriends that night to see "Casablanca" at the Harvard Square Theater, he mumbled something about Catherine and her recital, and declined.

Madaline felt a passing emptiness, but was not disappointed. She was not interested in "going out" with anyone right now. She wanted to focus on her studies. She did not need a repeat of her freshman year. She had dated a junior for almost four months. He had seemed so wise and worldly. He showed her around. He invited her to parties with other juniors who seemed so sophisticated. He took her to dinner at fancy restaurants in Boston. He seemed so perfect. Then he dumped her.

His idea of fun involved more than just spending time together. She enjoyed being intimate with him. He was a very passionate kisser and she learned a lot from him. Her boyfriends in high school had used their tongues when they kissed, but they were crude and inexperienced in comparison. He would caress her lips with his tongue and with his lips. He would explore every cavity of her mouth with the tip of his tongue. His tongue would press against hers and his lips would tighten around her mouth. When they embraced in this way, Madaline felt so safe. She knew that he loved her and would always protect her. She let his hands touch her in places where no one else had touched, except her doctor and her mother when she was young, but that she could not clearly remember. She soon forgot her paranoia about her breasts. His touch aroused new overwhelming feelings in her. She would feel dizzy and yet her senses would become crystal clear. She felt light as a feather and yet parts of her body felt like lead, unable to move. His movements would become more frantic and his hands would grope further beneath her dress. Madaline would panic and the spell would be broken.

She knew what he wanted, but she was not ready to give herself to him, or to anyone. Not yet. When this happened for the fifth time and she said "No, honey, not now," he pulled back from her. His face was contorted with frustration and anger. He stared at her in silence making her want to cry. She wanted to make him happy. She wanted him to love her. Why could he not love her for who she was, not for what she could do for him or to him? His face regained its composure. He said he was sorry. As he rose to leave, he said that he would call her. He never did.

*   *   *

Steve loved getting mail. He always stopped by the mailboxes on his way back from class to see what, if anything, had been delivered. There was usually some junk mail from the school announcing this change in the course offering or that speaker on whatever topic. Occasionally he would find a card from Catherine. She never included a return address, but he knew her handwriting and the cards were usually in a pink or lavender envelope. Even blindfolded he could recognize her cards—she always applied a few drops of perfume, Nordic Mist or something like that. She had told him several times what kind, probably dropping hints that he should buy her more as a gift.

He could usually count also on his mother to write. She would keep him up to date on what was happening around home—what new approach his father had taken on his research project—what the mother of one of his high school buddies had said when they bumped into each other near the cantaloupes—or that his grandmother, paternal grandmother, that is, who was visiting them for the month (Steve could sense the growing edge of tension in her handwriting), would not eat any vegetables except for peas. She would chew each one very carefully and then spit out the shells because "they were too hard for her to digest." "I am talking about pea shells, not orange peels or watermelon rind or peaNUT shells, just PEA SHELLS," she would continue.

Anyway, Steve always enjoyed getting his mother's letters. Even though she worked with his father and still took care of most of the household activities—vestiges of when the American Mom was married to the house—she still found time to write to her only son. The first week of Steve's freshman year, he had gotten a brief typed letter from his father saying how much he missed him around the house, then going on to talk about the progress he was making on their research project. Steve did not expect to get any more letters from his father. He was used to it. The summer he had gotten a job on a fishing boat at the Jersey Shore, his mother had written several times each week, often apologizing for her husband's failures as a correspondent.

One day in late February, after classes and a habitual attempt at studying in the library, Steve trudged through the fresh snow back to his dorm. His mailbox was empty. Steve blamed the college mail system that was notorious for delays. Harvard University Mail Persons—considered politically correct unless the Acronym was misused—were usually students enlisted as part of the financial aid program to help deliver the mail to all the dorms. They were bound by the oath, "to deliver the mail in a timely and professional manner," unless of course it was raining or snowing or they needed to study for a test or their girlfriend needed a ride home after class, or . . . However, the snow had not prevented all deliveries. Someone had slipped under the door a plain white envelope with "Steven Browning Harris" written on the front in a fine calligraphy. After putting down his backpack and removing his melted-snow-drenched sneakers—snow boots were not peer pressure approved—Steve opened the mysterious epistle. He discovered a simple, though elegantly engraved, invitation to a cocktail party for one of Harvard's Final Clubs.

His uncle, David, who had gone to Harvard back in the old days, as he referred to them, had told him about these clubs. Originally, Harvard men of strong social backgrounds were invited to join a club as a freshman. The following year, if they had proved themselves worthy, they would be asked to join a sophomore club, and so on until they were seniors and would be asked to join a "Final Club." Over the years, all of the clubs except the Final Clubs became extinct. There were nine remaining Final Clubs that now accepted men as early as their Sophomore years. One of the clubs tried to accept women, but their alumni, who provide over two thirds of the financial support for the club, vetoed this tampering with tradition, so these all-male bastions lumbered on un-swayed by the current political climate.

Steve felt honored to have been invited, but he was perplexed as to why. His parents were not by any means wealthy and he had not gone to a fancy prep school. Uncle David had told him that most of the Final Club members were white males who were listed in the Social Register. Steve had been unsure what the Social Register was or what it meant, but it had impressed him nonetheless. The cocktail party was scheduled for that coming Friday night. He decided to go check it out. He had heard this particular club referred to as "Utopia Unlimited" or "W" for short.

Steve arrived late at W. As he had been walking out the door, Catherine had called. She was upset that he had cancelled their date. She had been looking forward to seeing Fellini's latest film that had just opened. She did not like the idea of Steve joining a fraternity because she had heard stories about what those childish fraternity brothers did. Steve tried to explain that it was not really a fraternity and that he was only going to see what it was like. Catherine ended their conversation abruptly leaving a sour taste in Steve's mouth.

When Steve belatedly walked in the door, he was warmly greeted by Mark Haney, W's vice president. What surprised Steve about Mark was not that he seemed so hospitable or that he was wearing just boxer shorts with his blue blazer and Ralph Lauren tie, but Mark was black! As he looked around the room he saw other blacks as well as Hispanic and oriental looking men interspersed with the more WASPy looking guys. Mark grabbed him a beer and introduced him to some of the others. He met a Vanderbilt who spoke with a bit of the wired-jaw syndrome and the son of a Senator from Indiana whom he suspected was gay. He also met a member who had gone to a rival high school in Pennsylvania, a PUBLIC SCHOOL! Steve decided that this could be okay. He surmised that things had changed a bit since Uncle David's time.

Four weeks later, Steve had survived all of the getting-to-know-you events and was asked to join. He accepted.

His initiation was a memorable night for everyone except Steve. He passed out at the end and did not remember very many details the next afternoon when he finally rose off the sofa and stumbled back to his dorm room in his disheveled looking tuxedo. It had begun earlier that afternoon when he started to get ready. They had told him to be ready by 4:00 PM. At 3:50 he was showered, shaved, and dressed in his father's tuxedo. His father had outgrown it in the waist and thought that Steve might find some use for it with all of the formal dances at college. By 4:30 there was still no sign of his "Initiators" and he was growing nervous that he had somehow botched the instructions and this was part of the test that he was failing miserably. Around 5:00 he called the Club and was told to hang tight. Finally at 5:15, Mark and two other guys, one of whom Steve had never seen before, arrived dressed neatly in their tuxedos and carrying a large beer stein. They made no apologies. It was clear that they had started drinking earlier themselves. They took out a plaid blindfold and expertly bound it over Steve's eyes. The one that Steve did not recognize handed him the beer stein and instructed him to drink the W Punch. He said that once he had started drinking he should not stop. They would take care of him.

Steve expected beer. After the first gulp he stopped in horror. It was not beer. It smelled like ether. He was afraid they were drugging him and would abandon him in the middle of the woods with no clothes or money as his fear-monger friends had warned. He protested and they laughed. They insisted that he continue or it was over. Steve obeyed and finished off the whole stein. He learned later that it had contained two thirds vodka and one-third Cointreau. It was an 80 proof punch and it nearly knocked him out. His "protectors" led him out to the cars where several others were waiting, some of them in blindfolds.

The rest was only hearsay for Steve. As part of the initiation, they drove the group out to Wellesley. They told them that they were going to the Combat Zone in downtown Boston. For the blindfolded innocents they clarified for those still comprehending that this was Boston's red light district. En route to their misrepresented destination, they handed each initiate another beer to top them off. Near the campus, one of the blindfolded insisted he needed to take a leak. They helped him out of the car and he stood in the middle of a beautifully manicured lawn that could have belonged to the Dean. Curiosity got the cat, a young calico, that came up to investigate. They later told the initiate, who had been nicknamed "Peanut Bladder," that he had pissed on the Dean's wife's pussy.

Once at Wellesley, they found their way to the dining hall where a number of the White Hall young ladies were eagerly involved in their Friday evening meal. Mark and the other Protectors lined up the unsuspecting dupes and told them to drop their pants and to pump their hips as if they were making love to the air. They explained that the hookers wanted to see a good show. They told the performers that they should also shout out "squeeze me" and "eat me" and other expletives one would not repeat to one's grandchildren someday. It was childish, it was humiliating, it was disgusting. The Protectors were in hysterics urging on the inebriated cast. The girls were appalled. They had seen similar displays before from their immature intellectual neighbors, but this crossed over the boundary of decency. Most of the girls fled from the room leaving their half-eaten dinners for the kitchen staff to clean up later.

Among the first to escape was Catherine. She did not consider herself a prude, but she was mortified. She had quickly recognized Steve in the line-up in spite of the blindfold. She was certain that her girlfriends would also recognize his blond hair and broad shoulders. Her exit was so quick that she missed the lowering of the trousers and the display that followed. One of her more voyeuristic friends who stayed through the show gave her a full report later.

After three days had crawled by, Steve received a lavender envelope that carried no traces of Nordic Mist or any other perfume. It did carry a curt explanation of why Steve's calls to Catherine had not been returned. Catherine also made it quite clear that Steve would not be welcomed back at Wellesley, with or without his pants on. Twelve more phone calls and three letters from Steve went unanswered. Two months later, Steve asked Madaline out for ice-cream and to see a movie.

*   *   *

Because of the symphony of sounds conducted by the wind on the leaves in the trees and the small waves lapping upon the shoreline, Steve did not hear the gentle footsteps moving up the wooden dock behind him. Had the wind been absent, he still might have missed the soft creaking of the planks because of his labored breathing from the lengthy workout. Madaline adjusted her sweatshirt, savoring her surprise.

Steve and Madaline had only had two dates before the school year ended and they departed for their respective homes and summer jobs. During the summer, they traded a few letters and postcards. Steve missed the eloquence of Catherine's letters and he even missed the scent that lingered in his mailbox. Madaline's letters were not romantic but they always made him laugh. She had a unique approach of looking at the simple things in life and showing how absurd they could be. One letter was almost entirely about carrots. She ridiculed the name. Why would they name a vegetable, even though it is a root, after the rust on her mother's Oldsmobile ("car rot")? She made fun of her mother who bought a huge bag of fresh carrots because they were on sale and then forgot about them for several weeks while they aged in the vegetable drawer. One evening when her mother was deciding what to have for dinner, Madaline saw her take out the carrots and examine them. They were beginning to lose their firmness and their appeal. Madaline interjected a silly pun about "a peel." Her mother put the carrots back in the vegetable drawer and took out some frozen corn instead. Madaline asked her mother why they were not having the carrots and her mother explained that the carrots were not very fresh. Madaline asked why she was keeping them then and her mother responded that they were not bad enough yet to throw out. Two weeks later, Madaline found the unused bag of carrots in the trash.

In the two weeks they had been back in school, they got to know each other even better. They spent a lot of time together which was hard because they had no classes in common that semester and Steve's rowing and Madaline's editing work for the *Harvard Crimson* took much of their spare time. Some of their friends started referring to them as "S&M" which struck them as particularly ironic because they lacked carnal knowledge of each other, though they had seen the film together and they had kissed passionately that night after Steve had walked her home. In the process, Madaline learned one of Steve's greatest weaknesses.

As Steve settled his scull on the top shelf in the only remaining berth, Madaline swiftly moved in behind him. With flailing fingers and determination fueled by her chilling wait, she reached for his sides and tickled him mercilessly. Steve let out a muffled cry and with muscles taught he twisted around to confront his assailant. His shoulder smashed into one of the braces supporting the scull perched below his. When he recognized the culprit, though his shoulder was pounding and his heart was racing, he unclenched his fists and grabbed her firmly around the waist. He pulled her to him and planted a huge wet kiss on her uncertain lips. She had not meant to scare him so much and she did not know how he would react. They both started to laugh and Steve kissed her again, hard and long.

"Hi, Steve. Fancy running into you here."

"God, Madaline, you turkey. I could have broken your nose if I hadn't seen who it was."

"Whom it was"

"Geez, Lin, you scare me to death and you expect me to use good grammar. Give me a break. Speaking of which, my shoulder is killing me. I think you owe me a shoulder and back rub. Let's get out of here. It's getting cold."

*   *   *

Three days later, Madaline was sitting in her room and a piece of paper slipped under her door. She got up quickly and looked through the peephole. No one was in sight. She opened the door and looked up and down the hall only to find it deserted. She closed the door and picked up the paper. She recognized Steve's handwriting.

TO MY LOVE

Mountain passes choked with snow,
Raging waves and undertow,
Foreign legions armed with guns,
Motorcar that barely runs,
Doberman with gnarling teeth,
Lava flows from far beneath,
Four papers and five midterms,
Whooping cough or flu-like germs,
None of these my true sweetheart,
Could keep my Love and me apart.

CHAPTER TWO

Life is full of little ironies. Harvard was founded in 1636 for men. Radcliffe was founded in 1879 for women. As time passed, they became more and more interconnected. Professors from Harvard began teaching some Radcliffe classes. Radcliffe students began taking classes at Harvard. Classes became co-ed. Dormitories became co-ed. Bathrooms became co-ed!

By the time Steve and Madaline attended Harvard (women were still accepted to Radcliffe but graduated from Harvard, go figure!), everything was co-ed except the administrations and endowments. The Radcliffe campus is only a ten to fifteen minute walk from Harvard Yard where the freshmen live. In their sophomore year, all residential students (less than 10% live off campus) are assigned to one of the nine Harvard Houses or three Radcliffe Houses. Here comes that little irony . . . Steve was placed in Cabot House at Radcliffe and Madaline ended up in Kirkland House at Harvard, considered to be the jock house because of its proximity to the IAB (Indoor Athletic Building) and the athletic facilities across the Charles River. Junior Year, to no avail, Steve tried to switch to one of the Harvard Houses to be nearer the boathouse and Madaline's dorm which he was anticipating might become a regular stop on his commuter express.

Steve Harris and John Wood had been roommates since their freshman year. They were very different and rarely saw eye to eye. John grew up in a large family with five brothers and two sisters, Steve was used to having his own bedroom and bathroom. Ironically, John was socially inept, Steve was gregarious and easily adapted to different crowds. John was a stereotypical pre-med, Steve was majoring in "Undecided."

But, John enjoyed playing pranks, and so did Steve. This common thread helped them through the rough spots in their relationship and formed the basis for a long lasting friendship. Their Junior Year, they were assigned housing with two other guys, Peter Foster and Peter Johnson, who both enjoyed a good joke, too. They tried variations of "Pete" and "Peter" and "Petey" but as they got to know each other better, they ended up on a last name basis, "Foster" and "Johnson."

Initially, they directed their pranks towards each other, but soon expanded, looking for new victims. John had a fascination with shaving cream. He had worked as an orderly at St. Joe's, the local hospital, over the summer. One of his duties had been to shave the male patients before surgery. This was not so bad if they were having cartilage repaired in the elbow or a tumor removed from the neck, but if they were having a hernia operation or hemorrhoids excised, he had to shave places he had never even seen before. He reconciled himself to the fact that he wanted to become a doctor and this was part of the learning process.

In some ways, John preferred this to Morgue Duty. Whenever a patient died, the orderlies had to transport the CTB (Ceased To Breath) to the morgue in the basement. John had been warned by one of his friends in white that a few of the other nurses had morbid senses of humor. The year before, they had paged one of the orderlies to take a body to the morgue. When he arrived, the body was already in the body bag on the litter, hospital jargon for a rolling cart. The orderly had expertly maneuvered the litter, in spite of the shopping cart-like wobbly wheel, down the hall onto the elevator. In the basement he had yanked open the vaulted door of the large refrigerated room they used to store the bodies until the undertakers would claim them. Suddenly, the body in the bag sat up and screamed. It was rumored that the orderly wet his pants. The body had been a nurse in disguise intent on getting revenge on the orderly for one of his earlier pranks.

John had never seen a dead person before this job. The first day he was there, the Director of Nursing had asked him to go to the morgue to get the wedding ring off the finger of a Mrs. Jorgensen.

The family was concerned that it might be stolen. John panicked. He agreed to cover an extra half hour instead of eating lunch so that the other orderly on duty would remove the ring for him. The task at hand had suppressed his appetite anyway. John decided then and there that he would not consider Pathology as a specialty.

After hearing about the phantom nurse, John would usually check his bodies to make sure they were dead. Once in the elevator, he would jiggle the litter to see if the body wiggled naturally. If rigor mortis had set in, the body might not move the same. John would feel guilty on those occasions when he actually hit the CTB to make sure they were in fact dead. He worried that the undertakers might find bruises. It was not until later in an anatomy class that he learned his concerns were unfounded. Dead people do not bruise like the living because the blood is no longer pumping.

One evening, John was working the 3 to 11 shift with Anthony. Anthony had been an orderly at St. Joe's for eight years. He was studying by mail to be a medical technician. He was always overly precise and annoyingly officious. He wore designer glasses with his initials on the frame. His orderly whites were always freshly washed and neatly pressed. He never let John forget who was in charge, though John was not sure who had died and made him king. John had gotten tremendous hidden pleasure earlier in the evening when he had been helping Anthony lift Mr. Frangolini from his bedside chair back into bed after dinner. Anthony had instructed John to take the upper body while he would take the legs. John did not need his two years of college education or his four weeks on the job to tell him that the upper body was where most of the weight was contained, but he obligingly complied. As they lifted Mr. Frangolini's frail body from the chair, the blue lined padding—referred to as a "chuck"—which a nurse had placed on the chair in case of accidents came unstuck from his naked rear end. It had been temporarily glued there by a recent bowel movement, induced by the leathery pot roast and bland instant mashed potatoes from dinner the night before. The chuck slid off of Mr. Frangolini's bottom and continued its slow decent down the right leg of Anthony's pristine white pants. As Anthony jumped back, still holding onto Mr. Frangolini's legs, the patient's catheter came out and a pressurized spray of urine jetted about the room furthering the discoloration of Anthony's pants and shirt. John even saw a few drops running down Anthony's cheek, though they could have been sweat or more likely tears.

Several hours later, with Mr. Frangolini in his bed nestled in the third linen change of the day and Anthony freshly showered and wearing his spare pair of whites which were kept neatly folded in his locker, the orderlies were called to the Emergency Ward. Dr. Evans requested a morgue litter for room 2. John helped Anthony get the CTB, a 19-year old motorcycle accident by-product, onto the litter and into the elevator. Before the elevator doors could shut, John told Anthony that he had to help get someone back to bed at First Center. Leaving Anthony alone with the body, John headed towards the stairwell leading up to the first floor. After the elevator doors shut, he hustled around the corner to the stairwell connecting the ground floor to the basement. Because the hospital elevators were notoriously slow, John had plenty of time to get to the basement and position himself outside the elevator. The hospital basement is a maze of steam-pipes, electrical connections and hallways running between the boiler rooms, maintenance departments, storage rooms, some overflow instruction classrooms and the morgue. After 5:00 PM the basement is deserted. At 10:00 PM the basement automatically shifts to low-level lighting until morning. At 10:35 PM when the elevator door opened, the only noises in the basement were mechanical switches and rumbling steam pipes. When John came up behind Anthony who was backing the litter off the elevator and said "boo!" the bowels of the hospital reverberated with a dissonant blend of the screams of one terrified orderly who collapsed in fright onto the floor of the grungy elevator and the sadistic laughter of the other. Fortunately, Anthony's shift was almost over because he did not have any more uniforms into which he could change.

The next day, Anthony cornered John in the locker room and before John could break loose, he had emptied an entire can of shaving cream into his pants. It was a very long summer for John, but he learned a lot about the medical profession and more importantly gathered some new ammunition for College Pranks, Part III.

*   *   *

Shaving cream. John initiated Foster and Johnson into their rooming suite by filling their shoes with shaving cream three mornings in a row while they were showering. Not wanting to have Steve feel neglected, John included his shoes on day four. That night while John was sleeping, Steve helped Foster and Johnson shave off one half of John's collegiate attempt at growing a mustache. John finally woke up when they placed one of his hands in warm water. That trick never worked in camp either.

Steve and John and the Petes shared three bedrooms and a living room. They traded off on sharing the larger bedroom between two of them so that the living room could be kept for studying, relaxing and entertaining. There were two bathrooms on the hall that the thirty-eight residents shared. In the beginning of the year, the twenty men and eighteen women voted on whether to have single sex or co-ed bathrooms. Everyone except for three of the females voted for co-ed. The solution was to make the larger bathroom co-ed and the smaller bathroom for women only.

Steve had grown up with his own bathroom and was not used to sharing it, especially with women. It was a difficult adaptation for him to grow accustomed to shaved legs sitting in the stall next to him. Students sharing the same bathroom rarely dated each other because the mystery and illusion of glamour were shattered by watching him shaving or her putting on make-up in a moth-eaten bathrobe.

Occasionally an innocent victim would fall prey to their shower attacks. There was a large bucket in the janitor's closet that was rarely locked. This was used to dump cold water over the shower wall on each other. If they heard a high-pitched scream, they would run for cover knowing they had picked the wrong shower stall.

The showers also created some unintentional tension between the sexes. Apparently one of the guys who lived near the smaller women's bathroom did not deign to walk down the hall in the middle of the night. Foolishly, he failed to put the toilet seat cover back down after one of his stealth missions into the girl's room. One of the three co-ed nay-sayers discovered this egregious act and posted a sign on the door that said, "This bathroom is for women only. Men may not trespass. Whoever the ignorant faggot is who is not sure what sex he is, if you want to come to room 213, I will straighten you out."

Foster and Johnson saw this note as they walked down the hall around midnight to play some pinball in the common room as a study break. When they returned after 1:00 AM, they walked past the sign again. Just as they rounded the corner into the lower part of the small "r" shaped hallway, Johnson looked at Foster and said, "Bitch," referring to Alice who had written the sign. Foster, looking back at Johnson, saw Alice hiding around the corner in the short upper part of the small "r" with her back against the wall. When they got to their rooms, Foster had to grab a pillow to muffle his laughter because he was incredulous that Johnson could have said that at that very moment and that Alice could have been lying in wait there to catch any violators. Foster was not laughing the next day.

At 3:00 PM, Johnson heard loud knocking at the door. When he opened the door, he found Alice standing there with her boyfriend, a tough looking tackle on the football team. He glared at Steve and asked, "Is this the guy?" Alice said, "No." He grunted and told Johnson that his buddy had better watch out. Apparently Alice had thought that it was Foster who had called her a bitch and to her face. Steve, John and Johnson started teasing Foster that Alice was probably a black belt in karate and would kick down his door in the middle of the night. Foster dragged a mortified Johnson with him to explain what had happened. Alice and Foster never became best friends, but at least his door and his sanity remained in one piece.

*   *   *

After her first class in economics, Madaline decided that she definitely did not want to be an Economist. She also ruled out finance, investment banking, commercial banking, politics, manufacturing, anything to do with business, and anything even remotely connected with the economy. She felt that the "ic" most aptly described the rest of "economics."

Madaline briefly considered law. That loss of rational judgment quickly passed and she focused on engineering. But, most of the good engineering classes were at MIT and she hated the bus ride. As she steered away from the hard sciences, she started dabbling in other areas.

Madaline registered for a class in social biology. She liked the professor, an Indian named Ghandi, so she stuck with it. They covered such broad topics as the impact of the dwindling rain forests on the propagation of new species and the political risks of under-funding research for AIDS. With midterms approaching, Professor Ghandi abruptly switched gears once again. He lectured on the current theories relating to evolution.

He explained how the universe is comprised of a constant total of energy and matter. The only way new energy can be created is by the conversion of matter to energy, and vice versa. Einstein's Theory of Relativity states that energy equals the product of mass and the speed of light squared. A small quantity of mass can generate a large amount of energy. Some scientists believe that the world as we know it began with a big bang. All the energy and matter in the universe were compacted into a tight sphere no larger than a single star. This concentration of energy and matter defied all principles of physics that we accept today. Electrons and neutrinos and quarks and quasars were in constant flux. Electrons and protons melded together forming neutroids releasing more energy and allowing the cosmic mass to compact further until a single neutroid at the core erupted under the astronomical pressure. The electron and proton split absorbing energy from neighboring particles setting off a tremendous chain reaction. The particles repelled each other with a force estimated by one person to be the equivalent of 61,943,133,268,347,080,244,721,668,523,992,069,433,700,000,000,000,000,000 nuclear bombs, more or less. If anyone had been alive to hear this bang, it would have sounded like no tree you have ever heard falling in the woods.

As the particles disbursed out into the heavens, over millions of years, the reactions began to slow and particles cooled and came together to form intergalactic dust and comets and asteroids and planets and moons and stars and galaxies. Charles Darwin pioneered the concept of evolution that he described in his writings, "Origin of Species." He believed that human life evolved as a result of random mutation and natural selection. His associate, Thomas Huxley, used these ideas to address the widely accepted religious concepts of creationism. He posited that mankind is not an intentional creation of God, but rather derived from animal ancestors which were derived from even more primitive life forms. Man has achieved global superiority because of an opposing thumb and the ability to reason and remember. Man may continue to evolve if his ability to reason can keep his species from eradicating itself and others through destructive competition or greed.

At the end of his lecture, Professor Ghandi asked each student to prepare a paper on how different societies could ignore the scientific evidence and create other theories or beliefs to explain their existence. He suggested that those interested might want to attend the service that Sunday at Harvard Memorial Church where a visiting Theologian would expound on the latest Doctrine on Adam and Eve and creationism.

That evening after dinner, Madaline walked up to the Radcliffe Quadrangle to visit Steve. As she was walking across the Quad to Steve's dorm, she heard the fire alarm go off. This was not an uncommon occurrence for most colleges. Two weeks before this, Madaline's roommate, Ellyn, had been doing a cartwheel in the hall and had triggered the alarm with her foot as she completed an off-balance attempt. Some students regularly pulled the alarms as a joke. It is unlikely any of them knew that the Cambridge Fire Company #1 fined the University $600 for every false alarm.

Madaline located Steve in the swarming crowd of students gathered in the quad. She also spotted John over talking to one of the firemen.

"Wow, Madaline, you're not going to believe this. John's in a shitload of trouble. I can't believe he did this. Look at all these fire trucks."

"Whoa, Steve, slow down. Tell me what happened. Is everyone okay?"

"Sure. Yeah. Um, okay, let's see."

"Take a couple of breaths and start from the top."

"You know how John's pre-med, right, and how pre-meds can get a bit competitive. Well, John was talking to Jessica in her room. Jessica's pre-med also. Jessica was bragging how she had already finished her term paper for her bio-chem class. It's not due until the end of next week. John has been working really hard on it, but he's not sure he'll be able to finish on time. He was only kidding, but Jessica got really upset."

"What did he do, and why are all the fire trucks here?"

"Jessica was showing John her paper which was already typed, and John grabbed it and ran back into his room. Jessica chased after him calling him a 'super geek'. John locked the door behind him. Jessica kept calling him names and getting more upset. John thought this was pretty funny. He opened the window and stuck Jessica's paper on the ledge outside to hide it from her. Then he took our metal trashcan and dumped out part of the trash and lit what was left on fire. He put the can next to the door. After the fire was going, he unlocked the door. When Jessica opened the door, the open window and the vacuum of air from the hall caused the flames to leap up right towards Jessica. Some loose paint on the doorjamb started to curl up and burn. I was in the bathroom washing my hands when John came running in to get some water. We used the bucket from the janitor's closet. When we threw water on the basket and the doorjamb that had caught on fire, smoke billowed everywhere. Little pieces of mostly-burned ash started floating down the hall. Then the fire alarm went off. Someone screamed when she came into the hall and saw the smoke. After that, lots of people poured out of their rooms to see what was happening. Look, I can see Jessica's paper there on the ledge. I'd better find her and tell her that her paper didn't spontaneously combust."

"Steve, wait. Before you go, I need to ask you a question. Then I really need to get to the library to study. I know that you're not much on going to church, but I was wondering if you would go with me on Sunday. I have to write a paper and I have some questions already that I want to discuss with you afterwards. Do you mind?"

"Whatever will make you happy, dear."

"Thanks, Steve. I hope John gets off okay."

"Bye, Hot Lips." Steve kissed her three quick times before running off to find Jessica and to assist John in case he needed bail posted or an alibi or help cleaning up the mess.

John received a thorough reprimand from the fire chief and later from the Resident Assistant, and finally, a form letter(!) from the Dean of Student Affairs highlighting the seriousness of his playing with fire. John did not know that the worst punishment would come from Jessica, but he would not be the recipient.

*   *   *

Jessica is half Cuban. Her father had fled Cuba with his parents and sisters shortly after the Bay of Pigs fiasco. Jessica's mother had met her father when they were both studying at Harvard Medical School. Her mother had become an Ophthalmologist and her father a

Radiologist. Her two older brothers were also doctors (an Internist and a Dermatologist), but only the Internist went to Harvard. The younger one was mercilessly teased because he went to Yale Medical School instead. Her parents prepared her well for the rigors of pre-med studies while her brothers gave her the tools to cope with other pre-meds.

Two days after the fire, Jessica waited until she thought she heard John come back from class and close his door. She did not know that Steve, John, Foster and Johnson had all switched rooms the night before so that Steve and John would now be sharing the single room. It was actually Johnson who had gone into his new room where John used to live. Unlike the other two bedrooms, this one did not open up on the living room, only the hall.

Jessica crept out of her room and down to what she thought was John's door. She was armed with five pennies, a small hammer, a container of baby powder and her hair dryer attached to a long extension cord. She checked to make sure the door was locked. She could see the dead bolt crossing the small space between the door and the doorjamb. The door was locked. She entered phase one of her scheme. She stacked four pennies together and placed them carefully between the doorframe molding and the door. Holding them in place, she jammed in the fifth penny and using the small hammer gently tapped the fifth penny the rest of the way into place. With the five pennies wedged in there, the pressure against the deadbolt was too great for the occupant to turn the small knob inside in order to release the deadbolt to open the door. John, as she thought, had been successfully "Pennied-In."

Phase two. She opened the container of baby powder and poured a generous supply along the width of the base of the door. The doors were designed with enough height to pass over carpeting without binding, but none of the rooms had carpeting. With an evil grin of retribution passing over her mouth, she turned on the hairdryer blower to full power and ran it back and forth across the base of the door. A thick cloud of baby powder went billowing across Johnson's new room. Jessica's evil smile widened to a full sinister grin when she saw the door knob turning and could hear her victim struggling to open the lock which had closed so easily only moments before. Jessica stood there reveling in her victory. She heard steps coming down the hall.

As she turned to share the story of her conquest with the approaching audience, her jaw dropped in disbelief and despair.

"Please don't look so angry, Jessica. I didn't mean for the joke about your paper to get so out of hand. I am happy for you that you have finished it already."

"John. I think there is someone in your room."

"It's probably Johnson. We switched rooms last night. I'm in with Steve now."

"In that case, I think I need to apologize to Johnson. This was meant for you, you jerk." She showed him her handiwork. John started laughing and Jessica joined in. When Johnson heard the noise in the hall, he started banging on the door for help. Jessica put the baby powder, hair dryer and hammer back in her room while John knocked the pennies out with his key. Jessica returned in time to be greeted by a powdered Johnson wiping his eyes and surveying the settling blizzard in his room.

"Johnson, you look like you've seen a ghost."

"What the hell happened?"

"Jessica and I saw two guys standing outside your room. They ran down the stairs before we could see who they were. We didn't realize anything was wrong until we saw the baby powder on the carpet outside your room and Jessica noticed the pennies. You're lucky we came along when we did." John winked at Jessica. She tried not to like him, but she could not help it. Together, they cleaned up Johnson's new room while he took a shower.

Two years later, John and Jessica were married. During the service, John's grandmother passed out from the heat. Someone on the right side of the church yelled, "Is there a doctor in the house?" Half of the left side of the church stood up. John's grandmother was fine after she had a sip of water, and the service continued without interruption.

CHAPTER
THREE

Sunday morning, Steve met Madaline outside the church. Steve was a few minutes late and the service had started already. Madaline brusquely ushered Steve inside and they found some seats near the rear.

Madaline looked very devout in a simple blue dress with small white polka dots. Her neck was adorned by a single string of imitation pearls. The top button on Steve's white shirt strained to stay fastened around his muscular neck. It was the first time that Madaline had seen him wearing a tie. She liked it.

After a few songs and some scripture readings, one of the assistant pastors, whom Madaline had heard preach once before, rose to make announcements. She did not remember his name. The program which they had handed her as she was seated was of no help either because it listed three assistant ministers any of whom he could have been. It was not very important in the greater scope of things, but she felt disrespectful and somewhat irreverent not to remember his name. He had a neatly trimmed dark beard, so for lack of a better title, she thought of him as the "Bearded One."

There were quite a few announcements on this Sunday. The Bearded One invited everyone to stay after the service for coffee and refreshments in the recreation hall. He encouraged everyone to greet the person seated to either side and in front and behind. After the general murmur of friendly salutations to unknown faces, the noise subsided and the Bearded One continued. He announced that the Visitation Committee would be meeting in the Narthex at 2:00 PM to call on homebound members and those in the hospital. He invited anyone interested to join them. Madaline was very tempted to do this until she remembered the paper she needed to write and the reason she had brought Steve. She looked over at Steve who was yawning for the umpteenth time and she elbowed him in the side. He quickly covered his mouth while continuing his lion-like gasp for breath.

After thanking a few people for their help on various projects and listing the numerous events happening in the coming week, the Bearded One said, "It is with great pleasure that I now introduce to you the Reverend Doctor Marcus McPhinney. We are very fortunate to have him here with us today. He is in the United States for two weeks to visit his daughter and her family in Lexington. Dr. McPhinney is the senior pastor at the First Presbyterian Church of Glasgow in Scotland. He will be at the reception in the recreation hall after the service to greet everyone individually. Please join me in making him feel very welcome."

Dr. McPhinney had been seated behind the pulpit hidden from view. When he stood, he towered over the Bearded One. He appeared to be in his early sixties. He had longish wavy hair which was salt and pepper colored. And he had a beard. Madaline would have to come up with a new title for the Bearded One, but her attention was focused on other things now. That could wait. When Dr. McPhinney started to speak, a lovely thick Scottish brogue poured out. "I'm delighted to be here today. This church and this university dating from the seventeenth century represent magnificent symbols of the developing history of this young country. The church where I usually spend my Sunday mornings addressing a congregation not unlike this one was built in 1397. They believe that it was built on the site of an old Roman Temple that dates back to the twelfth century. History has always fascinated me. I am glad to see so many young faces out there this morning. The sad thing about history is that so many people do not like it because they are forced to study and memorize meaningless dates and places while in school. History should be fun. History has countless stories filled with many bewitching and bewildering characters and events. We can learn a great deal from our past.

"I would like to take us back in time today, even before the Romans decided to vacation on my island. It seems that the Romans were always bloody well causing problems back then. Just ask Jesus.

"It's hard to know exactly when—the Bible is not always very specific—but we reckon it was sometime around 6000 years before Christ breathed his first human breath in a dank manger in Bethlehem. The Book of Genesis reads, 'In the beginning God created the heavens and the earth. The earth was without form and void, and darkness was upon the face of the deep; and the Spirit of God was moving over the face of the waters.' I guess God must have been pretty lonely back then. After all, he didn't have much history to study and memorize.

"The first chapter of Genesis continues, 'And God said' "Let there be light;"" and there was light. And God saw that the light was good; and God separated the light from the darkness. God called the light Day, and the darkness he called Night. And there was evening and there was morning, one day.' In these words, God tells us that the six days and nights which were used to create the world were truly just six 24-hour periods. God's power is indeed unlimited and unquestionable. In under 9,000 minutes, he created mankind and gave us a nice place to live, and he had no work crews or computers or pre-fab materials to make his job easier.

"Genesis goes on to tell us about the rest of creation. On the second day—let's call it Tuesday—God created Heaven. On Wednesday, He separated the land from the sea and planted the Earth with plants and trees laden with fruit. On Thursday, the sun and moon and stars appeared.

"The expression, 'Thank God it's Friday,' has greater importance than many of you may realize. Without Friday, we would have neither fish in the sea nor birds in the sky. This is why many of our Catholic brethren celebrate the arrival of Friday by eating fish. Saturday morning, which many of you laze through either sleeping or watching those wretched American cartoons, is when God created animals. Later on in the day he decided to add one more animal, this one in His image and with power over the others. He called it 'Man' and formed it of the dust of the fields. Finally, God was able to take a break. On the seventh day, Sunday, he rested and declared that Sunday should be hallowed."

As Madaline listened to Dr. McPhinney, she realized that now she had more questions rather than fewer. The concepts of creationism which were so generally accepted differed significantly from the scientific fact. She could see why there was such a battle in many school districts, particularly in the more fundamentalist areas in the south, about how evolution should be taught in the schools.

Dr. McPhinney, his brogue becoming less evident to his listeners, continued with the story of Adam and Eve. He told how Eve was made from Adam's rib so that Adam should not be lonely. He told of the Garden of Eden with its lush plantings and abundant food. He described the river that flowed from Eden through the garden and then divided into four rivers, Pishon, Gihon, Tigris, and Euphrates. He said how Adam and Eve were naked and were not ashamed. He spoke of the tree of the knowledge of good and evil that God warned Adam and Eve to avoid, for if they were to eat of that tree, they would die that very day. Finally, he related how the serpent convinced Eve who then convinced Adam to eat of the forbidden fruit to be able to see good and evil as could God. Adam and Eve became ashamed of their nakedness and hid behind garments of fig leaves. God punished the snake by condemning it to crawl in the dust. He told Eve that woman would be subservient to man and would suffer great pain in childbearing because of her failure to obey His command. Finally, He chastised Adam for being influenced by his wife and sent him away from the Garden of Eden and its bountiful supply of food that God had arranged for them. From that day forth, man would have to struggle to grow and to gather his food.

Dr. McPhinney concluded with, "Because the hour grows late, we will save the stories of Cain and Abel and Adam's great-great-great-great-great-great-great-grandson, Noah. As you go forth into the world from this day forth, remember that God is a great and loving God, but that he has high expectations of His creations. Try to do that which is good. Render to no man evil for evil. Do not abuse God's compassion and willingness to forgive by sinning recklessly. Without God's goodness, we are merely dust. Let us pray . . ."

After the service, Steve and Madaline made their way to the recreation hall. Because they had been sitting at the rear of the church, they were able to exit quickly and make their way around the outside of the church. Madaline was charged with excitement at the prospect of asking a theological expert some of the burning questions necessary to complete her writing assignment.

When they entered the recreation hall, only a few people were there huddled around the two tables set up at the far end. One table contained four large coffee urns, coffee cups, spoons, napkins, sugar, tea bags (one of the coffee urns had hot water) and those little cuplets of cream which always spit a drop or two when the lid is peeled off. The other supported trays of finger sandwiches and homemade cookies. The women on the Ladies Auxiliary Committee must have been busy.

As Madaline filled her coffee cup, she heard three girls her own age protesting the concept of the rib and woman's imposed punishment of subservience to man. They concluded that the Bible had been written by men and that their sexist bigotry had corrupted the true meaning of the word of God. They agreed that God's greatest mistake was when She invented man. As Madaline was absorbing parts of this conversation, ignoring Steve's comments about the missing crust on the sandwiches, she wondered why God had created both man and woman. Why make it necessary for both a male and a female to reproduce? Cells and many small organisms can reproduce asexually. Even some trees and plants can do it alone. Why must man and other animals die off if unable to find a suitable mate? At this point she looked over at Steve who was munching away on an oatmeal raisin cookie. She looked at his crystalline blue eyes and his square jaw and blond hair. He noticed her look and smiled back, wiping the crumbs off the corners of his mouth. Madaline concluded that she was glad God had created man.

The recreation hall was filling and Madaline saw no signs of Dr. McPhinney. Their early arrival advantage was fast eroding. As Madaline's frustration was rising, so was the level of noise in the room. The pitch took a discernable jump as a large group entered at the rear of the room. Dr. McPhinney loomed over the others who swarmed around him in a reporter-like frenzy reminiscent of sharks. Madaline abandoned on the table her coffee, still too hot to drink, and surged toward the swelling crowd.

Madaline got close enough to hear others asking, "Why did God create Man to be so privileged over His other creatures?" and, "Why did God in His great power allow the serpent to use his sinister influence over Eve?" and, "Why did God put the tree of the knowledge of good and evil in the Garden of Eden if He did not want Adam and Eve to eat of its fruit?" Someone handed Dr. McPhinney a plate with a few sandwiches and cookies. He managed to eat one sandwich in small bites between answering questions. Before Madaline could get her questions heard, a woman who had been at Dr. McPhinney's side announced that he was thrilled to have spent time with them today, but would have to be going now. Without further adieu, the two broke free of the disappointed throngs, waved their goodbyes and disappeared through the door from which they had entered.

Madaline found Steve still standing by the food table which was feeling much less stress on its spindly legs thanks to the ravenous efforts of Steve and other new found fans of the Ladies Auxiliary Committee.

"God, I hate when that happens!"

"Watch your language, Lin. We're still in church."

With breathless indignation, Madaline continued, apparently unremorseful about her irreverent slip, "They tell us we'll have a chance to greet him after the service and I couldn't get within five feet of him. And besides, he is supposed to be an expert, and I heard him say that God devised disease and war and suffering and mosquitoes because Adam and Eve ate of the fruit of the tree of the knowledge of good and evil. Why would God make men and women suffer because of something Adam and Eve did? We had no control over them. And if he meant for all men and women to suffer, why is life so unfair for some people? I'm perfectly healthy and my cousin, Andrew, has cerebral palsy. How does that make sense?"

"Don't yell at me. I'm not the bad guy. I agree with you, it's crazy. I suppose in a biblical sense, we now know good from evil, so it's up to us to decide whether to go to war and whether to feed the homeless. God has left us on our own to fend for ourselves hopefully following some of the guidelines he gave us in the Bible. I can't figure out why he invented mosquitoes, though."

"There are a lot of things that don't make sense. Steve, you're one of the smartest people I know when it comes to understanding scientific principles. I'll bet you can't tell me when the beginning of time was and when it will end. How can we exist if time never began? And what about space—where does that end? It can't end, yet it can't go on forever either. That theory about space twisting around on itself doesn't work for me either, because if it twists around like a giant roller coaster eventually bringing you back to where you started, then what is outside of the giant amusement park?"

"I don't really understand how space or time work either. These are concepts that have eluded even our greatest geniuses. We think we understand that space is three-dimensional. Think back to your geometry class with the X, Y, and Z-axes. Every point in space is unique. The closest distance between any two points is a straight line. The physics class I'm taking this semester is just getting into the Theory of Relativity and how it can explain some apparent anomalies about time and space. We had a special guest lecture by Stephen Hawking who teaches in England. He is in a wheelchair because he has Amyotrophic Lateral Sclerosis."

"That sounds terrible."

"It is. It's ALS, Lou Gehrig's Disease. He can't talk, so he uses a voice synthesizer. He hypothesizes that time is a fourth-dimension that runs forward. He explains this through a complex theory about entropy and release of heat, but his layman's explanation is that we can remember things that happened in the past but not in the future because they haven't happened yet. It sounds pretty obvious, but try proving it scientifically. I find this all especially interesting because my parents have been working on a project for the past several years that involves time and, to some degree, space. I got a letter from my mother this week that said they had made a major breakthrough. My father's original premise was that they could freeze objects in time through neutralizing the movement of the electrons within a molecule. His greatest fear was that the atoms might collapse without the centrifugal force of the electron. He hopes that the polarity of the electron and proton would maintain the structure of the atom. I'm hoping that they will explain more to me at Christmas or this summer and that the classes I am taking now will help me to understand better. It would be neat if I could actually help them in some way."

"That's pretty exciting, but meanwhile I have this stupid paper to write. I have to relate scientific fact to the Bible. I think that I'm going to stick with scientific fact since Professor Ghandi is a scientist. I'll explain that the Bible was written before much of our current scientific knowledge was available and that translations and interpretations may have altered the original teachings of the Bible. I will point out the factual improbabilities of the biblical stories as written. If the world were only 8,000 years old, how can we be receiving intergalactic radio waves and light-waves from stars that are millions of light years away? Even on earth, how would one explain the carbon dating of fossils indicating existence millions of years ago? The Bible never discusses dinosaurs. I suppose that one could argue that animals were created on Saturday morning and Man in the late evening and that the passage of time in the Bible was interpreted a bit loosely. After all, the Bible says that Adam lived to the ripe old age of 930 years. He had a son at the age of 130. My mother stopped having kids when she was 34 and she said that was too old.

"Now as far as scientific fact is concerned, I won't rule out that a little divine intervention would be most helpful. Without some key guidance from God, the likelihood of all of the correct elements and conditions for life forming out of the cosmic soup would have been minuscule. I won't fail to point out, however, that the sheer number of galaxies and stars and planets would not rule this out. In fact, there may be many other varied life-forms out there somewhere, but I'll save that for another paper.

"I think I'll also raise the issue that different religions have portrayed the image of God, or in some cases, the Gods, in vastly different ways. Why would an all-powerful God represent himself differently to different people? How does that sound?"

"Lin, I think it sounds like a good start. You might want to cover all of your bases and conclude that although you support the scientific evidence, as scientists, nevertheless, we haven't been able to prove the existence of God, nor have we been able to disprove it. Now, let's go grab a bite to eat."

"How can you be hungry? You ate half the food at the reception. I think I'll skip lunch and get right to the library while this is still fresh in my mind. As you know, time can play terrible tricks on the memory."

*   *   *

Harvard has never been a super power when it comes to football, though you might think otherwise from the fanfare which surrounds the annual Harvard/Yale Game the weekend before Thanksgiving. Mercedes and Rolls Royces line the fields for the pre-game tailgating parties. Candelabras, bouquets of orchids, and lobster feasts adorn the portable tables. Men and women alike parade about in raccoon and mink coats oblivious to the glares of those who are refraining because of the momentousness of the occasion from tossing red paint on their coats of death. Younger spectators attired in crimson and blue sweatshirts and hats pass by each other hissing derogatory epithets under their breaths. Attempting to promote a spirit of tradition, they avoid profanity in these exchanges. One might hear a Yale undergraduate saying, "Oh, was that a Harvard Class ring I saw on your finger when you were picking your nose?" or, a female Harvard Business School student regaling a Yale Law School student with, "Try to bring up your grades, otherwise I might not hire you when you graduate."

Steve and Madaline were looking forward to The Game. As juniors, they would finally have real seats in the horseshoe shaped stadium. As freshmen, they had been seated in temporary bleachers in the open end-zone. As sophomores, they had been forced to hold their noses and make the three hour trip to New Haven where it had rained most of the second half.

Steve, John, Foster and Johnson loaded up their backpacks with the necessary provisions: pints of whiskey and cognac, a quart bottle of Southern Comfort, chewing gum, potato chips, cigars, "Go To Hell, Yale" buttons, and, oh yeah, blankets, gloves and hats. They caught up with the band in Harvard Square and followed it down John F. Kennedy Street toward the stadium. The entire band was wearing pink and green sunglasses that clashed miserably with their crimson blazers. Steve noticed that many of the blazers stuck further out on one side in the rear. This pseudo-mystery unveiled itself when a slender flutist paused to take a swig from her band-issued silver-plated grain-alcohol-punch-bearing hipflask. No wonder the band marching formations looked more like a herd of wildebeests; their rehearsal (AKA pre-party) had started at 10:00 AM. Steve's eavesdropping gave him reason to believe that for some, the party had in fact continued non-stop since 10:00 o'clock the previous night.

Steve saw Madaline and her roommate, Ellyn, and four other girls waiting outside of Kirkland House. When they spotted the guys, they joined in the parade. Madaline came up to Steve and grabbed him around the neck and kissed him hard as if to say, "I missed you this week. We have been studying too hard. I'm glad we can spend some time together today." Steve's kiss back seemed to say, "Oh, baby!" During the kiss, they were halted in the street together forming an obstacle around which the other parade participants had to swerve. When they had finished saying, "Hello," in this non-verbal way, they had to jog to catch up to the others in their group. Everyone seemed so festive.

When they found their seats they were disappointed to find that, although they were in the stadium, they were in the very last two rows behind a column that supported the Parthenon-like platform overhead. If it had been raining, they would have appreciated the protection, but on a chilly, yet sunny day, this deprived them of the solar warmth. By the time The Game had started, Steve and Foster had already finished off half of the quart of Southern Comfort. Madaline was not much of a drinker but she decided to join in the fun and sipped from a bottle of Bailey's Irish Cream that Ellyn had brought. She sometimes worried about Steve and his drinking. He would occasionally get so drunk he could hardly walk. He had thrown up once all over her favorite suede shoes. She did not want to ruin his fun, however, so she refrained as best she could from being critical. After all, it was the Harvard/Yale Game and they were expected to beat Yale for a change. There is no way she could have anticipated what was about to happen to Steve.

Toward the end of the first quarter, there was a sudden commotion on the field. During one of the plays that was a foiled interception by number 77 on the Yale team, the ground near the 35 yard line appeared to part and a small device came into view. Out of the device a large black ball appeared to grow. The referees gathered around to watch, uncertain what to do. The stadium grew eerily quiet as the crowd watched with great expectation. At the ball grew above the heads of the referees and the milling players, Madaline could read "MIT" in yellow letters all over what was apparently a giant balloon. Without warning there was a tremendous bang as the balloon ruptured spewing fragments of black rubber between the 20 and 50-yard lines. The referees and players dove for cover. When their hearts had resumed normal beating, the crowd burst into thunderous applause. MIT had scored another victory.

Madaline had heard about other pranks which MIT students had attempted, some more successful than others. Because MIT does not have a football team, they aspire to contribute in some way each year to the entertainment factor of the Harvard/Yale Game. A few years earlier, the morning of The Game, a Buildings and Grounds employee discovered a remote triggering device hidden beneath one of the stands. An investigation uncovered canisters of yellow paint buried throughout the field and wired to spray giant letters "M I T" upon command. The field had been under guard for four days to avoid such potential incidents. The perpetrators were never caught and their method of entry remains open to speculation.

MIT is known for its technically and mathematically inclined, though sometimes warped, geniuses. One of Madaline's favorite stories was about the MIT fraternity named "ATO." Their clubhouse was located on the Charles River opposite the Sheraton Hotel. The fraternity brothers managed to sneak onto the roof of the hotel and permanently short circuit the "S," "H," "E," "R," and "N" leaving an eight foot tall red neon sign blazing "A T O" visible to most of Cambridge and much of Boston. Madaline wondered to herself what these extraordinary minds might create if their energies were focused in other directions.

After the mysterious device was removed and the field cleaned up, The Game resumed. Because the stunt could be traced to neither the Yale nor Harvard supporters, no penalties were assessed.

After the excitement of the time-out in The Game, a rowdy group two rows down began to bellow out a rendition of "The Freshmen Down At Yale." Steve and his roommates joined in hoping their added volume would enable the blue pissants on the other side of the field to hear their serenade. Madaline and her friends looked on with mixed amusement and feigned shock; they had all heard it before but felt that as young ladies they should act reproachfully.

> Oh, the Freshmen down at Yale get no tail,
> Get no tail,
> Oh, the Freshmen down at Yale get no tail,
> Get no tail,
> To relieve their great frustration
> They resort to masturbation,
> Oh, the Freshmen down at Yale get no tail,
> Get no tail.

Oh, the Sophomores down at Yale get no tail,
Get no tail,
Oh, the Sophomores down at Yale get no tail,
Get no tail,
So half the Freshman Class
Has to take it up the ass,
Oh, the Sophomores down at Yale get no tail,
Get no tail,

Oh, the Juniors down at Yale get no tail,
Get no tail,
Oh, the Juniors down at Yale get no tail,
Get no tail,
To relieve that awful yen
They go out with Princeton men,
Oh, the Juniors down at Yale get no tail,
Get no tail,

Oh, the Seniors down at Yale, they get tail,
They get tail,
Oh, the Seniors down at Yale, they get tail,
They get tail,
For half a pint of scotch
Any Smithy'll spread her crotch,
Oh, the Seniors down at Yale, they get tail,
They get tail.

As the song continued, more and more male voices joined in with an occasional soprano or alto rising above the rest. People began passing their bottles up and down the row offering their bounty to their musical brethren. Steve and Foster continued to drain their joint bottle of Southern Comfort. Arms were linked in other arms and around shoulders as the multiplying rows of songbirds began to sway back and forth. A bottle slipped out of someone's hand and ricocheted through the wooden stands to the concrete floor below. A spat of profanity momentarily interrupted the song as the owner watched the last of the brown liquid seep between the shards of glass. Too drunk to mourn for long, the owner rejoined the song more boisterously than before.

Oh, the Section Men at Yale, they get tail,
They get tail,
Oh, the Section Men at Yale, they get tail,
They get tail,
If they see a piece of ass,
They just keep it after class,
Oh the Section Men at Yale, they get tail,
They get tail.

Oh, the Strikers down at Yale, get no tail,
Get no tail,
Oh, the Strikers down at Yale, get not tail,
Get no tail,
After two weeks on the picket,
They've forgotten where to stick it,
Oh, the Strikers down at Yale get no tail,
Get no tail.

Oh, the Overseers at Yale get no tail,
Get no tail,
Oh, the Overseers at Yale get no tail,
Get no tail,
To assume their lofty titles,
They must give up their gen-i-tals,
Oh, the Overseers at Yale get no tail,
Get no tail.

Kingman Brewster down at Yale gets no tail,
Gets no tail,
Kingman Brewster down at Yale gets no tail,
Gets no tail,
For they say his wife is frigid,
And he just can't keep it rigid,
Kingman Brewster down at Yale gets no tail,
Gets no tail.

Oh the Bulldog down at Yale has no tail,
Has no tail,
Oh the Bulldog down at Yale has no tail,
Has no tail,
After four years behind those walls,
He's damn lucky he's got balls,
Oh the Bulldog down at Yale has no tail,
Has no tail.

After the final verse, Steve swilled the last of the Southern Comfort and handed the upside down bottle to Madaline as a trophy. Madaline glanced at the bottle and noted that Southern Comfort was 100 proof. Madaline knew that Steve and Foster would be in a lot of pain that night. She was right about Foster.

*   *   *

The Game continued without too much excitement on the field. The history books would show that Harvard did win by a score of 10—6 beating the spread by one point. Few spectators in the stadium near Steve and Madaline were paying much attention to The Game, but then again, not many ever did.

After the third quarter, Steve decided that he needed to go to the men's room. He was sitting near the end of the row in the very last wooden bleacher. By this time, no one much was sitting in their assigned seats and the steps were completely blocked off by drunken visitors and clusters of gossiping loiterers. Steve decided to escape off the end of the stand and drop to the concrete below where he could more easily make his way past the remaining obstacles. Steve slipped under the metal railing and started to lower himself over the edge. Part way down, he hesitated. He heard a ripping noise. A dull throbbing sensation made its way from his back to his alcohol polluted brain. It dawned on Steve through the haze that the ripping noise was the skin on his back being shredded by the rough edges of the planks that served as scats for the wooden stands. Steve analyzed the situation with a growing clarity. He figured that his two choices were to pull himself back up thereby digging the edges of the planks further into the already mangled section of his back, or to lower himself the rest of the way thereby digging up clean patches of skin. Trying to ignore the noise, he lowered himself another six inches and then was able to swing free and drop to the ground. He tumbled into a heap under the stands and lay there thankful that he could not feel the pain, but knowing well that he would not be enjoying any of Madaline's special backrubs for a while. He was reticent to tell any of the others about his stupidity. He did not know that the expanding swath of blood staining his shirt would expose his secret.

Steve made it back from the men's room in time to see the bleachers empty as the students, along with those reluctant to lose their youth, swarmed onto the field. In spite of the mounted police guard, the mob managed to tear one goal post from its mooring. The triumphant vandals paraded their conquest around the field before some horseless officers appeared from nowhere to halt their celebration.

When Madaline saw Steve's back, she grabbed Ellyn and asked for her assistance to make sure Steve got home without further damage. Madaline had decided that the other guys would be of no use. The two girls each took an arm and led Steve staggering and swaying back to campus. He stumbled twice, each time pulling Ellyn down with him. Madaline managed to get them both up and going again with great difficulty. At the entrance to Steve's dorm, she thanked Ellyn and apologized for her skinned knees. She said that she would meet her later for dinner because Steve clearly was not going to be much of a date that evening. Madaline got Steve into the bathroom where she assessed the damage. She gasped when she saw the gash down Steve's back. She insisted that he go to University Health Services. He refused. She persisted. He won. Madaline gave up trying to reason with a drunk and instead found a stool for him to sit on while she tried to clean him up. She found someone in the hall who had gauze and adhesive tape in his room. While she was playing nurse, Foster rushed into the bathroom and vomited in one of the vacant stalls. Johnson, who appeared quite sober, followed him in. He forgot his mission of helping his namesake when he saw Steve's back. Madaline was quite proud of her handiwork. The gauze made an impressive looking bandage.

Suddenly, Johnson curled up his nose at the smell emanating from Foster's stall. "Gosh, Madaline, I'm sorry about the stink. Foster already chundered twice on the walk back. Geez, what a struggle that was."

"He looks pretty bad. I was worried about the two of them drinking so much. By the way, that's a great expression, 'chundered'."

"I learned that from my father. He worked in Australia before I was born and still uses some Aussie expressions. Chundered comes from 'watch under'. Pretty graphic, eh?"

"These guys should sleep well tonight. However, I'm afraid Steve won't be able to sleep on his back for a few nights. You may need to check his wound tomorrow and see if you can get him to go to the doctor. He can be so stubborn."

Steve emerged from his drunken stupor to respond somewhat ineloquently with drool dripping from the right side of his mouth, "I am not!" He then dropped his head back onto the edge of the sink.

"I'm going to try to get Foster back into our room and in bed with a big bucket near by. We sure have gotten good use out of the janitor's bucket here. Foster was such a pain on the way back here. He was grabbing at every butt in sight. It was really embarrassing. I wonder if he'll remember any of it tomorrow."

"Hopefully we can all forget this and just chalk it up to experience."

"I wish I had a girlfriend who was as understanding as you are. I wonder if Steve realizes how lucky he his."

"I guess you just learn to take the good with the bad. At least we beat Yale."

Three days later, John talked Steve into going to the clinic. His back was not healing well. There was no scabbing yet and the slightest impact would cause the wound to start bleeding again. Steve still had a headache, too, but it was more from lack of sleep than from a residual hangover.

The doctor examined and treated the wound. He took some blood and a sample of skin tissue. Two days later, he called Steve and asked him to come back to the clinic. The tests had indicated a likelihood of a genetic bleeding disorder called "Hemopalpacemia." The doctor would prescribe a medication that would help with clotting. He advised Steve to avoid any activities, such as climbing down the sides of stadiums, which might lead to an open wound. This was a rare disorder and not much was known about it. He would want to do some further tests if Steve were willing.

When Steve left the doctor's office, he could still hear the doctor's words echoing in his head, "Don't worry, we have absolutely no reason to expect that this is life threatening."

CHAPTER FOUR

December in Cambridge can be a numbing experience. The fifteen-minute walk from Radcliffe Quadrangle to classes near Harvard Yard can feel like an eternity. There is a small crimson shuttle bus that makes the rounds of the various campuses, but Steve usually managed to just miss it, especially when he was in a rush in the morning.

Somerville, the next town up from Cambridge, is the home of the renowned Steve's Ice-cream. This is where Steve took Madaline for their first real date after seeing "Play It Again, Sam." If someone chose to do a sociology paper on the trends of ice-cream, he or she might notice that, in Cambridge, the colder it got, the more people were visible walking down the sidewalks with ice-cream cones. The only reasonable explanation for this is that in colder weather, the ice-cream is less likely to drip and make a mess.

To say that Foster's room was a mess would have been too kind. As Steve walked past the open door, he saw the remains of a half-eaten ice-cream cone lying on the floor next to Foster's small metal trashcan with the Pittsburgh Steelers emblem on the side. John and Johnson had both complained to Foster about the mess and the situation had fleetingly improved. The stagnant smell which hung over his room would venture into the living room and adjoining bedroom with malicious stealth. As Steve looked more closely at the crusted cone, he saw a slight movement and the flicker of antennae. When he told

John and Johnson about the resident cockroach, they decided that immediate and drastic action was necessary.

John was assigned the auspicious task of locating a fish. The Stop and Shop was having a sale on cod, so cod it was. That evening, when Foster asked for company to the grille to get a bite to eat, his roommates all declined. Once he was gone, they invaded his room armed with the cod. Using a series of linked paperclips, which was all they could find, the olfactory terrorists secured the cod to the bottom of the wire bed-frame holding Foster's mattress.

When Foster returned with his evening snack, the living room was a scene of composed tranquility. Johnson let out a suppressed snicker that he managed to cover belatedly with an overly dramatic coughing fit. Foster went in his room and put the grease soaked paper plate with the remaining french fries on his dresser. He picked up his psychology textbook and rejoined the others in the living room.

The next afternoon when he came back from class, Foster noticed an unpleasant smell in his room. Steve observed him walking around with his Pittsburgh Steelers trash can disposing of the french fries, the empty soda cans, the partially eaten sandwiches, and even the decomposing ice-cream cone.

The following day, the smell persisted and grew nastier. John and Steve smiled at each other when they saw Foster gathering all of his dirty laundry strewn about the room and hidden in his closet. As he dragged his laundry bag out the door, they both burst into laughter when he asked where the laundry room was.

When the coast was clear, they removed the decaying cod trying not to laugh while they were holding their noses. That night, Foster sprayed his room with Lysol disinfectant. Nevertheless, the putrid smell of low-tide haunted Foster's room for weeks to come. Later, Johnson saw the janitor scrubbing the walls and floor of the hall garbage room. No one, almost, could understand why it smelled like someone had died in there.

*   *   *

Steve and his roommates often resisted the persistent callings of studies and sleep by staying up late at night to discuss almost anything, thereby avoiding both, with the later eventually winning out. This night's conversation was heavily influenced by the arrival of the Christmas season, already in full bloom in the shops and minds of anxious merchants.

As John walked into the living room, where his roommates were diligently making an effort to focus on the books in front of them, he announced, "Well, I just finished my last paper for the semester."

His roommates responded by throwing their books at the grinning speaker in rapid succession. John managed to dodge all but one that caught him squarely in the groin. The others laughed at his intense but passing agony, cognizant that the source of their own pain, the procrastinating pending paper problem, persisted. Steve, the first to feel some remorse for their vindictive reaction to John's happiness, conceded, "Sorry, man, we're just jealous. I have three more papers to go and my psych professor has alluded to the possibility of two more papers for his class. I think he may just be messing with our minds, but it's working. That Jessica sure has been a good influence on you. I'll bet she finished her papers last week. The two of you . . ."

Johnson, not to be outdone by a pre-med like John, interrupted, "Hey, Steve, don't forget that John and Jessica are both pre-med. John only had one class all semester that assigned papers. Come exam time, he may be singing a different tune. All of his pre-med 'buddies' will be studying all Christmas break. If I'm lucky, I'll almost be done when he's just starting. I have one term paper due on December 20th. The other is due in January, but I am nearly finished that one and should be able to get the last part done between Christmas and New Year's Eve. That means I'll only have two exams to study for."

"Obviously English is one of them, you and your dangling participles," retorted John.

"Okay, that means I'll only have two exams to study for, Asshole. How's that Mr. Dangling Participle?"

Steve, always the peacekeeper, jumped in, "Are you going to any parties this weekend? I'm going with Madaline to a party at the *Harvard Crimson* on Friday. I heard that there was a giant Pollyanna party on Saturday at Memorial Hall. They're having Paul Simon. You're supposed to come dressed as your favorite Christmas tree ornament and you're supposed to bring a wrapped gift for a boy or girl. The Big Brothers/Big Sisters have organized it. Allegedly Paul Simon is donating his time."

Foster, the tired, frustrated, over-worked, party-animal realist gave up pretending to study and put in his two cents worth. "I hate this school. I think the Administration is out to get us. They give us all this work to do and not enough time to do it. Then they organize all these great parties before Christmas so that we'll have a good time. But they schedule exams after Christmas so you can't even look forward to your Christmas holiday. If you go to any of the parties now, it means that you'll be that much further behind when you get back in January. I don't study my whole vacation, but I feel guilty the entire time I'm not. All of my friends finish before Christmas and they really rub it in. I'd rather be miserable now as I am anyway and get it all over before Christmas, then I could relax and enjoy Christmas for a change. This sucks."

"I think we're all part of some multi-year psych experiment," added Steve. "We're always reading these studies that they do with Harvard graduates over ten year periods to test the effect of smoking on alcoholics or breast feeding on children of prodigies. I'll bet that this is some perverted Pavlovian experiment to see if we will press the red button knowing it will cause pain in order to get the doggie biscuit."

"Maybe the Administration has been taken over by creatures from another galaxy and they are using us as guinea pigs. Perhaps our food is being drugged."

"That's right, it doesn't really taste like food, does it? It tastes more like chemical waste. Maybe it's imported from Chernobel in order to help the Russians with their foreign trade balance problems."

These nocturnal conversations would normally start out with an apparent direction, but would soon get lost in a rambling quagmire. Usually John or Johnson would be the first to stand up, hurl a ballistic insult at his conversational combatant and flee for the safety of his room knowing that it was better to attack and hide that to admit defeat.

The conversations would sometimes resume the following evening with opponents switching sides or lobbing new ammo to stimulate the debate. That Thursday evening, with only two weeks to Christmas, they were arguing about whether Santa Claus wore a red uniform because he was communist. After all, he distributed goodies to the masses. Foster reminded them that by rearranging the letters in "Santa," one could spell "Satan." John responded to Foster's scandalous remark by saying, "If we rearranged your face, it would spell "r-o-l-a-i-d-s.""

Just then the phone rang. In the spirit of the conversation, Johnson answered singing to the tune of *Here Comes Santa Claus*, "Santa got sunburn, Santa got sunburn. That's why he's all red."

The others started laughing and hurling new insults at each other until they saw Johnson's face. Steve asked what was wrong, but Johnson ignored him as he listened intently to the caller. The others looked at each other knowing that something ominous was happening, but not knowing what it could be. Johnson's voice sounded muted and dry when he spoke into the phone. "When is it?" Steve saw a tear running down one cheek and then the other. The only other thing Johnson said was, "I'll be there."

A heavy silence hung over the room as Johnson sat there with the phone still in his hand. When the blaring tone indicating a phone off the hook screamed from the earpiece, Johnson slowly replaced the receiver in its cradle. A moment longer passed and Johnson became aware that he was not alone. In a voice softer and even more strained than he had used on the phone, he said to no one in particular, simply, "My mother died," and he burst into tears.

None of the others had ever lost a parent. Steve's grandfather had died when he was three, but he was too young to remember that. No one knew what to say. They all started to mumble confused condolences distracted by their own thoughts of how they would feel if the phone call had been for them instead.

Johnson rose from the sofa and walked to the door of his room. He hesitated and then turned around. He said that he would have to leave the next day because the funeral was scheduled for Saturday. He then said, "Goodnight," turned and closed the door behind him.

The others sat there not knowing what to do. They heard some rummaging going on in Johnson's room followed by silence and then the intermittent gasps and wails of intense sobbing. They started into a halting conversation quiet enough that Johnson should not be able to hear what they were saying but loud enough that he would hear that they were talking and were not listening to him cry. They commiserated about what a terrible thing it was and how death seemed so unfair and could be so sudden. Then they decided they had to be practical for Johnson's sake. Foster related how Johnson already had his ticket home for Christmas. They resolved to call the airline the next morning to find out if they could switch his flight. They were concerned that his non-refundable ticket could not be exchanged. Even though he had booked the flight two months before and had gotten a very good rate, John felt that a death in the family was probably a valid reason to change a flight. They had a plan. Steve and John filed off to their room and Foster to his. They were hoping that things might not seem so grim in the morning.

Johnson never talked much about his family. Foster knew him better than the others, but never pushed with questions about home because he could tell that these questions made Johnson very uncomfortable. One night Johnson had had a lot to drink at a party. This was the exception rather than the rule for Johnson who usually stuck to Coke or Dr. Pepper. When they got home, Johnson wanted to talk rather than go to sleep.

He told Foster how his parents had gotten divorced when he was eleven. His two older brothers had moved with his father to Chicago. He and his younger sister had stayed with his mother in Louisville, Kentucky for almost three years before moving to Chicago to join the others. His father had gotten remarried to a seamstress who was only four years older than Johnson's oldest brother. Johnson and his sister never did get along very well with their father's new wife. They blamed her for their parents' divorce, even though Mr. Johnson had not even met her until he moved to Chicago after the divorce. Johnson told Foster how he missed his friends in Louisville and how they rarely got to see his mother. When Foster asked why they had moved to Chicago, Johnson grew quiet. When he finally answered, there was anger in his voice. He said that his mother was not always able to take care of him and his sister properly because she had a drinking problem. Months later, Foster had asked Johnson about a scar on his cheek. Johnson grew quiet and confessed with the same anger in his voice that it had been from an accident while he was living in Louisville.

After a restless sleep, the roommates gathered in the living room early the next morning. They asked Johnson for his ticket and what flight he would prefer. He mechanically responded that he needed to be in Louisville by 5:00 PM so his brother could pick him up at the airport and get him to the wake. John called the airline. He explained about the unexpected death of Johnson's mother and how he needed to change his flight. The airline service representative, Wendy, was very helpful and took all of the information. She said that the airline could switch flights for Johnson even though his ticket was non-refundable for a service charge of $50. John said that would be fine. However, when John explained that the new flight was to Louisville and not to Chicago, Wendy said that she was unable to switch destinations for a non-refundable ticket. She was very apologetic but explained that it was their policy and there was nothing she could do about it. When pushed, she agreed to check with her supervisor. When she got back on the phone, her response was the same. She found a direct flight from Boston to Louisville that would get in at 4:28. Her computer calculated that the cost for a one-way coach ticket booked for same day flight from Boston to Louisville would be $486. John asked if there were not some less expensive way to go. Wendy said she would check. A few minutes later, she finally said, "Ah hah! If we rebook the flight to Chicago for $50 and then add a one way from Chicago to Louisville for $277, the total cost would only be $327. The flight would arrive at 3:48. The flight to Chicago from Boston leaves at 10:15, that's just over an hour from now." To reserve the ticket, John gave the credit card number his father had given him in case of emergency.

When he got off the phone, he told Johnson who was attempting to pack that he was able to switch the ticket at no cost, but the flight would be leaving in one hour. They helped him finish packing while John called a taxi. There was not enough time to take the subway. Foster loaned Johnson $20 cash to pay for the taxi. They hurried him downstairs and gave him the best condolences they could muster. They also wished him a Merry Christmas but felt funny doing it. After the hurried departure, Foster complimented John on getting the flight arranged at no cost. It was then that John told them what had really happened. They all decided that they would split the cost among themselves and never tell Johnson. They would share many other secrets before they would graduate.

Two months later, Foster saw a report on Johnson's desk titled, "Investigation on Demise of Beverly Rachel Johnson." Since he knew Johnson was still in class, he picked it up, careful to remember how it had been laying on the desk. The report was a copy of a police investigation. It described how Johnson's mother had been burned to death in her bed. The cause of the fire was listed as smoking in bed. It said that the remains of Beverly Johnson were too badly charred to get any blood alcohol or other readings but it was suspected that she had been stoned on alcohol and drugs at the time of the fire. The report said that several bottles with shapes and styles used predominantly by local gin bottlers were found near the bed, one with trace amounts of gin remaining. The burn patterns on the bed led fire department investigators to conclude that an overturned bottle of alcohol was the initial source of the "quick-burn" fire. They also found numerous open bottles of barbiturates and amphetamines in the bedroom, bathroom and kitchen. Under additional remarks, the investigating officer stated that the house appeared to be in terrible disrepair and that he was shocked by the filth evident throughout the residence. When Foster got to the description of the body, he put the report down. "No wonder Johnson does not drink and is so damn clean," he said to himself.

Foster never mentioned the report to anyone. It was not something he felt he could discuss with the others and he was embarrassed to mention it to Johnson both because of what the report said and because he should not have seen it to begin with. He felt some pity for Johnson, but more importantly, he felt that he could be a better friend to him because he believed that he now understood more about what had helped influence and mold the Johnson he knew today.

CHAPTER
FIVE

Steve's parents met him at the train station. He had flown home for Christmas the past two years, but decided this year that the $120 round trip savings were worth the extra four hour travel time each way. Besides, he could use the train time to get some extra studying done before getting swept up in last minute Christmas shopping, parties with high school friends, and being a good son.

Steve was an only child. His father, William, had been 32 and his mother, Miriam, 34 when they had married. They had met while attending the California Institute of Technology in the Physics Ph.D. program. Most of their friends had already been married for as much as a decade. One friend had just had her seventh child the week before their wedding so had declined to attend. They knew that they wanted a family, but they were both immersed in starting their new careers. Four months after they were married, they were thrilled and somewhat surprised when Miriam's doctor confirmed that she was pregnant. One month later, their sadness exceeded their previous elation ten-fold when Miriam had a miscarriage.

Their despondency grew as Miriam's biological clock ticked away and nothing happened. Two years later, fate and an extra persistent sperm intervened. Steve was born after nine months of sickness with the final six weeks on total bed rest. They thanked God for a healthy son and decided that they would be satisfied with a happy family of three.

Steve would have liked a brother or sister. His parents devoted as much of their free time as possible to him, but he was always lonely since they worked long hours. He was jealous of other kids who had siblings. He was also jealous that they had a mother at home who would play with them and make them cookies and just be there when they got home from school. Now that he was older, Steve longed for siblings to share the eventual burden of caring for his parents as they got older. Steve's parents were in their mid-fifties and he had not even graduated from college.

As Steve rode the escalator up from the platform, he easily spotted his father in the crowd at Philadelphia's 30th Street Station. William was nearly 6' 4" tall and had wavy gray hair that he rarely cut. Miriam was barely visible at his side. Steve had been very proud when he had gotten as tall as his mother at the age of 12. That following summer he had passed her in height by a full two inches. Her hair was blond and she wore it in a short bob. Steve remembered that her hair had been darker when he was a kid, but so had his father's.

As he made his way through the milling passengers and their baggage, his parents came up to greet him. His mother reached up to give him a big hug and a kiss. His father also gave him a hug and a kiss. Steve remembered being embarrassed as a younger teenager that his father kissed him, but now he appreciated the affection.

His father grabbed his duffel bag and his mother placed a small gift in his hand. They both had huge grins plastered on their faces. His parents were usually very stoic so he knew that something unusual must be happening.

"Hey, I thought Christmas wasn't for another three days. I still have most of my shopping to do."

"This has nothing to do with Christmas," his father chided. "We have some very exciting news and we wanted you to share in the celebration. Now open your present."

Steve untied the red ribbon and removed the silver foil wrapping. When he opened the small white box within, he was perplexed to find a key.

Before Steve could utter the question that showed on his face as it was forming in his mind, his father jumped in, "We have discovered the key to the fourth dimension. We are only a few steps away from unlocking the secret of how objects pass through a sequence of events with the forward passage of time. Last month we had a major article published in the *Journal of Scientific Discovery*, and our premises have yet to be disproved by the scientific community. We have a copy of the article for you. That is why you need this key. In order for you to get to your copy of the article, you have to unlock the door to your new Jeep. You won't need to borrow your mother's station wagon anymore. We hope you like it."

Steve was speechless. He could not stop smiling, and wondering. Finally, he managed to say, "Wow! This is incredible. Thanks, Dad. Thanks, Mom." He gave them both a big hug.

William was pleased with the reaction. He continued, "But before we go home, we want to take you to dinner. Are you hungry?"

"Have you ever known me not to be?"

Miriam often had trouble getting a word in edgewise. But now, her adrenalin was pumping and she blurted out, "Your father and I would like to take you to a celebration dinner at Bookbinders. How does that sound?"

Dinner was delicious and it gave them a good chance to talk. Steve wanted to know how they could afford a new Jeep for him. Instead he asked about their scientific breakthrough. They responded that they would give him a full explanation after Christmas. Meanwhile, they wanted to know about him. How were classes? How was Madaline?

Steve told them about Johnson's mother and Foster's fish. He lamented about the last two losses his crew team had suffered ruining their perfect season. He apologized for not writing more often, but he had been very busy. He conveyed greetings from Madaline. He said that she was looking forward to meeting them sometime.

He did not tell them about their last night together. Steve had taken Madaline to dinner at Rotelli's. It was not fancy but it was very romantic. Steve had ordered a bottle of wine from the wine-list. He had never done this before so he was not sure what to do. His decision was heavily guided by the numbers in the right hand column. He found a nice bottle of red wine for $12.00. Maybe someday he would order one of the other selections that the waiter had suggested but which his wallet had vetoed. When he walked Madaline home, she invited him in. He had given her gift, a charm bracelet, to her when he had picked her up. He had been a bit disappointed that she had not given him anything. She made up for it now. She brought out four beautifully wrapped presents from under her bed. She handed them to Steve. He asked which one was for him and she said they were all for him. They had taken up almost a third of his duffel bag when he packed the next morning.

As they were kissing goodnight, they both got very passionate. Madaline surprised herself when she started to unbutton Steve's shirt. This was an unprecedented thrill for Steve. He got very excited and kissed Madaline wildly. He began to remove Madaline's dress. He had the back of her dress unzipped and he was grappling with the fasteners on her bra. He became almost frenzied as he struggled with the hooks. He cursed the designers who must get great pleasure from thwarting young men who have only seen a limited number of bras before. When he felt them give way his body rose to new levels of excitement. He loved Madaline very much and was overwhelmingly turned on by her increasingly nude body. He knew that tonight they would finally be making love and cementing their wonderful relationship.

At that moment when the bra straps receded from her back, Steve felt Madaline's mouth tighten up. She stopped returning his kisses. She buried her head in his shoulder and pulled him tight against her body. She resisted his further attempts at kissing and fondling. After a moment, she eased back from Steve and said that he had better get going since he had to get up early the next day. Steve asked if anything was wrong and Madaline mumbled something about the wine. After they had discreetly returned themselves to the sanctity of their clothes, they wished each other a Merry Christmas. Steve told Madaline he loved her. Madaline apologized and said that she loved Steve more than he could imagine.

Steve walked home with a smile on his face, but he was also feeling more frustration than the cold shower awaiting him at home could satisfy.

*   *   *

The day after Christmas, Steve joined his parents in their new lab. Over the years, their lab had expanded to take over the entire basement, eventually annexing the garage as well. While Steve had been at school, they had added a large cinderblock testing room off the back of the garage. It had displaced the part of the back yard where Steve's play-set and favorite climbing tree had been. Steve had not used the play-set in over ten years, but his parents had been reluctant to get rid of it. Perhaps they had been clinging to Steve's childhood as an extension of their own. Steve was pleased to see them expanding from their ever cramped quarters, but he did mourn the passing of "Oaky."

Steve's parents had been awarded a five-year federal research grant. These funds had paid for the new testing room and the computers and electronic gadgetry that filled the new space. The grant also allowed for only minimal living expenses for Steve's parents. It did not take into consideration a college bound child whose four-year expenses would approach one hundred thousand dollars. Steve was able to get a very good scholarship and compile several different loans to make up the difference. He would have to get a fairly high paying job upon graduation in order to afford the initial payments on his ten-year educational mortgage. That new stereo he had been eying would have to wait. But, he had a great new car, a Jeep Cherokee!

As his parents were showing him around they explained how they had converted an old electrical circuit box to use as their master switchboard. They said they had had to be extra clever because their funds had been running low and their request for an additional grant had been denied. Steve began to wonder with renewed interest how his parents had afforded such an extravagance as a new Jeep. His concern was interrupted when his mother proclaimed, "And this is one of our launch pads. We are just in time. It is now exactly 11:28 AM. Watch the center of the launch pad very carefully. If this works, it will conclude our tenth successful launch with only six failures."

Steve and his parents stood around the edge of the launch pad in silence. Steve did not know what he was watching for, but he could see the anticipation on his parents' faces, and he became equally excited. 11:30 AM came and went and nothing happened. Steve was getting warm, so he pulled over his head the teal, royal blue, and black argyle sweater that had been in one of the four boxes from Madaline. Her generosity had also included a Harvard mug, some cologne, and a rubber ducky, "for bath-time fun." Steve carefully folded the sweater and placed it on the file cabinet behind him. Meanwhile, William started to ask Miriam for a calibration check, but he was interrupted by a small static sparking on the launch pad. Instantly a pencil and a small gadget appeared from nowhere. Steve was bewildered, his parents delighted.

"Number sixteen a success, completed full 48-hour voyage,

standard time deviation less than .02 percent," William remarked as he wrote some notes on a clipboard.

Steve got over his shock and said, "Beam me aboard, Scottie."

William, grasping the reference, explained, "This is a bit different than a transporter. The object does not travel in space. It merely ceases to exist in its current structure as the result of a small, contained atomic reaction. The speed of the electrons in each of the affected atoms slows by approximately 99.93 percent. There is a dramatic compacting of the atomic structure as the centrifugal force diminishes. If the force is too great, the atoms may irreversibly collapse on themselves. If the force is too weak, we may lose the object because our re-activator may cause the electrons to over-accelerate. Our next project is to develop a variable power control for the re-activator." The gadget, which had reappeared with the pencil, William further explained, was the re-activator, resembling a TV remote control, though cylindrical in shape.

Miriam could see that Steve was confused. She attempted to clarify, "Our device can effectively freeze objects in time. We can make them disappear and reappear at a later date having aged only slightly. The objects still exist during this time period, but their atomic structure has changed so that they are not visible and so that wear and tear does not occur. We set off a small, contained explosion which effectively freezes all of the atoms. We include a re-activator device that has been preset with a radioactive isotope to initiate the second atomic reaction to restore the atoms to their original state at a pre-determined time. The half-life of the isotope has to be recalibrated to accommodate the slowing of the electrons."

"The possible applications are limitless. For example, once we have successfully tested the device on living creatures, we may be able to replace cryogenics and make it accessible to almost anyone. If a person has a terminal disease for which no cure currently exists, we can effectively freeze them and transport them to the future when a cure may have been found."

"We hope to have all of the final testing and modifications done by September when we are scheduled to present our findings at the annual meeting of the International Atomic Physicists Alliance. We have named the device 'MAMA' for 'Multiple Atomic Mass Activator'. We wanted to name it "STEVE" but we couldn't think of any clever acronyms."

William finished taking his notes and assumed control of the conversation. "We have learned so much about atomic structure and theory from this project. So much has fallen into place in the past six months. We believe that our study may even prove that some of the objects that were destroyed during World War II in Hiroshima and Nagasaki may still exist. At the correct distance from the epicenter, these objects may have received the right charge to reduce the electron speed by the correct amount. There may even be people who are frozen in time. There are many bodies that were never found. We believe that if accurate data were available, we could show that all of the missing bodies were either at the epicenter where they were actually destroyed, or were located in a radius around the epicenter where their atomic structures were altered. They may still be there lacking only a reactivation device to speed up the electrons' flight. We mentioned this possibility in a footnote in our article and it resulted in some very serious interest from the Japanese Government. We are trying to get clearance to apply for funding from Japan since our latest federal grant application was turned down. We have a lot more experimentation to do before we have exhausted the possibilities here. Come down to the basement and let me show you our Apple Particle Graphic Simulator."

Steve followed his father down a narrow wooden staircase to the basement. This was his parents' research office. Two walls were lined with computers and peripheral equipment. Along another wall was an office space with two desks facing each other sharing a single phone. There was a copy machine, a FAX machine, a typewriter, a large freezer and a safe. The remaining wall was covered by the furnace, the hot water heater, the washer and dryer and a white enamel washbasin. The dryer supported a laundry basket filled with unwashed clothes. The washing machine served as a makeshift stand for a large shredder. The washbasin doubled as an overflow filing cabinet and had stacks of papers spilling out of it. In the middle of the room was an older looking version of the launch pad Steve had just seen in operation.

Apple Computer had custom built the Particle Graphic Simulator (PGSimulator) for the Harris' research project. While the PGSimulator warmed up and began its initial field permutation series, William explained how the PGSimulator recreates the various internal and external forces affecting particles of matter. They could artificially adjust any parameters including the amount of centrifugal force on the electrons, the degree of attraction between neighboring or passing particles, or the effects of gravity from larger bodies. The PGSimulator was instrumental in determining the power of the blast that was needed to alter the electron speed in their target objects.

After a few moments, the PGSimulator beeped. William continued his explanation, "We can also use the PGSimulator for situational and sensitivity analyses of a myriad of forces. For instance, I have activated a permutation of the Big Bang Theory. I have fed in base standards for the initial volume of mass and the energy level generated by the boom and have included gravitational components and matter attraction levels. I have also incorporated energy to matter and matter to energy conversion factors as well as some other parameters. These base figures have been compiled from best guestimates by Astronomers and other Physicists over the years. Once these are input, we allow the computer to vary the factors within certain ranges and to track the results. We have also input as much as we know about how the universe is composed today. Our goal is to use the computer to vary the initial factors until it finds the most likely combination of factors thereby giving us an improved hypothesis of what factors helped to drive the Big Bang and how we ended up where we are today.

"The PGSimulator has a primitive form of artificial intelligence. This allows the PGSimulator to more quickly narrow down various components without doing an exhaustive matrix of possible combinations. Even so, the process is very time consuming. We try to revise our primary figures as the derived information indicates certain changes are warranted.

"Earlier this fall, I ran several lengthy simulations on the PGSimulator. One was terminated after 19 days by a power outage. We had no electricity for six whole hours and couldn't do any work. When the electricity finally came back on, we had to reprogram and start the simulation all over again. What a waste. Just one small example of how dependent we have become on electricity.

"The longest simulation took 45 days. The result was really quite impressive. The PGSimulator concluded that our basic theory of the Big Bang is slightly flawed. We had always believed that the universe was expanding consistently outward at a decelerating rate. The later part appears to hold water. The unexpected conclusion has to do with the consistency of the expansion. While the mass, on average, is expanding directly outward, individual particles, heavenly bodies, and even solar systems and galaxies are often bounced around by neighboring forces similar to a giant pinball machine. An entire galaxy may get catapulted back towards the center of the universe somewhat like you used to do at the skating rink by whipping the end person as you spun around. As that person shot out, you would rebound towards the center. Every action has an equal and opposite reaction, even with gravitational forces. The Earth may be taking a very irregular flight pattern as it follows the Sun around our fragile universe.

"Our next goal is to trace the effects of black holes. We hypothesize that these solar voids may be the result of premature contraction of the particles upon themselves. They may even be triggered by atomic explosions similar to the ones we are replicating upstairs but on a much grander scale. We believe that there is even a possibility that the magnitude of the explosions may be such that the speed of the electrons is not just slowed, but is actually reversed effectively sucking these masses and anything which comes into contact with them back in time, thereby leaving these powerful unexplained voids.

"Space, the final frontier. Time, the first and last frontier. Now, go wash your hands and help your mother set the table. I'll be up in a minute to make my special salad."

Steve spent the remainder of his Christmas holiday helping his parents in the lab and visiting friends. He neglected his studies because he felt he could learn more from his parents than he could from any book. At least it sounded like a good excuse at the time. The night before Steve had to leave to return to Harvard, he helped his parents place an ant and a mouse in small plastic boxes with little ventilation holes. They set the reactivation device for the least time their calculations would allow. At shorter intervals, the accuracy was crude. They expected the device should return in 8—10 hours. The next morning, Steve was in the lab at 6:00 anxiously watching. After almost two hours of waiting, his patience was rewarded. The device appeared along with the plastic boxes. Steve called his parents and when they appeared, he opened the larger plastic box and found the mouse on its side. It was dead. Deeply disappointed, he opened the other box. As he pulled off the lid, he glanced at the bottom of the box expecting the worst. There was no sign of the ant. Suddenly the ant emerged over the edge of the box and fell to the table. It was alive.

CHAPTER SIX

January in Cambridge can be even worse than December. A pall of depression and anxiety settle in over the Harvard Campus. Even the ice-cream salespeople lose their cherry jubilee smiles. The cold weather and impending exams keep even the most adventurous tied to their rooms, the library, the cafeteria or the pathways in between.

This year the gloom was even thicker than usual as its dismal cloak was crusted with fear. Three days after Steve had returned to campus, two girls in Quincy House were raped in their room. The following night, another girl was raped in the parking lot of Peabody Terrace, graduate student housing. The Harvard Police beefed up security, doubling patrols and adding security guards to each of the dorms' main entrances.

The investigations uncovered some discouraging news. A number of students in Quincy House were questioned. A senior male who wished to remain anonymous confessed to letting an unfamiliar individual resembling the police composite enter the dorm behind him. The police call this "shadowing." He did not get a close look at him, but he remembered that the suspect wore a purple bandanna around his neck and had on a Harvard ski cap. The ski caps are available to the general public at the Harvard Coop. The police felt that the purple bandanna, however, might prove to be a helpful clue. They decided not to release this information to the media.

Even more disturbing to the investigators was that the rape victim at Peabody Terrace had cried out for help when she was attacked. The assailant had pushed her into the snow between two parked cars and had held a knife to her throat. He had then used the knife to cut open her sweatpants and her underwear. His force upon her had been so great that the doctor later found gravel ground into her buttocks where the cloth had been pulled away. The victim recounted to the police in a trembling voice how she had seen several other people in the parking lot and near the entrance before it had happened. She could not say the word "rape." She could not understand why no one had come to her rescue. She would have helped someone if she had heard a cry for help. Why did no one help her? She then burst into tears and the nurse told the detectives that they would have to leave.

Madaline and Ellyn agreed that wherever they went, they would try to go together. Even this did not make them feel very secure. After all, the two girls in Quincy House had been together, and they were raped in the sanctity of their own room.

Madaline no longer surprised Steve by coming to his dorm unannounced. She asked Steve to please visit her whenever possible. She missed him after the two weeks apart and the roving rapist made her long even more for his reassuring male companionship. However, with papers to write and exams to study for, Steve was feeling the self-imposed pressures of academia. Without classes in Harvard Yard and no crew practice, he had fewer opportunities to be near Kirkland House and Madaline.

Feeling forlorn and neglected, Madaline decided to make the trek to Radcliffe Quad. She had not gotten a dose of Steve's lips or his blue eyes for four days and she was suffering from withdrawal. She considered asking Ellyn to go with her, but she really wanted some privacy with Steve, and besides, there had been no additional rapes since they increased the security forces. Madaline knew that Steve generally ate lunch when the cafeteria first opened, so she hurriedly threw some books and notebooks into her backpack, and set off for Radcliffe Quad.

She walked up through Harvard Square past the Harvard Coop. She thought about stopping to get Steve a new Harvard scarf which he had been eyeing, but decided that there was not enough time if she wanted to get there before lunch. Moreover, she was a bit angry with him for not visiting her more often. The scarf could wait. She continued up past the Cambridge Commons. The Commons was nearly empty except for a young mother with her two kids, one in a stroller and one running by her side. She also saw two homeless men sitting on one of the benches. It was a sunny day and warmer than usual, though it grew chilly as she passed through the shadows of the taller buildings along Garden Street. The thought of holding Steve close to her kept her warm inside her blue down jacket. She would go straight to the cafeteria and wait for Steve there.

After she stomped the snow off her boots and hung up her coat on the rack, Madaline entered the cafeteria. She saw John and Foster sitting with two other guys she did not recognize at a table. She went over to say "Hello." They exchanged greetings and chatted briefly about their Christmas holidays. They joked about not having seen each other since last year. When Madaline asked where Steve was, they pointed to a table in the corner and said, "Over there." Madaline sauntered over to where Steve was sitting with a pretty, young blonde.

"Hi, Steve. I thought I'd surprise you and have lunch with you, but I guess my timing is not so good."

"Oh, Madaline. Hi. Um, this is Tracy. She's in my French class." To Tracy, "This is Madaline. She's a friend of mine."

"I was just in the neighborhood and thought I'd drop by. Maybe I'll see you later."

"Madaline, why don't you grab some food and join us?"

Madaline thought about leaving Steve alone with this nymph. "I guess I do have to eat. Okay."

When Madaline returned to the table with her chef salad and cottage cheese, Tracy was gone. Steve had a sheepish look on his face.

"What happened to your friend?" Madaline loaded the word "friend" with as much sarcasm as she could fit in a one-syllable word.

"She had to get back to studying. She's only a freshman and is very nervous about her first set of exams." Steve munched nervously on a potato chip. "What a surprise. Why were you in the neighborhood?"

She ignored his question, not wanting to give him the satisfaction of knowing that she had trudged all the way there just to see him. "I hope I didn't interrupt anything." Again, she loaded "anything" with heapings of sarcasm, but this time she had three syllables to work with, and the result made the hair on the back of Steve's neck bristle.

Steve tried desperately to sweep Tracy under the proverbial rug. "Tracy wants to be an interpreter with the UN. She's the only freshman in our class. I think you'd like her. So, how's your studying going?"

"What did you mean by, 'she's my friend'? Are you embarrassed to say I'm your girlfriend? Or would you rather that she were your girlfriend?"

"Lin, no one could beat you. I love you. You're very important to me." Steve got up and walked around the table to where Madaline was still standing with her tray. He took her tray and placed it on the table. He kissed her gently on the lips. When she did not resist, he wrapped his arms around her and commenced a slow passionate kiss that must have continued for several minutes. When the kiss ended with a loud popping smack, the voyeurs at the next two tables burst into applause. Their cheeks reddened with embarrassment. Steve held Madaline's chair for her and they sat together, hand in hand.

After lunch, they relocated to the library. They spent several hours enveloped in their respective studies. Occasionally, Madaline would catch Steve staring at her above the edge of his book. Around 4:30, Madaline realized that it was getting darker. She told Steve that she needed to get going. He walked her to the ground floor and found an unoccupied space in the stacks. After making out for a few minutes, Madaline reiterated the need to go. They kissed once more at the entrance and Madaline fled into the cold.

As Madaline made her way back down Garden Street, she sensed that she was being followed. It was getting dark quickly and she realized that she should have waited for the small crimson shuttle bus. She periodically glanced over her shoulder and saw that a dark figure disguised under countless layers of clothing was drawing ever closer. As she waded through the deep indentations in the snow caused by absent traffic which had passed down the small cross street bordering the Commons, Madaline saw the shuttle bus cruising down the opposite side of Garden Street. She frantically waved at the bus to flag it down. Unfortunately, this was not a scheduled stop, so the little crimson shuttle bus with its faceless driver drove on, flashing its red brake lights as it disappeared around the corner in the distance.

The darkening shadows behind obstructions deflecting the yellow cast of the streetlights began to play tricks with her eyes as the sunlight faded. Madaline felt some moisture on her face. She thought that she had started to cry. Then a few more flakes of snow landed on her cheeks and melted against her face, heated by her warm breath and the burning fear within. She felt some comfort that she could see the twinkling lights of Harvard Square coming into view beyond the Commons. As she passed the Kiosk, where elderly gentlemen sold ice-cream and drinks in the summer and newspapers and cigarettes on days less dismal than this, Madaline's heart skipped a beat, or perhaps it was two. From behind the Kiosk loomed one of the homeless men who had been peacefully sitting on the bench that morning. He lunged at Madaline. She jumped out of his reach, panic stricken. She looked behind her in search of the dark figure that had been following her. The imagined stalker was now Madaline's best hope for salvation. He, or perhaps she, was nowhere in sight. Then she saw the huddled figure passing from view on the far side of Garden Street. Perhaps this kind person had crossed the street so as not to scare the solitary female making her way through the dusk. The vagrant lunged at Madaline again calling her a "wealthy bitch" and a "whore." Madaline screamed, but the noise was muffled by the quiet of the falling snow and masked by the roar of an MBTA Bus racing its engine on the far side of the Commons. He grabbed her arm, but she spun free. He caught onto one of the straps of her backpack. She turned to flee, but felt his powerful force restraining her. She twisted her arm out from under the backpack strap and scrambled away. A few yards from the Kiosk, she slipped on the ice and fell. She held her breath as she expected her attacker to pounce upon her. When nothing happened, she looked back and saw the despicable creature hovering over the captive backpack pulling out books and papers and scattering them about in the snow as he examined his bounty.

Madaline struggled to her feet. She vaguely noticed a jabbing pain in her left knee where she had landed on the ice. She began running. She was not sure where she was running, but she just kept running. Her legs were alternating below her body. Her breath was heavy, but she felt her energy was limitless. She could run until there was nowhere else to run.

She emerged from her daze when she recognized the lights of Hilles Library filling the void before her. Steve would be there. He would protect her. Steve.

*　　*　　*

The second time Officer Fisk came alone. He had set out only a half hour before with Officer O'Leary of the Cambridge Police Department, to investigate the scene of the alleged assault. Officer Fisk wore thick spectacles that made his eyes look very small. He reminded Steve of his parents' accountant who also would have looked quite out of place in a navy blue uniform with a gun, a nightstick, and handcuffs hanging from the thick black belt. The words "Harvard Police" were embroidered in yellow on the cap. As a freshman, Steve had been advised that if he were to commit a misdemeanor such as loitering or drinking in public, and if a Cambridge Policeman and a Harvard Policeman were both standing there, he should quickly run to the Harvard Policeman and submit himself to the historically more lenient punishment of the campus keepers of law and order.

After taking Madaline's statement, Officers Fisk and O'Leary had hastened to the Cambridge Commons. Since the crime involved a student but was not on school property, both officers were required. They apprehended the suspect sitting on one of the benches only a few feet from the kiosk still sorting the pens and pencils he had found in Madaline's backpack. Officer Fisk carefully gathered the snow-laden papers and books that had been discarded on the ground. He shook them off as best he could.

Officer O'Leary recognized the assailant as a homeless man known only as Ben who spent most of his time in the Commons and the subway. Officer O'Leary had arrested him himself on four previous occasions. The station had an active file on Ben. His offenses were never violent, but they continued unabated. The police usually transported him to the shelter when he was released, but he would never stay. He had been diagnosed as a manic depressive by a court-paid psychologist. The magistrate, who had grown tired of seeing his recurring face, suggested half seriously that they all chip in and buy him a one-way bus ticket to a warmer climate. They had tried to trace his family and his origins in vain. Officer O'Leary would have to make another entry in Ben's file that listed his last name as "Doe."

Officer Fisk returned Madaline's belongings to her and apologized that some of her notes were wet because the remaining traces of snow on the papers had melted in the heat of his squad car. He asked her to come with him to the Cambridge Police station to identify her attacker and to fill out some reports. As Madaline was explaining that she had a lot of studying to do and that she would have to reorganize all of her notes and that she really could not take time to do this now, she burst out crying. Through her tears, she continued her barrage of excuses. She felt that she really was not in a proper frame of mind to confront him that night. It had been pretty dark so she was not sure she could identify him. She did not want to be near a lot of people. She would not be able to sleep that night because his wretched face would haunt her. She did not want to be left alone . . .

Officer Fisk had been trained to deal with hysteria. He did not attack the inconsistencies in her excuses. Instead, he assured her that he would stay with her the whole time. He asked Steve to accompany them. He insisted that it would not take more than an hour or two and that she could identify her assailant hidden behind a one-way mirror. Choking back her tears, Madaline finally consented.

By the time Officer Fisk dropped Madaline and Steve back at Cabot House, it was after 8:00 PM. They had missed dinner, so Steve said he would go get a pizza. Madaline grabbed his arm and pleaded with him not to leave her alone. Steve suggested that she come with him. She refused.

Exasperated and hungry, Steve was relieved to find Johnson studying in his room. Johnson had done little besides studying since he had returned from home. His roommates were concerned about him and had invited him to go out with them, but he had consistently declined. They did not know how to help him. Steve was reluctant to ask for his help, but no one else was around. Steve rationalized that perhaps it might be good for Johnson if he could help someone else.

Twenty-five minutes later, Johnson returned with the lukewarm pizza. Even though he had eaten dinner in the cafeteria, he sat with Madaline and Steve and finished off two pieces while Madaline related her story. Steve could tell that Madaline was feeling better because she began to embellish her story to make it more dramatic. By the end, when Madaline was telling about the other characters they had scraped together for the line-up, both Madaline and Johnson were laughing. Perhaps misery loves company, or maybe we all need a jolt from time to time to remember that life can be very short and we need to savor each moment as it comes. Steve knew that everything would turn out all right, he hoped.

*   *   *

That night, fortuitously, was the semi-annual Quad Howl. After attempting to study for a while, Madaline had joined Steve on his bed where he was reading. Steve put down his book and turned off the reading light that was clipped to his headboard. They lay there holding each other without saying a word. Steve was unaware whether he slept or not, but the time passed quickly and he felt warm and secure. Madaline's mind was churning. She kept revolving through the same sequence of events, each time seeing the face that now had a name, and each time feeling a heavy weight pressing her down, trapping her so she could not escape. At one point, she got up and left Steve breathing heavily on the bed. She opened the door to the hallway and carefully looked each way, listening for any strange noises. She then scurried down the hall to the girl's bathroom even though it was further away than the coed bathroom that Steve always used. The bathroom was empty. She turned on the faucet and felt the stream until it grew warm and then hot. She pressed the metal tongue of the soap dispenser and meticulously slid her hands against each other to form a thick lather. She methodically rinsed and repeated this process two more times. Her hands felt clean, but she still felt clammy. Maybe it was her clothes or her hair or something else. She decided that if she washed her face, that would help.

Steve stirred as Madaline climbed back onto the side of the small bed, but he did not react to the lavender smell from the soap on the face that lay only inches from his.

Around fifteen minutes before midnight, first Madaline and then Steve became aware of a surging din emanating from outside Steve's window. They rose together and moved to the window. In the glow of the lights lining the walkways surrounding the Radcliffe Quadrangle, they could see a seething crowd of dark figures pulsating in and out of view. Suddenly a snowball returned to its fragmented origins as it hit the window with a loud thud, momentarily blocking their view. Steve slid the window open and was greeted by an arctic blast. Madaline shivered. Smiling at them from the crowd below was Foster's mischievous face, another snowball gripped in each glove. The window returned to its nest just in time to absorb the impact of another white projectile hurled from below.

Revenge was in order. Un-swayed by Madaline's protests, primordial man answered his calling. After all, it was the Quad Howl. Steve grabbed his down jacket and gloves and tossed Madaline's coat to her. When she stood there defiantly, he moved in for the kiss of persuasion. As his lips wrestled hers and his tongue suppressed any resistance, he reached around behind her and eased her arms into her coat sleeves. With this mission accomplished, he grabbed her by the arm and they set out down the hall with only one goal on Steve's mind, to wreak havoc on the aggressors. Foster must die.

As they left the sanctuary of the dorm, their padded bodies were pummeled with snowballs from numerous indistinguishable sources. Steve dove for cover, arming himself and losing his maiden in the process. He returned fire, aiming at nameless shapes, abandoning the concept of mutual deterrence. The battle continued, reinforcements shifting from side to side as preferable opportunities presented themselves. Steve catapulted a special mega snow boulder in the direction of a jacket that resembled Foster's. Before he could see if contact was made, he took a direct shot to the head. He tapped the side of his head to dislocate the melting shrapnel that had lodged in his ear.

This ear, Van Gogh-ed but for the composition of the missile, joined the other in recognizing the swelling cacophony of voices raised to the Trojan God of Liberation from the stress of exams and the futility of studying. Soon these ears were unable to hear these sounds, not because of spontaneous deafness, but because the vocal orifice residing between them had joined ranks and was not yet aware of its limitations. These ears could seek some comfort in the knowledge that they would have two days of peace and quiet while their neighbor was becoming well acquainted with the soothing benefits of Sucrets.

Madaline, abandoned, despairing, lonely and scared, staggered into the center of the Quad where she stood alone, a mute statue, unexplainably immune from the trajectories surrounding her. When the plaintive cries of her fellow students pierced her shattered shell, she joined in with a wail that would have made a rabid coyote flee with its tail between its legs. Even as the noise around her grew, she could hear the echo of her own howl reverberating in her head, but she did not recognize the voice. She screamed again and knew that it was hers. The more she screamed, the less she needed to. Finally, exhausted, she stopped. The noise around her had stopped. People were shuffling back inside their dorms, enjoying a stress free moment until confronted once again by the books that had been lying in ambush in their rooms.

Madaline felt an arm around her. She was startled. She relaxed when she realized it must be Steve. She jumped again when she turned and saw dark hair lining the face above her. Johnson calmed her down. He walked her back into the dorm with its heated halls. Once inside, he explained to Madaline that Foster had gone with Steve to the student health services in a taxi. They had tried to find her. Steve had been hit by a snowball in the side of his face. Apparently the snowball had some glass or a piece of rock in it. Steve had gotten a cut just below the ear that had been bleeding very badly. Steve had confessed that for more than a week he had not taken the medication the doctor had given him for his Hemopalpacemia. Johnson offered to walk Madaline back to Kirkland House but she decided to stay in Steve's room so she would be there when he got back. She also thought to herself that by staying there she could avoid for a while longer facing the real world where unknown faces named "Ben" waited for her in dark places.

CHAPTER SEVEN

Steve's cut stopped bleeding and he vowed to be more faithful about taking his medication. Madaline's wounds healed more slowly. She continued having nightmares and her hands began to shake, even before she had downed the five cups of coffee which she began drinking every morning to keep herself awake.

Harvard University Health Services offers counseling services free of charge to students. Ellyn and Steve both suggested that Madaline make an appointment with a counselor. Madaline's grandmother's first husband had been sent away to a mental institution after he was diagnosed with what Madaline remembered only as some terrible mental disease. Madaline had only been six at the time. She had been allowed to go visit him once before he had died. She would never forget the strange smells and the screaming she heard as they walked down the hallway, painted white but dark nevertheless. Her grandfather was sitting alone in his room, tied to his chair, and there was one long thin strand of drool hanging from the side of his mouth. She said "Hi, Grampa." He did not respond; he only stared at the floor. She had gathered her strength together and hugged him. Some of the drool got on the shoulder of her blue and white Sunday dress that she had worn just for Grandpa. She sat on the edge of the bed while her mother and grandmother told her grandfather about the weather and the new roof on grandma's house and that Mr. Bachich had passed on. Madaline learned later that that meant he had died.

After a short while, a lady dressed in white came in. Even her shoes and stockings were white. She told them that they would have to go. The next time her mother asked her if she wanted to go see Grandpa, she said that she was busy. Her mother never asked again.

Madaline decided that she did not want to go see a counselor. She was smart and she could work this out herself. Her psychology professor had said that it is important for a patient to confront his or her problems and to work them through rather than avoiding them. Madaline decided to take his advice, even though it had not been meant for her.

She would confront her fears directly. Officer Fisk had told her about the shelter where they usually took Ben and other homeless prisoners when they were released. She could get there easily by bus. Madaline gathered together her hat, her gloves, and her courage and set out for the Massachusetts Avenue Shelter and Job Services. As she sat on the bus, she pondered whether she should have called for an appointment. As she got closer to the stop, she concluded that it was inconsiderate not to have an appointment. These people were probably too busy to meet with her unannounced. She would go home and call. No, she was not making excuses.

The bus dropped her on the corner opposite the shelter. The bus stop to get back to school was on the other side of the street in front of the shelter. She would have to cross the street. When the walking sign turned from red to white she crossed to the bus stop. As she stood waiting for the bus, she stared at the entrance to the shelter. A man who looked much like Ben ambled down the street right towards her. She backed away. He passed by her without bothering her. As he passed, Madaline saw that the man was really a woman. Under the layers of old clothes and with her ragged wool hat pulled low over her head, it was hard to tell. The woman disappeared into the warmth of the shelter.

Madaline decided that since she was here, she might as well check it out. She wished that she had not worn her new hat and scarf that her mother had given her for Christmas. Her other hat worked perfectly fine and she had had it since she was in ninth grade. She would wear that next time.

Madaline walked towards the entrance. Suddenly two men appeared in the doorway. Madaline turned and walked back to the bus stop. When she glanced back at the shelter, the men were gone.

They had probably just been checking to see whether it was snowing. Once again, Madaline took a deep breath and headed back toward the single glass door. It was much lighter than it looked, and she was quickly inside instantly immersed in the chaos within. As she removed her hat, scarf and gloves and tucked them discreetly into a coat pocket, she watched as people of all sorts hustled about or sat listlessly. There was a lobby with tables where men sat and played cards. One man had a cigarette in his mouth but it was not lit. He looked up from his cards for a moment to assess the stranger by the door, but he had seen so many strangers come and go; he quickly lost interest and looked back down at his cards. Behind him, Madaline saw a large sign that said "No Smoking Permitted."

Beyond the lobby was a larger room with rows of long tables some of which were covered with empty dishes and others with dishes that were being emptied by the hungry people behind them. She saw two men and two women standing behind a silver counter serving food onto trays held by the anxious faces waiting there. Madaline thought to herself that the servers looked like homeless people themselves. She learned later that they were. Anyone who stayed in the shelter for more than one night was required to take a work assignment.

Madaline heard the door behind her open followed by a dull thud. She turned and saw an elderly women lying in a heap on the floor. Suddenly two women appeared from an office that was partially hidden behind the lobby bulletin boards. They started shouting orders. A large man dressed all in green appeared with a rolling cart. Three of the men stopped their card game and helped lift the woman onto the cart. The cart, the man in green, and the two women disappeared through a doorway off of the lobby. Madaline glanced in the direction of the office and saw a young woman not much older than herself standing in the doorway.

"Pretty amazing, huh?"

Madaline was stunned by what she had just seen and was not sure what to say. She felt pretty stupid just staring back at this girl.

"Hi, my name's Doris. You must be new around here. Were you sent over from B.U.?"

"No, I go to Harvard. I thought I would just stop by to see if I could volunteer to help. I'm not sure what I could do, but I wanted to do something. I thought maybe I could tutor in math or English. And I like to cook. My mother taught me some pretty good recipes."

"Well, um . . . I missed your name."

"Madaline"

"Well, Madaline, we can always use two more hands. But, I'm afraid we won't be needing your tutoring skills. Our main goal is just to get these people fed, keep them warm and clothed, and try to help them figure out what they are going to do when their 30 days are up."

"30 days?"

"No one is allowed to stay more than 30 days. Otherwise all of our beds would be filled with permanent residents and we'd have no room for people with emergencies. As for the recipes, we can definitely use help in the kitchen, but we have our own recipes we pretty much stick to. It's called, 'heat up whatever's in the big can.'"

Just then, one of the ladies and the man dressed in green returned to the lobby and came towards the office.

"Madaline, this is Lucy Kadanoff our Director, and George, our facilities coordinator. We call him 'Green Giant'. Lucy, this is Madaline, a Haahvad girl. She'd like to help."

"We don't get many people from Harvard. Why are you here?"

"I thought maybe you could use some help. I don't mind working hard and getting my hands dirty." Madaline looked at her hands. Her father had treated her to her first manicure two days after Christmas. She wondered if the Tahitian Sunset nail polish would survive. Lucy noticed that Madaline slipped her hands into her pockets.

Lucy continued, distracted by some shoving that was occurring at one of the card tables, "I would need a commitment from you. We spend too much time training new people who work for a few weeks and then get bored and stop showing up. If you are doing this just to add something to your resume, we don't want you. If you want to help people and can handle the hard work, Doris will help you fill out an application."

Lucy then hastened over to help George settle the brewing dispute. Madaline followed Doris into the inner sanctum of the office where she signed away her Sunday afternoons and Tuesday evenings for the next year, with time off in the summer for good behavior.

On the bus ride home, Madaline contemplated her experience. She had come away unharmed. The staff seemed nice enough, if a bit brusque, and they certainly needed help. Besides, this would indeed look good on her resume and it might give her some good information for an article for the *Harvard Crimson* or for a psychology or sociology paper. Madaline slept better that night. The next morning, she only had three cups of coffee and her hands were remarkably steady.

CHAPTER EIGHT

W had certain rules that had to be obeyed. When Steve had been initiated, he had sworn to uphold the principles of the club in a pledge that he had repeated as best he could, imitating the sounds coming out of the president's mouth. Later, in a more conscious state, he was allowed to read the pledge and learn what he had sworn to uphold. None of that will be repeated here as it is secret and not necessary for the telling of this story.

The club hosted several major parties each semester. Members were allowed to bring guests as long as they were female or did not attend Harvard. Undergraduate non-member males were only allowed in the subterranean guest room and the lower level bathroom and must enter by the side lower level door. Female guests were only allowed in the club after noon on Friday until midnight on Sunday or for special events. Female guests were allowed anywhere in the club during these hours.

The next two major events at W would both cause great emotional turmoil for Steve and have a cataclysmic effect on his psyche.

Saturday, February 12th was the annual Valentine's Dinner/Dance. Steve donned his new used After Six Tuxedo which he had purchased second hand at Keezer's used clothing store, known for its formal wear and selection of women's hats. Steve had torn the sleeve of his father's tuxedo at the club's Christmas party and had found it easier to buy a second tuxedo than to repair the old one. He had been carrying the jacket over his shoulder when he had left the party on the exceptionally mild evening for December. As he opened the ornate gate on the wrought iron fence that surrounded the club, someone threw a pretzel at him from one of the upstairs windows. As he spun around to see where the pretzel had originated, he snagged the sleeve on one of the long metal spikes which were integral to the design of the fence and which also kept intruders from invading their hallowed grounds. He would ask Madaline or his mother to mend it and then he would have a back-up tuxedo in case he needed one. He would have sewed it himself, but he once tried to restore a button to a shirt and it took him longer to attach the button than the button stayed attached.

When Steve picked Madaline up at Kirkland House, he was greeted by a radiant vision reminiscent of Cleopatra on one of her good hair days. He was pleased that she was wearing a pink skirt with a white silk blouse because he knew that there were pink and white carnation corsages at the club for each of the dates.

When they arrived at W, Madaline asked Steve to pin on her corsage for her. He managed to secure the corsage above her left breast even though his fingers were shaking. He was surprised at himself that the proximity of her delicate breasts could make him feel so nervous. He escorted her to the bar where he introduced Madaline to several of his fellow W's. Steve could tell from the slurred voices that some of the organizers had been happily imbibing while they prepared for the others to arrive. After a protracted conversation with Jason about the evils of mixing scotch and vodka, even though a Flaming Torpedo, Jason's favorite drink, combined these with limejuice and a banana for a very tasty experience, Steve rescued Madaline with a contrived excuse about showing her the new etchings in the billiard room. They made their way to the second floor. The ballroom was decorated with pink and white balloons and eleven tables with alternating pink and white tablecloths circled the dance floor. Steve noticed that there was one more pink than white table cloth. He wondered to himself why he bothered to notice such mundane, inconsequential things. Then as they walked into the billiard room, he was besieged by a totally consequential, entirely unmundane sight. Catherine, his Catherine, was standing arm-in-arm with Gunnar. She was wearing a floor length pink gown with a pearl trim at the waist where the off-the-shoulder velvet top met the taffeta skirt. She wore a single strand of pearls that draped down to the top of her unavoidable bosom. Steve noticed the corsage pinned over her left breast. He wondered if Gunnar had pinned it there, and if his hands had shaken. Gunnar was a tall, blond rower like Steve. He was from Sweden but had gone to high school in Washington, DC because his parents were somehow involved with the Diplomatic Corps. Steve had always liked Gunnar, but now he felt betrayed. How could Gunnar bring Catherine, his Catherine, into this sacred place, the same place that Catherine had condemned for their childish, offensive activities?

Without acknowledging their presence, Steve turned on his heels, swinging Madaline with him on his arm and spilling her Vodka Collins. Back in the ballroom, Steve explained to a discombobulated Madaline that he was feeling nauseous and wanted to go home. He was very sorry, but it happened very suddenly and could not be helped. A few minutes later, Steve deposited a still stunned Madaline back at her dorm and left without further explanation. He did remember to give her a kiss goodnight and to say that he would give her a call when he felt better.

As Madaline was washing the spots of spilled Vodka Collins from her skirt, she felt like calling Steve and telling him that she was very hurt at the thoughtless way he had treated her and that she would not marry him if he were the last man on Earth. She wondered whether she should suggest to Steve that he see one of the health service counselors that he had been pushing her to see. Steve had a lot to work out and she did not like being the victim. She had glimpsed the startled look on the face of the girl in the billiard room. She had seen that face before. She had seen it in a photo album that Steve kept in his room. The face had had a different expression in the photograph. Happy Valentine's Day, she sadly thought.

*   *   *

The following weekend, Gunnar walked into the bar where Steve was having a drink with Mark, the amiable Vice President, and Chris, a sophomore who had joined in the fall. Gunnar said "Hi" to the group and then pulled Steve aside.

"Man, I'm so sorry, Steve. I didn't realize. After we saw you last week in the billiard room, Cathy told me that she had gone out with you and had known you for a long time. I had no idea or I wouldn't have brought her. I hope you don't mind."

"It's not a problem, Gunnar. Don't worry about it. Catherine, ah, Cathy and I haven't gone out since last year. And you know I'm seeing Madaline now. Feel free to see her if you want. I hope that you have better luck than I did. She can be a bit unpredictable."

"Cathy told me that she didn't know which club you had joined. She was very embarrassed when you walked in. She said she had told you that she disapproved of the clubs, and there she was, next time she sees you, in a club, and the one you joined. I didn't see you at the dinner. Where'd you go?"

"Madaline and I had another party to go to so we couldn't stay. How was the dinner?"

"It was great until Max fell down the stairs and twisted his ankle. When Mark and Tim were helping him up, he threw up all over Tim's tuxedo. Mark said he got some chunks on his shoes, too. After that, most people left to go to Rendezvous for a nightcap. I left because I had to get Cathy to the last bus back to Wellesley. This was only our second date. I met her at a mixer at Wellesley a couple weeks ago. I can't believe you used to date her; she doesn't seem your type."

"She's not." Steve was getting annoyed at the conversation. Time to switch channels. Turning to Tim, Steve interrupted Mark and Tim's intent discussion. "Tim, would you like to help me initiate two new guys on the 5th?"

"Sure"

"Mind if I join you, too?" begged Gunnar, not to be left out or taken for granted by his friend.

"Why not? Let's get together next week to plan something outrageous."

CHAPTER
NINE

March 5th. Ten days before the Ides of March. Five days after Leap Day, but only once every four years or so. Approximately one out of every 365 famous persons was born on March 5th, and an equal proportion of famous corpses became that way on this otherwise nondescript day.

Madaline and Steve were studying in his room as had become their custom. Steve would usually sit on his bed both for reading and writing. He had one of those special cushions with arms for just this purpose. Madaline thought that it was a hideous shade of purple, but Steve had had it since his freshman year and there was no separating those two. Madaline would either lie on John's bed or sit at the desk under the window. Sometimes she would try studying on Steve's bed with him, but it was only a single bed and with books and papers spread out and the poor lighting from the single bulb . . . Madaline found it easier to concentrate if she had her own space.

Steve told Madaline that she looked very pretty. Having laid the groundwork, but without any sense of timing, Steve then asked Madaline if she could sew the torn sleeve on his father's tuxedo. W was having its initiation that night and he preferred not to wear his new used tux in case it got damaged. Madaline, having recently attended a Caucus on the Oppressed Gender at Radcliffe's Women's Center, replied that she had forgotten her sewing kit at home along with her Betty Crocker cookbook and her bare feet. Once on her soapbox, she waxed eloquent about how, as a big strong man, he should be able to do it himself. She would be afraid of that big bad needle in case she was to injure her soft little helpless hands. And besides, why did she always have to be the one to come to see Steve to study? Why couldn't they ever study in her room? She was tired of being taken for granted. When was the last time that Steve had brought her flowers or candy or perfume? And why had he stopped opening the door for her? She was a very special person, and no, she was not being hypocritical. She could have equal rights and still be treated like a lady. And no, that wasn't demanding the best of both possible worlds. When would Steve begin to appreciate her? Yes, there was plenty that she had done for Steve and she was not going to dignify that comment with giving him a list. With that, she stomped over to Steve's bed and pulled the purple cushion thing out from behind him and flung it at the floor, shouting, "And this thing is ugly, too!" as she stormed out the door.

Steve bemoaned the fact that he had not grown up with a sister to help him understand this kind of hormonal behavior. He picked up his purple cushion thing and settled back on his bed to ponder the preceding soliloquy, wondering how he fit into all of this. He decided that next time he would ask his mother to do his mending instead. Women. You can't live with them and you can't live without them, he concluded. If Madaline had been a fly on his cerebellum listening to these thoughts, he would have needed a team of seamstresses and tailors to sew the pieces of his shredded brain back together again.

On further reflection, guilt gave Steve the willpower to attempt the repair himself. Unfortunately, guilt did nothing to improve his sewing skills, so he soon threw up his arms in frustration and jettisoned the wrinkled tux jacket back onto the floor of his closet to be dealt with at some other time in his life.

In the living room, Foster was sitting, waiting. He was very uncomfortable in his rented tux that made him look like a cross between a penguin and a valet parking attendant at a suburban ethnic-cuisine restaurant. He had been waiting for nearly an hour for his initiators from W to arrive. Foster had heard Steve describing the camaraderie and wild times he had experienced at W and talked him into sponsoring him for membership. Steve was not sure about having one of his roommates involved with W, but he had complied with Foster's wishes.

Once attired in his new used tux, Steve headed for W. Tim was already there waiting, supplies in hand. Steve also saw Bruce and Alan who were still preparing for Foster's initiation. Steve could picture Foster sitting in the living room, hands folded in his lap, wondering if his deodorant was still working.

Gunnar appeared a few minutes later complaining about the lines at the pet store. They took a few minutes more to compose a lethal initiation punch, and then set out to see what was behind dorm number one.

Reginald Gregory Davenport, IV was a legacy. His father and his uncle had both belonged to W. Fortunately Greg was well liked because legacies are pretty much guaranteed acceptance, unless of course the initiating henchmen can convince the legacy to withdraw his membership without complaining to Daddy and causing a stink amongst the graduate board members. Greg was waiting in his room at Eliot House looking very dapper and hereditarily comfortable in his tuxedo that was most certainly not a hand-me-down from his father. He greeted his guests with a smile and offered them a cocktail. They declined his offer because they had to be back to the club by 7:30 and they had a tight schedule to keep. Nevertheless they were impressed by his cool in the face of grave uncertainty. Maybe no one had told him that initiations had changed since his father and uncle had been heralded into the annals.

As Steve was tying a blindfold around Greg's head, he noticed that there were flakes of dandruff on his shoulders and sprinkled throughout his light brown hair. Steve mused that even the well-bred can have physical afflictions. Steve also spotted a large number of gray hairs interspersed with the darker ones making the overall color appear lighter than otherwise. Steve had never before seen someone younger than he was with so much gray hair. When he had been home over Christmas, his mother had spotted a wiry gray hair sticking out from his nest of blond hair. Without warning, she had snagged it and yanked it from his scalp. She made a disparaging remark about being like a bad wine and getting old before one's time. She then disappeared to her room where, unbeknownst to Steve, she kept his baby book with a record of all significant events in his life. She opened to a clean page and taped her trophy carefully across the top, labeling it "First Grey Hair" and citing the date.

Once Greg was blindfolded, they took a couple of swings at his face to see if he would flinch. The integrity of the bandanna passed the test. They then filled a plastic beer cup to the rim from the thermos containing their special concoction. Greg was instructed to finish the punch in the same manner in which they had all done when it had been their turn. Greg drained the glass without a protest. Clearly he had grown up in a family where before dinner cocktails even for the youngsters were part of the daily ritual. His composure was momentarily disturbed when a rumbling belch escaped from his digestive tract. He mumbled a slightly slurred apology as he belatedly brought his hand to cover his mouth.

Meanwhile, Gunnar opened his backpack which had a delightful informality about it surrounded by the aspiring gentlemen in their black uniforms. He pulled out a plastic bag and undid the twist tie that kept the contents from spilling. He took the empty plastic cup back from Greg and emptied the contents of the bag into the cup. He placed the cup back in Greg's hands and told him that they had a chaser for him with a special crouton at the bottom. Greg drank from the cup and handed it back to whoever would take it. The others watched as he swirled the "crouton" and the last of the liquid around in his mouth, a perplexed look on his face. The silence was shattered when Greg exploded with, "What is this, a fucking fish?" followed by thunderous laughter from the others.

As Greg examined the goldfish with his alcohol numbed tongue, Gunnar handed back the cup and told him to spit it out. They did not have the heart to make him swallow it after he had French kissed it. The fish took its final voyage down the toilet in the hall rather than down Greg's esophagus.

The group made its way out to Gunnar's waiting Saab, careful not to let Greg trip over the cement blocks in the parking area, and headed for dorm number two.

Brian Abbott did not answer his door when they first knocked. Finally, a tall, thin figure with red hair that was matted on one side cautiously opened the door in response to their repeated banging. He explained that he had not slept much the night before. He did not explain why. He said that he must have laid down for a rest while he was waiting and dozed off. They gave him a moment to brush his hair, put on his jacket and find his missing keys. Brian nearly gagged on the potent punch, but he managed to get it down. Steve and Gunnar watched in horror as the slimy "crouton" swam into his mouth and Brian proceeded to chew it up and swallow it. Steve was certain that he could hear the bones crunching. They decided to wait until later to tell Brian what it had been in case the news might prompt a weak stomach to soil Gunnar's car upholstery. They then guided him back to the Saab where they dumped him in the back seat where Tim was waiting with Greg.

Since it was originally Tim's idea, he explained to their incapacitated passengers that they would be going to the Ritz downtown for a drink. Gunnar drove around Cambridge for a while carrying on a rehearsed conversation with his sighted cohorts about the various landmarks they were passing on the way to the Ritz. After they grew tired of this ruse, Gunnar pulled up behind Widener Library and the others piled out. They waited while Gunnar parked.

Widener Library had been donated to Harvard University in memory of Harry Elkins Widener who drowned in the great Titanic disaster of 1912. There had been one condition with this gift from Mrs. Widener—that all students at Harvard learn how to swim. Swimming lessons, alas, would not have saved poor waterlogged Harry. Nevertheless, generations of Harvard students have made their way to the Indoor Athletic Building to take the mandatory test. The less buoyant would often take the dreaded lessons before squeaking in the week before graduation to qualify.

The Harvard Library system houses the third largest collection of books in the country after the Library of Congress and the New York Public Library. It is also home to the Harry Elkins Widener Memorial Room. Ignoring the I've-seen-it-all-before-and-I-don't-like-the-looks-of-this glare of the bespectacled, gray-haired first floor front, I'm-only-six-months-away-from-retirement librarian, the five tuxedos made their way to the second floor and the Widener Memorial Room. Tim found a large empty table and helped Gunnar set up a tablecloth, candlesticks, wine glasses, napkins and silverware. Even though the Reading Room was populated with a healthy number of readers, a heavy silence hung over the room interrupted only by a steady flutter of turning pages.

To maintain the illusion for the sensory-deprived beneficiaries, Steve said in a hushed voice, "I wonder if this section of the restaurant is closed. Oh, wait, I see some other diners. They look like they're having a very romantic time. We'd better keep it down so we don't disturb them. Why don't we go ahead and sit here. It looks like the waiters are busy." As Brian sat down with Tim's help, he knocked over his wine glass with a load clang. More eyes turned towards them intent on deciphering the extraordinary scene transpiring in their midst.

Steve spotted John's friend Jessica surrounded by books and papers at a table in the corner. While the others made quiet conversation, he hurried over, explained the situation to her and asked for her help. Jessica came back with Steve, and in the best hoity-toity voice she could muster, she apologized for their inexcusable wait and asked for their order. Gunnar jumped in and ordered a bottle of their best Sauvignon Blanc for the group. A minute later, Jessica was serving wine from the bottle that appeared out of Gunnar's backpack, peering over her shoulder in case a librarian should appear thus ending her pre-medical career with this foolish escapade.

When a series of "shushes" and "quiets" erupted, they decided to chug the rest of the $6 wine and move on. Jessica watched from her academic enclave while they gathered up their supplies, careful not to bang the silverware together thereby making their guests suspicious and arousing the wrath of the literary masses.

Next, they told the initiates that they were going dancing. They walked down JFK Street to Strawberries Records. As they jostled their way into the crowded store, they headed to an open space near the bay window overlooking the street. They told Greg and Brian that they were in a club and that they should start dancing. Gunnar found the stereo that was playing a Guns 'n Roses CD as background music and cranked up the volume. Many of the shoppers and a few passersby on the street stopped to watch the two blindfolded and tuxedoed dancers in the window flailing away under the bright lights.

When an unseen hand, probably belonging to the store manager, turned the volume back down, the spectators watched a moment longer while the dancers were guided away by three other tuxedoed guys with huge smiles and tears streaming down their faces.

Un-swayed, they moved back up to Harvard Square in front of the Harvard Square Theater. Occasionally Steve or Gunnar or Tim had to catch Greg or Brian as he tripped over some object that got in his way, even though they could not always see the cause of their clumsiness. The punch and the wine were taking their toll.

Once in position, Gunnar produced two picket signs and a stack of fliers. Tim had drawn pictures of Fidel Castro and Muammar Qadhafi and written "STOP OPPRESSION" underneath. Brian was instructed to hold the two signs while Greg distributed the fliers. Usually people avoid the teenagers and old men who are paid a flat fee to hand out a stack of coupons or fliers, but curiosity about the well-dressed, blindfolded political activists caused Greg's pile to shrink rapidly. When some of the recipients started circling back to shout angry obscenities at Greg and Brian, the others emerged from hiding and ushered them to safety.

Tim looked down at the remaining samples of his handiwork.

"Stop Oppression. The US has trampled the Cuban and Libyan communities for long enough. Castro and Qadhafi are caring leaders who have struggled to develop their countries in spite of blockades and overt aggression by the US military. The Bay of Pigs and the Gulf of Sidra are markers of US paranoia and brutality. Without Soviet support, these regimes may fall. Please write to your congressmen and send donations to: Dictators Support Fund, P.O. Box 666, New York, NY 10000."

On further reflection, Tim decided that perhaps the caricature of Hitler in the Dictators Support Fund Logo was taking it a bit too far. Oh, well.

They stumbled their way to the parking space where Gunnar had left his car. After they piled into the car, Tim explained to Greg and Brian that they would now be heading back to Cambridge. Gunnar then maneuvered his car through Cambridge onto Storrow Drive and headed into Boston. After parking in a lot that charged $2.50 for each half hour with a maximum of $18 per twelve hour period, plus city parking tax, (of undeniable concern to the student budgets), the group fought the traffic and the streetlights to head towards the Ritz. On the way, Gunnar stopped to buy some cigars and Tim took Brian into a McDonalds to use the restroom. Somehow Steve and Greg got separated from the others. Steve felt stupid asking for directions to the Ritz with a blindfolded guy dressed in a tux holding onto his arm. It was getting late, and Steve was getting tired of all the fun. He saw a subway entrance and decided to head back for Cambridge. Steve tried to ignore the probing eyes on the subway, but he could not ignore Greg's pleas for a bathroom. As they mounted the stairs into Harvard Square, Steve recalled that the Harvard Coop, straight ahead, had bathrooms on the Mezzanine level. When they got to the tiny bathroom and Greg asked for help, Steve made a hasty decision. He broke the steadfast rule of never removing the blindfold until the swearing in. He made Greg promise not to tell. Once Greg was finished and had washed his hands, Steve replaced the blindfold and they returned to W, with no one the wiser.

Gunnar, Tim and Brian arrived nearly an hour later. They had searched for Steve and Greg with no luck. They had continued to the Ritz, expecting to find them there. While standing in line to be seated in the Lobby Bar, Brian let out a loud moan and then vomited all over the back of the full length Chinchilla coat waiting in line in front of them. Steve never heard the rest of the story, but he learned third hand that Brian had been walking around with his zipper down the whole time and had eaten part of a flower arrangement in the lobby when no one was watching him. "Sometimes these kids from Nebraska have no manners," Gunnar had remarked as they fled through the revolving front door with the doorman yelling after them.

Gunnar, Tim and Steve had drunk very little before returning to W. Gunnar had been driving and the other two were happy to postpone their intake until they were safe in their comfortable castle. Because of what happened later that night, Steve swore that he would never drink alcohol for the rest of his life. He managed to keep his pledge for the next six months passing up many temptations. After that, he had no choice in the matter.

CHAPTER
TEN

Madaline had returned to her room feeling very fussed. Steve could be so dense sometimes. In a funny sort of way, she liked getting mad at him. He always seemed so surprised when she would yell at him for something he had done, or more likely had not done. She was happy that Steve could make her so crazy. She had read in a Cosmopolitan Magazine that the more you care for someone, the more they can hurt you and make you angry. She liked being in love, and she especially liked being in love with Steve. Sometimes she worried that Steve knew how much she really loved him. She did not want Steve to think that she loved him more than he loved her. She had to find that shifting equilibrium where she could be coy and yet let Steve feel just secure enough. Madaline did not want Steve to get too lazy with this relationship. She was going to make him work for it, and she knew that she had to make this extra struggle worthwhile for him. Her one greatest fear was that once she had given herself freely to Steve and they had made love, that Steve would lose interest in her because the chase was over. Or worse than that, what if she was no good in bed? How could she know if she was any good? How does one measure such a thing? She knew that Ellyn had slept with her old boyfriend, or at least that is what Ellyn had implied, however, she could not imagine asking Ellyn what she did to be "good" in bed. She had talked about sex with her girlfriends in high school and they had all shared what they did while making love, including her. But most of them were making things up, including her. What if Steve was into S&M? After all, that is what some of their friends jokingly called them. She was glad that Steve had not been more demanding of her. She knew that he was anxious to make love to her. Sometime soon. Maybe.

Madaline found a notice slipped under her door. It announced that Harvard would be sponsoring a Conservation Competition. Prizes of $500, $300 and $200 would be given after each of the next two months to the three residential houses that decreased their electricity consumption by the greatest percentage over the corresponding month of the previous year. The prize money was to be used for a party for the house members. Harvard only has twelve residential houses including the three at Radcliffe Quad, so the odds were pretty good.

Before Madaline climbed into bed later that night, she turned off the night light which usually burned all night. She decided that she would practice for her part in the competition. She thought it was a great idea. Harvard would save thousands of dollars in energy costs, fossil fuels would be spared, and a bunch of students would get to eat some pizza and drink some free beer. As she climbed into bed in the dark, her feet got tangled in the sheets. She kept pushing, trying to get her legs down under the covers. She got more and more frustrated. She felt like a klutz. Finally she gave up and climbed out of bed. She tripped over her shoes as she fumbled for the light-switch.

Once she could see, Madaline returned to examine her bed. She pulled back the covers and discovered that she had been short-sheeted. Ellyn, it must have been Ellyn, had removed the fitted bottom sheet and hidden it under the blanket. She had tucked the top sheet in at the top of the bed and folded the bottom half back up to look like the cover sheet. No wonder she had been unable to get her feet to the bottom of the bed.

What a night for Ellyn to become a prankster. She should not have been telling Ellyn about all of Steve's shenanigans. Now she was mad at Ellyn and she was even madder at Steve. She fumed at both of them while she remade her bed. She turned on the nightlight and climbed into bed. "Who cares about some damn competition," she thought as she stared at the shadows on the ceiling.

*   *   *

Steve sat at his table enjoying the soothing effects of the scotch in his tumbler. His parents were teetotallers, so Steve had not gotten much exposure to different types of alcohol until he got to college. He had drunk plenty of beer at parties in high school, and he once got very drunk and threw up after drinking vodka straight from the bottle. He had discovered Southern Comfort his sophomore year, but after the Yale Game, he vowed to try something else. Southern Comfort was too sweet and went down too easily.

This was Steve's fourth scotch that evening and his fourth scotch ever. He was slowly deciding that this would be his new drink. He was glad that Mark had bought him the first one. Steve watched as Mark climbed on his chair and nearly fell. He raised his drink to the room and downed the whole glass. Steve determined from the color of the drink that Mark was probably still drinking scotch as well, but Mark looked like he had had a few more than Steve. Mark began to tell a very raunchy joke while hoots and jeers were shouted about the room. "What's your left hand doing in your pocket?," shouted one. "Show us your joke," shouted another. The waitresses from the catering company were clearing the dishes from the dinner off of the tables. Steve could see them giving disapproving glances at each other. He felt a brief embarrassment, but then decided that they had probably heard much worse over the years.

A box of cigars with a "W" imprinted on the labels was being passed around. Steve did not like cigars, but he took one anyway in case someone wanted one later. Steve finished his drink and meandered downstairs to the bar for a refill. When he returned, the jokes were getting even more disgusting and the hecklers were dominating. A large poster board with an ornate sketch of the clubhouse was being passed around for signatures. The walls were covered with a history of such posters dating back to the beginning of the century. Steve watched Ramon, the new member who was sitting next to him, sign the board. Steve could not decipher from Ramon's signature what his last name was. The "Ramon" was barely legible as well. Steve made a concerted effort to have his signature more legible so that his descendants might be able to locate his signature on the wall someday. He felt very proud that he had joined such a wonderful organization and was making such good lifelong friends. He could always come back to visit Cambridge and they would welcome him at W. Some of the older alumnae who came regularly were treated almost like celebrities by the undergraduates.

As Steve was carefully signing the board, Reginald Gregory Davenport, IV stood on his chair to tell a joke as was the custom for all new members to do. Brian would be excused from this exercise because he had passed out hours before and was sleeping on a sofa in the guest room on the lower level. As Greg hoisted the glass to his mouth, he leaned his head back to chug the contents. The force of his movement propelled his whole body backwards over the backrest of the chair. Gunnar, sitting in the chair beside him, was too slow to prevent the fall. He did catch one leg as it slid over the back of the chair. Greg's upper body landed with a loud clamor on the wooden floor below. Silence briefly filled the room as everyone froze, aghast that an accident might mar their fun filled evening. Gunnar swung around onto the floor next to Greg. After blinking his eyes a few times, Greg said, "Wow, that was quite a trip. I don't think I finished my joke." He tried to sit up, but Gunnar held him down. He asked one of the waitresses, who was transfixed by the scene, to get some ice from the kitchen. They wrapped it in a white linen napkin and Gunnar held it to the back of Greg's head where a large bump was forming. Gunnar motioned to Steve to help him. The two blond juniors hoisted the wounded sophomore to his feet and assisted him down the stairs to the living room. They sat Greg on a sofa and tried to assess the damage. They heard the roar of laughter resume upstairs as the crisis was quickly erased from the short-term memories of the drunken masses.

Gunnar and Steve decided to walk Greg home. They felt responsible since they had been the ones to mix the original punch and each had bought him a drink later on. When they got to his door, they found some keys in Greg's pocket. As they were fumbling with the lock, the door opened and one of Greg's roommates let them in. They dumped Greg on his bed and the roommate said that he would take care of Greg. The roommate looked at Greg's eyes and said, "At least he doesn't have a concussion." Steve chastised himself for not thinking to check for that, but then he remembered that he did not know how.

On the way back to W from Eliot House, they passed by Kirkland House. Steve considered stopping in to check on Madaline, but decided that she might get even angrier if she saw how drunk he was.

He marched on with Gunnar, letting Gunnar talk while he partially listened.

As they came near the clubhouse, Steve and Gunnar both looked up when they heard their names. Steve saw Foster, Tim and Ramon, the new member who had been sitting next to Steve at dinner. They had climbed out of one of the dormer windows on the third floor and were sitting on the ledge with their drinks, shouting at the girls passing by.

In the past, Steve had occasionally climbed out a second story window onto the roof over the entryway to watch the passersby, but he had never seen anyone on the third floor roof before. It looked very dangerous with their legs hanging over the edge. Steve shouted back, "Come on down, you idiots."

Foster yelled back, "Come on up, you chicken shit." Foster was holding a beer bottle in one hand. He swung the bottle to try to spray some beer at Steve below. As he was flailing about, they all heard a loud wrenching noise. Suddenly the gutter below their legs gave way and went crashing off to the left. Steve and Gunnar watched in horror as Foster and Tim lost their grip and slipped off the roof. They saw their shadows plummeting across the lit ballroom window on the second floor. Steve felt the ground actually shudder when their bodies hit the ground. Out of the corner of his eye, Steve could see Ramon hanging onto the lip of the dormer window. He could hear Ramon screaming. He did not hear Foster or Tim screaming.

CHAPTER ELEVEN

When Steve had been nine, his family had adopted a cat. To be more accurate, the cat had adopted Steve's family. The family had gone to church together that Easter morning. Christmas and Easter are usually the only two times each year that the entire family of three would venture out together to the Bryn Mawr Presbyterian Church. Most Sundays, Steve would sleep in, undisturbed by his parents who were either sleeping themselves, or sitting in the family room reading the Sunday paper. Sometimes Miriam would go to church alone and leave William there reading by himself, content with his coffee in his "Best Dad In The World" mug which Steve had given him for father's day when Steve was five. William constantly thanked him for the mug that caused Steve unending embarrassment because he remembered that it was his mother who had bought the mug, wrapped it up and then asked Steve to print his name on the card. Even at nine years old, Steve did not feel he deserved credit for his mother's good intentions. When Steve was ten, the mug was found mysteriously broken in the kitchen sink. Four days later on Father's Day, Steve gave his father a new "Best Dad in the Universe" mug that he had bought himself with his own birthday money.

As the family drove up the driveway in their Sunday clothes, they were greeted by a large scruffy black cat with a single splotch of white fur on his left side. The cat refused to yield to the car, so William, who always drove when they went anywhere together, jammed on the brakes. The cat remained there, statuesque, blocking their way to the garage. Steve scrambled out of the car and around to the cat. Fluffy, the cat with which Steve had grown up, had been hit by a car and killed over a year before. Steve's parents had resisted his periodic pleadings for a new cat or a dog. This was Steve's chance. He and the cat magically joined forces and quickly overpowered his parents' futile resistance. Steve swore that he would feed the cat and walk it every day. The cat rubbed against both of their legs and purred as loudly as he could when they weakened and petted him. Steve's parents gave in. They negotiated for Steve to clean out the litter box in lieu of the daily walks. When Steve discovered that the cat had an extra toe on one foot, his father explained about genetic deformities and mutations. Steve decided to name the cat "Genetic Deformity" and call him "Genny." Steve's parents thought that this was a bit odd, but at least preferable to his other choice, "Funky Foot."

The vet that gave Genny his distemper booster shot said that Genny appeared very healthy, for a sixteen year old cat, as best as he could figure. Steve's parents were concerned that Steve would become emotionally attached to Genny. They explained to their young son that cats often do not live to be even as old as Genny was then. Like Steve's grandfather, Genny might be too old and his heart might give out. Steve said that he understood. But Genny did not die of old age.

For Miriam's birthday, they had gone to the William Penn Inn for dinner. Steve wanted the double chocolate sin cake, but William whispered to him that they had a birthday cake for his mother waiting at home. They drove home in high spirits, looking forward to the cake, and Steve hoped ice-cream, too. As Steve was walking toward the back door, he saw a lump on the step. It was Genny. He was bleeding from the mouth. When Steve leaned over to try to help, Genny raised his head slightly and let out a brief squeaky meow. Steve caressed his head. He heard Genny purring. Then the purring stopped. Genny had died.

The next morning, they buried Genny in the back yard. In the light of day, they were able to figure out what must have happened to Genny. He loved to climb on roofs. He must have been on the roof of the garage and slipped off. Perhaps he was swatting at a fly or a moth and his aging sensors miscalculated the edge of the shingles. They found a matt of fur and a pool of blood near the garage. There was a trail of blood leading to the back door where Genny had dragged himself in search of human assistance. The size of the dried patch of blood on the top step and the door mat indicated that he must have lain by the back door for a long time waiting for his master and watching the last of his nine lives wither away.

*   *   *

People came running from everywhere. Steve stood there frozen in disbelief watching the escalating activity. Finally, he was aware that Gunnar, who was still standing at his side, was shouting to Ramon, "Hang on, Ramon." A light and then two faces appeared at the window on the third floor. Strong hands reached out and grabbed Ramon's arm that was swinging beneath the window. The front door flew open and bodies surged out into the front courtyard. Other faces peered out the windows from the ballroom. A girl on the street screamed. Several others must have joined her as the screaming grew in intensity.

As Ramon was lifted to the opening in the window, a small shadow plunged toward the ground below him. Ramon had been so scared since the gutter gave loose and he was left alone on the roof that his hands were like vice grips on the ledge and the glass which he had been holding. As they pulled him up, his grip relaxed and the glass met the fate that could have been for Ramon. Two of the frenzied spectators were pelted by the shards of glass ricocheting off the slate walkway below.

Steve realized that his legs had started moving. He was heading toward the gate and the commotion beyond. He heard that same girl screaming. He heard himself breathing. He heard the thoughts in his brain smashing into the side of his head trying to get out. He did not want to think. Maybe he should head inside to the bar and order another one of those magnificent scotches. His legs did not cooperate. He continued on toward the mass of bodies hovering around the space where Foster and Tim had disappeared. He could not see much because of all of the people. The only lighting was from a yellowish streetlamp and the intermittent bright lighting that poured out of the front door every time someone else came out to join the crowd.

Steve pushed his way in closer. Then he saw them. The fence. He heard more screaming. He knew that it was he who was screaming.

He heard sirens. He heard screaming. He heard voices. What were they saying? Why were they talking to him? What was he saying? He heard a voice. It was not louder than the others, but he heard it anyway. It said, "He's dead."

Steve was sitting on the ground. He watched the blue uniforms guiding people away. He watched the white uniforms hovering around the bodies. They brought in different equipment. A second ambulance arrived and more red and blue lights began flashing. Steve watched while four shapes in white lifted a limp body off the metal fence where it had been impaled on the decorative spikes. Steve threw up on the ground beside him. He felt dizzy. He welcomed the sour taste in his mouth. He felt that he deserved some punishment for allowing this to happen. He had been having so much fun with Tim earlier that day. And Foster was his roommate. They always picked on Foster. He was a real character and could always make them laugh. He tried so hard. If he could talk to Foster now, he would tell him that he loved him. Steve did not have a lot of close friends. He had always wanted a brother. This year had been good for Steve as he had gotten to know Johnson and Foster better. Steve began to cry. The tears blurred his already hazy vision. He could see more people rushing about and hovering over one of the bodies. Soon, a rolling cart was brought in and the body and the hovering white uniforms moved with it until it disappeared inside one of the ambulances. The ambulance sped away. Steve could not hear the siren. It was not loud enough to be audible over the screaming in his ears. Suddenly he started choking. The screaming stopped. He regained his breath, but he did not start screaming again. He spit. He still had that taste in his mouth. Where was his handkerchief? He usually carried one. He should have worn his other tux. He went ahead and blew his nose on the sleeve anyway.

Why were they taking so long? What were they doing? How would he tell John and Johnson? What would Madaline think? Would he be the one who would have to tell Foster's parents?

He stopped crying. His head was still pounding. He saw the other body rising on the rolling cart. The group moved past him to the second ambulance. The letters on the front of the vehicle looked like, "e c n a l u b m A." Steve realized that it spelled "Ambulance" backwards. Good. His brain must be working again. He looked at the group as it passed. He saw the body on the cart. He looked carefully to see who it was, but he could not see the face. They had a sheet covering the face. How could he see who it was if they had a sheet over his face? How could he breathe like that? He should get up and take the sheet off so he would not suffocate. Steve tried to get up. He fell back down landing squarely in the vomit that he had unceremoniously deposited there.

After the crowd began to disburse, Steve gathered his wits about him. He started to analyze the situation. He began to get overwhelmed so he decided to focus on one issue at a time. He was very proud of himself. He had a plan. He reached an important decision and he concluded that it was a good one. He would get his tux dry cleaned in the morning. And, he would take his father's tux to the tailor to get the torn sleeve repaired. Then he would have two tuxes if he needed them. "Yeah, that's it. That's what I'll do."

*   *   *

When Steve called Madaline the next day it was almost noon. Somehow, he had gotten himself home and cleaned up. After taking four aspirin, he had gone to bed. The next morning, he could not separate his nightmares from the horrors of reality during the previous night. As the cold truth dawned on him, he felt a wave of nausea rising within. He dry heaved, but he had nothing left to vomit. He needed to eat. He needed to call the police and the hospital. He dialed Madaline's number.

"Hello."

"Madaline, I'm so glad you're there."

"I'm not talking to you."

"Lin, listen, I need your . . ."

"You can be such a jerk sometimes. Yesterday, you were acting like a real idiot. You . . ."

"Madaline," Steve pleaded.

"What?" she retorted, still sounding angry.

"I think Foster is dead."

"That's not very funny."

Steve got choked up and simultaneously annoyed that Madaline was not being more supportive. He tried to continue but could not.

"Why are you doing this to me? I'm still mad at you. This is a sick joke if you're trying to say you're sorry about your attitude yesterday."

Steve regained his voice and corralled his thoughts. "I'm not kidding. Foster and Tim fell off the roof of the club last night."

"Oh, my God."

"I have to call the police to find out what happened. I needed to call you first."

"What happened?"

"I don't know. They were fooling around on the roof. I saw the whole thing. It was unbelievable. I don't think I'll ever be able to sleep well again. I need a hug so badly. I heard someone say, 'He's dead.' I thought maybe I was imagining it, but they took someone away with a sheet over his head. It was supposed to be a fun party. If I had been faster, maybe I could have caught them. I was the one who proposed Foster to W. If I hadn't he might still be alive. He'd probably be sitting here belching and making fun of my hangover." Steve started to cry.

"Steve, honey, it wasn't your fault. Let me call the police and see if I can find out what happened. Maybe you had a bit too much to drink and imagined it all. Foster is probably asleep at the club waiting for his hangover to go away so he can come home and make fun of you. I'll give you a call back. Go take some aspirin and drink lots of water. Don't worry, honey."

Madaline pieced together the story from the person who answered the phone at W, a desk clerk at the Cambridge police station, and a ward secretary at Massachusetts General Hospital. When she realized that Steve had not been hallucinating, she hailed a cab and went to be with Steve. She could not confirm his fears over the phone.

Foster was the lucky one, or so the doctors said. Tim, only 19 years old, landed squarely on the wrought iron fence that surrounded the clubhouse. The spikes gored his stomach, his spleen and his left kidney. But, these injuries were superfluous. Death was attributed to the massive cranial bleeding and the broken neck that he suffered when his head flung into the rungs of the fence. Tim never knew what hit him and he died within moments of the impact.

Tim had been looking forward to being an usher in his sister's wedding that June. Mary was his only sister and he had been so happy that her fiancé, Carlo, had picked him to be in the wedding party. The wedding pictures looked slightly out of balance with six bridesmaids and only five groomsmen, but Mary had refused to let Carlo replace her brother. The wedding album has one picture of Mary, looking strikingly beautiful in her beaded wedding dress, standing alone holding a framed picture of Tim. It was his graduation picture from high school and was the most recent picture they had. Mary was not ashamed of the tears streaming down both of her cheeks. She would later show this picture to her oldest son and tell him, just one more time, why he had been named Timothy.

Fosters parents flew in from Pittsburgh to be with him at Massachusetts General Hospital. He was in the critical care unit. His fall had been partly broken by the branch of a Japanese maple tree. Unfortunately, the beer bottle that Foster had been holding fell undisturbed to the ground where it landed on the edge of the walk. The bottom of the bottle shattered. The neck and a large protruding spike of glass remained intact and came to rest in a space between the slate blocks of the path. Foster landed directly on the upturned spike of the bottle, severing the lateral portion of his spinal cord. The only blessing in this was that he could not feel the pain from the cracked femur that was protruding through the flesh and skin of his thigh. The doctors had to wait for his blood alcohol level to decrease before they could safely operate to assess the damage to the spinal cord. Massachusetts General Hospital has its owned world-renowned neuro-surgeon on staff. At the time of Foster's accident, Dr. Herpels was speaking at a conference in Lake Tahoe. His surgical team was highly skilled and practiced. They handled the three hour and forty-eight minute surgery with only a brief telephone consultation with their chief.

Shortly after the operation, the team leader told Foster's parents, who were taking turns pacing in the blue and yellow flowered waiting room, that their son's operation had been a success and that he was resting comfortably. Yes, they could see him in a couple of hours. Yes, once his broken leg had healed, he should be able to walk again.

The surgeon and his team had missed a small lesion in the parietal lobe at the rear of the cerebrum where a tiny shard of glass had splintered off. Three days later after Dr. Herpels had returned and examined Foster's chart and condition; he ordered emergency surgery to investigate the exorbitant swelling and discoloration adjacent to the injury sight. Dr. Herpels discovered the lesion and the resulting nerve tissue damage. He did the best he could. Foster would feel minimal pain. They would be able to release him from the hospital in a few weeks time. Dr. Herpels ordered intensive occupational and physical therapy programs to help Foster adjust to his new condition. Foster would never walk again.

*   *   *

When Madaline arrived, John and Johnson were with Steve in the living room. They all looked concerned. Steve looked ill. Madaline dreaded having to report her news, but there was no way to soften it.

Madaline spent the day with Steve. She had planned to write a sociology paper that day and finish her psychology readings. The four of them sat around for a while not saying too much. They got into some heavy discussions about death and dying. They discussed the government's plans for long term care. They talked about different relatives and friends with disabilities whom they knew. They made a list of what they could do to help Foster with his course work and organizing his stuff. They formulated a plan about how he could get around. The college had a special van for disabled students. They figured if they could get him through this semester, he could finish his recovery over the summer and return good as new in the fall for his senior year. After all, a second call to the hospital revealed that the operation had been a success. Everything was supposed to be all right.

Then Steve remembered Tim. He excused himself to his room. Madaline joined him after a little while. She left John and Johnson alone. Johnson had seemed very shaky, but she figured that John could take care of him while she looked after Steve.

Madaline climbed onto the bed with Steve. She hugged him tightly. After a while, he slept in her arms. She listened to his heavy breathing. She imagined what it would have been like if Foster had called her with the same news. What if he had died? She did not know Tim, but it made her very sad, nonetheless. When Steve awoke, he told her about the evening. He told her about the wine in Widener Library and how Brian had thrown up at the Ritz. He even laughed once. Madaline could tell that he needed to talk, so she just listened. He talked on about the dinner and the faces the waitresses made when someone told a bad joke. He could not remember any of the jokes, but he never was any good at remembering jokes. Finally, he talked about Tim. He told about his sister's wedding and how Tim was on the volleyball team. He wondered what the volleyball team would do without him. He talked about Tim's girlfriend, Annie. He wondered if she knew yet. He wondered what Tim must have thought as he flew through the air. He wondered why God would allow this to happen.

When Steve fell asleep again, Madaline carefully slipped her arm from under his neck and climbed out of bed. There was no sign of John or Johnson, so she left without a word. She was pleased that Steve had needed her. She was sorry that it had to be for such a terrible reason. She felt very sad and lonely. She started to cry, for the first time that day.

CHAPTER TWELVE

Steve's eight man crew boat received a respectable second place in the final heat of the Head of the Charles. They were nosed out by the University of Southern California in the final leg. Steve had been hoping that they would qualify to race at Henley. He had never been to England and had been looking forward to going with his teammates and showing the world that they were the best. Unfortunately, the eight men from USC disproved that theorem before they had a chance. Perhaps if he had been sleeping better and had not gained those four pounds from eating two depression desserts every night, they might have been victorious. Steve hoped that his teammates did not blame him for their loss. The coach had made a comment at weigh-in, but no one else had said anything. He had tried to resist the desserts, but he found that the chocolate cake and éclairs and chocolate ice-cream in particular made him feel better, at least while he was eating them. Afterwards, he was usually disgusted with himself.

Madaline had come to watch the Head of the Charles. She had given him a good luck kiss before the race. Steve was pretty sure that he saw her standing on one of the bridges waving and yelling as they passed underneath. He was glad she was there. She had been a wonderful support system, encouraging him to continue his life and not blame himself for what had happened to Foster and Tim. Madaline was waiting for Steve when his boat coasted into the dock back at Newell Boat House.

"Wow, that was quite a race. I think the judges had a bad angle. You guys beat them by a full second."

Steve gasped, "We should have beaten them." The ride back up river had been at a more leisurely pace, but Steve was still short of breath.

"Well, I'm very proud of you. I think you did great."

"Was that you on the bridge?"

"Why, did you see another gorgeous girl watching the race? Yes, it was me. The view is great from up there and I was able to get a good peek down your shirt."

"I thought I saw you. I was glad it was you. Sometimes there are teenagers up there who spit on us during practice. One time I had a giant hocker land right on my shoulder. I was rowing, so I could only watch as the glob of phlegm slid down my shoulder and across my chest into my lap. It was repulsive. I would hate to have that happen during a race. It can be very distracting. I have noticed that the boat seems to go faster under the bridges. I wonder if everyone is pulling extra hard to get us past the spit bomb danger zones."

"I finagled my way into covering the Head for the *Crimson*. Normally I do not work on the sports desk. I was able to trade Kissinger's speech with Jim Wright who normally covers the rowing events. Now, Mr. Harris, would you kindly give me a quote for my readers."

"I love you."

"That's wonderful news, but I'm not sure my editor would consider that very relevant to today's near victory."

"How about, 'If not for the courage of the fearless crew, the minnow would be lost'?"

"I don't think so."

"Okay, try this on for size. The high-pressure zone and northwesterly breezes on the Charles River this morning provided a considerable advantage to the team from Southern California where similar weather conditions prevail. If a surely unintentional wave created by the USC coaches' launch had not crossed the bow of the Harvard eight, the superior talent and strength of Coach Ian Spinner's rowers would have prevailed. Make sure you spell Coach's name right. When he gets upset by little things like a typo, somehow we end up being the ones to run the extra laps."

"You don't want me to mention the little inboard engines on the

USC boat? Or maybe that they were on the short side of the race course?"

"Hey, stop teasing. That wave may look little to you, but it can really make a difference. If the officials had seen it, the USC team would have been disqualified. The coaches' boats are required to keep their wake behind all of the competing boats."

"Okay, honey, I'll use your quote. I may even spice it up a bit. You know, artistic license and all that."

Steve changed and grabbed his books from his locker. He accompanied Madaline back to her room. Since the accident, they had started studying in Madaline's room. Steve was spending less and less time around Cabot House. He and his roommates no longer had their late night discussions. Without Foster there, it felt wrong. Steve would go home and usually straight to his room.

Steve and John would occasionally throw a Frisbee around the quad and he still had meals with John and Johnson. But, Steve felt especially uncomfortable around Johnson. The two Petes had been roommates before blocking together with Steve and John for their junior year. Johnson had never quite bounced back to his old self after his mother died. Now, he rarely laughed. If anyone asked how Foster was doing, Johnson would usually walk away without responding. He started skipping classes and staying up all night in his room. Steve was worried about him.

Steve and John continued to share their room. Even after Foster's parents came and removed Foster's clothes and books and his stereo, they left his room untouched almost like a shrine. John was spending a lot of time with Jessica, so Steve could often get to sleep without having to talk with either of his roommates. He kept thinking, "Maybe Senior year will be better when Foster comes back to school." Steve did not know then that he and Foster would never see each other again.

CHAPTER THIRTEEN

The end of junior year was uneventful. Steve was sad to say goodbye to some of his friends who were seniors and would be graduating and going out to face the "real" world. Some of his best buddies from W, like Mark and Kevin, would be leaving and moving to such exotic places as Denver and Hong Kong. Steve, on the other hand, would be heading back to Philadelphia for the summer.

Steve liked Philadelphia. All of his high school friends lived there. The best soft pretzels and cheese steaks in the world could be found there. He knew his way around. What more could he ask for?

But Philadelphia was not exciting or exotic. It was just home. Whenever he told someone he was going home to Philadelphia for the summer, he could not help thinking of W.C. Fields who said, "First prize, one-week in Philadelphia. Second prize, two weeks in Philadelphia." Steve would be there for almost twelve weeks. He decided he should not complain about twelfth prize because he would be receiving another prize before then.

Steve and Madaline planned a pilgrimage to Maine to go camping for eight days as soon as Madaline's last exam was over. Steve would have two days to prepare and pack for their excursion because his exams were scheduled earlier. Madaline told Steve that she did not want to hear "boo" from him during those two days. It would be hard enough studying without hearing the chipperness in his voice knowing that he had already completed three fourths of his college degree.

Those final days of junior year ticked away in an agonizing blur. Steve met Madaline outside her last exam with a bottle of once chilled sparkling grape juice. They sat under a tree and laughed and joked and called their professors nasty names. They did not even notice that the bubbly was rather flat and left a bitter after-taste. Steve joked that he was looking forward to when he could afford some real champagne that came with a cork, not that he would ever drink any. He blamed alcohol for Tim's death and Foster injuries. Madaline made a huge popping noise with her finger in her cheek and Steve kissed her with an even louder pop.

That night as they drifted off to sleep in their own beds, they both dreamed of what life would be like in the future. They imagined getting married and having kids. They bought lots of cars and big houses. In their own dreams, Madaline had a horse and Steve had a plane. They each came home from work and their spouse greeted them at the door with their slippers and dinner was waiting for them on the table. Music played throughout and the world was a happy, peaceful place.

Their alarms jarred them awake at 6:45, synchronized the night before. Steve wanted to get an early start, and after all, he had been packed and on idle for almost two days.

Steve had made a deal with Jason. Since Jason would be working in Cambridge and living at W that summer, he did not need his Isuzu Trooper. Steve's new Jeep Cherokee was still in the garage in Philadelphia. So that Steve would not have to travel to Philadelphia and drive the Jeep the three hundred miles back up to Cambridge, he agreed to pay to have new tires put on the rear and have the Trooper simonized in exchange for borrowing it for the eight-day camping trip. To seal the deal, Steve bought Jason his favorite drink, a Flaming Torpedo. When the banana was gone and the bottom of the glass was almost showing, Jason agreed to drop the wax job. Steve felt slightly guilty about his newfound nefarious negotiating skills and the tools of his trade.

Steve drove down to Kirkland House in the borrowed Trooper. Jason had just had it painted metallic red and had put a Mercedes emblem on the front hood. There was a little green Christmas tree hanging from the rearview mirror. The pine fragrance that it advertised barely helped to mask the smell of 48,000 miles of cigarette smoke. Jason was one of the few people Steve knew who still smoked. Smoking had gone full circle from being hip in the sixties to being scorned today.

Steve noticed that the fuel gage was almost on empty, but he figured that he had no grounds for complaint. He would be sure to return the Trooper with a full tank of gas and maybe a six-pack of beer, or at least a thank you note. Jason was pretty cool to let them use his vehicle.

The drive to Mooselookmeguntic Lake in the upper Longfellow Mountains took nearly seven hours. The roads in that part of Maine are very narrow and windy as they meander their way through the lower ranges of the Longfellows up close to the Canadian border. Madaline and Steve marveled at the spectacular scenery. A road sign several miles before Wilsons Mills read "Mooselookmeguntic Lake—16 miles." As they passed through the center of Wilsons Mills, they took seriously the sign that said last gas station for 42 miles. From the looks of the roads and the dearth of civilization, they decided to fill up the tank, check the oil and add water to the radiator. They also stopped in Patterson's Grocery to fill up the cooler with sodas, apple juice, eggs, milk, cheese and frozen hotdogs. Steve gave Madaline a riveting look when she picked up some beer. Without hesitation, she placed it back on the shelf. They finished off their mental list with bread, cookies, fruit and an assortment of canned goods. As they pulled out of town and read the parting sign, "Come back soon, in one peace," they felt content with the world and ready to hurry up and relax.

The final dozen miles to the lake took over an hour. The road alternated between macadam, asphalt, gravel and dirt. A few miles out, they had to stop and move a fallen birch tree that was blocking the road. As they passed by other lakes on their way through Massachusetts and New Hampshire, Madaline asked Steve how he had picked Mooselookmeguntic Lake. Steve explained that his parents had gone there shortly after they were married and said that it was one of the most beautiful places on earth. As they got closer, Madaline remarked that things must not have changed much, especially the roads, since Steve's parents had been there.

When they finally arrived, excited and tired, they checked in at the ranger's station that doubled as the registration desk for the campground. In exchange for the $25 registration fee that was good for a full week, they were given a map, a guide booklet and a key to their own private outhouse. Steve glanced at the guidebook while the female ranger recorded their vehicle information in her leather-bound logbook. The guidebook had sections on "Snake Bites," "Caution With Fires," "Care of your Outhouse," and "The Woods After Dark," to name a few. Steve turned his attention back to the logbook. It looked like it had been around forever. He asked the ranger how old it was and she replied that it was the original for the station. She further explained that the station had opened in 1947.

Steve's parents had been married two decades later. The ranger allowed Steve to look for his parents' signatures. They were easy to spot as there were only a few dozen other names logged that year. Steve wondered if the same log would be there for his kids to sign. Steve would have been quite surprised to learn that Mooselookmeguntic Lake would be even more isolated and pristine when his kids would become adults.

Steve had rented a tent, two sleeping bags and some other camping equipment from the Army/Navy store in Boston. He was hoping to borrow these things, but no one he knew, understandably, had these things with them in Cambridge.

By the time they located their private "dunny" with the help of the map and a little luck and had found a smooth spot to set up the tent, it was nearly dark and they were thoroughly exhausted. They were too tired to bother cooking anything, so they munched on fruit and cookies and enjoyed the first cold sodas of their first vacation together. Their campsite had a superb view out over the northwestern section of the lake. Through the gaps in the trees, they could see the reflection of the moon growing brighter on the still water as they finished up their evening snack. They walked down a small sloping path leading to the water's edge. They stood there, arm in arm, gazing up in sheer delight at the plethora of stars blanketing the night sky. They were ecstatic when a shooting star, their first ever, rocketed across the constellations. Their childish glee atrophied as they saw the second and third and fourth shooting stars painting shining paths across the fairy dust horizon. The silence was interrupted by a splash in the water where a fish forgot that it could not fly. The disturbance awoke a bullfrog whose deep-throated rib-bits were joined in chorus by a cacophony of crickets and other creatures of the night.

After fidgeting about in her sleeping bag for a few minutes trying to accustom herself to sleeping at ground level, listening to Steve's already heavy breathing, Madaline joined Steve in a deep sleep, anesthetized by the clean mountain air, and did not awaken even once until the tremendous crash outside the tent.

*   *   *

Steve and Madaline both sat bolt upright in their sleeping bags. They looked at each other, unfocused terror showing in their sleepy eyes. Because they had each heard the noise, they knew that it was not a dream. They listened, uncertain whether to move or hide, and they heard more clattering noises outside the tent. Steve carefully unzipped the front flap and peaked outside. The sunrise was reflecting on the water below splashing vibrant patterns of reds and purples across the shimmering waters. Steve stepped out of the flaps and stubbed his toe on a protruding rock. Fear of the unknown intruder kept him from cursing up a storm. As he peered around the edge of the tent, he saw the source of the noise. There were three faces staring back at him, the beady eyes surrounded by the dark circles of the bandits' masks.

Steve and Madaline had left the cooler and a bag of groceries on the picnic table that came with their campsite. The crash that had awakened them was the cooler encountering the hard ground after being pushed off the table by the team of raccoons. They were busily munching away on the picnic breakfast that the humans had so kindly left out for them. Steve lunged at the masked marauders clapping his hands together painfully aware of the pine needles sticking into his bare feet. The raccoons hesitated a moment, staring at the spectacle confronting them. They then leisurely bounded off the far side of the picnic table hauling with them an unopened bag of cheese curls, a partially eaten bag of marshmallows, and a mangled king size loaf of white bread, leaving a trail of slices behind them.

Steve returned triumphantly to the tent where his maiden was waiting for him. He had cast out the villains and had suffered only minor injuries. Madaline examined his stubbed toe and kissed it to make it feel better since there was not much else she could do to help.

They abandoned thoughts of further sleep. They would have all week to relax. After they hastily dressed, they ventured outside to assess the damage to their supplies. The carton of milk had burst open and had nearly drained on its side. There were some claw marks on the package of frozen hotdogs, but they appeared relatively intact. The glass bottle of apple juice had survived the crash miraculously unscathed. The carton of eggs had landed on the ground and four of the shells had cracked. Most of the cans were still on the table, but Madaline found a couple which had rolled down the path toward the lake. The biggest loss was the packet of fresh ground coffee that had been ripped open and scattered all over the table and the ground. Steve was able to salvage a little that was left in the packet and scoop some of the grounds off of the table. They could have coffee that morning, but they would need to restock. Steve needed his coffee.

While Madaline started breakfast, Steve headed back to the ranger's station to find out where they could get some new supplies. The ranger on duty was a surly looking man whose ample uniform and its bulging contents had probably prevented him for years from seeing his feet while standing. Steve explained his problem and the ranger said that there was a supply depot on the northeast tip of the lake. As Steve turned to leave, the ranger grunted after him that if he had taken the time to read the guide booklet, which he himself had written, he would have seen the section about, "Protecting Your Food and Yourself." He advised that Steve might want to leave his supplies in the car at night or the Depot might have to open an account for him. Steve thanked the ranger and left massaging his wounds from the verbal lashing.

When he got back, Madaline was nowhere to be seen. He could see some raw eggs in a fry pan on the Coleman stove. Madaline had managed to salvage most of the contents of three of the cracked eggs. When Steve shouted her name, he heard a subdued response from inside the tent.

"Madaline, where are you?"

"In here."

"What's wrong? You sound upset."

"I was trying to get that damn stove to light. I tried the starter and then I tried some matches. I think the fuel line must be clogged or there is no gas. As I was lighting another match, getting very frustrated,

I saw a large stick near the picnic table move. It was a God damned snake. I hate snakes. I can't stand them. They make my skin crawl. I'm going to have nightmares about them crawling in my sleeping bag and slithering across my face. My psychology professor would say that I am having a very Freudian reaction, but I don't care. I hate snakes."

"Which way did it go?"

"You think I hung around to watch where it went? You must be crazy."

"I'm not big on snakes either. Let me take a look at this great guide booklet and see if it has any advice about snakes. Let's see, it has a section on snake bites. Let me try the index. Snakes, page forty-two under *wildlife*. I guess they count as wild. Okay, 'Snakes are in the Colubridae Family.' Fascinating, but who cares? 'Most snakes found in the Longfellow Mountains belong to the seven species of domestic garter snakes. The females range from 20—30 inches in length while the males are shorter and thinner. They can be identified by the three light stripes running the length of their bodies, one on the back and two on either side near the belly.' Did it look like that? Did it have three stripes?"

"I don't know. It was big and long and slimy."

"Gross. Let's see, it says, 'the babies are born alive in litters averaging 18 in number. The young eat earthworms while adults eat frogs, fish and salamanders. They are virtually harmless to humans. Occasionally you will spot a common milk snake or eastern ribbon snake sunning itself on a rock. These, too, are harmless if not disturbed. The timber rattlesnake is indigenous to this area, but it is rarely seen by humans. If you are bitten by a snake, see section 3, *Snake Bites*.' It looks like we don't have too much to worry about. Look at it this way. I've never seen a snake in the wild. You can tell your grandchildren that you survived an encounter with an evil serpent in the wilds of Maine."

"See if you're still so smug if you 'encounter' a snake while you're brushing your teeth or taking a leak behind a tree." Madaline examined a broken fingernail. "I guess I'm just a little city girl. I'm not cut out for this stuff."

"Come on, I think you'll get to like it. I found out where we can get some more supplies. The ranger also mentioned that we can rent a sailboat at the Depot. Won't that be fun? I've never sailed before and I've always wanted to."

The sign at the Depot said, "Sailboats For Rent—Sunfish, $7 per hour, $22 per day—Lasers, $11 per hour, $35 per day. Security deposit required. Must have experience. Collision Waiver $8/$14." Steve decided that a little white lie about sailing before would not hurt anybody. How hard could it be?

Soon they were launched in a blue and white sailed Sunfish. The fourteen-year old kid wearing red high top sneakers who rigged the sail looked at Steve suspiciously as they boarded the boat and Steve fumbled with the tiller and the rope for the sail. The kid had called the rope a "sheet," but that did not make any sense to Steve. While Steve was contemplating this anomaly, a gust of wind filled the sail and the boat took off from the shore before the kid could reclaim his vessel from this captain of dubious experience.

Steve had studied the principles of sailing in the aerodynamics section of one of his physics classes. A sailboat can move almost straight into the wind using the same diffusion of wind principle that holds airplanes aloft. Steve had merely to convert this theory into practice and they would be sailing. After hitting his head twice on the boom—"good name," Madaline commiserated—and nearly losing Madaline over the side when he "came about"—he had heard that terminology used during the America's Cup Races—Steve started to get the hang of things. The gusty wind propelled them back and forth across Mooselookmeguntic Lake's ashen blue waters. They could see two other boats out on the lake, a Laser sailboat and a rowboat supporting two aging fishermen. Madaline helped lean out over the water to keep the sailboat stable whenever heavy winds would come from the side.

After a while, Madaline began to relax and forget about the morning's bouts with Maine's prodigious wildlife. She found that if she held onto the mast she could lie across the bow and keep her feet near the cockpit where Steve was stationed. She enjoyed the intermittent warming rays of sun which helped dry her out after a particularly aggressive wave lapped over the bow. She was in this position when a powerful gale careened down the lake behind Steve's back and drove its unseen force squarely into the Sunfish' sail.

The Sunfish reared up as the sail bent over toward the choppy water. Madaline rolled off the side and disappeared into the darkening waters. Steve tried to release the sail to keep the boat from going over, but as the sail swung out, the precarious angle of the Sunfish caused the sail to catch a wave and get trapped in the water thereby pulling the boat the rest of the way onto its side. Steve lost his balance and landed in the water between the deck and the boom. By then, Madaline was nearly 50 yards behind. Having recovered from the initial shock of the cold water, she had to laugh out loud when she saw Steve flop into the water. Her merriment was short-lived, however. The sky behind them flashed with light and a reverberating boom ensued. Steve and Madaline both turned to the source of the audio-visual commotion. The entire southern sky was the color of charcoal. As the gusts of wind grew more excited, the waves crested over into white caps. The lake soon looked like a sea of ice-cream sundaes with whip cream spilling everywhere.

Madaline started toward the boat. She was glad that she had taken the available swim lessons at the IAB. She did not need them to pass the swimming test, but she felt it was a good opportunity to learn some new strokes. One stroke was a lifesaver's breaststroke done keeping the head above the water. She used this now so that she could keep an eye on the boat that kept disappearing behind the swells. She saw Steve right the boat, but as the sail swung out of the water, the wind filled the sail and blew it over the other way. When Madaline caught up, she helped Steve turn the boat into the wind and steady the one side while Steve climbed on the centerboard to leverage the sail out of the water. Soon they were both back in the boat, dripping wet, cold and out of breath. Another burst of lightning and they were reminded of the danger of their situation. The mast of the sailboat would make a perfect lightning rod, and they would make perfect toast.

They looked to see if anyone was coming to help them. In the distance they saw the other sailboat nearing the dock of the Depot. There was no sign of the fishermen. They realized that they were probably alone on the twenty-mile long right wing of the butterfly shaped lake.

Careful not to flip again as he turned back toward the dock, Steve held on tight to the tiller and the sheet as the boat surged into high gear driven by the pounding winds. Suddenly the water around them began to spray as if little depth charges were being set off all around them. Then they began to feel smacking all over their bodies. They were being bombarded by hail. Madaline shouted over the noise of the wind and the pounding of the hail on the deck of the Sunfish, "I thought it was June. This is crazy."

Steve responded, "It's unusual but not impossible. I'll explain later. Get back in the water and try to protect your head under the edge of the boat."

After a few minutes, the hail turned to rain and they climbed back on the boat. They were both shaking by now. Steve managed to direct the boat back to the dock. As they neared the dock, the kid in the red high tops appeared in the doorway and watched as Steve smashed into the side of the dock unable to battle the wind any longer. The kid gave Steve that same disapproving look. "My great grandmother can sail better than you. It's a good thing you bought that collision insurance, buddy. Most people don't need it."

Steve and Madaline dragged themselves out of the boat and abandoned it to the care of the 14-year old critic. As they stood on the dock, feeling secure on dry land (well, a wet dock), the rain grew warmer and felt soothing on their cheeks. They hugged each other and their shivering subsided. They waited a few more minutes as the kid stowed the sail and hoisted the Sunfish onto its padded wooden cradle. They watched the wind and the waves and the rain and were in awe of the power of nature.

Back inside the Depot, they surveyed the available goods and selected a few items from the sparsely stocked shelves. Steve pulled his wallet out of his pocket and laid three wet five-dollar bills on the counter. The cashier gave Steve an annoyed look and laid the three bills on the back counter to dry. The eyes led Steve to believe that she must have been the mother of the unforgiving boat boy.

As they climbed into the Trooper to return to their tent, they were swept with guilt as they dripped on the gray striped upholstery. Hopefully Jason would understand that it could not be helped. Hopefully it would dry without leaving a mark and Jason would never find out about their stupidity.

By the time they got back to their campsite, tiny rivulets of water were flowing around their tent. As they ran for the protection of the canvas, they realized that they should have brought some of the food with them from the Trooper. Oh, well, they could go back and get it later after the rain had stopped.

They were relieved to find that the inside of the tent was bone dry except for the small puddles that were forming under each of their feet. Steve was impressed by Madaline's dexterity as she modestly changed into dry clothing within the confines of a large towel.

They settled down ready to enjoy an afternoon of reading and talking and playing cards. They were thankful for the feel of warm, dry cotton against their skin and the rhythm of the rain against the roof of the tent was hypnotizing.

As the afternoon light faded and the rain persisted, Steve wrapped himself in the plastic trash bag in which the Army/Navy store had stowed his sleeping bag. He dashed out to the Trooper and leapt inside. He gathered together some cheese and crackers and a six-pack of cola. The can goods were useless because they could not light the Coleman stove inside the tent and cold Spaghettios were not Steve's idea of haute cuisine.

They decided to go to bed early because they had been burning the flashlights all afternoon and they were afraid that the batteries would be getting drained. Madaline sat on her sleeping bag brushing her hair trying to restore some life to the limp strands. Steve used the rainwater that he had collected in a pan outside the flap of the tent to brush his teeth. He spit out through the flap figuring that the rain would wash away the residue.

Steve usually washed his hair everyday. The swim that morning had been refreshing but had not been an acceptable substitute for a nice warm shower. He refrained from complaining because he had talked Madaline into the camping trip and his macho ego would not permit him to admit weakness or failure especially since Madaline appeared to be coping fine. He put on his best stoic face and zipped up the flap.

When Madaline climbed into her sleeping bag, Steve slid over and squeezed in beside her. The sleeping bag was designed for one person so it held their bodies tightly together. Madaline laughed playfully because she had never had joint occupancy of a sleeping bag before. Steve managed to roll over so that he was on top of her, pinning her body in the close confines. Steve stared deep into Madaline's soft hazel eyes. He combed her just-brushed hair with his fingers. He moved his fingers to her unsuspecting lips and then he lowered his head gently until his lips melded together with hers. He kissed her cheeks and her neck. He heard her rapid breathing and imagined her purring. He arched his back slightly to kiss her shoulder and then he heard the rip. The fabric constrictions of the sleeping bag released their grasp as the zipper gave way to the strains of passion. Steve grumbled something about "Army/Navy," "deposit," "zipper," and "bonehead." Madaline missed the rest.

Steve rolled free of the gaping sleeping bag to inspect the damage. As he rolled away, he knocked into the left wall of the tent. The impact was enough to pull one of the plastic tent spikes free from its muddy hole. Without the assistance of the missing spike, two others on the left side gave way under the pressure and the tent collapsed on its exasperated inhabitants. Steve pushed the canvas off his face and scrambled about for the flashlight. Madaline found it first where she had tucked it near her sleeping bag in case she needed to venture out in the dark to their private facilities.

As Steve was groping about in the dark, he felt a puddle of water on the floor of the tent. The puddle appeared to be growing. When Madaline turned on the flashlight, they saw that the front flap had torn open as the tent collapsed and half the floor was now under water. Steve's sleeping bag and most of their clothes were soaked to varying degrees.

In bare feet, they fled for the Trooper. Steve stubbed his toe again, perhaps on the same rock. This time he did curse up a storm, using some words whose meanings Madaline could only imagine.

Steve wanted to apologize to Madaline. He wanted to explain that camping was normally fun and these things did not usually happen. He wanted to tell her that he loved her. Instead, he decided to go to the bathroom.

He left Madaline sitting alone in the passenger seat of the Trooper wearing her pink shorts and *Harvard Crimson* T-shirt, trying to find a comfortable position to endure the rest of the night.

As Steve opened the door to their private outhouse content that he had a dry place to relieve himself, he was greeted by two eyes leering back at him. Before he could react, his nose went into olfactory overload. He had surprised a skunk that had been taking shelter from the relentless weather outside. Steve staggered back to the only other dry spot for miles.

"Oh, my God! You stink! Get out of here! You smell awful! What is that? It smells like skunk!"

Steve dejectedly got back out of the car and stood outside feeling nauseous from the fumes. Madaline lowered the car window slightly to talk to him.

"What happened? It still stinks in here."

"I'm going to demand our money back from that ranger. We were supposed to have a PRIVATE outhouse. He did not say anything about sharing it with vermin in inclement weather. I don't know how it got me so bad, I didn't even make it through the door. Talk about foul smelling outhouses . . ."

"I need to go to the bathroom, too."

"I recommend the one in Kirkland House."

"Don't tell me you're not having fun, Steve."

"Oh, yeah, this is lots of fun. I'm glad you like my new aftershave."

"I heard that tomato juice is the only way to get rid of the smell."

"Too bad we don't have any, and I doubt the Depot has night time hours."

"We have that Bloody Mary mix Jason gave us. That has tomato juice in it."

"Hey, good thinking. It's definitely worth a try."

"I'll get the mix out of the back. You're going to have to get rid of those clothes. Get some others out of the tent. The only positive thing is that your eau de skunk after shave has overpowered that terrible cigarette smell in here."

Steve felt very silly sitting on a log near the tent totally naked rubbing Bloody Mary mix all over his body. The benefit of the Bloody Mary mix was diluted by the bombardment of raindrops washing it away. When the bottle was empty and the rain had finished washing him clean, Steve put on some fresh clothes. He did not care if they got wet. He was just happy that he could now smell himself again without wanting to vomit.

Madaline allowed Steve back in the Trooper and only made a slight grimace at the residual odor. The Trooper had already taken on a skunky aroma from Steve's first contaminated visit and Madaline was becoming desensitized herself.

Madaline and Steve both looked at each other and in harmony said, "Boston!" They both laughed for the first time in what seemed like a long while, and they meant it. They envisioned warm showers, clean sheets and hot food.

Since Steve was already wet, he clambered back out and did his best to fold up the collapsed tent and drag it to the Trooper. Madaline had to get out to help load it as it was too heavy for Steve alone since he had not taken the time to remove the sleeping bags, clothes and other paraphernalia still inside. As they stuffed the tent through the back hatch, mud got everywhere. They would have to spend several hours at a car wash getting Jason's Trooper back in shape before returning it. They had plenty of time, however, since their vacation was being terminated a week early. Maybe they would go down to the Cape for several days and relax on the beach and stay in a bed and breakfast to make up for the camping fiasco.

Even though it was late and still raining lions and Great Danes, they started the engine and bid farewell to Mooselookmeguntic Lake and the campsite from Hell. Steve would drive for a while and then Madaline would alternate. They figured that they could make it back to Cambridge by early morning even if they drove very slowly. They had enough gas to make it most of the way, and by then, they should be able to find an open station without too much trouble as they would be back in civilization.

The rain made it hard to see the road signs. Steve was relieved when he spotted a sign for Wilsons Mills and knew that they were heading in the right direction. In the daylight, the roads through the Longfellow Mountains had been tricky. At night in the rain, they were treacherous. Steve had to rely on the solid and hatched white lines down the center of the road because there were no lines on the outside edges.

As they rounded one turn, a small truck veered past them, perhaps heading to the Depot with more supplies. They saw no more traffic for the next half hour as they wound themselves through the mountains. The rain was easing up and Steve was beginning to relax though he was feeling quite tired. The worn, oversized tires on the Trooper were still having problems gripping the rain-slicked road. Steve wished that he had bought the new tires before the trip.

As they rounded another curve, slowing down to only 25 miles an hour, a large tree that had fallen diagonally across the road suddenly loomed in front of them. Steve jammed on the brakes, but they began to hydroplane. He pulled the steering wheel hard to the left and one of the tires caught some pavement just before they plowed into the tree. The Trooper swerved to the left and they barely missed the tree. But, before Steve could get the brakes to hold and bring it to a stop, the right side of the Trooper smashed into a large branch attached to the fallen tree flinging the right side of the Trooper up into the air. Madaline screamed. Steve stopped breathing as he pulled helplessly at the non-responsive steering wheel. The Trooper landed with a crash and a thud on its left side and skidded along the road into the ditch. As they slid off the road, Madaline could hear the canned goods in the back flying about colliding with each other and the sides of the rear cabin. Steve could not hear anything.

When the Trooper landed on its side, Steve's head crashed into the side window and he was knocked unconscious. His seat belt had kept him from bouncing off the front windshield and the steering wheel, but he had no protection on the side. When the Trooper came to a stop, Madaline was suspended by her seatbelt in the air hanging precariously over Steve's limp body. After the barrage of scraping metal and banging objects, the silence that hung in the air was eerie. Madaline could hear her own heavy breathing, but little else except the high-pitched whistle as the air escaped from one of the tires.

When Madaline called Steve's name, there was no response. In the dim light, Madaline could see a thin stream of blood flowing from Steve's nose across his left cheek into his darkening hair. With blinding fright, she wondered whether Steve had been taking his medication for his bleeding disorder. She could not remember what it was called. She would have to get help, quickly.

Madaline managed to find the release for her seatbelt. As she unclasped the belt and began to lower herself, her head was jerked upwards and pain shot through her scalp. She raised herself back up by pushing with her left foot on the edge of Steve's seat. The pain subsided. Using her fingers to investigate, she discovered that a large clump of her hair had been pinned between the edge of the door and the frame of the car where it had bent in when the Trooper hit the branch. She tried to pull her hair free but only managed to get a few strands loose. She was trapped. She had resisted acidulously for so long the temptation to cut her hair. Now she was faced with the bitter irony of one more advantage of short hair for women.

Madaline felt a surge of panic welling up inside of her. She was tired and cold and she felt her knee beginning to throb where she had smashed it against the glove compartment. She mentally distanced herself from the pain and the urgency of her situation. She began to pull together the facts as if she were looking at a word problem on the SAT or a homework assignment from the logistics section of her applied mathematics class. Her mind wandered momentarily as she pictured herself safe at home doing a homework assignment, and enjoying it!

The facts of the problem: she was stuck. Steve was injured and bleeding. It was raining and dark. It was probably around 3:00 AM and they were in the middle of nowhere. She could not count on someone passing by for hours. She needed to get her hair free. She could try to bend the metal. No. She could cut her hair. Yes. What with? Steve carried a Swiss Army knife with him, but he was unconscious and she could not reach his pocket. She tried breaking her hair. She was able to do a couple strands at a time. She stopped. This would take forever. The cigarette lighter. She could just reach it. She pressed it in to heat up. She waited. It popped out. She held it to a clump of her hair. She heard a sizzling noise, and then was struck by a putrid smell. It reminded her of burning flesh. She was not sure why she would know what burning flesh smelled like. She moved the lighter about to different parts of the trapped hair. It was working. Her hair was coming free. She heated the lighter one more time and completed the job. She was free. Now to help Steve.

Trying not to step on Steve who was beneath her, she reached up and found the handle for the passenger window. She started to lower the window but it jammed about six inches down. She rolled it back up and lowered it again, but it stopped in the same place. She fumbled around on the ceiling that was now on her left side and found the overhead light switch. The dim glow cast enough light that she could see the door had been crumpled enough by the impact with the branch that the window could no longer track smoothly down into the engineered cavity in the door. She was trapped.

Madaline looked about for something with which she could smash the window. She decided that the canned Chunky New England Clam Chowder Soup would work best. She needed to cover Steve to protect him from the flying glass. She looked at his face now that she could see better in the faint light. He appeared to be sleeping peacefully except for the still trickling blood on his cheek and the unnatural angle of his head where the seat belt was still partially supporting his body, letting the head dangle free. Madaline turned to the back of the Trooper to find a sleeping bag or some clothes to shield him. She heard the rain pelting outside. It sounded louder as she leaned over into the back. She looked around the mass of the tent and saw what looked like muddy pavement. The back door on the Trooper had been knocked open when the Trooper landed on its side. She would not have to break the window after all.

Madaline turned her attention to Steve's bleeding. She needed his medication and she needed an icepack. She was leaning against the cooler. She pried off the lid and felt about inside. There was cool white fluid on everything. The milk had spilled when the Trooper had flipped. She wanted to cry.

Her fingers felt something cold. The hotdogs were still partially frozen. She crawled back into the front and laid the hotdogs next to Steve's cheek and nose. They slid off. She needed to secure them in place. She undid the lace from her sneakers and tied the package against his head.

Next the medication. Steve carried his medication in his pocket. He was supposed to take a single pink pill with every meal and at bedtime. If he was bleeding, he was supposed to take two of the little white ones to help with clotting. Madaline tried to lift Steve a little so that she could get to his pocket. Too heavy. He was dead weight and she could not budge him. She would have to try to lift the Trooper back off its side.

Madaline crawled into the back and cleared loose clothes, cans and the spare fuel tank for the Coleman stove away from the storage compartment. Inside she found a tool kit, a can of oil and a flare, but no jack. Where else would Jason have kept the jack? Madaline pulled herself out through the opening in the back door. She stood up next to the overturned Trooper and surveyed the scene. The rain was steady but not hard. Madaline brushed the wet hair out of her eyes and felt where her long strands had been severed. She was feeling very lonely and very helpless.

Madaline had been told a story about her great grandfather. He had lived until three months before his hundredth birthday. He had been a carpenter and had worked until he was 74. When he was 95, he had been taking a walk by himself using his cane only to keep his young wife of 87 happy. He had come upon three teenagers in a parking lot trying to dislodge a Volkswagen Beetle from a cement parking barrier over which they had driven and gotten trapped. They were trying to lift the small car and shove it backwards, but it was too heavy. Her great grandfather had picked up a long two-by-four that had been lying in a pile of wood near the parking lot. He walked over to the teenagers and used the board as a lever to pry the Beetle off the cement block. The teenagers were in awe of his wisdom and offered to buy him an ice-cream. He normally avoided dairy products because of a problem digesting lactose. Madaline had recently learned that cow's milk is 5% lactose which is a carbohydrate made of one molecule of glucose attached to one molecule of another sugar, galactose. Unless the body can process this compound, the molecules stay attached and no energy is derived. Her grandfather accepted their gift, nevertheless, because he appreciated their appreciation so much. He was sick for a week after that strawberry cone, but he spent the next four years telling that same story.

Madaline saw a large branch that had broken off the tree as it crashed into the road. She wedged the heavier end under the top of the Trooper and pushing up with her shoulder and both her arms; she raised the top of the Trooper until gravity took over and flipped it back on to its four tires with several jarring bounces. Madaline was able to wrench Steve's door open. The hotdog ice pack had fallen off and Madaline could see the blood caked on the side of Steve's head. She tied the hotdogs back in place and adjusted Steve's head to a more comfortable position back against the headrest. She reached into his pocket to get the medication. She had never had her hand in his pocket before and felt like she was trespassing, and yet was exhilarated by doing it. She found a crumpled Kleenex, some change, and half a roll of lifesavers along with the pillbox.

Madaline had never given a pill to an unconscious person before. She wondered how she would get him to swallow them. She remembered how they had given pills to their German shepherd, Rusty. They would hide it in a piece of meat. If that did not work, they would pry open his mouth and stick the pill in the back of his throat. She got the two white pills ready. She did not think that the meat thing would be very effective, so she pulled his chin down while she held his forehead with the other hand. She dropped one of the pills, but it landed in a fold in Steve's shirt and was easy to find. She pushed the two pills with a finger to the back of Steve's tongue. She felt Steve gag and then swallow. The pills were gone. Mission accomplished.

Madaline went back to the storage compartment and got the flare. She tried to read the directions on the flare but the print was too small to see under the overhead light. She walked around to the front of the Trooper and held the flare up to the headlights. She twisted the cap and a reddish flame burst from the top of the flare. She took two small branches and propped the flare in the roadway by the Trooper. She got back in the Trooper by climbing through the backdoor, over the tent and into her seat. She sat there exhausted and contemplated what more she could do.

She was mesmerized by the flare. Even though the rain was beating down on it, it continued to burn brightly. She wished that she could be as strong as the flare. She had read about people in plane crashes who had traveled through winter snows for days to go for help. Maybe she would wake up and this nightmare would end. She would be at home in bed and she would be warm and dry.

She did not know how long she stared at the flare. She thought her mind was playing tricks when she saw more lights. The other lights were moving and then they stopped. A shadow came between her and the flare. Then she saw the face of a ranger looking in at Steve through his window. It was the heavyset ranger who had written the guidebook and had given Steve a hard time about his carelessness with their supplies. He was out on his nightly patrol and seemed excited to have found an emergency where his rangerly skills would be needed.

The ranger radioed for help and then attended to Steve. With Madaline's help, the ranger carried Steve from the Trooper to his Range Rover. Madaline was impressed by the ranger's tremendous strength hidden under the layers of doughnut-derived padding. They drove for a few miles to a field. A few minutes after they arrived, a helicopter appeared from the direction where the sky was growing brighter. Steve was transported to the hospital in Portland and released two days later. The Trooper was towed to the garage in Wilsons Mills where the bodywork was done and two new tires installed, replacing one that had gone flat during the accident and the other as Steve had promised Jason. Madaline drove Steve back to Cambridge in a rented car. They rested there for a few days before heading off for the summer to their respective homes. They would have to work extra hard over the summer to make up for all the unexpected expenses.

They were sad to say goodbye and their parting kiss was long and passionate. They would try to forget their camping adventure, but unfortunately, this would not be too easy—they had both contracted agonizing cases of poison ivy.

CHAPTER FOURTEEN

Two weeks later, Steve was feeling like a retread tire, looking better on the outside, but still a bit weak on the inside. He had been sleeping late and hanging out with his high school buddies. He had been down to Wildwood, New Jersey and the beach only once. He had driven in his Jeep Cherokee with his best friend from high school, Paul Garvey. The salt and sand had irritated his poison ivy so much that he had scratched it until he was bleeding in several places. He had to make a special trip along the boardwalk to the pharmacy to stock up on the little white pills for his Hemopalpacemia. Paul had to drive home while Steve lay down in the back.

It was Monday morning at 7:20 and Steve had already hit the snooze alarm twice. He did not want to be late for his first day on the job, but his body was objecting to the thought of being vertical before noon. He was not aware how he got into the shower, but when the cold water hit him in the face and pelted his chest, his body switched into high gear and his mind eventually followed. The hot water soon joined forces with the cold and his goose bumps subsided. He grabbed the bar of soap off the rack and noted the green stripes. His mother had gotten him the "manly" soap. He switched on the autopilot so that he could begin charting his day. While he was deciding what clothes to wear and which route he would take to work, his hands began their routine pattern for soaping his body. His right hand armed with the soap started with the left arm, down the outside and up the inside to the armpit. The soap had an extended session there. After a detour over the left shoulder to the back, the soap then traveled across the chest and swirled down to the stomach. A transfer was made to the left hand and the process was repeated for the right arm. The soap was then airborne to meet the left foot as it was raised. Up and down each leg and then to the genitals and the patch of light colored pubic hair that rose to his navel. He lingered a while as he gently massaged this sensitive area, wondering if it would have a chance to experience the joys of love making with Madaline. He went back on autopilot and the soap disappeared around to the rear where it effectively cleansed both buttocks and the indentation between. He rinsed the soap and placed it back on the rack. A quick shampoo and he was out of the shower, drying himself in less than four minutes. If he could get it down to three minutes, he could get an extra minute of sleep each day.

After putting on a clean pair of khakis, a pressed shirt, and a flowered tie, Steve proudly climbed into his Cherokee. It only had 650 miles on the odometer from a few short jaunts at Christmas time and the trip down to the shore. He was very proud of his first set of wheels. He had thanked his parents at least once every day. He wondered again where they had gotten the money for it. He could not help noticing that his mother had been wearing some new dresses and his father was sporting a Rolex watch. These things stood out because they were so unusual for his parents. He would have to ask them, but in a way that would not sound ungrateful or critical.

Steve headed down the Schuylkill Expressway towards Center City. He continued on past the Center City Exit towards the airport and took the Passayunk Avenue Exit into an industrial section of South Philadelphia. Referring twice to the map and his directions, he arrived at Joe's Fortune Cookie Factory with ten minutes to spare. "More sleep tomorrow," he thought.

Steve reported to Mary Ng, the plant Personnel Manager. When he asked directions to her office, he was very embarrassed because he was not sure how to pronounce her last name. He asked for the Personnel Manager's Office hoping that the person guiding him would say her name. He did, but it was of no help.

"Mary's office is the second door on the left down that hall," was all he said.

Steve avoided saying her name at their first meeting during which he filled out an Internal Revenue Services Form W-4 and an Immigration and Naturalization Services Form I-9. The rest of the summer, he never heard anyone say her last name, so he ignored his training in respect for his elders and called her "Mary," as did everyone else.

After several days of "learning the ropes" and doing a lot of sweeping and cleaning, Steve was promoted to the folding machine. A machine would cut out small circles of cookie dough and bake them until they were almost done. The conveyor belt would pass by two ladies who would lay a small strip of colored paper imprinted with a profound piece of wisdom on the middle of the circle. Steve's machine would fold in the two sides and give a blast of heat that would dry the cookie dough and allow it to retain its shape when it discharged onto the cooling trays. Steve had to regulate the blast of heat so that the cookies got enough heat to retain their shape, but not so much that it would burn the cookie.

Steve liked the smell of the factory and he liked the people who worked there. He used his breaks to wander around the factory floor to learn how the other steps of the production process worked. He presented several ideas, some better than others, to the production foreman, Henry Wong. He suggested that they cook the cookie a little longer before folding and then use cold air rather than a hot blast to solidify the shape. He believed that this would save energy, make the folding machine more comfortable to operate and give the cookie a fresher taste. They experimented and the taste did improve. It took two weeks to retool the machinery and they had to halt production for one day, but everyone agreed that the result was a better cookie. He also proposed that they inject a blast of air into the finished bags of cookies before sealing the bags. This would give the cookies extra protection and reduce the breakage factor significantly during shipping.

After Steve had been there for three weeks, Henry Wong appeared, accompanied by a short fat man with a bushy mustache and long thin black hair which he brushed up over his head to mask the naked scalp on top. Over the hum of the machinery Steve could hear Henry say that Mr. Weinstein had been very impressed by Steve's ideas and he wanted to thank him in person. Steve tried not to smile as Mr. Weinstein kept pulling his pants back up onto his hips as he talked. Mr. Weinstein explained how he had reviewed Steve's application and how pleased they were to have such a capable person on their team. Steve kept glancing at his folding machine. He thought that he heard it starting to squeak. Then he realized that every time Mr. Weinstein said a word with an "s" in it, he whistled slightly threw the gap in his two front teeth. In a strange way, he liked Mr. Weinstein. He had an air of confidence about him, and he certainly was saying nice things about Steve.

Steve concluded that he must be the accountant. Trying to impress him, Steve recalled some jargon from his business class in high school. He babbled, "I realize that this is a bottom line oriented company and we must have our debits equal our credits and the variable cost factors for each component on the balance sheet such as energy consumption can have an inverse impact on the return to the stockholders." He looked at Mr. Weinstein to see if he had made any sense.

Mr. Weinstein smiled, flashing the gap in his teeth and continued, "I would welcome any other suggestions you might have. We encourage all of our workers to feel a sense of responsibility for our small operation." He patted Steve on the back and waddled off toward the hallway with the offices.

Henry watched with Steve until Mr. Weinstein was out of sight. "Mr. Weinstein is very impressed with you."

"Well, I hope he tells the boss. Maybe I can get a raise. I have some big repair bills to pay off."

"Steve, that was the boss. That was Joe Weinstein. He is the one who started Joe's Fortune Cookie Factory twenty years ago. The bottom line you were talking about is his bottom line. He owns the company."

"You're kidding. I thought he was the accountant or something. I always thought that Joe was Chinese."

"No, I think he was born in Brooklyn. But, he does go to China once every two years to renew our rice batter and fortune slip contracts."

"You mean we import our fortunes from China?"

"That's right."

"Well, that explains a lot. Half the time they don't make any sense. I suppose that could be part of the appeal. I know that I always look forward to the fortune at the end of a Chinese meal and I am usually disappointed. If you want another suggestion, I think that we should make up our own fortunes here. We could become known as the fortune cookie company with the best fortunes in the world."

Steve did get a raise and he also got a new job. He was put in charge of writing and printing the new fortunes. Their supply would run out in two months and Mr. Weinstein would not be renewing the contract. He also decided to start producing his own special recipe for rice batter. Mr. Weinstein would be taking his holiday in the Bahamas this year rather than in China.

Steve set up a suggestion box so that all of the factory employees could participate in writing the new fortunes. He had fun coming up with his own and adapting many of the suggestions. He decided to print facts about China on the backside of the fortune so that they could be educational as well.

Some of Steve's favorite fortunes included,

"Make peas, not war, but be sure not to overcook them."

"You take the high road and I'll take the low road, and we'll see who gets arrested first."

"If being lucky means you have lots of luck, let's hope that it is not all bad."

"Why are parents happy when babies belch, but angry when their teenagers belch?"

And the inevitable handwritten, "I'm a prisoner in a fortune cookie factory. Please rescue me."

Steve hoped that his good fortune would continue.

*   *   *

Neither Madaline nor Steve was stellar correspondents. Steve was surprised and delighted to get a letter from Madaline written on North American Consumer Products stationery. He had enjoyed the letters she had sent the previous summer when they were just getting to know each other and could hardly wait to get to his room to read the new arrival in private.

"Dear Sweetheart,

"I hope that you have recovered from that dreadful poison ivy. I miss you. I got poison ivy in places that have never seen the light of day. I miss you. In some ways, I miss the pleasure pain paradox of scratching when I knew I should not. I miss you. I wish I could be there to scratch your poison ivy . . .

"I miss you. They say that absence makes the heart grow fonder. I don't know how mine could grow any more. I am counting the 5,011,200 seconds left until we see each other again. It keeps me busy. I just read an article in one of my mother's magazines that says that people should not get married until they are at least 24 years old and have dated for more than one year. It also says that between 18 and 22, people's sense of who they are and what they are looking for in a mate changes the most, especially for people in college. I agree that what was appealing to me as a freshman is not what I want now, but I can't imagine wanting anything other than you. Perhaps my tastes have just matured more quickly than most people's.

"I dyed my hair red. Just kidding. I did put some red highlights in and the sun has made them quite bright. I think you might even like it, but it will have faded by the time I see you. Maybe I'll take a picture. I keep a picture of you on my nightstand. I give you a kiss every night before I go to bed. Do you have a picture of me? Do you want one? Do you miss me? I can't hear you.

"I read a very interesting fact. Did you know that 93.4% of all statistics are inaccurate?

"How are you enjoying the business world? I have been to three different Chinese restaurants with my friends and I keep looking for a message from you in one of the fortune cookies. Have they taken you prisoner? Are you being shanghaied? Have they taught you how to use chopsticks yet? How do they get those fortunes inside the cookies? Why don't people wish upon fortune cookies when they break them open like they do with a drumstick?

"Question—How many ants does it take to screw in a light-bulb? Answer below.

"I hate my job. NACP hired me as a temp for the summer in the accounts payable department. You remember how much I hated economics. This is worse. All I do all day is process bills and talk to vendors who are calling to complain that they have not yet received payment. Did you know that they spent $382.25

last year on paperclips?! And I wonder what this bill for $3,285.00 for a Jacuzzi is for. It was approved by the Vice President of Marketing. I wonder if they are going to install it in our lunchroom for the clerks to use. Ha! Maybe I'll set up a new vendor on the computer. I wonder what code I should give Madaline Wallace Enterprises. At least I'm getting a paycheck and I can buy all the laundry detergent I want at cost in the employee shop. They just released another new and improved product so maybe I can get the last of that skunk smell out of my sweatshirt . . .

"Answer—two, one male and one female.

"In case you hadn't figured it out from my subliminal messages, I miss you. I can't wait to see you in September. They should write a song about that. I should get back to work now. More bills to pay . . . I love you.

"Your adoring buttercup,
"Madaline"

Steve folded the letter and put it back in the envelope. He would read it 23 more times that week even though he had already memorized it. He liked looking at Madaline's flowing handwriting on the formal business stationery. He decided that he would write back right away. His intentions were good, but he kept putting it off until tomorrow. After all, he was not a very good correspondent.

*   *   *

Every day when Steve came home from work, his mother was busily preparing dinner. While they were eating, Steve's parents would take turns telling him about the new breakthroughs they had made that day. They were at a very exciting stage where everything was falling into place and they were rapidly testing the various applications of their theories. Steve was very happy for them and listened with great interest though he did not understand much of what they were talking about. As Steve listened, the sickening realization dawned on him that perhaps he would need to spend another five years in school after he graduated from Harvard. He would need a Ph.D. in order to really understand and help his parents. Five more years. That sounded even worse than the chants at political conventions of, "Four more years."

One sweltering hot Thursday evening in August, Steve's parents had been especially excited and had decided to go to Le Bec Fin to celebrate. They had invited Steve, but he had declined, preferring to stay home, watch TV, and enjoy the air conditioning.

Steve fixed himself some leftover spaghetti and poured a large glass of his father's sun ice tea. He settled down in his father's recliner and watched a rerun of "The Partridge Family." He only vaguely remembered seeing Susan Dey, Danny Bonaducci, and Shirley Jones the first time around.

When the closing theme song had finished, an episode of one of those sensationalized true life stories began where the cameraman chases around real cops filming their escapades. Steve switched channels. He found a movie just beginning—"Halloween." He had never seen it, but he sadly recalled how Foster had told him that when he had seen it he had locked his bedroom window and checked in the closets and under the bed. He remembered that it was about a crazy guy who goes around killing regular teenagers in regular houses in regular neighborhoods. As Steve watched, transfixed, he felt very regular.

While the movie was progressing and more bodies were littering the screen, the late evening sky grew darker and darker. After it ended, Steve sat in the recliner, afraid to move. The news came on and Steve watched even though he was not paying attention. He jumped when he heard a noise at the front door. He relaxed when her heard his mother's voice saying, "We're home, dear."

Steve told his parents how scary the movie had been and asked about their dinner. His mother was very chatty after her two glasses of Chardonnay. Steve interrupted and said that he had to get to bed because he had to work the next day.

Steve climbed the carpeted stairs with trepidation, carefully turning on the lights ahead of him keeping a sharp eye out for any evil that might lurk beyond. Steve heard noise behind him. Out of the corner of his eye, he assessed that it was his mother following him up the stairs on the way to her room. He turned his attention back to the dark shadows and the unheard noises. As he reached the top of the stairs and stretched around the corner into his room for the light-switch, two hands grabbed his shoulders from behind and a camouflaged voice yelled, "Boo!" He flung around to fend off the attack. His mother was standing where the attacker should have been. She was wearing a devilish grin. Steve reached back and turned on the light. His mother's teeth sparkled in the light like the new double string of pearls that she wore around her neck. Steve's fright metamorphosed into anger as he realized his own mother had used the opportunity of his confessed vulnerability to play a mean trick on him. His own mother! What had come over her? She had never been much of a prankster and she certainly was not a malicious person. Maybe it was the wine. Or, maybe she was a repressed prankster and Steve had been genetically endowed with her humorously sadistic tendency.

Without a word, Steve spat bullets with his eyes and stormed down the stairs to the kitchen where his father was finishing off a bowl of butter pecan ice-cream, his favorite. Steve complained to his father who failed in his efforts to hide his amused reaction to his wife's outrageous behavior. Steve had too much adrenalin flowing from the movie and his encounter with the maternal monster to see the humor. Steve accepted the offer of some butter pecan ice-cream. After several bites he began to enjoy the taste and his heart slowed down to a sub-traumatized rate.

He was feeling better, but he was still furious at his mother. How could she? He wished his father a good night and stomped up the stairs straight into the hall bathroom. He turned on the light and closed the door with a bang. He hoped that his mother knew how upset he was. Steve picked up his toothbrush and uncapped the Crest toothpaste. He applied a strip of toothpaste to the brush and stuck it in his mouth. As he began an up-and-down motion with the brush, he looked at his image in the mirror. How could such a big guy, his age, be frightened by a movie? He was safe in his own home and his parents were here to protect him.

Suddenly, behind his own image in the mirror he detected a slight motion. He froze. The shower curtain began slowly moving to the left. His legs felt weak. He swallowed hard and tasted some toothpaste as it passed down his throat. A hand appeared. He was too frightened to turn around. Maybe if he did not move, the hand would leave him alone. He used to do that as a child when he was lying in bed and he heard a scary noise. He figured that if the intruders thought he was asleep, they would not have to kill him because he could not identify them.

The curtain stopped moving and the hand disappeared. Steve turned around inch by inch. He still held the toothbrush to his mouth. Without further warning, the shower curtain flung the rest of the way open and Steve's heart skipped two beats. His mother was standing in the bathtub wearing the same grin she had before. She had been lying in wait for her victim all this time savoring the moment when she could torture her only son.

Steve would finally laugh about it when he told Madaline on the phone. But that was two weeks later. He was late to work the next day for the first time because he slept through his alarm having finally drifted off to sleep around five in the morning. If he could not trust his own mother, whom could he trust?

*   *   *

Since Steve had never written back to Madaline and she had sent another loving letter in the meanwhile, he decided to call her. It was great to hear her voice again. They laughed and giggled. They called each other cute names. They complained about their jobs and told of their adventures with their friends. After nearly an hour, Steve glanced at his watch. The time had flown and his phone budget had been depleted three fold. Before he released a machine gun barrage of kisses over the phone to Madaline and hung up, he invited her to Philadelphia. His parents would be receiving an award in early September and Steve wanted Madaline to be there. If she would take the bus or train from North Carolina to Philadelphia, she could spend a week with Steve and then his parents would drive them both to Cambridge. She said she would think about it. The letter that Steve received two days later included the arrival time and number of her Amtrak train.

CHAPTER FIFTEEN

Strange things seemed to be happening around Steve's neighborhood. Mrs. Yoder who lived across the street from the Harris' called to say that she had seen the same black sedan sitting outside their house three times while they were out. She called back later that day to say that it was there right again right at that very moment. When William pulled the curtain back to look out the window, he saw a black Lexus pull away from the curb. He could not see the driver. Two days later, as Steve left for work, he noticed that their trash had been picked up while all the other neighbor's trash was still sitting by the curb.

The following day Miriam came home quite upset from shopping. Steve overheard her telling his father that she had been followed in the store by an oriental man who wore sunglasses even though it was a cloudy day. She noticed that he did not buy anything. He followed her out of the store and she saw him get into a black car. On the way home, she saw the black car in her rearview mirror. She got scared and stopped at her friend Peg's for a cup of coffee even though she had milk and ice cream in the car. As she drove home from Peg's, she spotted the black car once more. When Steve asked what was going on, his father said not to worry. The tone of his voice did not reassure Steve.

That Friday evening, the Irish setter belonging to their next door neighbors, the Carlsons, was found dead in their back yard. It had been strangled.

Steve began to have bad dreams. The shower curtain would slide open and a dead dog would be hanging in the shower. Steve would hear barking and the dog would become alive. Its teeth would turn into knives that would be dripping blood. He would try to run away, but he would slip on the blood on the floor. He would watch as the dog mangled his parents and dragged them by the throat into the tub. When he would run outside to escape from the dog, a black car would be sitting in the driveway. The door would open and the dog would leap out. It would have Madaline's head clasped in its bloody jaw. As the dog leapt on top of him, he would usually wake up in a cold sweat.

Steve started sleeping with the light on, which he had not done since he was six years old. When his parents asked about the light, he made up a lame excuse about how he was used to sleeping with a light on at school where there was a light just outside his window. He hated to lie to his parents, but he was too embarrassed and disturbed to tell them about the nightmares. Soon reality would produce more fodder for his nocturnal horrors.

*   *   *

Saturday morning when Steve came down for breakfast, his parents were huddled over a modified version of MAMA, the Multiple Atomic Mass Activator. They had added an additional set of keys and a small external antenna. Before Steve could pour some Captain Crunch into the bowl, his father grabbed his arm and led him down to the basement.

"Your mother is a genius."

"I knew that, Dad. Now, can I go eat my cereal?"

"In a minute. I want to show you what your mother just finished putting together. I believe that she has proved her initial postulation about the non-linearity of the fourth dimension. It all makes sense. Think of a straight line in one dimension. To get from one point to the other you must pass along the straight line. If you add a second dimension giving you a plane, you can get from one point to the other by leaving the line and circling around to the other point never coming into contact with the rest of the line. The shortest distance, as you know, between two points is a line, but why always travel the shortest distance. Time is also tied in to the other three dimensions. If time were the only dimension, just as the line, we could only travel along that one dimension. The other three dimensions give us the ability to jump around by leaving the straight line of time.

"Apple Computer has expanded the capabilities of our Particle Graphic Simulator. The artificial intelligence has been upgraded and the processing time decreased by a factor of one thousand. It cost a fortune, but it's giving us unbelievable potential for new discoveries. Your mother has run a series of simulations about the big bang theory. She has shown that over a million year time period, there is a very high probability that individual galactic bodies will occupy the same location within the universe more than once. Two bodies cannot occupy the same space at the same time, but at different times, the same bodies can occupy the same space, or at the same time, different bodies can occupy different spaces. Time and space can generate parallel worlds through either space or time. Your mother is running further tests to see when earth most likely occupied this same location in the past. This is still an inexact science because of all of the variables. We are amazed at the advances the artificial intelligence has generated in the program. We are hoping to reduce uncertainty to a manageable level."

"I'm a bit confused, Dad. What does all this mean?"

"We are not limited to moving objects forward in time. We should be able to travel into the past as well as into the future. The possibilities are limitless. Our tests with living creatures have been far more successful since our Apple upgrade. We transported a cat ten days forward. Other than a slight dizziness, the cat was fine. It was the first time I have seen a cat walk and fall over on its side. I couldn't help laughing. Great reaction for a scientist, huh? The cat was fine after a few minutes."

"That's fantastic! You and Mom are really amazing."

"The trouble now is testing our theories. We tried sending a pencil back 230,000 years. It disappeared from our launch pad and the computer indicated a successful launch, but we have no way of verifying it. We have not determined how to bring things back from the past. When we transport into the future, eventually we catch up to whatever we transported. We have modified MAMA so that we can calibrate our settings more accurately and even input variables for settings that will be determined by the artificial intelligence in the PGSimulator. Now, go get your Captain Crunch. I don't know how you can eat that stuff."

"Dad, I have to ask you a question. This upgrade to your PGSimulator must have cost a fortune. I have noticed some other new equipment in the lab, too. I know that you have been having some budgeting problems with your grant. And Mom's new pearls and my Jeep. You are usually very careful with your money. I love my Jeep. Don't get me wrong. I know that it's none of my business, but how can you afford all of this?"

William glanced around the room as if he were looking for a distraction or a way to change the subject. His wife was banging around upstairs so he could not rely on his customary crutch. He had trouble looking Steve in the eye as he finally responded, "You're right Steve. Have a seat." They both sat down on the two rickety office chairs.

"As you know, we were running out of money from our five year grant. We budgeted well, but new technology and the unexpected advances we were making created a need for additional very expensive equipment. We had gotten so far and we didn't want to have to give up or settle for a partial victory because of a shortage of a few dollars. We applied for additional funding to the government and several other US development groups. We offered to join forces with a group of scientists at Cal Tech who have been operating a parallel grant. We were turned down by all. Your mother and I became desperate. We started using some of our personal retirement savings to keep the project going. Out of the blue, I was contacted by a fellow named Hideki Minamoto who said he represented a group called SWAN. He said they were funded by the Japanese Ministry on International Trade and Industry known as MITI. Their mission is to track down scientific and commercial developments worldwide and to provide funding and other support including limited technological, application development, and marketing assistance. He must have gotten a copy of one of our confidential grant applications because he knew a great deal about our project. It sounded good until he got down to specifics. They would require one hundred percent ownership of all commercial applications. We could present to the scientific community and accept accolades for our discoveries, but we would need to mention MITI as co-sponsor and owner of all patents and patent rights. Our federal grant prohibits that type of arrangement. We turned them down."

William yelled upstairs, "Miriam, please come down here. I'm telling Steve about the Saudis."

The two men waited while Miriam came down the stairs. She gave her husband an inquisitive look, but did not say a word. William Harris continued, "Your mother and I are not proud of this. We weighed the alternatives and felt that this was the best approach. Through two of your mother's university friends and the International Atomic Physicists Alliance, IAPA, we put out feelers. In less than two weeks, we had inquiries from France, China, Iraq, Khazakstan, Taiwan and Saudi Arabia. We ruled out Iraq and Kazakhstan immediately. We felt that Kazakhstan was too unstable with all of the changes going on in that region. We felt that negotiations with the Chinese would take too long and we did not want to risk offending the Chinese by going with Taiwan. That left France and Saudi Arabia. Our research lapsed for several weeks while we met with representatives from the two countries. In the end, we had to go with the best offer. I must admit that it was partly out of greed. The Saudi group offered one million dollars in additional funding as well as a sixty thousand dollar personal honorarium. Our bank account was almost empty, and, I guess we have been a bit excessive spending the windfall, but we have been so happy about our progress. Anyway, the Saudis required no public recognition. Their only demand is to receive limited domestic rights to any non-military applications. We would be required to train up to three of their scientists. We have a two-year window before they would require access to the technology. That keeps us from flagrantly violating the terms of our federal grant. I hope that you understand why we had to do this, Steve."

"Wow. You've really entered the big league. The whole world wants access to what you're working on. I'm glad I'm on your team. In a way I'm relieved. All this time, I couldn't imagine where you had gotten the money for the Jeep. Please forgive me for imagining the worst. It's great that the Saudis were so generous. I guess they'd be happy to know that some of the money was spent on a gas guzzler."

Miriam had been listening patiently. She said, "Steve, we love you very much." Then she turned and climbed back up the stairs. Steve had the feeling that this situation might be even more involved than what his parents were telling him. He had great faith in both of them and decided not to question them any further. He was sure that they knew what they were doing. After all, these were his parents. His mom and his dad. They always made sure everything turned out all right.

*   *   *

Steve's parents had not taken a real vacation since the former president had been sworn into office. They had driven the six hours to Cambridge numerous times to deposit Steve in the fall, retrieve him in the spring, or to watch an important crew race. They had each attended several scientific conferences, but they never arrived early or stayed late for the tours, golf days or formal dances which were tacked on. They never attended the same conference because they could not justify the extra time and money to hear the same things and someone needed to continue working. As William or Miriam sat next to a stranger in coach or lay alone at night listening to the rambunctious conventioneers in the hall returning late from the bar with old or new friends, he or she would imagine the joy of being there with his or her best friend who would be alone at home wondering how the other was doing.

When the envelope from IAPA arrived, Steve's parents were surprised and pleased. They danced around the kitchen like four year olds, holding each other's hands and spinning in a circle laughing until they became dizzy and had to sit down. The envelope contained two airline tickets to Nassau in the Bahamas and a letter from a member, Raul Pascal, who chaired the Membership Affairs Committee. He thanked them for their hard work and stated that IAPA wanted to recognize them in advance for their achievements that they were looking forward to learning more about at the Annual Meeting in September. The tickets were for the following weekend from Thursday afternoon until Tuesday morning—just long enough to relax, but not too long to keep them from finalizing their work before September's meeting.

Steve considered having a party while his parents were gone, but decided to just take it easy instead. He would be too nervous inviting a bunch of wild and crazy college age kids into his parents' house with so much expensive stuff around. Besides, he could never be quite sure when some unknown object or creature would reappear in the lab. This would be difficult to explain to his friends.

Saturday morning, Steve was awakened at 11:00 AM by the phone. "So much for sleeping in," he thought. It was his best friend, Paul.

Some strange guy had given Paul a jet ski and a pair of box tickets to the Phillies/Cardinals home game for that afternoon. Steve listened, not quite sure why Paul was telling him this. Once Steve had shaken the sleep from his brain, he understood what Paul was babbling about. Paul was inviting him to a baseball game that afternoon. Steve had nothing planned, so he accepted.

Paul asked Steve to drive since his car had gotten two flats that morning and he only had one spare. It was most peculiar. That morning when he woke up, Paul saw his car tilting to the right in the driveway. When he investigated, he found a nail in each of the passenger side tires. He concluded that he must have driven through a pile of nails the day before.

An hour later, Steve picked up Paul at his house. They only lived three blocks apart. Paul wanted to beat the traffic down to Veteran's Stadium. As the traffic grew heavier near the exit where Steve normally got off the Schuylkill for work, Steve thought that he could smell the baking cookie dough. Maybe Joe Weinstein was experimenting with his new batter, or maybe Steve was going through weekend work withdrawal syndrome.

Steve was now fully awake and psyched for the game. Nevertheless, he was troubled by part of what he thought he remembered Paul saying through the cobwebs of sleep.

"So, where did you get these tickets again?"

"Like I told you, some strange guy gave them to me along with a new jet ski. He said I had won some marketing contest. He told me that the jet ski would get delivered on Monday."

"What did you do to win the contest?"

"I just answered a bunch of questions. He came up to me at the mall and asked my name. He said if I would spend a few minutes completing a questionnaire that I would definitely win a prize. He was pretty insistent, too. He said I'd be making a big mistake if I didn't do it. I wasn't doing anything, so I figured what the heck."

"What kind of questions . . . ?"

"He asked me what I do on weekends. He asked me who my best friend was. I lied and said you." Paul flinched as Steve swung the back of his right hand at his chest. "The guy asked what sports I liked. He asked if I had a car and what kind. He asked what types of things we did together. He asked questions about my family and then he asked me about your family. Some of his questions were kind of weird. How would I know how much money my father makes let alone how much your parents make? When he asked me if you had told me about any strange happenings lately, I got weirded out. I told him that I had to go. That's when he told me that I had won. He gave me these two tickets and told me about the Jet Ski. The Jet Ski is a Kawasaki 650. It comes with a trailer. I tried one down the shore last year. It's great on the waves. I had trouble standing up, though. But now, we can practice all we want."

"Why did you say that he was strange?"

"He kept looking around while he was talking to me. Right after he finished with me, I saw him head out to the parking lot. Also he . . ."

"What did he look like?"

"He was oriental, probably in his forties."

"Japanese?"

"Maybe. And he wore a really expensive silk suit that seemed strange for a guy filling out questionnaires in the mall. Oh, and he said that if I didn't take you to the Phillies game that I would not get the Jet Ski. I asked him why and he said that the sponsors were promoting friendship as part of their campaign. So, you won, too."

"Well, the Jet Ski should be fun and it's a great day for a game." Something did not make sense, but Steve could not pin it down.

The Phillies beat the Cardinals four to three. However, Steve and Paul did not see the last five runs scored. In the third inning, while munching on a $3.00 hot dog, Paul spoke in a garbled voice, "Lots of strange things have been happening lately. Someone broke into our house and stole the TV and my high school yearbook. Those were the only things they took. And this morning, when I looked out the window, I spotted a guy across the street getting into a black car. He looked a lot like the strange guy at the mall. When I came out the door, the car had already gone. The thing that was so strange was that he was wearing a business suit and yet he was carrying a hammer. Go figure."

Steve got the eerie feeling that someone had gone to great lengths to get him out of the house. He grabbed Paul who was stuffing the last of his hotdog in his mouth and said, "Let's go." Paul was unable to protest with his overloaded mouth so he followed along in disbelief. When he had managed to swallow a bit, he spit out, "Hey, these are great seats. What gives?"

Steve replied, "I've got to get home. You can come now or walk."

Paul sensed something in Steve's voice that kept him from objecting further. When they found Steve's Jeep Cherokee lodged somewhere in section H of the packed parking lot, Steve and Paul both stopped dead in their tracks. The Cherokee was tilting to the right. Both passenger side tires had been slashed. After a string of profanity that this publisher was loathsome to reprint, Steve growled, "This is no coincidence. My parents are in the Bahamas and I'm stuck here."

Steve's parents had ordered an optional full-size spare tire for the Jeep Cherokee. The dealer had thrown in the donut-size spare tire at no extra cost. Steve had kept the donut tire in the back because he was too lazy to take it out and since the garage was occupied by part of the lab, there were few other places to store it. Steve and Paul cranked up the side of the Cherokee and had the two new tires on in less than fifteen minutes. As they careened back up the Schuylkill toward the Main Line, the donut tire caused the Jeep Cherokee to veer to the right as it screamed a high-pitched complaint about the speed.

When they got to Steve's street, everything looked normal. There were no black cars parked outside of Steve's house. The front door was closed and no windows were broken.

Steve told Paul to wait in the car while he checked the house, then he would drive him home and they could watch the rest of the game at Paul's house. Steve briskly walked up the front walk trying not to show his fear to Paul who watched from the curb. He tried the door. It was locked. Good. Steve used his key and went inside leaving the door open behind him. At first glance everything looked fine. Steve walked down the hall to the kitchen. He froze when he saw the basement door open and a light shining from below. He was certain that he had not left any lights on. He crept forward to investigate. He heard the scuffling noise behind him too late so he was not able to turn around quickly enough to ward off the blow. Something large and hard struck him on the back of the head and the shoulder. He crashed to the carpeted floor in the hallway knocking down two framed pictures as he went.

Before the black chilly air swallowed him, he heard a voice but the words were indistinguishable. Nevertheless he recognized the accent. He had heard a close approximation before. One of his crew team members was from Osaka.

No more thoughts. Darkness and fitful sleep are the wretched gifts that postpone pain.

*   *   *

Paul. The Police. His parents. The FBI. They all kept asking him the same questions. No, he did not see what the guy looked like. Yes, it was definitely Japanese. No, he knew the difference from Chinese—he worked in a Fortune Cookie Factory. Yes, he thought there were at least two of them. No, he had not touched the computers since his parents had left. Yes, he had a terrible headache. And yes, he was certain the neighbor's murdered dog, the black Lexus, the jet ski, the trip to the Bahamas, the flat tires, the missing year book, and MITI were all tied together in some twisted evil plot to sabotage or steal his parents' project.

When Steve had not returned to the Cherokee, Paul had gone in to investigate. He found Steve unconscious on the floor with a dented brass umbrella stand on the floor next to him. He called 911 and got ice from the freezer to attend to Steve's injury. He was unable to get the bleeding on the back of Steve's head to stop, so the police had called an ambulance when they arrived a few minutes later.

The police asked Paul some questions and then combed the house in a routine robbery investigation. The back door lock had a few scratches on it and the door had been found ajar. Obviously these were professionals. The police were stumped when they found the TV and stereo and all the computer equipment in the basement still in what appeared to be their proper places. They surmised that perhaps Steve had startled them and they had fled before they were able to take anything. They found a smoldering cigarette burning a black stripe into the mahogany hall table. They figured that the burglar had put the cigarette down when he had picked up the umbrella stand by the door and had forgotten about it in the excitement. They noted how neat the house appeared except for the terrible disarray of files strewn about the floor in the basement and the pile of dirty clothes in Steve's bedroom.

The police visited Steve at the hospital after he had regained consciousness to ask more questions. Paul tried to respond to the questions to save Steve from the exertion, but the police wanted the answers straight from Steve. At Steve's request, they notified his parents in the Bahamas. Back at the police station, they completed their report and then closed the file. "Insufficient evidence/ insufficient damages."

Steve's parents were able to switch their flight to Sunday morning at 7:20. So much for their relaxing vacation. They went straight to the hospital to see Steve. The doctor agreed to discharge him if he avoided any undue stress and stayed in bed for two days.

Paul had returned to the hospital to be with his friend. Since Steve was feeling much better, Paul began to tease him about the flap in the back of his hospital gown and how silly he looked as he was wheeled to the exit of the hospital in his white gauze turban.

Steve was disappointed at how unsympathetic his parents were. He realized how anxious they must have been to see what damage had been done. He hoped that they did not blame him for what had happened. He probably should have called the police rather than trying to be a stupid hero himself. Hindsight is 20/20.

Hindsight is 20/20! Even though Steve's head was still throbbing and his shoulder ached, his mind began racing. His father had begun to explain how they could move objects back in time as well as forward in time. If he could travel back in time to Saturday morning, they could set a trap and catch the intruders. He could change the present by altering the past. He would spend as much time as possible with his parents to learn how their equipment worked and to complete the testing. He would be a hero. His parents would be so proud.

When Steve's parents realized the nature of the burglars' focus, they called the FBI. A team of six was assigned to investigate. They identified the brand of cigarette that the police had found—Dunhill International. They determined where their car had been parked and the type of tire—Goodyear GS-D—standard on the Lexus LS400. Footprints proved there were three inside the house. Perhaps a fourth waited with the car. There were three cigarette stubs near where the car had been parked. Again, Dunhill. The depth of the indentation from their shoes in the soil and the shoe size gave them rough estimates of the heights and weights. Two of the men were probably between 5' 6" and 5' 9" and were quite slender. The third was significantly taller and heavier.

The house was clean. There were no prints anywhere. They did manage to get two partials off the cigarette butts near the car, but they were insufficient to generate a SYSCOM computer match.

Steve's parents inventoried their equipment and files as best they could. Large segments of their working files and test results were missing. The file where Miriam kept her latest records on her Time Parallax Theory had been untouched, presumably the result of Steve's interruption. An early prototype of the re-activator was missing along with the remains of their supply of uranium 235. It was not enough to make a bomb of any significance, and their supply of plutonium remained intact. Fortunately, all four of their current working re-activators had been in time limbo generating more data for their testing matrices. One had returned early that morning with a perfectly healthy gerbil. They watched as a second returned on schedule with a still frozen ice cube transported from two weeks in the past. Steve had been instructed to supervise that return which had been sent before they knew about their surprise vacation.

Their vacation. Steve had insisted that the vacation had been part of the complex scheme to get them all away from the lab and the office. William went to his desk to get the letter from IAPA and the Membership Affairs Committee. It was not where he had left it. He flipped through the other papers on his desk. It was gone.

They thought hard trying to remember the name of the membership chairperson, a name that had been unfamiliar to them. Miriam remembered the first name, Raul, but they drew a blank on the last name. William pulled out his Rollodex and spun around to the card for IAPA. He asked the receptionist for the name of the chairman of the Membership Affairs Committee. She responded without hesitation that Peter Swanson was chairperson of the Membership Committee and Gregor Razvinski was chairperson of the External Affairs Committee. William asked the knowledgeable receptionist if a Raul somebody chaired a committee. She said no. Could she check membership for that name? After a moment she responded that the computer indicated that there were no current members with that name but past membership included a Raul Pascal. William asked for his address and phone number. The receptionist responded that his file was marked "deceased." He thanked her and hung up.

*   *   *

During the next three weeks, Steve rushed home from Joe's Fortune Cookie Factory to work with his parents well into the evening. They got the files back in order as best they could and recreated the test results from memory. Steve developed a more accurate tracking system and began copying selected documents for safekeeping. With Steve's help, his parents were convinced that they could make up lost time and be prepared for their presentation at the IAPA Annual Meeting.

Henry and Steve's other friends at the factory had been concerned that Monday morning when Steve called in sick and said he had been attacked. Tuesday morning when Steve arrived, they greeted him with a get well card and some special ointments for his wounds. Henry appointed himself as Steve's mentor and instructor in the martial arts. Steve declined Henry's offer, whereby Henry pulled rank. Steve spent every lunch hour with Henry learning the philosophy of power and the cognitive wherewithal to control it. Steve was a quick learner. Henry was proud of his pupil. Soon, Steve would have the mental strength and the physical skills to protect himself from undisciplined aggression.

When the yellow school buses began to appear on the roads again, Steve sadly said goodbye to his newfound friends at Joe's Fortune Cookie Factory. They gave him a small farewell party. He was ceremonially presented with a card on which they had each written a special fortune for him. Steve was pleased to see Joe Weinstein at the party. Mr. Weinstein was rarely seen in the plant. The boss pulled Steve aside and said that he wanted to give Steve his own fortune to remember them by. He handed Steve an envelope. Inside were ten crisp one hundred dollar bills, a fortune to a college student and enough to pay off the last of the repair bills on Jason's Trooper. It had been a very hot day and Mr. Weinstein was sweating like a pig. As he bid Steve farewell, he gave him a big slimy hug. Steve appreciated the gesture, though he now craved a shower, the sooner the better. His own clothes had already been permeated by his own perspiration streaming down his body throughout the day.

As Steve drove away from the plant, enjoying the first cooling affects of his Jeep Cherokee's air conditioning unit, he felt a burning emptiness inside. Then he pictured Madaline's face and that emptiness was filled with love and joy. He would be picking Madaline up at the train station later that evening. Oh bliss, oh rapture. Oh rapture, oh bliss.

CHAPTER
SIXTEEN

The late summer temperatures soaring into the 90's had prompted residents throughout the Delaware Valley to turn on their air conditioners and stay inside watching TV or playing Nintendo. The Philadelphia Electric Company's main switching station was overloaded and straining under the pressure. Implementing an experimental programmed grid switching procedure they were able to prevent a total black-out of the region. Instead, within the 42-grid network, the sweating technicians were able to initiate brown-outs sequentially in each of the 42 sectors, two at a time for 45 minute periods. The switching station itself was operating on reduced power which is why there was no air conditioning to cool the hard working technicians.

The red-cheeked conductor on the 6:55 PM out of Washington, DC was tired of dealing with angry passengers. The train had been sitting on the tracks in northern Delaware without moving while their grid was shut down for its designated period. They had enough power to operate the communications system and the ventilation system, but not the air conditioning. The silver capsules each containing scores of passengers turned into giant outdoor grills, slowly roasting their contents from the inside out. The conductor allowed the passengers to lower the windows but due to safety regulations would not allow them to detrain.

The passengers cheered when the engine rumbled and the sluggish wheels began to turn. The vents filled with blasts of cooling air and irate passengers settled down to weather the last of the trip.

Ten minutes later, the train coasted to a stop and the cool air was replaced by blasts that surely must have been imported from Hell. The train erupted in an explosion of rage. Lawyers started demanding names and addresses. Young macho males threatened the conductor. One svelte young lady tried to seduce her way off the train. Everyone was yelling. But the train stayed still. They had entered another designated grid and would have to wait the remaining 35 minutes until adequate power resumed.

The conductor in Madaline's car used this time to reassess his decision not to accept the early retirement plan that had been offered to him in July. Monday morning, he would call headquarters to ask if the option were still available—that is, if he survived until Monday morning. He had to break up one fistfight that fortunately did not involve him. This time when the train started to move there was only scattered applause. The pessimists and the realists expected the train to stop again at any minute.

Fortunately for the sanity and safety of the conductor, the train did not stop again until it reached Philadelphia. They finally pulled into Philadelphia's 30th Street Station shortly after 10:00 PM. The conductor apologized for the delay and made his standard announcement thanking the passengers for riding Amtrac. He felt like a hypocrite. He knew that once he had retired he would never board a train again.

When Madaline climbed the stairs into the main station, she saw Steve anxiously waving from the waiting crowd. She knew that she did not look her best but she was too hot and tired to do anything about it. She wanted to make a good impression on Steve, but she was sure that he would understand.

Steve had showered and applied two splashes of his father's cologne before he had left for the station. Now, he was covered by Madaline's perspiration as they embraced. This time he did not mind. He was back together with his very special girlfriend. She did not sweat, she glistened. Everything would be great now. After all, what else could go wrong?

*　　*　　*

The big day had finally come. William was awake at 6:00 AM pacing around the kitchen. Miriam eventually joined him unable to get back to sleep with the ruckus downstairs and her own anxiety blended with unadulterated glee. Tonight was their opportunity to demonstrate to the scientific community—their peers, the same ones who had said it could not be done—the results of their nearly half decade of dedicated scientific exploration, research and application.

At 7:30, Steve heard the upstairs toilet flush and figured that Madaline must be awake, too. Steve had been oscillating in and out of sleep all night long, ignoring, and then forcibly encountering the metal bar which ran across the center of the fold-out sleep sofa in the family room. Around 3:00 AM, he had placed a hex on chivalry wishing it were dead. He regretted having bestowed his bedroom on his beautiful guest and cursed the engineers who had designed the sleep (ha!) sofa.

When Madaline sauntered into the family room to check on Steve, she was wearing a peach-colored satin bathrobe over her potentially risqué nightgown hidden underneath. Steve immediately chastised himself for even considering denying her every creature comfort.

Madaline looked radiant. She had brushed her long flowing hair until the oils from her head had coated each strand giving them a rich luster. She had applied a thin coat of tinted lip-gloss and her customary eye enhancers. She wore mascara and a deep aquamarine eye shadow that made love to her hazel eyes. The mask of brilliance shining from her face helped camouflage the exhaustion that burrowed deep within her soul and flowed from her eyes on lesser days. Today, her elation at being with her beloved overshadowed the misery that she harbored inside. She smiled softly upon seeing Steve contorted across his place of rest.

Madaline was torn whether or not to share her burden with Steve. She had not slept well since the day she first did it. Now, more than ever, she was terrified what Steve might think. She had always been the one with the impeccable moral fiber. How could she have let this happen?

The vision of Madaline waiting at the breakfast table inspired Steve to break his shower record of three minutes, six seconds including shampoo and conditioner. As Steve came back downstairs, the smell of fresh brewed coffee filled his nostrils. He joined the others at the round table in the kitchen for blueberry pancakes, turkey bacon and pineapple juice. The conversation was light and comfortable. They talked about the weather and what they would do that afternoon. They asked about Madaline's summer. She talked about her job and her new friends at North American Consumer Products. She chatted about her experience riding a motorcycle for the first time and the latest movie she had seen with her girlfriends. She talked about everything except what was most pressing in her mind.

The others had a lot on their minds, too. They kept the conversation at a safe distance from the IAPA Meeting, just ten hours off, to which they were all invited. A foreboding feeling was shared by each of the Harris' that tonight's festivities might not go exactly as planned.

After breakfast, Steve and Madaline packed a picnic lunch into a 34-quart Igloo Cooler. Miriam watched with fascination as they microwaved chicken legs and gathered together bags of sour cream and onion chips and dinosaur shaped chocolate chip cookies. She remembered twenty-five years before when she and William, her boyfriend at the time, had gone on a picnic. She had cooked the entire day before making fresh biscuits and her mother's special recipe for chutney. She had packed everything in a wicker basket that had pouches for the silverware, glasses and a red checkered table cloth. How things had changed!

Steve finished off the preparations by spreading chunky peanut butter and marshmallow fluff on white bread to make two fluffernutter sandwiches. Madaline threw in some paper napkins, plastic forks and knives and two cans of cold Dr. Pepper. She tried not to think of their last portable food adventure at Mooselookmeguntic Lake.

As the sun peeked through the scattered cloud covering, Steve maneuvered the Jeep Cherokee into the parking lot for Fairmount Park off of Bells Mill Road. He explained to Madaline that Fairmount Park is the longest inner-city park in the country. Steve favored this particular stretch of the park where it bordered the Wissahickon River because it was an easy walk to the old covered bridge and the statue of the American Indian.

Steve and Madaline walked along the dirt trail each holding one handle of the cooler. They walked slowly, enjoying the warming sun and the closeness of the other. After about twenty minutes, they found a large rock by the water's edge. They pulled the two sodas out of the cooler and lowered them into an eddy on the upstream side of the rock. The sodas were already cold and the cooler performed well, but they wanted to commune with nature and avail themselves of its bounteous offerings. Even though the water was not as cold as the interior of the cooler with its frozen icepack, the Dr. Peppers still refreshed them when they finally retrieved them after a short nap in the warmth of the soothing sun.

"I can see why turtles like to sun themselves on rocks. That felt great."

"I could sleep here all day, except those tiny black ants keep crawling up my skirt. The sound of the water bubbling over the rocks is very soporific."

"I'm so glad you were able to come by way of Philadelphia. It means a lot to my parents to have you attend the meeting. I really wanted you to meet them. They have heard so much about you. They're very nervous about tonight, but they're also very proud of their discoveries. And besides, I'm glad to have some quiet time to spend with you before we get back to the rat race of school. I can't believe that this is our last year of college."

"Yeah, pretty soon we'll have to grow up and start looking out for ourselves. We'll even have to get jobs."

"Oh, horrors." Steve laughed. "Actually, I'm kind of looking forward to the interview process. I had a lot of fun this summer at the factory. I know that I don't want to do anything like that for a permanent job, but it was a good experience. They were so nice to me. The boss even gave me a nice bonus. I was concerned about being able to pay the balance of the repairs for Jason's Trooper, but now I think I have it pretty well covered." Steve did not notice the peculiar expression on Madaline's face. "Darn, I forgot to bring my fortunes with me. I wanted to show you the fortunes that each of my co-workers wrote for me. Some of them were pretty funny. One of them read, 'May you always be healthy, wealthy and eat fries.' They know that I love McDonald's french fries. Did you know that french fries were actually invented in Belgium?"

"I knew they invented Brussels sprouts."

"Pommes frites and baby cabbages, what a combination! Anyway, another fortune read, 'May you find a beautiful woman and live happily ever after.' I love it when fortunes look like they are going to come true. I hope that the latter part turns out as well as the former part. I feel so lucky."

"Steve, I have something that I have to tell you." Madaline's voice started to quiver as her eyes filled with tears.

Steve looked at Madaline unsure what to say. He had a dreadful premonition that Madaline was going to say that his fortune was not going to come true. Perhaps she had met someone else over the summer and was leaving him. "What is it, Lin?"

"Please don't hate me. I don't know why I did it. It was so stupid. I wanted to help you." Madaline started to sob. Steve leaned closer and tentatively put his arm around her, still uncertain where this conversation was going. Madaline continued, mixing tears and quick gasps for breath with her words. "I have broken one of the Ten Commandments. I am a terrible, horrible sinner. I wish I hadn't done it. I don't know what to do."

Steve was growing impatient. "Madaline, what did you do?"

"I stole. I'm a thief. I'm evil. And now you don't even need my help. I did it for nothing."

"Madaline!" Steve tried not to lose his patience. "Lin. Tell me what happened."

"You know how you were so concerned about paying Jason for the repairs and the new tires? I decided that I should pay for half. Why should you always have to be the one to accept responsibility? I'm a big girl now. I tried to get a raise, but they said that was not possible. They said that they might be cutting back their workforce and I was lucky to have gotten a job for the summer. I tried to get an extra job for evenings or the weekends, but all of the jobs were already taken by other kids who had gotten there first. Trying to find a summer job in the middle of June is impossible. I got so frustrated. Every day, I sat there and wrote checks for thousands of dollars for all sorts of crazy things. I think that I wrote to you about some of them. Imagine, $2900 for a first class ticket to Seoul, Korea. I saw fares in the newspaper for $850. The economy seats get there just as fast as the first class section. And $300 in one month for yellow pads. If people would save their junk mail and write on the back of the paper that is only printed on one side, then we could have saved lots of money, not to mention a few trees in the process.

"I saw so much waste and no one seemed to care. My supervisor told me not to question what the executives spent and to stick to doing my job. No wonder corporate America is having trouble competing with the Japanese and Koreans. Wait until we start having to compete with over a billion Chinese.

"Dick Huffman is the Manager of the Household Cleansers Division. He is a real jerk. He would send a requisition for petty cash through inner-company mail. The morning after he sent it, he would call up and complain to my supervisor that he had not received his money yet. He demanded that someone hand deliver it. Guess who had to do that? Right, the low man on the totem pole. It would take me nearly an hour to get over to their building and back so I would usually miss lunch. After this happened for the third time, I suggested to Ms. Faunstable, his pompous administrative assistant, that he send over a supply of requisition forms and any time he needed petty cash he could call and we could then deliver it through inner-company mail and he would have it the next morning. Remarkably they listened to my idea and sent over a stack of signed requisition forms each for $1,000. They sent them to my attention. I got to thinking. If I processed one extra form and forged Mr. Huffman's name and cashed it for him, no one would know the difference. We had already been audited by the internal auditors in conjunction with an outside audit by Ernst & Young. I noticed that they reviewed all expenses over $10,000 and only did a random check of lesser amounts. Even if they noticed a discrepancy, all the petty cash amounts were for $1,000 and they would never be able to track it. I coded it as a normal disbursement and charged the amount to the Household Cleansers Division. They say that many of the best criminals were geniuses and many of the best geniuses were criminals. I wouldn't say I'm a genius by any means, but I think that I figured this one out pretty well. The bank teller didn't even question it when I brought in an endorsed petty cash check. Secretaries often cash checks for their bosses. It was so easy the first time; I did it two more times. Steve, I stole $3,000 and you don't even need it."

"What are you going to do about it?"

"I don't know." Madaline's voice was barely a whisper.

"I guess you have three choices. You can keep the money and be miserable the rest of your life and risk going to jail if you get caught. You could try to return the money and hope that they forgive you or don't find out. Or you could give the money to charity and appease your conscious."

"What do you think I should do?"

"Well, the money is not yours. I don't recommend keeping it. I appreciate your desire to help me out even if you did get a bit overzealous. Now, we just need to try to repair the damage. I don't think that giving it to charity is the right answer either. You're not Robin Hood. That money belongs to the shareholders of North American Consumer Products. Even if they don't spend all of their money wisely, it's not for you to determine where any excess goes. So, I guess you have to return it."

"How?"

"I don't know. You're the one with the criminal genius. Just think backwards."

"Steve, I am not a criminal. I made a mistake. I know it was a big mistake. I still can't believe I did it and I'll certainly never do it again. Do you believe me?"

"Of course I do. I know you only meant to help. You are a good person. Any of your friends at the shelter would attest to that. Don't worry, I still love you."

Steve was disappointed that Madaline would have this flaw in her character. He had created an ideal image in his mind and had placed her high on a shiny white pedestal. Nevertheless, he felt partly to blame. If he had not had the accident and if he had not shared his monetary woes with Madaline, perhaps she would not have been pushed to do this egregious act. He did love her but he could not help thinking less of her. He would try to forgive her. He would try to forgive himself.

CHAPTER
SEVENTEEN

Around 6:00 PM, Steve started to get hungry again. The gastronomic effects of their early afternoon repast were beginning to fade. Dinner would not begin until after 8:00. He decided to wait as a form of atonement. Besides, he could not find anything particularly appetizing in the well-stocked kitchen.

At a quarter to seven, the glitterati began to appear in the downstairs hall. Steve and William looked stunningly handsome in their Henry Ford Black Tuxedos. Madaline appeared in an off-the-shoulder mid-calf floral gown. Her hair was woven into a nest atop her head and was interspersed with sprigs of baby's breath. She wore no jewelry and yet she sparkled.

Miriam appeared last. She wore a pale blue sequined dress and navy blue spiked heals. She also sported a small navy blue chapeau that was pinned to her blond hair at a distinct angle. She looked elegant and her demeanor demanded attention in spite of her diminutive size.

The spell only flickered momentarily as they entered their chariots, the well-traveled family station wagon and Steve's Jeep Cherokee. William had pre-packed the rear of the wagon with all of the necessary equipment for their presentation that left little room for passengers. He had made a list and had checked it twice. He was leaving nothing to chance. Steve was perfectly happy to drive separately in case the evening wore on too long and he and Madaline wanted to make an unobtrusive departure.

Steve's parents had reserved parking at the Bellevue. Their lot was full so Steve found a space in a garage across from the hotel on Broad Street. By the time they located his parents, the wagon had been unloaded with the help of a well-trained bellhop.

The Bellevue is one of the premier hotels in Philadelphia. The tasteful decor and the "Fully Reserved" sign by the front desk gave no hint that the Bellevue had been closed and had even changed its name for several years because of the infamous outbreak of Legionnaires Disease in 1976 which had caused the death of 29 individuals staying and working at the hotel.

As they entered the Liberty Room, Steve was impressed by the grandeur of the banquet room. The table cloths were pink and the linen white. Each table had a flower arrangement of roses and pink and white carnations elevated on a narrow long stem vase to allow for eye contact with those on the opposite side of the table. A string quartet played Strauss in the corner. Steve had not expected such gracious amenities from a bunch of scientists.

They registered at a welcoming table by the door. Steve had mixed feelings when he saw that he and Madaline had been assigned to the head table along with his parents. It was quite an honor, but he was not sure that he wanted to be on display. Also, it would be harder for him and Madaline to play footsie with each other.

Steve and Madaline were each given pre-printed nametags with just their first names. It was intended to convey a friendly informal feeling, but Steve felt it was hideously incongruous with their formal attire and the elegant atmosphere of the Bellevue. Nevertheless, he affixed it to his right lapel, hoping that the sticky glue would not leave a residue on his tuxedo.

Steve recalled arguing with Foster about which side a nametag should be on. Steve had contended that the right side was correct since when shaking hands upon meeting someone, the right side is turned forward along with the right hand making it easier for someone to read the tag. Foster had argued that the left side made more sense because it just did. Thinking about Foster made Steve sad. Steve looked at Madaline and her smile in response to his glance helped ease his sorrow.

The dinner was sumptuous. A spinach salad with a light Dijon dressing was followed by a coconut sorbet to cleanse the palate. Next came a bouquet of fresh seafood, adorning a bed of crushed ice surrounding a silver chalice containing a spicy red cocktail sauce. The flock of waiters returned, this time with a lemon sorbet. Madaline asked how sorbet and sherbet differed. Steve learned the answer from the white-haired woman in the green silk dress seated to his left. Sorbet contains milk or cream while sherbet does not. Steve thanked the woman who introduced herself as Mrs. Bartlett, wife of the Executive Director of IAPA. Her nametag read "Maud." Mrs. Bartlett complimented Madaline on her hair and informed them that the ladies in her gardening club back in Trumbull, Connecticut would be most interested in her creative use of baby's breath.

The main course consisted of a superb chateaubriand, braised carrots with a hint of ginger, an unusual rice pilaf, and a tomato aspic molded in the shape of a star. Steve had completely forgotten his earlier hunger by the time the dessert arrived. A blend of white and dark chocolate mousse was nestled in a thin milk chocolate basket and drizzled with a raspberry sauce and topped with pralines. Steve did not need any encouragement to finish off the last few bites of Madaline's when she was sated.

As the last of the tables was being cleared, Dr. Harold Bartlett rose to the microphone with a great flourish. Maud Bartlett grabbed Steve by the arm and interrupted his conversation with Madaline about marsupials. "My husband is about to speak. Be sure to listen," she instructed the young guests.

Dr. Bartlett cleared his throat, twice for emphasis. The room, filled to capacity with nearly 250 physicists and their spouses and guests, gradually quieted down as he began, "On behalf of the Executive Committee and the Officers of IAPA, I am pleased to welcome you all to our 40th Annual Meeting. This is a record crowd that I attribute to three factors. First, the ladies on the Development Committee did a remarkable job organizing this event. Would you ladies please stand and accept our thanks."

Enthusiastic applause filled the chamber. "I, for one, was especially impressed by the engraved invitations and the pre-event organization. Thank you again, ladies. You may all be seated now." Steve watched as Mrs. Bartlett lowered herself back into her chair. "Second, we are pleased to see the membership in IAPA growing at such a healthy rate. In the past year, we have approved applications for nearly two hundred new members bringing our worldwide membership to just less than two thousand. I would like to take this opportunity to welcome those who have traveled the farthest to be here. We have representatives from Canada, Mexico, England, Germany, France, the Netherlands, Sweden, Saudi Arabia, Egypt, China, Australia, and Fiji. According to our archivist, this meeting here in historic Philadelphia has more countries represented than any meeting to date. Thank you for making the trip. I am sure that you will find the meeting most informative and intriguing. As you all know, tonight kicks off three days of symposia, lectures and work groups. Be sure that you have registered for these events before you leave tonight as space is limited.

"Finally, I attribute tonight's attendance to the excitement which has been generated from advance leaks about the nature of tonight's keynote presentation by Dr. William Harris and Dr. Miriam Harris." Steve began to applaud thunderously. When Mrs. Bartlett turned in her chair to register her disapproval, Steve halted, but by then the rest of the room had taken over with a surge of energy. Across the table, Steve's parents beamed at the deafening recognition. They shot nervous glances at each other. Steve felt vindicated and very proud.

"Based on that response, I think that we will postpone the business meeting until the luncheon tomorrow and without further adieu, ladies and gentlemen, I present to you Dr. and Dr. Harris."

As the room repeated it previous ovation, Steve's parents accepted the podium from Dr. Bartlett. While Miriam adjusted some of the equipment displayed on a long table adjacent to the podium, William advanced to the microphone. Even though Steve's parents were peers in their profession and their work together, Miriam usually deferred to her husband in social situations and for public presentations. She did not enjoy public speaking and she believed that her husband's imposing figure gave greater credibility to what he was saying. She enjoyed her relationship with her husband. Some might have called it quaint, others, old-fashioned. All she cared about was that her husband still opened the door for her and would protect her if anything went wrong. William Harris had been an athlete in college, not unlike their son, though her husband had been on the basketball team and had done track and field events in the spring. She could still feel the power in his body when he wrapped his arms around her at night. As she made the final adjustments, she listened with admiration as her husband addressed the audience.

"Thank you for inviting us to speak tonight. We are much honored to be standing here before such an esteemed assembly of scientists. Our intention is not to gain recognition for our discoveries, rather to share them with you so that we as a cooperative organization can draw on each other's expertise to make further advances in our field to the benefit of all humankind." Miriam Harris smiled at her husband's politically correct substitute for "mankind."

"We will be conducting an in depth workshop beginning tomorrow morning at 10:30 for those wishing to pursue the specifics of our findings. Being passed out now are copies of the two articles that have been published thus far, one in the *Journal of Scientific Discovery*, and the other more recently in *Scientific American*. We will have additional handouts at tomorrow's workshop.

"Rather than give you a lengthy discourse about the premises for our findings and the procedures whereby we have tested and modified our theories, we will be following the old adage that a picture is worth a thousand words.

"Ladies and gentlemen, mesdames et messieurs, we are about to demonstrate to you for the first time that the concept of travel through time is not just the deranged hallucinations of science fiction authors but indeed a verifiable scientific phenomenon. The secret and the power are contained within our tiny friend, the electron.

"Please watch carefully as my wife makes scientific history." Miriam removed a brown and white guinea pig from a small, ventilated box. They had chosen a guinea pig because of its titular appropriateness. The guinea pig had been injected with a mild tranquilizer to keep it from scurrying off the launch pad and spoiling the presentation. Miriam attached the re-activator to a small hook on the collar that surrounded the guinea pig's neck. She dialed a setting and flipped a switch on the re-activator. A knife dropped by a tardy waiter shattered the silence as the spectators were glued to the scene anticipating either a failure or a miracle. Miriam moved to the portable activator and pressed the start button. The coordinates had been meticulously pre-set and checked and rechecked.

A split second after the button was pressed, a bright flash emitted from the location of the guinea pig. As the burn spots on the retinas of the audience cleared, their eyes refocused on an empty launch pad. A muffled gasp echoed throughout the room.

William broke the resurging silence, "Please keep your attention directed to the launch pad. In 180 seconds, Howie, our furry little time traveler, should return to us. While we have all aged three minutes, he will have been suspended in time, unaware of anything unusual. Our recent success rate with living creatures has approached one hundred percent."

Glancing at his watch, William stopped his monologue and turned back to the launch pad. He tried to appear calm, but the growing patches of moisture under his arms belied his condition. His reputation, their reputations as scientists rested on this demonstration. No one would take their monumental discoveries seriously if they could not show them in this forum. He would be a laughing stock.

No one was laughing when 181 seconds later, Howie reappeared apparently unfazed. Bedlam broke out as suspicion and fascination swept through the large room. Steve's parents watched with visible glee as their peers marveled and debated among themselves. Steve reached over and took Madaline's hand. They smiled at each other. Steve could feel the stress flow out of his body.

Hands began to flail in the air and shouts of "Dr. Harris, Dr. Harris" filled their ears. William pointed to a large rugged looking gentleman sitting at the nearest table. He stood and tried to speak but could not be heard over the din. William calmly reiterated, "Silence, please," into the mike until the turmoil settled down. The imposing gentleman tried again, "This looks like a magic trick I saw on the TV recently. How do we know you didn't use mirrors or some other deceptive means?" He spoke with an accent that sounded almost English but which was a bit rougher, somewhat tainted with a southern twang. Steve decided that he must be from Australia.

"If you come to the workshop tomorrow, we will repeat the demonstration and you can stand on any side of the launch pad you like. We have nothing to gain from showing you tricks. This has taken us nearly five years to attain. Science is the only true magic."

More hands shot up. William pointed to an oriental gentleman sitting two tables over. "I understand also you have been able to send objects back in time, not just forward. Explain and demonstrate please." Steve's parents exchanged quizzical glances. They had not yet released any information about Miriam's advances in proving the non-linearity of time. How could this man know about this? Or was he just extrapolating and made a lucky guess?

William responded, "Our presentation tonight involves linear time travel. If you have questions about other aspects, please see me afterwards and I will try to answer your questions." The man looked at his two colleagues with disgust and sat down. Steve watched as they leaned in to talk among themselves. Something did not seem right to Steve. Suddenly it dawned on Steve what was wrong.

Dr. Bartlett had announced that there were representatives from China, Australia and Fiji. He did not mention any other Asia-Pacific countries. Steve looked around to see if there were any other oriental looking guests. He could see none. He turned his attention back to the three men. They were still in heated conversation among themselves. Steve casually got out of his seat and walked over closer to their table as if he were heading to the door and the bathroom beyond. He paused to get a closer look. They all turned around and stared at him. The man who had asked the question wore a thin mustache. Steve noticed that his feet did not quite reach the floor. To his left was a much larger man who had a mean scowl and was completely bald. The third man wore glasses and had a long scar that ran down his cheek from his left eye to his chin. Steve continued out the door and waited in the hall until the door had closed behind him.

Steve was certain now. Those men were not from China. He had spent most of the summer with a factory full of men and women who were first and second generation Chinese. Henry Wong had complained to him one day at the factory about how he hated it when whites mistook him for Japanese or Korean. "We do not all look alike," he had protested. "You can usually tell from the eyes." Steve knew that the Japanese had totally segregated their society for generations and it was not until the beginning of the Meiji Restoration in 1868 that Japanese society once again came into contact with other cultures. They believed that they were a pure race and intermarriage was strongly discouraged.

Steve was confused. What did this all mean? Why would Japanese men come to a conference and pretend that they were Chinese? Unless . . .

Steve reentered the room and returned to his seat. He whispered to Madaline that something very strange was going on. He pointed out the three men and told Madaline not to let them see her looking. Steve tried to get his parents' attention, but they were busy answering questions.

He felt an unrestrained urgency as he rifled through his pockets for something with which to write. He would send his father a note. His father would know what to do.

He asked Madaline and she handed him a small gold colored pen. Now the note. He could use a napkin, but they were linen. Madaline saw his dilemma and handed him the white card marked "1" which had been mounted over their table on a small wire stand.

Steve scribbled his message on the card,

> "Dad—DANGER. Chinese men are Japanese. LEXUS.
> Robbed house. Want re-activator. Be careful. I'll get help.
>
> Steve"

In an excited whisper, Steve asked Madaline to hurry to the concierge and have them call the police. Mrs. Bartlett turned around and in her best librarian imitation shushed them.

Madaline and Steve both ignored her and stood up. Madaline headed for the door and Steve moved over to the podium. William became distracted by Steve and looked annoyed. Steve reached out his arm with the note. He watched the Japanese men out of the corner of his eye. They had stopped arguing and were carefully watching Steve's actions.

William finally extended his arm and took the note from Steve. He continued answering the latest question. Steve implored him with his eyes to read the note. Miriam moved over next to her son to investigate his troubled countenance. Steve pulled her aside and explained as best he could what was happening. Meanwhile William glanced at the note as he continued to talk.

Madaline took the stairs to the first floor rather than waiting for the elevator. She did not understand why Steve was so upset but she knew he was serious. The concierge was busy giving descriptions of local restaurants to one of the hotel guests. Madaline interrupted. When the concierge said he would be with her in just a minute, Madaline paused and then demanded assistance. The concierge apologized to the guest and turned his annoyed attention to this rude intruder. She explained that she needed the police because there were some suspicious characters at the IAPA Meeting in the Liberty Room. The concierge looked even more annoyed, if possible, when he realized the nature of the unmitigated interruption. To appease this pushy female and to remove the nuisance from his presence he agreed to call the hotel detective. After dialing two numbers and mumbling something into the phone, the concierge turned his attention back to the guest without a further word to Madaline.

Several minutes passed before an attractive young man in a well-tailored business suit approached the desk. "What can I do for you, Bill?" Madaline noted how he looked more like a hotel guest than a detective. She figured that this was intentional.

"Hi, Drew. This young lady seems to have a concern. Perhaps you can help her."

The hotel detective turned to Madaline. "Hello, Ma'am. My name is Drew Appenzeller. How can I be of service?" He looked up and down her body noticing her thin waist and the smoothness of her well tanned naked shoulders.

She observed his vertical survey and avoided mentioning Steve, or "boyfriend" or anything else that might dissuade this man from helping her. After a hurried explanation of the situation as best she could with the limited information she had, she led Drew Appenzeller back to the Liberty Room. As they entered the room, she quickly scanned the scene to assess any changes. Steve was off to the side talking nervously with his mother. His father continued to respond to questions from the podium.

Madaline pointed out the relevant suspects. Drew said, "Everything looks under control to me. I don't see any suspicious behavior." Madaline looked up pleadingly into his eyes. "Okay, if it will make you feel any better, I will go ask them a few questions. If you're wrong, this could be very embarrassing for me, and for you."

From their respective corners of the room, Steve and Madaline watched as the detective approached the table where the allegedly Chinese guests were sitting. Drew looked at them carefully. The young lady had told him that they were really Japanese and were pretending to be Chinese. He could not tell for sure. They were dressed nicely and did not seem to be disturbing anyone.

Madaline saw Drew lean over and start talking to the man with the glasses and the scar. At one point, she saw Drew and the three men all turn in her direction as Drew pointed his finger at her. Why did he do that? He was young and probably inexperienced, but to identify her seemed very foolish and could endanger her if she was right. And if she was wrong, Drew was making sure that she would be embarrassed in the process. She became upset at Steve. Why had he put her in this no win situation? What was really going on?

Before she could finish her thought, she heard a loud bang and watched as Drew tumbled backwards crashing onto the table behind him. He landed in the lap of a man wearing a turban. A woman sitting across the table screamed. The man in the turban was stunned. As blood flowed from Drew's chest onto the white folds of his galabiyah, which resembled a silk nightshirt, the man next to him yelled, "Mon Dieux! Il a été touché par un balle! Help! Help!"

Meanwhile, the three Japanese men had flown to their feet and had shifted to the front of the room near the podium. The bald man made no effort to hide the large barreled gun which he held in his left hand. "Sinister," the Latin word for left. How appropriate, thought Madaline, her brain clouded and filtering out other thoughts.

As the audience interpreted the noise and the nature of the unexpected entertainment, and as more people saw the gun at the front of the room, they began a stampede for the exits. Chairs crashed to the floor and entire tables were knocked over. Screams arose from those less agile who were trampled in the melee.

In the confusion, William grabbed the portable activator and the re-activator from the launch pad. He threw them in a canvas case and passed it to Steve. The last words he heard his father say were, "Hurry, son. Protect these. God speed."

Steve scrambled behind his mother and around the scattered chairs and tables. He made his way through the mob toward the door where he had last seen Madaline. As he moved past one overturned table, he heard a voice calling his name and demanding assistance. Maud Bartlett was on the floor and her green silk dress was trapped under the table. She had fallen and she could not get up. Steve's natural inclination was to stop and help, but his father's words echoed in his ears. He continued toward the door and safety beyond.

As he neared the door he heard a scream. He turned to see the source. The man with the glasses and the scar had his arms around Miriam and was struggling to subdue her. Steve watched in shock as his father lunged towards his mother's captor. William looked tremendous and fierce looming over the smaller man. A moment from the impact, a shot rang out and the lifeless body of William hurled past its intended target and crashed into a cart containing two pots of coffee, one with an orange cap indicating decaf.

Steve saw the bald man, outstretched gun in hand, nod to the little man with the thin mustache. An evil smirk spread on his pudgy lips. He had conquered the white giant with a single shot. They still had the woman and they could force her to tell them what they needed to know. The equipment and the papers they had stolen had proved useless. Now, there would be nothing to stop them. Even their government did not know of their plans.

Steve wanted to vomit. He tried to twist back to help his parents, but the mass of the mob convulsing towards the door carried him through. As the mob opened up into the larger space of the hallway, Steve broke free. He was dazed. His father had been shot and his mother was being kidnapped. William had told him to protect the equipment. He wished that he could have protected his parents instead.

Something grabbed his arm. He jumped and swung around to fend off the attack. He barely restrained his fist, inches from Madaline's face.

In the hallway, people were screaming and crying. A blur of tuxedos and dresses of all colors lined their path. Steve and Madaline fled down the stairs to the front with Madaline leading the way. Once through the revolving door and onto the street, Steve had to pause. He felt the blood rush from his head and he sensed the pavement rising to meet his face. He felt a hard tug on his arm as Madaline pulled him back to his feet. She had such incredible strength enveloped in that smooth body.

Madaline had heard the second shot and knew that in some way, they were now the target of these murderers. With both hands, she backed Steve into an alley and told him to wait for her there. She reached into his pocket and pulled out the keys. Her mind flashed back to the deserted road in Maine when she had reached into Steve's pocket to get his medication.

Madaline hurried down the street and ran across to the parking garage. A few moments later, she emerged behind the wheel of Steve's Cherokee. As she swerved out onto Broad Street, she glanced at the entrance to the Bellevue. She saw two police cars arrive and skid to a halt outside the passenger-loading zone for the Bellevue. The drivers and passengers in blue bounded across sidewalk and disappeared inside. At the same time, she saw coming out one of the other doors the stocky bald Japanese man who had been behind the gun that had discharged its small lethal contents into the chest of Drew Appenzeller. He seemed unfazed by the presence of the police cars. He looked intently up and down Broad Street searching through all of the activity of a Saturday night in the city. Madaline did not slow down to observe his further actions. She screeched to a halt in front of the alley. Madaline reached across to swing open the door. Steve appeared from the alley and tumbled into the front seat next to her. The door swung shut as Madaline jammed the accelerator to the floor and maneuvered her way through the light traffic back toward the Schuylkill Expressway. Steve flinched when Madaline roared through a red light, but he withheld any criticism. He admired Madaline for her gumption and was thankful that she was at the helm.

The color began to flow back into Steve's face. His heart was still racing nearly two kilometers a minute. Steve started to explain to Madaline as best he could what had transpired at the Bellevue and why. When he tried to tell Madaline about the second shot and how he had left his mother in the hands of murderers, his voice cracked and she could feel the Jeep shake as his body shuddered. Madaline tried to make a joke about how Steve always showed her an exciting time, but her humor was ill conceived and Steve relapsed into silence except for giving occasional directions.

As they approached Steve's neighborhood, Steve leapt forward in his seat and his face lit up. "Eureka! I know what we can do. We'll go back in time and change everything. We can keep Dad from getting shot and we can have these bastards arrested before they can do any harm."

"Steve, that's not possible. Your parents' research has only accomplished forward travel through time."

"No! Mom had made tremendous advances on the concept of non-linear time. She has the Apple PGSimulator programmed for analyzing when this point on the Earth last occupied the exact same space in the universe. If we hook up MAMA and program the PGSimulator to activate the atomic reaction the moment we are in a parallel location, we should be able to jump back in time. We'll put in a variable setting requesting the transfer to wait until there is a recent time period that corresponds. If we can go back a day or a week, that would be enough. The only problem is that if we go back a whole year, we would have to do junior year all over again."

"If that happens, maybe we could save Foster and your other friend . . .

"Tim."

"From falling off the clubhouse."

"What do you think?"

"I guess it's worth a try, if you think it will work. I wouldn't mind spending some extra time with you. Maybe we can go somewhere other than Mooselookmeguntic Lake for our vacation, or at least we can go when it's not raining."

Madaline turned down Willow Lane and pulled the Jeep Cherokee into the Harris' driveway. They grabbed the canvas bag and ran into the house. Steve had trouble getting his key in the lock. His hands were shaking, but at least he had a plan.

In the basement, Steve powered up the equipment. He was praying that he would remember enough of what his parents had taught him. He keyed in some components and ran a system interface to connect MAMA to the PGSimulator. He removed the portable activator and the re-activator from the canvas bag and placed them on the launch pad. He ran a lead wire from the PGSimulator to the two devices so that the blast level could be automatically calibrated by the artificial intelligence at work within the Apple brain.

Steve was relieved that the system accepted his password and his input. He would be projecting a series of simulations through the network to select an optimal setting. All that remained was to set the radius for the launch arena. Steve knew that he would have to transport the PGSimulator with them in order for the machine to make the final adjustments in calibration as the blast was occurring. The machine would not have time to pre-set these amounts because it would not know which simulation would be applied until the match occurred at the last second.

Steve did not know which equipment in the lab was tied into the system, so he set the radius on 50 meters. This would encompass the entire house and lab and most of the yard, plus parts of the neighbors' yards.

Steve's mind had been on hyper-drive. He could think of nothing else besides saving his parents. They meant the world to him. He had no other family.

Before he pressed the activation button, he took a deep breath and pulled Madaline close to him. He gave her a deep searing kiss on the lips. Her presence gave him great comfort. Without her, he could not have done this. He would probably still be in an alley in center city Philadelphia.

"Lin, I don't think you should come with me. My parents have not completed their experiments and they have never transported humans in either direction. This is very risky. There is no guarantee that it will work at all, and it may well kill me in the process. I think it would be better if you waited here for me. You can take the Jeep and drive down the block where you can watch. You need to be at least 150 feet away."

"Steve, I love you very much. I don't understand most of this, but I don't want to be here without you. Please, I want to go with you."

Steve did not need to be persuaded. He was too afraid to insist on going alone. He pressed the activation button and they waited. The hard drives moaned as they began the simulations. Perhaps as many as a billion would need to process before a match might be made. The transfer could take seconds or perhaps hours or even days or perhaps it might not work at all.

Steve and Madaline leaned against the table in the center of the room that served as the launch pad for smaller objects. As Steve's adrenalin began to subside, he began to think back to the horror of the evening. His parents were perhaps both dead and he was fleeing into the past on a mission with little likelihood of success or even survival.

He had worried about caring for his parents when they were older. Now they might never have a chance to enjoy their old age together. Steve could not shake the guilt that somehow he should have protected them.

Madaline looked at Steve and saw a tear run down each cheek. She was worried about him. She was too frightened to be concerned with her own safety, but she could not stop thoughts of never again seeing her parents or eating ice-cream or even breathing from darting through her mind. She directed her attention to Steve's pain in order to shield herself from her own.

Madaline reached her arm around Steve's shoulder. He started as if awakened from a dream. He wiped both of his cheeks and his eyes with the backs of his hands. He looked at Madaline, words failing him. His emotions were being thrashed all over the place. He was devastated about his parents. He was nervous and excited about their impending, unprecedented trip through time. And, he was thankful that he was not going alone.

He felt an overwhelming crush of love for Madaline, both wonderful and painful. He wondered how something so special could also hurt so much and at such strange times.

Steve maneuvered his arms around Madaline and held her in a tight embrace. After a few soothing moments, he began to wildly kiss her on the lips and the face and the neck. He moved his head lower and kissed the small mounds of her bosom that showed above the edge of the floral pattern of her gown. He used his tongue to gently caress the warm silkiness of her skin.

Madaline felt moistness between her legs, and her head felt light and dreamy. She ran her fingers through Steve's hair and gently massaged the back of his neck. With both her hands, she cupped Steve's head and raised his lips back to hers. Her tongue darted out to meet his. In the warm space engulfed by their mouths, their tongues parried back and forth, lunging and thrusting like the metal foils at the fencing match she had attended with Steve. Her tongue ventured about exploring the dark recesses of her boyfriend's mouth. She felt an uncontrollable desire invade her body and her soul. She could fight it no longer. Her animal desires were primitive and base and carnal in nature. She was ashamed of these feelings and yet felt a great relief to succumb to their powers.

While her tongue continued to occupy Steve's, her fingers roamed across his chest. Her energies were highly focused and her senses were acute. She could feel the texture of the studs and the buttons on his ruffled shirt as she deftly undid their grasp. She mused over how men's buttons were the opposite of female's, perhaps to make the opposing partner's job easier.

Madaline felt Steve's strong hands move to the zipper on the back of her gown. As his guiding hand slid down and the dress fell away from her chest, she felt a flash of insecurity. She had always been embarrassed by the size of her chest. When she was a teenager she had longed to look less like a boy. Perhaps that is why she still kept her hair so long. What if Steve did not like her chest? What if he found her unattractive? What if she did not know how to make love?

When Steve undid the hook on the back of her white lace bra, she was ripped away from her negative thoughts. An aching passion overtook both their bodies. Madaline felt detached from her hands as she watched them undo the belt and zipper on Steve's pants and slide them to the floor. She watched as Steve moved the re-activator from the center of the launch pad and hoisted her onto the table.

While her hands explored the newly exposed regions of Steve's body, she looked around. Their fancy clothes had looked so out of place in the lab and yet looked even more incongruous in heaps on the basement floor. Madaline had imagined this moment in many varied ways, but it was always in a bed with soft pillows and romantic lighting. The acrid smells of the subterranean room filled her nostrils instead of the sweet scent of fragrant candles in her dreams. The table was hard and cold on her naked back. Something rough was sticking into the back of her left leg. She managed to shift her body to the right and the roughness disappeared. Her mind turned back to her love-making. When she felt the hardness of Steve's penis pressing against her belly, her breathing became short and irregular as she fought the panic that was building inside.

Steve's tongue moistened her ear and probed inside. Madaline felt a shiver course through her body and goose bumps sprang to attention. She heard his comforting voice say, "I love you, Lin." The panic subsided and the excitement skyrocketed. Her body shook with anticipation. She heard a voice that sounded like her own. It said, "I love you, too. Please be gentle."

As Steve kissed Madaline, she felt the coarseness of his beard burrowing into her supple skin. The abrasion was a welcome pain, kind of like the sensation that one feels when scratching a mosquito bite.

Steve raised himself above Madaline. His hand gently moved one of her legs aside and then fumbled between them. Madaline froze as she felt a sharp pressure where his hand had been. As Steve inched his penis into her, Madaline gasped. Steve stopped when he saw the grimace on her face. Madaline gritted her teeth and whispered between breaths that she was okay and that he should continue. She felt the rest of his length slide up between her legs. She found it hard to breath and the initial pain persisted. Steve started to pull away from her again. She felt the firm penis between her legs sliding out, but then it started back in again. Steve began a rhythmic pumping motion that grew in intensity. After a short while, Madaline could hear his breaths coming in shorter gasps. Steve's body was sliding against hers. She could feel the sweat but she did not know if it was hers or Steve's. Suddenly his muscles tightened up and she felt the foreign object inside of her press against her insides as it swelled beyond its size. She sensed several bursts of hot sticky liquid splashing against her. Suddenly, her legs and arms tensed up. A trumpeting orgasm swept through her body. She shook from the inside out. Her vaginal muscles clamped down on Steve's penis and she felt waves of pleasure pulsating through her body and causing her head to reel. She heard a metal canister crash from the table to the floor. When she could breathe again, she started to laugh. She felt wonderful. She was in love and she had just shared that love with the most important person in the world to her. As Steve lowered his tired body onto hers, she reveled in the ensuing warmth and confinement. The residual pain could not be ignored yet its cause could not be regretted.

They lay in that position for several minutes waiting for their breathing to return to normal. Steve recalled reading about soldiers heading off to war who made love to their girlfriends for the first time the night before they shipped out. He wondered if Madaline would have resisted again if she had not sensed the omnipresent danger.

Steve said, "Lin, you were incredible. Thank you. I love you so much."

Madaline responded, "You were incredible yourself, the best I've ever had." They both laughed. Steve rolled over and lay next to Madaline. She took his hand and played with his fingers. She lovingly kissed each of the tips. Madaline could not help but wondering whether this would be just the first time they made love together or the last time as well.

Their breaths became longer and more relaxed. Madaline noticed that they were breathing in harmony. They were in sync. She had never felt closer to anyone. She heard Steve begin to snore slightly and then she heard a tremendous crash, the sound of breaking glass overhead.

Steve and Madaline both sat upright on the table. They heard the sound of individual pieces of glass joining the others on the ground. Steve pulled on his underpants and bounded for the steps. At the top, he pressed the knob for the lock and swung the deadbolt into place.

He scrambled back down the steps where Madaline was dressing. He pulled on his pants and listened. They both heard the sound of footsteps creaking across the kitchen floor above them. They watched as the knob to the cellar door slowly turned. Someone else was in the house. They were not alone.

CHAPTER
EIGHTEEN

Steve and Madaline were frozen in their places. They held their breaths while the mysterious figure behind the door tested its strength. The door shook at its hinges and then it reverberated as a heavy object was smashed against it repeatedly from behind. Steve looked about the room, searching for some means of defense. His heart was racing and his mind was at a full gallop. He was thankful that his father had installed the fire tested steel door at the entrance to the cellar. He had taken precautions to protect the house from an accidental malfunction of one of the explosive devices. Most of the testing now occurred in the new lab, but some tests were still done in the underground office space.

Without warning, the banging stopped. They heard footsteps across the linoleum in the kitchen followed by silence. Steve knew that they could not relax. The intruder or intruders were most likely regrouping for a further, more vicious onslaught.

Behind Steve, he heard a click and a bell. The PGSimulator had locked onto coordinates and was programming MAMA with the relevant settings. The transmission would start momentarily. Steve reached for Madaline's hand and then he blacked out.

*   *   *

The amount of empty space in an atom is immense. An atom may have as few as one electron. An electron travels at very high speeds. Its path is heavily influenced by the nucleus which is comprised of a single proton and a neutron in this smallest of atoms. The attraction of the electron and the proton keep the electron from flying off into space. The orbit of the electron would appear random in nature to a miniature spectator or one with a very high-powered microscope and very fast eyes. A time-lapse photo of the electron would show that over time its path overlaps on many occasions.

A molecule is comprised of many atoms and a cell is comprised of molecules. Cells are the building blocks of living organisms. The Earth is also made of atoms and molecules of many varieties. The Earth in turn is just one planet, on the smaller side, in a rather inconsequential solar system centered on the Sun. And, the Sun is just one star out of billions in the Milky Way Galaxy which is just one of countless galaxies making up the Universe. The distance from the Earth to the Sun is 93 million miles. The distance to the next closest star is over 250,000 times that far. There is a lot of space in between, not unlike the amount of space, relatively speaking, in a single atom.

While the electron will frequently occupy the same space it has occupied on many previous occasions, the stars and other heavenly bodies dwell in a far less controlled environment. There are many external forces affecting each individual mass. The Earth is most obviously affected by the Sun, around which it orbits, somewhat like the electron and its nucleus. The Earth is also influenced by its closest neighbor, the moon, hence the tides. Other bodies, though larger are more distant and therefore their impact is less remarkable or traceable.

When Steve set the parameters for the PGSimulator, he was naive to expect that their time transfer might only be a day or a week. The trajectory of the Earth around the Sun would have to be offset by a comparable shift of the solar system within the galaxy or within the universe. Not inconceivable, just unlikely.

*　　*　　*

Steve lay on the floor unaware if it was day or night. He did not know if he was tired. He did not know where he was. He did know that he had a headache and that something heavy was on his leg. He tried to lift his head to see, but his head would not cooperate. It was dark and there were no sounds. He lay still, aware of time passing, but without any sense of urgency. His headache subsided and he succumbed to sleep.

Through his dreams, Steve heard a noise. The noise became part of his dream. It was a moan. He was trapped. He could not move. Was it him moaning? No.

Steve knew he was awake. He had been here before. Where was it? The darkness was complete. He had a sense of motion. He heard it again. The moan. He lifted his arm and reached to where his leg had been. He could feel nothing there except that sense of motion. His hand touched something soft. It was large and it was moving.

Madaline opened her eyes. She was sure they were open though her vision deceived her. Was she blind? Was she deaf? The silence was unbearable. She tried to talk. It sounded like a moan. Her ribs ached. She needed to go to the bathroom. Something was pressing up into her. Madaline felt something touch her shoulder. She tried to scream, but another deep moan is all that came out.

Madaline shifted her weight off of the lump below her. She tried to sit up. She was dizzy and it was hard to orient herself to know which way was up or down. As a child, she had always harbored the fear of becoming blind. Her neighbor had been blind, the result of Diabetes. Madaline hated that long white pole. Madaline despised the dark. Why had her world turned black?

Her head was spinning, but the rotations were slowing. Then she felt it again. Something touched her. It was a hand. Madaline remembered where she was. She was with Steve. She reached out for him and found him next to her on the floor. She felt his leg. That is what had hurt her side. She had been lying on his leg all that time. All what time? How long had they been there? Where were they?

Madaline tried to talk again. This time words came out. "Steve? Steve, are you all right?"

"Man, I've been hung-over before, but this takes the cake. I fell off my bed. What time is it?"

"Steve, we're in the basement. Remember the dinner, the gunshots, and the computers. I think we had a blackout. All of the power is off. I don't think that it worked."

"I think I broke my leg. I can't find it."

"Don't worry, honey. I was lying on it. It's probably asleep. Let me try massaging it."

"Ow, I'm beginning to feel it. The tingling. I think I can move it now. See if you can find a light switch. There should be one at the bottom of the steps."

"I can't see anything. Where are the steps?"

"Tell me what you feel."

"I feel the side of a, it feels like a file cabinet."

"What else?"

"Okay, I feel a rug on the floor and metal legs for, I think it's a wash basin."

"Okay, continue to the right along the wall from the wash stand. The stairs should be about five more feet."

"Got it. Where's the switch?"

"Attached to the vertical board at the left of the bottom stair. It's about shoulder height, I think."

"Found it. Nothing. It doesn't work."

"Okay then, we'll have to go upstairs and see if there's more light. There's a flashlight in the kitchen if it's dark out. It's weird not knowing if it's day or night."

"What about the noises? The guy we heard upstairs?"

"Shit, I thought that was a dream. Try to find something we can protect ourselves with."

After a concentrated search, Steve found a piece of PVC pipe. It would not be as effective as a metal pipe, but it would have to do. At least it was lightweight.

Steve and Madaline were becoming more comfortable in the dark. They were developing a sense of where things were. Steve mustered his most heroic voice and told Madaline to wait there. He carefully climbed the stairs on his hands and knees, awkwardly carrying the pipe with him. When he reached the top of the stairs, he reached up and undid the deadbolt. He swung the door open. It must be night, he concluded. Only a dim light shined in from the outside and the house was enshrouded in gloomy shadows.

Steve listened for any clues about the intruder. He thought he heard breathing but he could not be sure. Steve's muscles were tense, ready for action. A few languorous seconds passed, and then a huge dark figure lunged around the corner and struck out at him. As Steve ducked to avoid the blow, he felt a sharp pain in his cheek and a nauseating agony permeating his shoulder. He held onto the stairs and applying all of the knowledge he had accrued from his martial arts lessons with Henry that summer, he grabbed and twisted, catapulting the significant mass of his attacker over his back. The body cascaded down the steps shaking the entire staircase with each impact.

Madaline barely managed to back out of its path before the body came to rest in a broken heap at the bottom. A metallic clinking persisted a moment longer as the wielded gun dislodged from the limp fingers and skidded across the basement floor ricocheting off the launch pad table base.

Mastering the natural urges of fight or flight, Steve pulled himself together and stood defiant to any further aggression against himself or his loved one. Nothing. The attack had ended. The assailant was defeated. Good had triumphed over evil. Steve felt immortal. Then he felt pain. His cheek and his shoulder informed the nearby synapses that they were not happy. Steve touched his cheek and felt a warm secretion. His Hemopalpacemia pills were in his room. He would have to get them soon.

Madaline responded that she was unharmed, so Steve felt his way into the kitchen and found the cabinet where the flashlight was stored. A flick of the switch proved that the batteries were strong. At least one thing had gone right.

Steve decided that they would restrain their still unidentified assailant as best they could and call the police. In the same cabinet as the flashlight, Steve found a pair of scissors and an unopened length of clothesline. Miriam had intended to start air-drying her clothes in order to conserve energy, but she never quite got around to it.

Back in the basement, Steve found Madaline huddled in a corner shivering. It was not cold. He wrapped his arms around her and hugged her tight. The scissors fell from his hand and clattered to the floor. Steve realized that he was shivering, too.

A moan came from the human heap. Steve shined his light in its direction. The beam cast upon an unwelcome face and reflected from the bald head. It was the Japanese man who had shot the hotel detective and his father. He had followed them to the house. Or perhaps he knew where they lived. Maybe he had been here before.

Without further delay, Steve handed Madaline the PVC pipe and the flashlight. He unwrapped the clothesline and squatted beside the bald man. He had studied knots as a tenderfoot in the boy scouts, but now that he needed them, he could not locate any in his available memory. He wrapped the line around the man's wrists and pulled the rope through his legs. Suddenly the man's leg swung up and kicked Steve in the chest. Steve could not see where he landed because Madaline dropped the flashlight. Steve expected the worst. He did not know that Madaline had dropped the flashlight so that she could use both hands to swing the PVC pipe down toward the spot where she had last seen the bald head. A moment later, the flashlight shined in Steve's face. He was stunned but had sustained no further injuries. When Madaline turned the light back on the bald man, Steve could see some blood on the side of his skull. He was unconscious.

Steve recovered the end of the rope from under the dead weight and then tied the two feet together and ran the rope up to his thick neck. He fashioned a slipknot that would tighten around his neck if the man struggled to free himself. Not bad for innovation, he thought. As a last touch, he took the handkerchief from his back pocket, twisted it and wedged it between the man's teeth, tying it off in the back. He knew that it was silly to gag an unconscious man, but he did not want him shouting any warning or advice to his partners in crime especially since Steve would not be able to understand if he was speaking Japanese.

Steve took the flashlight back from Madaline and walked over to the desk. He picked up the phone and dialed "911." There was no answer. Steve tried again. This time, he noticed that there was no dial tone. The man must have cut the phone lines. Burglars usually did that, Steve had read somewhere. He would go to the neighbors' house and call from there.

Steve was worried about Madaline's safety. He had tied the knots securely, but he could not be sure they would hold. He could send Madaline to the neighbors' house, but it was late at night and the Carlsons had been very edgy since their dog had been murdered. They might not react well to a stranger banging on their door. Besides, his accomplices might be lurking about.

Steve scoured the floor for the bald man's gun. He found it resting in a corner next to the washing machine. He cautiously picked it up and handed it to Madaline. She resisted taking it but Steve pressed it into her hands. Neither of them had ever touched a gun before. They had once attended a rally in Harvard Square supporting gun control measures pending in the Massachusetts legislature and Steve had objected several years ago when William had purchased a gun "for protection."

The gun. Steve would get his father's gun, too, in case the bald man's cronies showed up. Steve left the flashlight with Madaline. Fortunately he knew the house well. He had hidden in nearly every nook and cranny when he was a child. Now he had to logically reason where his father would have hidden the gun.

Steve found it in only a few minutes. It was on the top shelf of his father's bedroom closet. The bullets were another story. Steve's father had stored the bullets separately to avoid an accidental shooting. Rummaging in the dark, it took Steve over half an hour to find the bullets. He found them among pill bottles and extra tubes of toothpaste in the master bathroom medicine closet. Steve hoped that the moisture had not in any way affected the viability of the bullets. He had recently learned that medicine closets are the worst place to store medicine. The steam from the shower or bathtub can damage pills over time even though they are "protected" with childproof caps. He would have to remember to tell his parents that. Steve bit his lip and returned his concentration to the gun.

He removed one bullet from the box and placed it in the gun's chamber. He counted out six more bullets and dumped them in his pocket. He returned the box to the shelf.

Steve guided himself back down the stairs, sliding his hand along the railing. He made his way to the front door and looked through the peephole. Forty feet down the front walk, parked in the street, Steve saw a familiar sight. Through a break in the clouds, the quarter moon shined its light down upon the polished body of the black Lexus.

Steve did not know whether the bald man had driven it by himself or perhaps the other two men had more recently arrived and were hiding in the shadows. Taking advantage of the intermittent moonlight, Steve headed for the side door leading out of the family room. This was much closer to the Carlsons and he could sneak behind the garage.

He opened the doors slowly and slipped outside. He held the screen door as the hydraulic retractor pulled it closed, careful not to let it bang against the metal doorframe. Steve held his breath. The chorus of crickets continued its concert undisturbed by any foreign sounds.

Steve scurried across the brick patio to the shelter of the garage. He moved behind the garage avoiding the compost heap and the stack of bricks left over from the patio that had been built eight years before.

He felt perspiration dripping down his brow and his face. He did not realize that the sweat on his face was mixed with blood that was flowing freely from the gash in his cheek caused by the bald man's gun when he had lashed out at the top of the basement stairs. Had it been brighter outside, Steve could have seen that the collar of his white ruffled shirt was turning a deep crimson color.

The hand that held the gun felt clammy and tingly. He imagined himself in a war zone where people fear for their lives as they sleep in their own beds, and roof top snipers make crossing the wrong street a potentially dangerous decision. Steve had always felt blessed that he had been born in a country at a time where war was not a daily way of life. The video arcade at the mall was the closest he had ever come to the "real" thing.

As Steve approached the six-foot high stockade fence some of the events of the past month began to gel. All of the mysterious happenings could be tied to the three Japanese men and their black Lexus. They had tried to lure Steve and his parents away so that they could steal the "time machine." When they realized that the technology was not so simple, they needed to steal one of his parents as well. His mother was probably still alive because they would need her. Steve felt some relief at this realization.

The Carlsons' dog had not been so lucky. They had probably strangled him one night in case he was to sound the alarm by barking. These men had been here before on several occasions and they were ruthless. They might even be in the Carlsons' yard now. They had been there before.

The clouds were clearing and the moonlight was shining more steadily. Steve crept up the side of the fence and peered over hoping that he would not see a Japanese face staring back. He did not. What he did see was far more startling.

CHAPTER NINETEEN

Madaline sat on the floor as far from the bald man as she could. She held the gun in one hand and the flashlight in the other. Madaline was staring at the blood on the side of his head when suddenly his eyes popped open. Madaline stifled a scream. The man meticulously surveyed the room memorizing the layout as best he could in the restricted lighting. He stared back at Madaline unable to see her clearly behind the glare of the flashlight. He could tell that it was the girl from her shoes and the folds of her skirt at the bottom. He saw no sign of the boy.

He started to cough and then to choke. Madaline raised herself to her knees, uncertain what to do. When his choking subsided, she deciphered his gasp from behind the handkerchief of, "Water."

Madaline had seen a coffee mug on the desk. With the flashlight she was able to find it without taking her eyes off of the man for very long. At the washbasin, she turned on the faucet and some water trickled out into the mug.

She was feeling a bit more confident since he was injured and tied up and she had his gun. She also controlled the only source of light. He was helpless and relied on her even to drink.

Since his hands were tied, she would have to hold the mug for him. She tried to pour some water into his mouth, but it ran down his face. The handkerchief was in the way. In order to untie it, she would have to put down the water and the flashlight and the gun. She made sure that the gun was out of his reach behind him. Once the knot was undone, she quickly picked up the flashlight and the gun. He had not budged. Madaline then picked up the water and tilted the mug for him so that he could drink.

She did not want to put the gun and flashlight down again, so she left the gag off. Steve could put it back on when he returned.

Madaline returned to her spot near the far wall. They sat for a moment staring at each other. Madaline asked him his name and he responded, "Yuki." Then her captive lowered his head to his chest. At first Madaline thought that he had gone to sleep. Then she noticed his jaw working. He was chewing on the rope leading from his legs to his neck.

Madaline shouted, "Stop that!" Yuki ignored her and continued chewing. What should she do? Where was Steve?

Madaline again demanded, "Stop that or I'll have to shoot you!" She did not believe in violence and could not believe that she was actually saying these words.

A few chews later and the rope snapped. Madaline watched in horror as the rope around his feet began to loosen as he wiggled them. She had watched Steve tie him up and realized that he had used one single piece of rope relying on the integrity of its entirety. Once the feet were loose, it would only be a matter of a brief moment before his hands would be free, too.

She still had the gun. "Stop or I'll shoot. I mean it." Where was Steve?

*   *   *

When Steve looked over the fence, it was not what he saw that surprised him; it was what he did not see. The Carlsons' house was gone. It was not there. It had completely vanished. Steve saw their tool shed near the fence, but where the house had been, there was an empty field. The field was huge. Near the middle he could see a stand of trees and at the far side the beginning of a forest. This was unbelievable. Perhaps the blow to his head had been harder than he thought, or perhaps he was still dreaming. He tried pinching himself and it hurt. Then he wondered why pinching himself in a dream would not hurt. Nothing made sense.

Unless, maybe the time transfer had actually worked. Maybe they had actually gone back in time. He wondered if they had gone back a week or a year. Or perhaps even longer. Maybe the Carlsons' house had not been built yet. If that were the case, then they had gone back at least ten years which was much more than Steve had planned.

Steve sat down and tried to think. He was feeling lightheaded. He rubbed his cheek because it hurt. He pulled his hand away to look at it. Even in the faint light, he was certain that he saw blood on his hand. He definitely needed to take one of his pills. He needed to get back to the house.

He picked himself up and brushed off his seat. The grass had been covered with fresh dew. It must be nearly morning. Then he heard it. A moment later he heard it again. It was a scream. It sounded like Madaline.

*   *   *

Madaline was afraid to turn the flashlight away from Yuki, but she needed to find something else to use to protect herself. She knew that she could not pull the trigger. She had covered a story for the *Harvard Crimson* about an attack on an abortion clinic in Somerville. Her editor had asked for an angle about the hypocrisy of the attackers who used violence to protest the taking of innocent lives. Madaline found that her sympathies leaned towards the protesters and her angle was the need to sometimes bend one's principles when greater goals are at stake. Madaline was a pro-lifer who on further introspection found that she did not even support capital punishment.

Madaline saw that his feet were free and his hands were coming from behind his back. On the inside of his left arm, she saw a tattoo. However, she was unable to discern what it was. Yuki stood and started to walk toward Madaline who was still kneeling. He hovered over her. She could now see the tattoo more clearly. It was a black serpent coiled around a skull and crossed bones.

Madaline aimed the gun at him. She heard him say, "Gimme gun, girl." She held her breath and started to squeeze the trigger. Then she stopped. This man would not hurt her. She had given him water. But he had shot the hotel detective. She was confused. Then it was too late. He grabbed the gun from her hands and then she heard the explosion as the gun went off.

Blood splattered on her face. She screamed. The flashlight crashed to the floor and went out. Darkness swept over her as her head hit the floor.

*   *   *

Steve held her head in his lap and mopped her forehead with a damp rag. It was the handkerchief that had been in the bald man's mouth. Madaline felt dizzy but she heard Steve talking to her. "Baby, are you all right?"

Madaline managed to respond, "I've felt better." Steve felt the lump on her head where she had hit the cement floor after she had fainted. The fright had been too much. She had forgotten to breath. In the glow of the flashlight, Madaline could see the bald head attached to the body lying next to her. Blood was coming out of his mouth. He was dead.

Steve had returned just in time to see the bald man freeing himself from the ropes. Steve had taken a few quiet steps down the staircase to get a better angle. He had seen Madaline take aim and held his breath. When the bald man had grabbed the gun, Steve had no choice. He aimed his father's weapon that had been meant to protect the family. He fired one shot. It had been deafening in the confines of the cellar.

When silence recaptured his head, Steve spent several minutes frantically searching the floor for the flashlight. When he found it, he tried banging it. Darkness. Then he twisted the cover slightly. The light came back on. He turned and directed it to the floor. He saw two motionless bodies lying next to each other. His heart skipped a beat. What if he had missed?

Steve force himself to take the bald man's fetid wrist and feel for a pulse. He could not find any beating, but he was not very good at finding pulses.

He turned his attention to Madaline. He found his handkerchief on the floor and wetted it with the drippings from the washbasin. When Madaline began to move, Steve was elated. He had been so concerned. He had even forgotten about his own bleeding.

As soon as Madaline could move, she wanted to get away from the body next to her. As her dizziness diminished and her eyes cleared, she saw the dark patch on Steve's cheek and the staining on his shirt.

Together they stood and then helped each other climb the stairs, each saving the other once from falling backwards. The climb to the second floor seemed to rival the trek to the pinnacle of Mount Everest. Neither had done it, but they could both imagine how it felt.

When they got to the hall bathroom, Steve automatically reached for the light-switch. There was still no power. While Madaline held the flashlight, Steve sorted through the bottles in the medicine cabinet and found the one with the little white pills labeled "Diagnosis—Hemopalpacemia—take one to assist clotting. Call doctor if bleeding persists after twenty minutes. Use only as directed."

Steve popped a pill and heaved a sigh of relief. Steve closed the medicine cabinet with a flick of his wrist. They stared at the reflection in the mirror. The flashlight gave an eerie glow. Madaline's hair had come undone and hung loosely at the sides of her head. The remains of her makeup could not disguise the pallor of her skin underneath.

Fresh blood still trickled over the patches of dried blood caked to the side of Steve's face. His shirt looked almost brown in the yellow light of the flashlight. As their eyes scanned further down their disheveled bodies they could see that much of his shirt was still white.

Madaline saw it first. When they shifted slightly to the left, Steve was then able to see it. On both of their chests, they still wore their nametags. Steve stood to Madaline's right. Steve wore his nametag on his right lapel. Madaline's was affixed above her left breast. All that was visible in the mirror were the inside halves of the nametags. Even though the capital E's and the D were backwards, it was very clear what it said.

Staring back at them from the mirror were the names, "ADAM" and "EVE."

CHAPTER TWENTY

Steve and Madaline were both overcome with exhaustion. They moved into Steve's room. Steve removed his jacket and his bloodstained shirt. He imagined that he would not be having much use for formal wear in the near future. He dropped them on the floor and they both collapsed onto the bed.

Steve was awakened fourteen hours later by what sounded like the television. He could hear, "The Mate was a mighty sailing man, the Skipper brave but sure. Five passengers set sail that day for a three hour tour, a three hour tour."

It could not be the TV. It was someone singing.

"The weather started getting rough. The tiny ship was tossed. If not for the courage of the fearless crew, the Minnow would be lost. The Minnow would be lost."

It sounded like Madaline. Where was she? Steve was alone in his bed.

"The ship stuck ground on the shore of this uncharted desert isle, with Gilligan, the Skipper, too. The millionaire and his wife. The movie star, the professor and Marianne, here on Gilligan's Isle."

Steve traced the sound down the stairs. He found Madaline in the family room. She was sitting on the floor in front of the big screen TV. She was staring at the blank screen. "Good morning, Lin. Or should I say afternoon?"

Madaline did not respond. She began rocking slowly back and

forth. She continued to stare straight ahead. Then she began singing again, "Now this was the story of our castaways. They're here for a long, long time. They'll have to make the best of it; it's an uphill climb. No phone, no light, no motorcar, not a single luxury. Like Robinson Caruso, it's primitive as can be. So, join us here each week my friends. You're sure to get a smile. From seven stranded castaways, here on Gilligan's Isle."

"Pretty funny, Madaline." Steve laughed, but Madaline remained in her near catatonic state. As Steve stared at her, she began to cry. At first it was just short sniffles, but it escalated into long drawn out sobs. She began shaking uncontrollably. Steve took her in his arms and tried to comfort her. She began to hurl questions at him between her sobs.

"No, I don't know where we are."

"Yes, it is incredibly weird."

"Yes, I have seen over the fence."

"No, there is no electricity or phone or water." Steve tried to add some levity. "But at least we have a motorcar."

"Yes, there is a dead body in the basement."

"No, I wish it were a dream, too."

"No, I don't know what we are going to do. But I think we should probably start by getting something to eat."

Steve helped Madaline up off the floor and they walked into the kitchen. Steve looked in the pantry to see what there was to eat. Madaline opened up the refrigerator. Steve returned carrying two boxes of cereal. "How about a feast for our first morning in paradise. Would you prefer Shredded Wheat or Captain Crunch?"

No response from the inside of the refrigerator. "In light of your nautical theme this morning, perhaps you would prefer the latter."

Madaline appeared from the bowels of the refrigerator holding a crisp red apple. In her best imitation of the wicked witch from the *Wizard of Oz*, Madaline mimicked, "How about an apple, my precious?"

Steve remembered the apparition from the night before when they saw the names of Adam and Eve in the mirror. He caught her reference to the forbidden fruit in Genesis. He was relieved that she seemed to be regaining control over herself. "Very clever. But I think you're tempting me with the wrong apple. The Apple Computer is really the forbidden fruit. Just ask any IBM employee. And it was really their PGSimulator that got us into all this trouble. But now we have no electricity so it can't help get us out.

Steve's voice turned bitter and hard. "We have already been led down the path to sin. I killed a man. I will have to live with that guilt. But I know that I would do it again. I couldn't stand to look at him. I saw him shoot my father. I couldn't let him harm you, too."

Madaline saw the tears coming down his face and it was now her turn to hug him.

After a few minutes, they sat down to their breakfast. Steve could taste that the milk and the orange juice were already losing their coldness. He would have to try to get the electricity back on soon. They would go exploring after breakfast. They would find someone who could help.

Madaline took a big knife and cut the apple in two.

*   *   *

Soon they were done eating. They were both famished but their need to assess their situation was overpowering. Before leaving the house, Steve tried the telephone and several light-switches one more time. Nothing.

They decided to take the Jeep Cherokee and see if they could find someone who could help them figure out what was happening. They headed for the front door.

As Steve reached for the doorknob, he hesitated. "Of course. The fuse-box. I need to check the circuit breakers. Maybe they all tripped when MAMA was activated. The power surge might have overloaded all of the circuits. I'm such an idiot. I should have thought of that before."

"What if that's not it."

"I'm sure it is. It has to be. What else could it be?"

"Where are the circuit breakers?"

"The main panel is in the garage. Let's try there."

A quick inspection showed that all of the circuit breakers were still set. Steve pulled the lever which disengaged the metal knife that completed the circuit for power to the house. He raised the lever slowly and watched for arching as the knife made contact with the metal support plates. After several tries, Steve gave up. There were no sparks flying between the metal contact points. The only possible answer was that there was no electricity coming to the house from the electrical pole outside. Philadelphia Electric Company would need to make the repairs.

They returned to the front door to resume their exploration.

The door opened to a nice warm sunny day. There were birds singing and butterflies of all varieties lazily flapped about continuously altering their course at the whim of the gentle breezes.

The view out the front door was at once beautiful and at the same time horrifying. The black Lexus was still parked at the curb, a horrible reminder of the tragic night that they had survived. They would have a lot of explaining to do to the police.

Across the street where the Shepards had lived in a large stone colonial with a circular driveway, there were three deer grazing in a field of clover. At the sound of the door, the deer raised their heads in concert and examined these strange creatures that had caused the disturbance. Their ears twitched back and forth in the breeze attentive to any other signs of potential danger. After a moment two of them returned to their meals while the third continued its watch.

Steve wondered where the deer had come from. The Philadelphia suburbs have a large population of whitetail deer. Many are even found within the city limits, in particular in Fairmount Park and in and around the Schuylkill Valley Nature Center. But, these deer were somehow different. Their legs appeared shorter and their snouts were longer and fuller.

Steve started to speculate that perhaps the time/space equalizer had somehow failed and they had ended up in a different location than Willow Lane. They might be nowhere near Philadelphia. This thought was confirmed when Steve looked down the street.

Not far from their house, the paved macadam ended in a curved diagonal. The same thing happened in the other direction. Just beyond the pavement there was not even a dirt road. It looked like the McNichol's yard the one summer when they went away and the lawn mowing company had misplaced their service request.

The curb on the far side of the road ended just as abruptly as the pavement. Steve realized that the changes all occurred a little more than 100 feet from the house. He had set the radius on 50 meters. All of this had been transported with them, but they had not landed where they were supposed to. Where could they be? At least this meant that they had not necessarily gone back more than ten years.

Steve looked at Madaline, thankful for something familiar to greet his eyes. He had been through a lot the past 24 hours, but Madaline had been right there with him the whole time. When everything else was going wrong, he thanked God that this wonderful relationship was going right.

Madaline returned Steve's adoring look and said, "Toto, I don't think we're in Kansas anymore." They both laughed for the first time in what felt like ages. Tears started to roll down their cheeks, but for a change, they were not tears of sorrow.

Steve responded by humming the theme music from "The Outer Limits," "do, do, do, do, do, do, do, do." Again they laughed.

Then Steve said, "My best guess is that the transfer coordinates did not take into account the rotation of the Earth and that we ended up somewhere in Western Pennsylvania or maybe Colorado. The scenery is pretty enough to be either. Smell how fresh the air is and look how lush all the vegetation is. We're going to have a tough time getting the house moved back to Philadelphia along with the yard and part of the street. Both our neighbors lost their fences and I'll bet that there is a big ditch about 50 meters deep where the house used to be. At least it will give the neighbors something new to gossip about."

"How far back in time do you suppose we went? I don't feel any younger."

"Well, you wouldn't no matter how far back we went, even if we went back before you were born. Remember the ice cube? It didn't melt when it was sent forward in time. The transferred objects do not experience the passage, and presumably the reversal of time." He paused, deep in thought. "I've got an idea. Perhaps the final coordinates will be registered on MAMA. I heard the PGSimulator loading the coordinates just before we were transferred. Come on, let's go take a peek."

Steve and Madaline headed into the house and started down the stairs. Even though it had been sunny outside, the basement was still shrouded in darkness. Steve retreated to the kitchen where he found the flashlight.

In the basement, they found MAMA still on the launch table. They avoided looking into the corner where the body of the bald man still lay. They would have to take care of that later.

Steve shined the light on the keypad. There was no reading appearing on the LCD screen. He scanned the keys and found one labeled "Settings."

He pressed it once. "It looks like it says, '50.0 meters'"

He pressed it again. "I can't quite read it, but it looks like it says . . . Oh, my God. It looks like, '82.83 years'." Steve's heart sank. No wonder the Carlsons' house was not there. By the time the fortieth annual meeting of IAPA came around again, he would be over one hundred years old. It would be years until his parents would even be born.

Madaline looked stricken. Her parents thought that she was on her way back to school. She was only supposed to take a three-day detour in Philadelphia. This could not be happening. Madaline felt as if the world was pressing in on her from all sides.

Steve saw her panicked look and tried to lift her spirits. He smiled and said, "Well, at least we'll be able to make a fortune in the stock market by selling short when 1929 rolls around. And perhaps we can warn the President Roosevelt about Pearl Harbor."

Steve looked back at the illuminated numbers on MAMA in disbelief. As his eyes focused they widened in horror. He could barely get out the next two sentences, "Wait a minute. Let's take this up in the light and take a better look at it."

* * *

The Earth's path has overlapped on numerous occasions, however, at any one time, such as the night of the IAPA Meeting, the likelihood of parallel space coordinates diminishes significantly. For instance, if you have a room full of seventeen individuals, the odds are very good that at least two people will share the same birthday. However, if you pick a specific individual and try to find a match, on average, you will need 365 other people in the room.

Steve and Madaline were luckier than they might have been. That night, at the moment of the transfer, the Earth had only been in that same location on two other occasions. The first had been 628,552,000 years ago more or less. The other had been 8,283 years before the 40th Annual IAPA Meeting. If the more recent overlap had not occurred, Steve and Madaline would have landed in a volcanic inferno where the Earth's atmosphere was so hot that rain vaporized before it could fall.

If Steve's parents could have witnessed the complete technical success of their applied discoveries, they would have been stupefied. However, they would not be born for another approximately 8,228 years.

Madaline followed Steve as he bolted up the steps two at a time. In the sunlight, Steve and Madaline took one last look at the numbers. There was no denying it. The screen read, "8283 years." That pre-dated civilization. They had gone back to the time of Adam and Eve. This realization struck like a bullet to the heart. Once again, their minds blazed with the image of their nametags in the mirror, but this time, it was no joke.

Madaline fainted.

CHAPTER TWENTY-ONE

They lay in bed together, holding each other with restrained vice grips, trying to regain some sense of security. The world as they knew it had ceased to exist. They would never again see anyone that they knew. They were completely on their own in a new, or rather old, and strange land. The time/space equalizer had operated perfectly. The house was in the exact location where it would be built over eight millennia later. William Penn and his fellow Quakers who moved to America to escape religious persecution could no longer claim to be the first white settlers in Pennsylvania. Steve and Madaline were the uncontestable winners in that category.

Neither one could sleep. They had been so exhausted, but they had only been awake for a few hours before the sky had started growing darker. They had used the flashlight a few times as they cleaned up from dinner and made their way upstairs, but they decided that they had better conserve as much of the batteries as possible. There were no corner drugs stores selling replacements.

Steve was worried about Madaline. She seemed morose, and nothing he did could cheer her up. Normally she laughed at his stupid jokes, but now they only seemed to irritate her. Steve felt like an invisible wall was growing between them and that Madaline was sinking behind it.

Steve sneezed. "I feel like we are just beginning a camping trip that is going to last for the rest of our lives."

"Let's hope that this one goes better than our last try. There's no one to pull us out of the ditch this time. Maybe I should drive." A devilish grin passed over Madaline's face and then it was gone. Her expressions had become fleeting and muted.

Steve sneered at Madaline and got out of bed. In the hall linen closet, he found an extra blanket. It felt like it was going to be a cold night. They had no five-day forecast from the Acu-Weather System to guide them, but these were never terribly reliable anyway.

The previous night, thanks to an early Indian summer, they had sweated profusely while they had slept, unable to combat the humidity and heat without an air conditioner or even a fan. They could not even take a cool shower because the water pipes were empty. The intake end of the pipe now led to solid dirt rather than a public system water main.

"We should make a list of what we need to find and try to prioritize it. I would put water at the top of the list. We'll also need to plan for food. The refrigerator is practically useless and the cupboards will soon be empty. I wonder if Dominos delivers." Madaline did not laugh.

"Let's see. We don't need the phone. There's no one to call. Think how much money we can save." Again, Madaline did not laugh.

Madaline broke her silence, "I don't want to have to be so practical. Why should we have to deal with everything? We're still kids. We haven't even finished college yet."

"You're right. It doesn't seem fair. I remember reading a bumper sticker once that said, 'Life's a bitch and then you die.'"

"You know, in a way it's kind of funny." Steve stared at Madaline as she climbed out of bed and rummaged through her overnight bag. He did not know what to expect given her erratic behavior. He was afraid that the stress was too much for her. He realized that it was probably too much for anyone.

Madaline returned clutching a stack of dollar bills. "Remember what we decided I should do about my little transgression with North American Consumer Products? I had figured out how I was going to return this money. At Christmas time, I was going to go visit my old department. I was going to ask my best friend, Susie, for copies of a bank deposit form, an expense report, credit report, and inter-departmental transfer reports, allegedly for a paper I was working on for school. I would then deposit the money into their account, process the correct paperwork, pre-date the forms and hope that the timing discrepancy was not picked up in the year-end audit. That way the fiscal year end would balance and no one would be the wiser and all harm would be undone. Sounds great, huh? So, now what do I do?"

"Well, they say that you can't take it with you. I guess they were right. That money has absolutely no value to us unless we need it to start a fire or wallpaper the bathroom."

"It's a shame. If I could just find a good stable bank and make a long term deposit at say 3%, in eight thousand years, I could pay back NACP, pay off the national debt and buy Switzerland and all of the Caribbean with change to spare." Madaline's voice changed. "I hope that my parents don't have to suffer because of what I did. It's bad enough that I just disappeared without leaving a note. I guess they'll figure out that something extraordinary happened from the pit where your family's house used to be. Or is that, will be but then won't be? This tense thing is going to be tough to get used to."

"I think a lot of things are going to be tough to get used to."

There was a long period of silence while both Steve and Madaline wandered about in their own thoughts.

"Steve, I can't get to sleep. I'm too worried."

As Steve climbed on top of Madaline, he cooed, "I know something that will take your mind off of things . . ."

Steve and Madaline made love for the second time. The urgency of the first time was missing, but the level of pleasure for both reached new highs. For a few minutes, Madaline relaxed and allowed the spasms of ecstasy to drown out the remnants of pain. Steve found the sensations more fantastic than anything he had imagined. As he achieved his orgasm, he shouted with joy. Madaline joined in the crescendo of sheer rapture, momentarily rising out of her depressed state.

Then they heard a noise. It sounded like the front door slamming. "Oh, no, my parents are home," thought Steve. His mind was numb from the preceding moments of glory. They were making love in his parents' house. This was not acceptable. Where could they hide?

Then his delirium evaporated and his heart was seized with the increasingly familiar pain. It was not his parents coming home. His parents would never be coming home. Not while he was alive.

Then, what had caused the noise?

*   *   *

Steve took the flashlight and his father's revolver from off the nightstand. A check of the front door and the whole downstairs showed nothing out of order. It was not until the next morning after breakfast that they found out what the noise had been.

Steve decided that they needed to bury the bald man before his body decomposed and began to smell. Madaline had told him that the man had been named "Yuki." Steve had preferred not knowing his name. As soon as possible, Steve wanted to eliminate any unnecessary reminders of the trauma they had been through. Perhaps that would help Madaline's psychonosema. Madaline's behavior was pushing Steve to the brink of depression as well.

Steve was uncertain how they would get the body out of the house into the backyard. Yuki probably weighed nearly 200 pounds and would be dead weight, no pun intended.

Steve figured that a pulley system could help hoist him up the stairs from the basement. He found two pulleys in the workbench in the garage. Madaline accompanied Steve downstairs to hold the flashlight while he secured the clothesline under Yuki's arms. As they approached the corner in the basement where they had left the body, their eyes lit up in terror. There in the corner was a dark patch of dried blood, but no body!

CHAPTER TWENTY-TWO

Madaline and Steve did not discuss the missing body at length. It was worse than a ghost story and could make them shake even in broad daylight. They decided to lock the doors at night and to carry both guns with them whenever they left the house. Certainly Yuki could not survive in the woods alone and seriously injured, but they should not take any unnecessary risks.

Steve hoped that he would have more luck with project number two for the day. They needed water. Steve remembered that a small creek ran through the backyard of Paul Garvey's house just three blocks away. They gathered together some buckets and empty bottles. The water would certainly be drinkable since man-made pollutants had not yet been invented. There was some concern about beaver fever, but they would have to take this risk.

Since the Jeep Cherokee had four-wheel drive, they decided to take that even though it was a short distance. It would make carrying the water back easier. They would need water for drinking, for bathing, and for cleaning.

Finding Paul's creek turned out to be more difficult than Steve expected. There were no street signs or familiar landmarks. None of the trees were even the same. Steve had to gauge in his mind how the streets ran and how far in which direction relative to his house.

The Jeep Cherokee ran well across the meadows and fields. It nearly got stuck in one hidden ravine where the frame lodged momentarily on a deteriorating log. Steve circled the area where he was convinced the creek had to be. It had disappeared. Steve did not know that the creek would not be formed until shortly before Paul's house was to be built in 1957 when the developer paid to divert a small stream further north in order to make his properties more salable in a highly competitive, semi-saturated market.

Steve would have to try something else. He stopped the Jeep and got out. He surveyed the area trying to assess the natural lay of the land. Based on the positioning of the sun, he figured that the stand of trees at the base of the sloping hill was to the west. The trees appeared to meander in a curving fashion as far as the eye could see.

His hunch paid off. He stopped the Jeep at the edge of the trees and started into the woods. Less than 50 feet into the cool shade, he saw the earth slope down to the edge of a swift flowing stream. Steve was relieved. This was further than Paul's house, but it was still within walking distance. Steve realized that the gas in his fuel tank would not last forever. The gauge was already dipping below a quarter of a tank.

After they had filled all of the containers, they drove home slowly, trying not to spill their precious water as they rumbled over the uneven ground.

Steve was fascinated as he analyzed the changes that would occur over the coming years. The source of their water flowed along what would one day be Lancaster Pike. Even before the man-made structures would dominate the countryside, hills would disappear and reappear elsewhere, rivers would change their course, and animals would continue to evolve. Some day, he would live again to see it all.

*   *   *

Steve's bladder was ready to burst. Being a guy, he did a guy thing. He walked across the short segment of street, which they now referred to as "Main Street," to the Carlsons' property-to-be and picked out a single tree which had a broad girth. He positioned himself behind it, lowered his zipper, and relieved himself.

Earlier in the day, Steve had needed to have a bowel movement. He had gone into the downstairs powder room and done his duty. When he was finished, he lowered the handle and the toilet flushed, emptying out the reserve tank. The tank did not refill. Steve wondered what Madaline had been doing. He felt uncomfortable asking. This was not a very romantic topic.

There were two major toileting issues. Water was one. They could use water from the stream to flush the toilet. Carrying enough water for this purpose could become quite tedious, especially as winter approached.

Of greater concern was the destination of the sewer pipes. The house had been hooked up to the public sewers, but the sewage plant, intermediate pump houses, and pipe networks no longer existed.

Steve recalled with longing their private outhouse at Mooselookmeguntic Lake. Then he remembered the skunk and his nose automatically recoiled into a P.U. pose.

They would have to build an outhouse. There was extra wood in the garage. Digging the pit would be difficult, but feasible. They could even get fancy and move a toilet seat from the house out to the outhouse to make it seem more like home.

But there was one problem. There always seemed to be a problem. Steve remembered reading somewhere that a treatment of lime must be added to an outhouse at least annually. This would help the waste to decompose and decrease the likelihood of the spread of disease. Why Steve had been reading about outhouses he could not imagine. But there it was, lodged in his memory, shouting at him, "Where the hell do you find lime?"

Probably from limestone. There was a quarry over in Whitemarsh. Perhaps they processed limestone. Steve smiled. His brain was still operating on Eastern Future Time.

"Shit, too much to deal with," Steve decided. He would continue using the tree as appropriate and flushing as best he could until he could come up with a better alternative. Meanwhile, they needed to think about finding food.

*   *   *

But first it was lunch time.

Steve found Madaline in the kitchen. She was sitting at the kitchen table polishing the stainless steel silverware. Steve mused to himself about how forks and knives and spoons were referred to as "silverware" no matter what they were made of. He interrupted her from her futile task, "are you hungry?"

"I think we'll have tuna fish. I'm in the mood for seafood."

"That sounds good."

"Steve, sit down. I'll prepare the meal."

"I can help."

"No!" Madaline then lowered her voice. "I can do it. You relax."

Steve watched as Madaline pulled the mayonnaise and lettuce out of the dark refrigerator. "At least now we don't have to wonder if there's anyone in there turning off the light when we close the door."

Madaline smiled, but only for a brief moment.

Steve figured that the mayonnaise would only be safe for another day or two at most. The refrigerator was now only a few degrees below room temperature and a small pool of water was forming beside the freezer section. They would have to start eating the frozen foods for dinner before they went bad.

Madaline found a can of tuna fish packed in water in the cabinet over the sink. She placed the can in the electric opener and pressed down on the lever. The can let out a whoosh as the vacuum seal was punctured, but that was the only noise.

Madaline faced Steve with a look of disgust on her face. "This can opener is broken."

"Madaline, we don't have any electricity."

"Oh."

Madaline turned back to the counter. "Then we'll have hotdogs."

"Lin, I think that we should eat the tuna since it has been opened."

"It's not open. That's the problem," she practically screeched at Steve.

"Madaline. I think there's a manual opener in one of the drawers. Let me open it for you."

"No, I can do it." Madaline rummaged through three drawers before finding the hand crank can opener. A few minutes later, she plunked in front of Steve a plate with a tuna fish sandwich, three pickles and some ranch style chips on it. She had cut away two corners of the bread where some blue mold was forming.

After eating in awkward silence, Steve decided to inspect the house. He left Madaline in the kitchen cleaning up.

Steve walked through the entire house except the basement. He noted all of the things that were of absolutely no value to them. These were ironically the things that thieves would consider most valuable had there been any thieves to steal them. The televisions, the radios, the stereo and compact disc player were high on this list. Even if they had electricity, the televisions and radios would have been useless. No one was transmitting, at least not on this planet.

Sitting under the television in the family room was the VCR. If there had been electricity, the indicator would have shown that there was a tape loaded. Next to the TV was an empty box from the video rental store. His parents loved old movies. The box had a small sticker which said "North by Northwest." Steve hoped that his parents would not get penalized for a late return.

It would have been nice to have some music. It was terribly quiet all the time. The only sounds were of nature and each other's voices. Steve had once thought how he could never grow tired of Madaline's lilting, warm voice. Now, it tended to grate on his nerves. All of her sentences seemed to start with, "So what are we going to do about . . . ?" Why should he always be expected to have the answers? She was a Harvard woman, part of the new generation. One time she even roared at him. Let her figure some of this out.

Meanwhile, Madaline was thinking, "How could I have let Steve get me into this mess? I could be back in Cambridge now, sitting in a nice warm classroom learning something useful. I could go to a new movie tonight and call my parents when I get home. But, no! Here I am in some pre-historic hellhole trying not to use up all the toilet paper. What do we do when we run out? I refuse to use leaves. This isn't fun anymore. I want to go home." She wept as she cleared the dishes off the table.

The list went on. The washer and dryer, all the lamps and overhead lights, the fans and air conditioning, hairdryers, curling irons, and the electric toothbrush. Madaline and Steve were both glad that they had their own manual toothbrushes that they used at school. They did not relish trying to brush their teeth with the tiny brush attachments for the electric toothbrush. They also realized how important it was to keep their teeth in tip top shape. Their dentists would not be making any house calls.

In the garage and the workroom, Steve spotted the electric weed-wacker, the power-vac, the electric garage door opener, and a selection of tools ranging from electric drills and a new table saw, to the electric paint sprayer. At least the mower was gas powered, for whatever good that would do.

It became painfully evident to him that their society had become totally dependent on electric and gas powered gadgets. Even the oil furnace had an electric starter. They would need to manually start the furnace and hope that the fuel lasted through the winter. If only his father had opted for solar heat, but it had not yet been cost effective for the northeastern part of the country, and so, he had not seriously considered it.

They would try to use the fireplace as much as possible. There seemed to be no limit to trees around. Then Steve remembered that his father did not have an ax. He had given it to the Good Will Thrift Shop when he had gotten his new gas powered chain saw two Christmases before.

When Steve got back to the kitchen everything looked neat. Steve glanced about and saw a myriad of other useless items: the toaster, the blender, the electric stove, the refrigerator, the microwave, and the dishwasher. Even the faucets were useless. Some things, like the electric carving knife, could still serve a purpose even if not in the original manner intended.

Madaline was sitting back at the kitchen table staring at a fork. She looked at Steve and said, "We have a problem."

Steve felt uneasy. "What is it?"

"We're out of dishwasher soap."

Steve tried to be patient. "Lin, the dishwasher doesn't work. We don't have any electricity."

"Oh, right." Without a further word, Madaline stood up and walked to the dishwasher. She opened the door and pulled out the carefully stacked dishes. She put them in the sink and reached for the faucet. When no water came out, she shouted, "Bastard!" and stomped out of the room.

Steve was flabbergasted. He could understand Madaline's frustration, but he felt unjustly accused and was nonplussed about how to remedy the situation. As he scrubbed the dishes with the cold water from the stream his thoughts turned back to food.

*   *   *

Steve rifled through the cabinets in the kitchen and the pantry taking a mental inventory. There were boxes of cereal and pasta and cake mix. There was flour and sugar. There were bottles of various juices and a myriad of sodas. There were canned goods of all sorts stacked in neat rows. His mother enjoyed shopping, but she could not be bothered to go too often, so she stocked up.

Steve figured that they could finish off the frozen and refrigerated goods in the next two days. The food in the cabinets should last them an additional three to four months if they planned their meals carefully. A mental calculation placed them right in the coldest part of winter as their food ran out. If there were only one mouth to feed, the supplies would last until spring. But, there were two of them. Clearly they would need to start supplementing their supplies.

Steve went to the desk in his bedroom and took out a piece of lined paper. He needed to make a list. He had to be organized.

Now, where does food come from? The grocery store. Wrong answer. The farmers' market. Wrong again. The gas station mini-market. Wrongo. Go back to the source.

Okay. Meat. Meat comes from animals. Chickens, cows, pigs, fish, deer, turkeys. One deer could get them through much of the winter. Two guns and approximately thirty bullets could kill from zero to thirty deer. Steve had never shot anything before. Oh, yeah, except for Yuki. Deer hunters always used rifles, not handguns. They would have to save some bullets for protection. At least there were plenty of deer.

What if they shot a deer? They did not have a freezer. The meat would go bad. How did they do it before they had refrigeration? Once the lakes and rivers froze they could fashion an ice box with large blocks of ice. If they packed extra blocks in sawdust, they would even last into the summer. Steve was beginning to crave a cold soda. He hated warm Dr. Pepper and warm Coke was even less appealing.

In eighth grade, Steve's class had gone to Williamsburg, Virginia for a long weekend. He remembered seeing dried fish and smoked turkey and ham. SMOKED! They could preserve meat by smoking it. What exactly did that mean? They had smoke houses in Williamsburg. Maybe by hanging meat in the smoke house and burning wood for several days in the smoke house, it would dry out the meat and preserve it. If they could find any meat, it would be worth a try. They could use the tool shed as the smoke house. It was metal so it would not burn even if they lost control over the fire.

Chickens, turkeys and cows. These were all domesticated farm animals. Farmers did not invent these animals. They must have found them in the wild. Steve had heard of wild turkeys, but never wild cows or chickens. And there was "the other white meat." Pigs could be wild. They might be tough to catch, however. Steve had witnessed the greased pig contests at the Bloomsburg County Fair and knew how smart pigs could be. He would have to start searching for farm animals. They would have to start a farm. Steve hated animals. Oh, well, that's life.

Steve wondered what kinds of animals were indigenous to good old Pennsylvania. If his parents had saved his old fishing rod and tackle, fishing would be a whole lot easier. He could even fish in the winter if he needed to. He had seen ice fishermen perched over their holes in the ice trying to stay warm with their steaming thermos of hot coffee. Steve could almost smell the hot coffee. He would love a cup. Maybe he would go smell the can of fresh roast as a fix.

Steve was beginning to feel better. He was making a plan and with a little luck and a lot of hard work, they should be able to keep meat on the table.

Vegetables. Farms again. Steve hated gardening. His father had tried to convince him it was fun. Steve almost fell for the Tom Sawyer act, but when he felt the moist soil in his hands and got a whiff of the fertilizer, he realized that this was not his cup of tea. Steve would even enjoy a cup of tea, though he preferred coffee. Steve shook his head. Back to planning . . .

They would need seeds. Steve left his room and headed for the tool shed. He thought he had seen, yes, there they were on the top shelf. Good news. Packets of Burpee seeds: tomatoes, green beans, zucchini squash, butternut squash, cucumbers, pumpkins, nasturtiums and daffodils. Bad news. The expiration date read two years ago. Well, two years before two days ago when their clocks still ran. Hopefully they would still be good. They had to be.

Steve read the directions. The tomato packet read, "For best results, start seedlings in an egg carton indoors beginning in March. When seedlings are 2-3" high, transplant outdoors in direct sunlight and fertilize soil liberally. Water 1-2 times per week depending on rain."

Steve leafed through the other packets. All of the seeds required planting in the spring. He would have to wait another six or seven months before he could start planting and then they might have vegetables, IF the seeds were still viable. Yikes!

A balanced diet. What were the four main food groups? Fruits were lumped with vegetables. Maybe they could find berries or apple trees. If they could plant the seeds they could grow trees nearby. The apple they had for lunch . . . Steve made a note to get the core out of the trash and save the seeds. Maybe these could be planted in the fall. He would save some and plant the others.

Breads and high-fiber things. That had to be one of the other groups. How does one grow wheat or oats or barley? They had some bread left, but the grains were processed. Maybe one of the cereals would have "whole grain" marked on it. Maybe Madaline would have some ideas.

Ice cream. Steve loved ice-cream. Cookies and cream or butter pecan. Steve resolved that he would have to learn to live without certain things—like almost everything he was used to having! Life sucks and then something else goes wrong.

*   *   *

With his notes in good shape, Steve decided to look for his fishing rod and then get Madaline's input. He hoped that she was learning how to cope better. She was definitely acting weird.

Steve pulled down the attic stairs and climbed up the narrow steps. He instinctively reached for the pull cord for the light. When nothing happened, he mentally kicked himself and then returned to his bedroom for the flashlight.

In a corner sitting next to an old croquet set, he found the fishing rod and his tackle box. Memories of sitting on a dock with his father dangling his feet over the water flooded back to him. His poor father. Steve picked up the rod and box and then saw his old archery set. He grabbed the bow and quiver of arrows. Even though this was a kid's set, it might still come in handy.

Laden with his goodies, he lumbered downstairs. There was no sign of Madaline. He shouted her name. No answer.

Through the dining room window, he saw some movement.

Madaline was walking toward the street. She stopped at the mailbox and put something in. She raised the red flag indicating that there was a pick up for the mailman. What could she be doing?

Steve snuck out the family room door. When he saw Madaline return to the house, he hurried out to the mailbox to investigate. Sitting in the white box was a letter addressed to Durham, North Carolina. It was for Madaline's parents. Steve's heart wanted to break. He knew that the Wallaces would never again hear from their daughter, and he was saddened because Madaline could not yet accept that fact. He did not care what the Postal Carriers' Oath read; this letter would not go through.

Steve closed the lid on the box and returned the letter to its dark premature destination.

*   *   *

Steve found Madaline in the kitchen. She had pulled all of the spices out of the cabinet and the spice rack and was carefully putting them back.

"Hi, honey. What are you doing?"

"I'm rearranging the spices."

"What was wrong with the way they were?" Steve felt that his mother's legacy was somehow being tampered with.

"I'm putting them in alphabetical order. I already fixed the records and the CD's. Now we should be able to find whatever we want much quicker. We need to be efficient, you know."

Steve wanted to explain that the records and CD's were basically useless, but he did not want to derail Madaline's sense of purpose. Steve's mind dwelled on the irony of alphabetical order.

Steve talked while Madaline continued with her task. "Do you realize how much power we have?" No response.

Steve continued, "Alphabetical order can be whatever we decide. We can set all new rules. We could start the alphabet with 'g' and end it with 'f'. If we ever start a rental company, we can call it 'G to F Rentals'.

"And, we can completely change grammar. We can fix English so that it makes sense. If we decide that "i" comes before "e" even in neighbor and weigh, we can make it that way. We can pronounce "bough" and "rough" and "dough" all the same way. I guess at this point that English really is the international language.

"What else should we change?"

Madaline turned to Steve and responded, "I need to change my underwear. I've been wearing the same pair of panties for three days now. That's totally unlike me, you know." She turned back to her spices.

Steve looked at his watch thankful that he had recently purchased a new long life battery. It was nearly 5:00 o'clock and they had not had lunch yet. "Lin, how about a late lunch or an early dinner."

"I've already eaten."

"Oh. What did you have?"

"Nothing, yet."

"Well, why don't we eat together?"

"Okay." Madaline turned triumphantly. She had completed the organization of the spices. Everything would be all right now.

Steve reached into the freezer section of the refrigerator and grabbed the first thing his hands touched. He slammed the door trying to retain any last vestiges of cool air within. His hand gripped a soggy cardboard box with a picture of a rugged fisherman in his yellow all-weather gear. The label indicated that ten frozen fish sticks were contained inside. Steve doubted the validity of the adjective. Nevertheless, it was food and he was famished.

Before Madaline could get to the cabinet containing the fry pans, Steve suggested, "Let's barbecue for a change." Madaline seemed pleased.

The gas grill was stored by the side of the garage. The meter on the tank read half full. They would luxuriate tonight and then save the remainder for wintertime when it was more difficult to start a wood fire. He was thankful that his father was a match collector. He had matchbooks from such exotic places at the Mandarin Hotel in Hong Kong and Maxim's in Paris. The three full shoeboxes of matches would keep them burning for some time to come. After that, Steve figured that he could use the grinder in the workroom to generate sparks. In only two days, Steve had already advanced to the level of Cro-Magnon Man, a hunter who may have been the first to use fire. Steve mused that hindsight can help keep your butt warm.

The fish sticks were unlike any Steve had tasted before. The charred flavor partially masked the freezer burn. At least the open flame helped crisp the soggy breaded coating. Madaline dispensed a large quantity of ketchup on each of their plates. She did not want to deplete their supply of canned vegetables and had not bothered to look in the freezer where she would have found formerly frozen succotash, peas and carrots, and oriental style mixed vegetables. When Steve asked about the ketchup, Madaline responded that fish sticks tasted good with ketchup and back in the early 1980's Ronald Reagan had determined that ketchup constituted a vegetable for purposes of school lunches. So, there!

After dinner, Madaline disappeared again, so Steve did the best he could to clean the dishes with a minute ration of dish detergent.

Fall was approaching and every day was getting shorter and shorter. By the time Steve had dried his hands, the last rays of the sun were barely evident in the west. Steve could not remember going to bed before 7:00 PM since he was an infant and he could not really remember that. There was no television and there was no light by which to read. What else could he do? The last major blackout Steve could remember had not been so bad because the phones had still worked and he called some of his friends and talked about the blackout. At least he could still talk.

Where was Madaline? Steve thought that he heard someone talking. He followed the noise up the stairs. He heard Madaline's voice coming out of his parents' bedroom. When he got to the door, he could see her dark shadow sitting on the edge of their bed, holding their bedside phone to her ear. She was talking. To whom? This was really scary.

"Finished eating . . . batter fried fish. Steve cooked it on the outside grill. He's not a very good cook, you know . . . I'd better not talk to long; I don't want him to know that I'm using the phone. He can be very strange sometimes . . . I can barely hear you. You're going to have to speak up . . . Never mind. Nothing seems to work very well any more. I've got to run. Bye. I love you very much." Madaline replaced the receiver on the nightstand. She noticed Steve's shadow in the hallway but did not react.

Steve said, "Let's get some sleep." A few minutes later, Madaline went into the bathroom and closed the door behind her. Steve had carried up a bucket of water so they could wash up and brush their teeth. The sink still seemed to be draining fine.

When Madaline got in bed, she lay on the far side of the bed from Steve. Steve rolled over to kiss Madaline and she turned her cheek to him. After Steve pecked her cheek, he rolled back and tried to go to sleep. His mind was troubled and he felt very lonely. He needed Madaline and he did not know what to do to help her. Steve listened as Madaline's breathing grew heavy. How could she rest so peacefully? Sleep finally carried him away nearly two hours later.

They were both awakened by a mysterious scraping noise accompanied by squeaking. As the perception of reality became distinct from his dreams, Steve sat up in bed. A moment later, Madaline sat up as well.

The moon had been waxing and the sky was clear. The noise was coming from outside.

Steve was distracted by a motion on the floor. A dark shape was gliding across the patch of carpet illuminated by the moonlight. It was only a shadow. Steve looked at the window in the direction of the noises and saw another smaller dark shadow.

It looked like a mouse crawling up the outside of the screen window. Steve arose from the bed and approached the window. He reached out his hand to knock the mouse off the screen. Just as his hand got near the window, the mouse leapt at his hand. It was on the inside! It was coming at him. And it had wings!

Steve ducked and the bat soared past him. Madaline screamed as it swooped near her head. Steve cowered as the bat swept back and forth across the room. It was barely visible as it moved in and out of the shadows. It came remarkably close to them, but never touched them. Steve had read that bats helped keep the mosquito populations under control eating up to 300 per hour. He also knew that they could have rabies. What was rabies? Would this have existed before man? Steve would have to check in the old encyclopedia in the morning.

Meanwhile, they needed to get rid of this bat so they could sleep. Steve saw the bat flying toward the window repeatedly and then veering off at the last second. He scooted over to the window and pulled up the screen. He watched as the bat completed another lap. But it did not fly out. Instead, two more bats flew in. Madaline screamed again.

The air was turbulent with the beating of the bats wings. The three bats gave the impression of a battalion of birds because of their irregular flight patterns. Madaline dove under the covers. One of the bats veered at the wrong instant and was caught under the covers with her. Steve heard her muffled cries as he flung the screen back down. Suddenly Madaline burst from under the covers and her screaming filled Steve's ears and brain leaving no more room for thoughts.

The sheet began bouncing next to Madaline's leg. She fell sideways off the bed to escape the Draculian beast in bed with her. Steve raced to the bed and trapped the bat with the sheet. He tugged the end of the sheet free from the bottom of the bed and carried his prisoner over to the window. He raised it enough to fit the sheet and its contents through. He held one end of the sheet and dropped the rest. The bat fell from its confines and flew off. Steve pulled the sheet back in and lowered the screen again. One down, two to go.

Steve managed to trap one more when it landed on the wall. It looked so much smaller when its wings were tucked at its side. He could see how it could sneak in the smallest places. First thing in the morning, he would patch the half-inch square hole in the window screen. As he carried this one to the window, the remaining bat swooped right across his face. Steve could feel a gust of wind from the passing wing. Then it disappeared.

Steve's nightmares deviated from the norm that night. While his feet were weighted to the floor he tried frantically but in vain to escape from the huge black wings that were trying to suffocate him. He felt millions of tiny teeth ripping holes in his neck. Everything was dark. Then he woke up.

CHAPTER TWENTY-THREE

Everything always seemed better in the daylight. Steve never did find the other bat. He patched the screen with part of an old torn screen he found in the workroom. He checked the rest of the windows in the house and everything seemed secure.

The encyclopedia in the family room did not assuage his fears about rabies. Rabies is an infectious disease that attacks the nerve cells in part of the brain. He had already caused enough unnecessary brain damage in his life from drinking too much alcohol. He did not relish having rabies further incapacitate himself or Madaline. Furthermore, he did not look forward to sharing his residence with other species, especially the nocturnal winged kind that frequented dank musty caves.

Steve decided to start hauling wood back to the house. They would need it for cooking and for heat when the weather began to turn. He took his father's chain saw out of the garage and put it in the wheelbarrow he had found in the shed. After he told Madaline where he was going, he set off for the woods. He wondered what Madaline would be doing in the meantime.

There was gas in the chain saw and in addition there was a 2 1/2 gallon can of mixed gas sitting nearby. That would cut a lot of trees, but once the gas was gone, the chain saw would be virtually useless. Steve did not plan on drilling any oil wells in his spare time. He would need to weigh the benefits of siphoning some gas out of his Jeep.

As Steve was walking along with the wheelbarrow leading the way, he realized that they did have one more source of gas. The Lexus. He would need to smash a window to get inside to release the gas cap cover since a previous try on the door handle had proven it to be locked.

Steve cut down three trees, severed the branches and carved them into two-foot lengths. His shirt was drenched by the time he took a breather.

He started to load the wheelbarrow and discovered that he would only be able to fit from three to five logs depending on size for each of the long trips home. It would take nearly 20 trips to transport his cuttings.

Steve was thirsty so he decided to take a brief detour to the stream. He found a large rock outcropping at the water's edge. He crouched down and rinsed his face. He cupped his hands and scooped up a cool refreshing drink. He avoided swallowing the tiny bugs that were gliding along the surface of the water. With a light puff, he was able to blow them off the surface and they drained with some overflow down the sides of his hands.

Steve pulled off his shirt and dropped it in the water. While it lasted, he was still using deodorant out of habit and preference, but his shirt smelled nonetheless. He swirled it about in the water watching a thin film rise to the surface and get carried away by the gentle current.

He pulled his shirt out of the water and decided to rinse his dungarees and underwear while he was at "the laundry." Even though no one else was around, Steve still felt very modest. He remembered reading the passage about Adam & Eve and how they had fashioned aprons out of fig leaves to hide their bodies because they were ashamed. Steve was not sure why he should feel ashamed, but he did. Probably his puritan upbringing, he concluded.

He thought about the futility of wearing clothes except for warmth and wondered how long his clothing would last. At least he would be able to wear some of his father's clothing with some minor adjustments when his started to fall apart. He did not think that he would be having much need for his tuxedos, however.

When the wash cycle was done, Steve laid the dungarees and underpants next to his shirt on the rock to dry. Steve lay down next to his clothes and closed his eyes. The warm September sun felt good on his naked skin. Steve began to think about school and his classes and his friends there. It all seemed so far away. This seemed like a bad dream that would not end.

Steve racked his brain for ideas. Then it hit him like a brick. He had the power. He could get them out of this mess and back to help his parents. There were just a few things he needed to check on back at the house. Why had he not thought of this before? All he needed to do was . . .

Steve's thoughts were cut short by an unsettling sensation. He thought that something had brushed against his leg. Through his closed eyelids, he pictured Yuki looming over him. His eyes popped open. No Yuki. Then he felt it again. It was crawling over his foot. A snake! He hated snakes.

He did not move. He could not even feel himself breathing. The five foot long snake slithered across his leg and looked him straight in the eyes. Its forked tongue lashed in and out of its mouth.

The gun! Steve had left the gun with the chain saw and wheelbarrow. How could he be so careless? They had that rule for a reason.

If the snake bit him, he would be dead and Madaline would probably follow suit soon after. She needed him. His muscles tensed slowly.

Before Steve could finish formulating his attack plan, the snake swung its head to the left and continued it journey off his body and onto his clothes. It stuck its head under the elastic on his underpants and then maneuvered its way to the opening for one of the legs. Steve watched while the snake's body slimed through his underwear, over his dungarees and down the side of the rock.

A moment later, Steve realized that he was breathing again. He quickly put on his clothes even though they were still damp. He tried not to think of the snake in his underwear. It gave him the creeps. He knew that snakes were not slimy, but his mind convinced him that he could feel against his skin inside his underwear the slippery residue left by the snake. He shivered.

"No wonder most women complain about doing laundry," Steve said out loud. It reassured him to hear a voice, even if it was his own. He counted his blessings that he was still alive.

Steve hurried back to the logging site. At least there were no environmentalists around dressed as spotted owls and chaining themselves to trees. Then again, Steve would have welcomed some company. Anybody. His mind turned back to Yuki. Well, almost anybody.

Steve grabbed the two handles on the wheelbarrow and turned it towards home. He was anxious to get back to the protection of four solid walls, so he practically ran. After a while, his arms grew weary from the weight of the logs. The wheel bounced over a series of roots. Steve's foot got caught in between two of them and he tripped, losing control of the wheelbarrow as he fell. The logs tumbled and rolled in all directions.

Steve picked himself up and brushed off the dirt. After all, he had just washed. He began to gather the logs back on the wheelbarrow. As he leaned down to pick up the last one, the sun reflected off something in the grass. Steve picked it up. It was a piece of cellophane. It reminded Steve of the plastic wrap that surrounds new packs of cigarettes. Neither Steve nor Madaline were smokers. Steve tucked it in his pocket and tried not to speculate. What if they were not alone?

Steve surmounted the last hill leading to the house. As he came over the crest, he spotted the house. Steve froze in his tracks. A huge black cloud of smoke was forming over the house. It was on fire!

Steve imagined Madaline inside burning to death while Yuki jumped around outside taunting her. The anger in Steve became intense. He flung the wheelbarrow aside and hurtled himself down the hill toward the house. As he came closer he could see that the roof of the testing room and the entire garage were engulfed in flames. Panic and nausea both fought to see which could be the first to overtake him. Where was Madaline?

He saw her. As he circled the garage keeping his distance from the pulsating heat, he glimpsed Madaline's form through the smoke. She was standing on the far side near the back patio holding an empty bucket. Madaline had used all of their water to try to extinguish the flames, but now there was no more water and Madaline was stymied.

Madaline saw Steve running towards her and recoiled as he pounced on her. She was afraid that he would beat her for her stupidity. She had started the fire. Instead, Steve hugged her ferociously and planted a bumper crop of kisses all over her.

"Thank God you're all right," Steve breathlessly blurted out.

"I'm so sorry. It was an accident. I was trying to help."

"What happened?" There was no anger in Steve's voice, only pity and concern.

"I wanted to fix you a nice dinner. I've been so glum lately. Women are supposed to be the fairer sex but I haven't been fair to you at all lately. I've been blaming you for everything. I found a nice steak in the freezer. The meat still looks good, so I decided to try barbecuing it. I was going to make a big Caesar salad and put strips of steak in the salad. But I've never used a gas grill before. My father always does the grilling at home. Why is that?"

"Why is what?"

"Why is it that women do most of the cooking indoors, but as soon as the cooking goes outdoors, suddenly it's the men who are the experts? Anyway, I turned on the grill and I could smell the gas so I knew it was working. Since I did not see any flame I decided that you had to light it. I got a match from the kitchen and lit it. I stuck it through a small hole underneath and suddenly there was a loud explosion and the top of the grill blew off."

"Oh, my God."

"I used up all our water. I threw it all on the fire. And it didn't do any good. The shutters and the trellis on the garage caught fire. I ran into the kitchen to get some water to put it out. By the time I got back, the fire had reached the edge of the roof. I threw on an entire bucket and it put out most of the fire on the shutters. By the time I got back with the second bucket, the roof was burning. I couldn't get enough of the water onto the roof. I kept trying. Really, I did." Madaline sounded so morose.

Steve and Madaline turned as one when a loud cracking noise preceded the collapse of the roof of the testing room. A terrible noise followed as metal and glass within were crushed by the steel supports and partially burned wood that had been the roof.

There was no water, no fire trucks, not even a shovel to throw dirt on the fire. Fortunately, the wind was now blowing steadily from the south, forcing the flames away from the main house. But, if the wind shifted, the fire could spread across the portico between the garage and the house.

If Steve could chop down the portico, he could save the house from the spreading inferno. Alas, he had left the chain saw at the logging sight. Even if he had an ax, that might be too slow.

Steve rushed inside and appeared a moment later with the crocheted afghan from the family room sofa. His mother had sat in front of the TV and occasionally glancing down had magically created each of the 120 squares of varying color that she had then pieced together as a gift for his father. If need be, they could use this to help smother any flame that might venture across the portico.

Steve and Madaline stood, helplessly watching as the fire consumed more of the adjoining buildings. A fireball erupted from the garage as the can containing the remaining mixed gasoline for the chain saw exploded. Steve despaired as he thought of the valuable objects that were being wantonly consumed by the fire. Steve knew that his father religiously paid the homeowner's and fire insurance bills. The salesperson had promised that an adjuster would be on-sight within 24 hours of any disaster with a check in hand. Ha!

Suddenly Madaline crumpled into a heap at Steve's side. She had unceremoniously fainted.

Steve knelt beside her. He reached for her hand to comfort her. The back of her hand felt strange, sort of puffy and dry, yet almost spongy. Steve examined it and saw blistered skin surrounded by red patches. The damage continued up most of her forearm. The pain had been intense but Madaline had stoically kept it to herself.

Steve knew that ice was the best treatment for a burn, but they did not have any. His mother used to use butter before the powers-that-be decided that this either impeded healing or could cause infection. Steve did not remember which. He figured that the best thing he could do for now was to soak the burned area. But he had no water.

Steve was torn with a terrible dilemma. He needed to go get water, but he also needed to tend to the fire in case the wind shifted. Otherwise, they could lose the whole house. But Madaline would be suffering dreadfully from the burn if he could not give her some relief . . .

Club soda! There had been a bottle of club soda in the pantry. Steve would soak her arm in this until the fire subsided and he could get some fresh water. Whew! He had a plan. As he ran into the pantry, he wondered what else could go wrong.

*   *   *

That night, after he gently held her head up while she took three aspirins, Steve tucked Madaline in bed. She was in tremendous pain, but there was nothing more that Steve could do to make her comfortable.

After Madaline had recovered consciousness, Steve had carried her inside to the family room. He was disappointed that his parents were not drinkers because he could have used some alcohol to dull the agony. He propped her arm up on pillows and told her to rest. He then made the trip by foot to gather the wheelbarrow and head to the stream for water. He did not have the heart to tell Madaline that his new Jeep Cherokee, and their only means of automated transportation, had been destroyed in the fire. The good news was that the flames had died out before the wind had shifted back towards the house.

Steve managed two trips for water—he wanted extra on hand in case another fire came along—and retrieved the five logs from his aborted first logging run before his shadow left him alone with the dusk. The steak that Madaline had been preparing was in charcoal heaven, so Steve opened a can of chunky soup which he served cold to Madaline. "This isn't so bad," Steve tried to convince himself, as he ate alone at the kitchen table. He resolved to go hunting soon.

Even though Madaline seemed exhausted by the ordeal of the fire and her burns, Steve reveled in the fact that she seemed to be emerging from her depression. Her sense of humor was returning and she did not seem so fatalistic about their situation, even though things were far worse than they had been that morning. Steve would need Madaline's help now more than ever. Steve tried to maintain as cheery a disposition as possible to aid Madaline in her delicate mental transitioning.

Steve slept alone in the guest room so as not to disturb Madaline's sleep. The bed in his parents' room was much larger and more comfortable, but Steve could not bring himself to sleep in his parents' bed.

Two nights later, they made love for the third time. It was wonderful. Madaline and Steve were a team again. Steve reckoned that there was no team more capable or with greater potential on Earth.

CHAPTER
TWENTY-FOUR

A week after the fire, Steve woke up early. His mind was troubling him. He remembered that he had forgotten something. What was it?

Steve lay still, trying to think. Madaline was sleeping peacefully at his side. Her naked shoulder was visible through the folds of the blanket that covered the rest of her body. Steve had been worried about her burn. The skin around the burn had turned a deep purple shade and then began to fade. Steve scrubbed the burn area every day, removing the layers of dead skin. Tears would come to Madaline's eyes but she would not protest. On the fifth day, a white gooey puss began to ooze from part of the burned area above the wrist. That area was the slowest to heal. Madaline never regained the sensation to touch on the back of her hand and part of her arm, but she did regain full use of her extremity. The ragged scar served as a constant reminder of the dangers of their new environment.

If there had been any electricity, a light-bulb might have gone on over Steve's head. He suddenly remembered what he had forgotten. When he had been rushing back to the house before the fire, he was in a hurry to see if MAMA might still operate. He had resigned himself to the fact that none of his parents' fancy equipment would work because there was no electricity. He had forgotten about battery power. What if he were able to rig enough batteries to initialize the PGSimulator and reverse the settings. Maybe he could transport them back to the future. After all, forward transports operated on a different principal and were much less risky. He knew exactly how many years they had gone back, so he could set precise coordinates for forward travel without worrying when the Earth had occupied the same space coordinates in the future. There was still hope. Most of the important equipment was in the basement and had not been damaged by the fire. Steve shouted with joy. Madaline opened her eyes and saw the delight on Steve's face.

Madaline mumbled, still half asleep, "Not now, Steve, I'm trying to sleep. Can't you wait until tonight?"

"Lin, your boyfriend is a genius."

"Where is he? I'd like to meet him."

"Honey, I think I can get us back. Batteries. We need lots of batteries. I need your help. We have to search the whole house for any kind of battery. If we have enough power, we can ship ourselves back where we came from. I'm gonna nail those bastards who attacked me and my parents." Steve leapt out of bed and started a whirlwind ransacking of the house in search of 9-volt, AAA, AA, C, D, watch, and any other kind of battery he could find. The battery from the Jeep Cherokee was toast, but the Lexus battery was in good shape. This would generate a lot of power.

Steve was on a mission and he could not be stopped. Okay, he did stop once for breakfast. His own battery was running on low and Madaline enticed him with Wheaties cereal dripping with clover honey and sprinkled with raisins.

Madaline found four batteries in the tie rack in Steve's father's closet. Steve added these to his collection from two portable radios, the flashlight, three clocks, the answering machine, three smoke detectors, the cordless phone, the TV remote, and a remote powered dune buggy that he had gotten for a birthday present two years before. He decided that the watch batteries would be pointless and he liked knowing what time it was. He had second thoughts about using the flashlight batteries and removed all of the size D batteries from the pile.

Other than the car battery, he was not left with much. He needed more power. If only the Jeep's battery had not been destroyed. Steve sat on the floor with his legs crossed in front of his little battery pile. Discouragement was written across his face in thirty-eight languages. Their only hope was if he could build a giant battery. He had learned how in a high school science class. All he had to do was remember . . .

*　　*　　*

Steve's memory failed him, so he resorted to the collection of books lining one wall of the family room. Surrounded by a collection of physics texts from nearly two decades of combined scientific education was a twelve-year old World Book Encyclopedia which Steve's parents had gotten him for his ninth birthday. Steve had wanted a G.I. Joe but he had smiled and thanked them anyway. It was not until he began partially plagiarizing his papers in junior high school that he really appreciated the gift. Now, it served as his only reference on how to make a battery.

He found "battery" sandwiched by "battering ram" and "battle" on either side. It started off with, "Battery is a device that produces an electric current by chemical action." He read on about "Dry Cell Batteries" such as those used in his flashlight, and Storage Batteries commonly used in automobiles.

The Voltaic Cell was described as one of the earliest and simplest battery cells discovered sometime around 1800. It consists of two plates called "electrodes" which are dipped in a weak sulfuric-acid solution called "electrolyte." The negative electrode is usually made of zinc and the positive electrode of carbon. The acid, which is neutral, generally splits into positive and negative ions when it is dissolved in water. The sulfuric acid consists of hydrogen, sulfur and oxygen. The zinc plate serves as the fuel until it dissolves. Energy is transferred along a connecting wire and then back through the solution. Steve learned that he could increase the voltage by connecting cells in series or increase the amperage by connecting them in parallel.

Steve glanced through the rest of the section and then returned his mind to the problem at hand. He had the knowledge, now he needed the components. He would need containers for the liquid, water and sulfuric acid, connecting wires and zinc and carbon plates. Containers and water were the easiest. He had seen a bottle labeled "sulfuric acid" in the workroom and there was plenty of wire available in various forms. The sulfuric acid was limited, but might prove adequate. The real problems were the two electrodes. Steve figured he could create a carbon plate by compressing charcoal. It might not be too efficient, but it should work.

It all came down to zinc. The battery would not function without this key component. Steve collapsed back on the sofa disgusted.

Steve had gotten his hopes way up. Even if the battery was not strong enough to operate MAMA and the PGSimulator and transport them back to the future, at least they could have powered the battery and the CD player and even the electric knife. But these luxuries would have been short-lived. As soon as the CD player wore out, that would be the end. Even if Steve could invent a battery or at least create one from future knowledge, he would not be able to reproduce a new CD player. He did not have the knowledge, the tools or the materials necessary. At this point, Steve was not even sure that he would be able to find enough food to keep them alive through the winter.

Steve wished that he had gotten a job on a construction crew like his friend Paul had that summer. At least he would have learned some useful skills. What would happen when the house began to fall apart? What good would knowing how to make a fortune cookie do? How could he be so smart and know so little?

During their Spam and canned baked bean dinner, Steve broke the news to Madaline, "Once again, I have failed you, my love. I can't even make a simple battery. Some scientist I would have made."

"At least you thought of it. And at least you tried. I think you're wonderful."

"Thanks for saying that, but I feel awful. That was our last hope. There I go, cheering you up again."

"Well, maybe it's for the best, Steve. I had a concern that I was afraid to mention because you seemed so excited. You had wanted to go back to the future and arrive sometime shortly before we left so that we could help your parents and Foster and Tim, right?"

"Right."

"Well, if we had done that, we would have arrived when the house and you and I were already there. There would have been two of us and the house would have landed on, or in, or whatever itself and would have been destroyed. We know that this did not happen because we were there. We can't change history. We have to get used to being history. Maybe this was our destiny. Without us, it's possible that mankind might never have started. Maybe we are like Adam and Eve. Maybe Dr. McPhinney had been right about creationism. Don't look at me like I'm crazy. Think about it. It may be possible."

"I don't seem to be missing any ribs."

"You don't need to take all of the stories in the Bible literally. It's their message that counts. I was right by your side when we were transported and we need each other. I have been so weak and you were the strong one who got us through the last few days. And it was my fault that Yuki got loose. He tempted me. I felt sorry for him. It wasn't an apple, but he did convince me to loosen his gag so he could have some water. And remember the serpent on his arm. There are too many coincidences. This is too weird."

But Madaline, in the Bible, this all takes place in the Holy Lands, not in Philadelphia. How do you explain that?"

"Maybe they weren't so good in geography by the time they got around to writing the Bible. Don't forget that the first capitol of the United States was in Philadelphia. Pennsylvania is the link between New England and the rest of the America. Maybe our descendants will vacation in Europe and make a wrong turn coming home. I don't know. It just all seems too amazing. How would you explain it?"

"When all else fails, ask questions. Good strategy. How the heck should I know? I'll write to Ann Landers and see what she says. Meanwhile, tomorrow I have to go hunting. I'm getting sick of this canned stuff and we really should save it for winter anyway. How does Venison Harrisienne sound?"

*   *   *

Steve woke up early the next morning. He had not slept well at all. His brain was still filled with fleeting memories of the dream that had filled his last moments of sleep.

Steve had been married to a large battery named "Bertha." The pews of the church were filled with all different appliances, all of which were running throughout the ceremony. Steve could barely hear the minister over the grinding, the revving and the blaring music. Steve's family had not made it to the wedding because none of their car batteries had worked. When they left the church, the guests threw sulfuric acid at them. For their honeymoon, they traveled to Europe. Everyone stared at Steve as he walked down the street or sat in a cafe with his wife, big Bertha Battery. She was constantly yelling at him. He wished that she would run out of energy. Her charges were all false.

She kept screaming with her Germanic accent, "You dim wit. You packed everything we needed except you forgot the kitchen zinc, the kitchen zinc, the kitchen zinc."

Steve wiped the sweat from his brow and mouthed, "Zinc, damn it." Without disturbing Madaline, he climbed out of bed and got dressed. He did not worry about wearing bright colors because he did not think that there would be too many other hunters around who might mistake him for a deer. Steve gathered his father's gun and counted out ten bullets. He could not risk more ammunition on his first hunt.

In the kitchen, he grabbed a pack of crackers that he stuffed in his jacket pocket. He could snack on his breakfast while he waited in hiding for his prey.

When Steve walked out the front door, he felt the chill in the air. The sun had not yet risen over the crest of the trees and the dew was heavy on the grass. Even in the diffuse light, the reds and yellows and oranges of the turning leaves was breathtaking. He paused to appreciate their beauty.

A slight movement caught his eye. A solitary doe was gracefully munching away on the clover in the Carlsons' yard near to where he had seen the three deer when they had first arrived in their new epoch. Mr. Carlson had refused to hire a lawn fertilization service. He would do it himself. Repeated laps with his green spreading machine had conquered the dandelions, but the clover reigned triumphant. Mrs. Carlson tried to console her husband that perhaps the clover would bring them good luck. Steve mused that even though they had lost part of their yard and some of the clover with it, they were indeed lucky. They still lived in the twentieth century.

Steve kept his eyes on the doe. He could not believe his luck. He thought that it might take all day to track down a candidate for slaughter. Instead, his target had sought him out. Thank God for clover.

Steve raised his gun and pointed it at the deer. It was less than 100 feet away so it should be an easy shot even without a rifle. The doe did not seem to be frightened by his presence. Steve lined up the far sight at the end of the barrel in the center of the "V" and debated whether he should aim for the head or the heart. The doe raised its head and looked at Steve, still chewing the grass and clover that appeared in excess at the sides of its mouth. Steve looked back at the large brown eyes, the pathways to the soul of innocence. Steve's hands trembled. He lowered the gun. He had forgotten to put in a bullet. He had not expected to begin his hunt so soon.

With a bullet in the chamber, he again raised the gun and set his target in his sights. The doe had shifted to the left and presented him with a clear shot at its left flank and the heart. He pulled back the hammer. The trigger made a loud click. The doe raised its head, its ears twitching. The doe faded and Steve saw the face of Yuki staring back at him. He closed his eyes and pulled the trigger.

When he opened his eyes, the doe was no longer standing in the Carlsons' yard. His aim had been true. The doe was dead. Steve wondered if killing would ever get easier. He hoped not.

CHAPTER
TWENTY-FIVE

Over the next few weeks, Steve and Madaline were very busy. A small trail began to wear through the fields and woods between the house and the stream. They converted several trashcans and one of the bath tubs to water storage. In the basement, the washing machine, wash basin and a file cabinet lined with plastic trash bags were also converted for this purpose.

Steve and Madaline finished transporting the logs which Steve had already cut and felled four more trees to supplement their fuel supply. Some of the wood was stacked in the living room and family room near the fireplaces and the rest was stored near the back door.

The work-shed was cleared out and used as a smoke house. Madaline, using her limited skills acquired in the lab for her first year biology course, meticulously dissected the body of the doe and hung it to dry in the smokehouse on hooks fashioned from metal clothes hangers.

Part of the house was closed off so that they would not have so much to heat in the winter. They carried the bed from Steve's room and put it in place of the TV and stereo in the family room. Other than the tub in the hall bath that they still used as a basin for bathing, they no longer used the upstairs except for storage. Steve removed the banister and nailed a canvas tarpaulin over the top of the stairs. To allow them to get upstairs easily, he cut a hatch in the tarp that could be re-secured with four hooks. They figured that during the coldest part of the winter, they would live in just the family room. The fireplace could be used for both heat and cooking. They could melt snow in buckets or break blocks of ice off from their stored supplies. Before the first heavy freeze, Steve would remove all of the "S" traps from beneath the sinks and the tubs to prevent any water damage to the pipes. They would also try to winterize by blocking off all unused doors and windows with furniture and spare clothing or blankets.

Everything seemed to be going just great. Steve even came home one afternoon and found a fresh bouquet of flowers on the kitchen table. He had forgotten how certain amenities could compensate for other difficulties. After that, until the first snow came, Steve brought Madaline a bouquet of flowers every day. If he could not find flowers, he created an arrangement out of pinecones, evergreen branches and dried leaves, occasionally mixing in birch bark or holly branches for variety. It seemed to cheer her. It seemed to cheer them both.

While Steve had proven to be a successful hunter, Madaline displayed her acumen as a prodigious gatherer. Every day during her trips for water or wood, or during one of her lengthy forays exploring new areas, Madaline would search for various items of use. She would come home laden with pine needles—excellent for starting fires, globs of a gooey mud-like substance—helpful for patching or sealing cracks in the walls, and even containers of honey. Even though she said she was careful, Steve noticed the swelling from the multiple bee stings. She never complained.

One day, she came back very excited and asked Steve for the wheelbarrow that he had been using to gather more wood. She would not explain what she needed it for. It was a surprise. That evening when Steve came in from splitting some wood with a metal wedge and a sledgehammer, he was greeted by a sinister smile. It was carved in the face of a large orange pumpkin. Inside was a small candle that Madaline had molded from some bees wax from her favorite hive. Dinner began with a warm pumpkin soup and ended with pumpkin pie. The soup was delicious. Steve was afraid to tell Madaline that the pie tasted more like bitter sweat potato pudding on a graham cracker crust than pumpkin pie. It was fun as a change nevertheless and he praised her efforts. It was a good thing that Steve liked pumpkins because they would be eating a lot of experiments over the next month. Madaline had found a large field of wild pumpkins and they would continue maturing until the first heavy snow. Madaline was careful to save some seeds. Next year, if all went well, she would not have to go as far for their orange delights.

Several days later, Madaline returned from another trip, this time even more emotional about one of her finds. Her excitement was permeated with fear and it was clear to Steve that she had been crying. She was too hysterical even to tell Steve what she had found. He had to follow her to see.

Steve followed Madaline as she cantered through the field behind the house in the opposite direction from the stream. As they entered the woods, Madaline slowed to a trot and then a walk. Steve was winded but Madaline, though still agitated, seemed unaffected by the cross-country run. As they neared a glen, Steve heard a low buzzing noise. He caught up to Madaline who was standing and staring at a tree overhead. Wedged in the crotch of a tree where two large branches met fifteen feet off the ground was the body of Yuki. Flies were swarming over his face, crawling in and out of his orifices. His shirt and business suit were shredded and he was covered with dry blood. He was not wearing any shoes. He must have climbed up to protect himself from the animals.

Steve thought that he saw movement in his legs. He could not possibly be alive. What could it be? He moved closer to inspect. His eyes focused on the source of the movement. The open gashes in his legs were covered with writhing maggots. Steve turned away trying to contain his dry heaves.

Madaline had not seen the maggots but she could empathize with his horror. When she had heard the buzzing and looked for its source, the sight of the dead Japanese man had petrified her. She had seen him too many times in her nightmares. Now her dreams would take on a more realistic and equally horrifying image. At least he was dead. Their greatest fear, ironically from one of their own species, had now been eliminated. She could leave the gun, Yuki's gun, at home. Now, Steve and Madaline truly were alone in their new home.

*   *   *

The weeks passed, the days grew shorter, the nights grew colder, and the shampoo ran out.

"Stee-eeve! There's no more shampoo. I'm in the tub and I'm freezing cold. Would you please look and see if there's any more anywhere."

Steve shouted up the stairs through the open canvas, "I already checked. That was the last bottle. At least you'll be happy to know that there are two more bottles of conditioner."

"Steve, I know this is not your fault and I know there is nothing you can do about it, but this is going to drive me crazy. I have gotten used to washing only twice a week and the dirty cold water no longer makes my skin crawl, but I can't imagine not shampooing my hair. It already begins to itch two days after I shampoo. We don't even have that much soap left, and I refuse to use laundry detergent in my hair. If we don't keep clean then our clothes will get dirty that much faster. And our sheets have not been washed in three weeks. We've run out of clean sets. Everything feels so dirty. Even the water we heat to clean the dishes doesn't always get all the crud off. I'm afraid I'm going to grow a curly little tail living like this. I can't stand it. What are we going to do about it?"

Steve had wandered back into the family room out of earshot about halfway through Madaline's tirade. When Madaline did not get a response, she decided to take matters into her own hands. It was the only thing that she could think of. She did not care if Steve did not like it. It would serve him right.

With her mind made up, she climbed out of the tub and patted herself dry trying not to inhale the overwhelming smell of aged mildew in the towel. She put her same rancid clothes back on and went into Steve's bedroom. In the desk she found a pair of scissors. Back in the bathroom, she hacked away at her hair, her long beautiful hair, until there was little left. If the hair had been clean, she would have saved it to stuff a pillow or weave a rope. Instead, she threw the clumps of clinging hair into the trashcan by the sink. Two days later, the hair would be gone, incorporated into the lining of a rat's nest.

When Madaline walked into the family room, Steve gasped in horror. He thought that some terrible tragedy had befallen Madaline. Madaline laughed at his response. It was a harsh laugh, triggered by embarrassment along with amusement at Steve's dramatic reaction. It had produced the desired affect. Steve felt sorry for her, and his guilt could be used to her benefit. More importantly, however, was the practical result that she no longer had so much hair to care for. She had become a modern pre-historic woman, a real trendsetter.

*   *   *

"Steve, do you believe in abortion?"

Steve swallowed before he had finished chewing his mouthful of dry cereal. He was getting used to eating cereal without milk or sugar. His goal for the spring was to find a wild goat or cow and learn how to homogenize or pasteurize or whatever it is one has to do to milk. This was not one of his top priorities; however, because he figured that by late February their substantial supply of cereal would be depleted. He would like having milk anyway. He was already getting bored with drinking only water.

Madaline and Steve often had lengthy intellectual conversations, but rarely did they begin over breakfast. Steve preferred to lie awake at night when the darkness dominated and other activities had been curtailed. He could talk for hours before he got sleepy. His mind was not so quick in the morning. "Abortion?"

"Yes, do you believe in abortion? We've never talked about this before."

"I'm not sure that this is a very productive or relevant conversation. I usually avoid this subject at all costs. There is no way to win an argument about abortion. Most people have their minds already made up and even the most well intentioned debate could only lead to hurt feelings." Steve took another bite of cereal, hoping to end the discussion.

"I want to know what you think. I won't get mad, I just want to know."

"Why, Lin, what do you think? Are you pro-life or pro-choice?"

"Nice try, but I asked you first. I'm not going to give up on this one, so you better go ahead and answer me."

Steve put his spoon down. "I guess I tend to be on the conservative side. Even though I believe in capital punishment, I strongly believe in the value of life. I don't regret shooting that guy, Yuki, because I sincerely believe that he would have hurt you if I hadn't. I must admit that I felt some satisfaction in getting revenge for my father and for that other man, the detective, who he shot at the dinner. Nevertheless, I think about it every day. I wondered if there could have been some other way. When his body disappeared, I felt some elation because I figured that maybe I hadn't really killed him, though I was scared to death that he would still try to do something to us. I'm still haunted by his face. I think that it would be the same way with an abortion. I think that the guilt would be unbearable. It would be ending the life of an innocent child. There wouldn't be the threat like with Yuki, and I would always wonder what the child might have been like if he or she had grown up. I guess what I'm saying is that I don't like the idea of abortion."

"Are you saying that a woman does not have the right to decide what she can do with her own body?" Steve could not tell if Madaline was angry or just being argumentative. She often liked to play devil's advocate.

"I think that a woman should control her own body, and the best way to do that is to not get pregnant. Too many people use abortion as a form of birth control. I guess that I do believe in abortion under certain circumstances like rape or incest or if the mother's life is in danger. Some people are having abortions if testing done in utero shows that some genetic defect might exist. I read an article about how people may start opting for abortions if the tests show that the fetus is the wrong sex or has the wrong color eyes. Look out Hitler . . ."

"You don't know what you're talking about. Men are always trying to run women's lives. You'd make a terrible father. I wish that I could have an abortion." Madaline started to cry. Steve stared back at her, shell-shocked.

After a few moments, Steve managed to ask, "Why would you want an abortion?"

"I think I'm pregnant, you idiot."

Now Steve knew, without any doubt, that Madaline was mad at him. He had said the wrong things. He had been insensitive. He hated heavy discussions in the morning. How was he to know that it had not been hypothetical? "Maybe you're mistaken. How can that be?"

In her most sarcastic voice, Madaline shot back, "Well, a little sperm, one of yours, takes this long trip and visits one of my little eggs. Then your sperm mercilessly attacks the poor little egg until she can't resist anymore." Steve handed Madaline a paper napkin and she blew her nose.

"That's not what I meant. How could you be pregnant? Weren't you taking the pill or something?" A gnat flying across the table between them plummeted to the surface in a death spiral. Steve surmised that it must have been an innocent victim of the vicious look which Madaline had aimed at him.

Madaline was too angry to cry. "Why should it always be the woman's responsibility? No matter what, you should have been wearing a condom. How do I know who you've slept with and who they've slept with? You could be a tramp for all I know. If I have AIDS, you can forget about that sweater I was going to knit for you for Christmas." Madaline stopped shouting. Her voice dropped to a whisper, "No, I'm not on the Pill. You were the first person I ever made love to. I hadn't planned that first time in the basement. I got swept away with all the excitement. I loved you so much I didn't think about it. After that, the whole thing seemed so weird. I didn't have anyone to ask. Besides, where would I get a diaphragm or a lifetime supply of the Pill anyway? The drugstores here don't carry my size." Madaline tried to smile.

"So there you have it, Mr. Conservative. We're not even married and you're going to be a father. What would my grandmother say?"

"Well, this is certainly going to make the headlines for today's news. I don't know what to say. Even if we could have an abortion, I wouldn't want to get one, would you?"

"It would be ME getting the abortion, Steve." After a pregnant pause, Madaline continued, "But, no. I would want to keep the baby. I love you, Steve. Besides, I was getting tired sleeping through the night without interruption. We should start making the mailing list for birth announcements. Okay, I'm finished. That was easy." Madaline looked nervously at Steve, still uncertain how he would take the news as it sunk in. It was hard to tell from his face what he was thinking. Madaline had suspected for several weeks so had more time to adjust to the situation.

She also had more to fear. There were no hospitals or doctors. What if something went wrong? What did she know about having a baby? What if she had a craving for ice cream and pickles?

Steve looked at Madaline. She looked so different from when he had first met her. Her eyes were the same, but little else. Her short hair had a wild look about it. He missed the long strands that hung down below her shoulders. He looked carefully at her face. She looked tired. Her cheekbones were very pronounced. She looked so thin and drawn. What if she was not eating enough? What if the baby were getting malnourished? Steve would have to start searching for more food that afternoon. He needed to find more fruits and vegetables. And he definitely needed milk for the baby, not just his cereal.

Madaline had left Steve speechless. Now he did the same to her. "I think that we should get married."

The silence was unbearable. Steve got out of his chair and moved over next to Madaline. He looked deep into her beautiful eyes and said, "I love you." He bent down beside her on his right knee and continued, "Will you please make me the happiest man on Earth and let me be your husband?" He was pleased with his politically correct wording.

Steve looked up at Madaline. He saw her really smile for the first time in a long, long time. It was a big beautiful smile. Steve's heart ached for joy. She only said one word and then they kissed.

"Yes!"

CHAPTER
TWENTY-SIX

The Invitations would have read,

> "The parents of Madaline Elizabeth Wallace and Steven Scott Harris, if they could have been here, would have hereby cordially invited you to witness the somewhat belated vows of holy matrimony, though there won't be any priests, ministers, Justices of the Peace, sea captains, or other qualified persons there to officiate, and to celebrate their entering into a lifetime commitment to each other, since they really don't have any other choice.
>
> This Saturday, approximately 2:00 PM. Wedding and Reception to be held at the home of the Harris Family. Directions—it's the only house on the block, you can't miss it.
>
> Dress warmly; bring your own food and beverage. The couple has registered with Energizer and Duracell.
>
> RSVP to RR#1, Box 1, Harrisburg, Wallacesylvania, USA

In the attic, Steve uncovered the gown box in which his mother's wedding dress had been vacuum-sealed. Unfortunately, Madaline and Steve's mother were not even close in size. Madaline towered six or seven inches over the older woman's head. Steve offered to help with the alterations, but Madaline smartly refused. She had seen Steve's attempt at repairing his torn tux. Madaline had to remove the zipper and sew in a patch of material that she cut from a linen tablecloth. She used the same material to lengthen the dress. In Steve's mother's sewing drawer, Madaline found a roll of lace that finished off the bottom of the dress nicely. The dress was still tight in a few places, but Madaline had no plans to diet before the wedding in order to look her best. She had already lost too much weight and was growing concerned about her nutritional intake. Her mid section had not yet started to expand with the baby, so the lines of the dress still hugged her narrow waist.

Madaline had often dreamed of this day. She had marched down the aisle a thousand times in her daydreams. This dress was not what she had envisioned, but she was delighted, nonetheless. She would be the talk of the town. She was getting married.

Steve found his not-so-new-anymore used tuxedo in his closet. He did the best he could to iron out the wrinkles in his white pleated shirt. This would probably be the last time he would ever need this outfit until someday when his oldest daughter would get married. But that day would never come. There would be no one for his daughter to marry. Except for one of his sons. Dear God.

The wedding was short and simple. Steve waited by the fireplace as Madaline glided in from the kitchen. He hummed the wedding march. She looked beautiful. The billowing white veil covered her head and helped Steve to forget his longing for her flowing, radiant hair.

They spoke their own vows to each other promising to love and cherish until death did they part. Steve took his Harvard ring off of his little finger and slid it onto Madaline's ring finger. He said, "This ring signifies my love for you, never ending." He then handed her a magnet that he had gotten off the kitchen refrigerator. It had a small carrot glued to it. "Since I could not give you a diamond, the least I could do was give you a carrot. I would have made it two carrots, but I didn't want to be too pretentious and make the other girls jealous." They laughed and they kissed. They kissed and they laughed. Together they shouted, "And we now pronounce us husband and wife." They threw rice at each other and then fell onto the bed laughing and exhausted. They would clean the rice up later. Wasting food was not an option.

Two hours later, the marriage had been consummated more than once. As they lay in bed wrapped in each other's arms and their own thoughts, Steve laughed and said, "I guess that computer dating service is going to go bankrupt now. The species, 'singlus personus humanus', is now extinct." He placed his hand on Madaline's stomach. "That is, until our baby is born. I wonder if it will be a boy or a girl. Should we use cloth or disposable diapers?"

Steve and Madaline often joked about things that would have been normal in the late twentieth century in Philadelphia. They found that it helped keep themselves sane, but it also made them sad. There was so much that they did not have, but at least they had each other.

The role of the wedding cake was played by two Tasty Cake chocolate cream-filled cupcakes. They fed each other a bite and then smashed the remains into their partner's face. Then they licked it off of each other making loud slurping noises and laughing. It was easier and a whole lot more fun than going to the sink in the bathroom to wash.

That night, Steve said a special prayer. He did not consider himself very religious and rarely prayed except in church. He asked God to bless this marriage and to give them strength. He also begged God to take care of his unborn child. He should have included Madaline in his prayer.

*   *   *

"Good morning, Mrs. Harris. And how are you on this fine morning?"

"I am quite well, Mr. Harris. And how would you be?"

"I, too, am well. Thank you kindly for asking. I have been doing some thinking about our honeymoon . . ."

"How about Tahiti?"

"Good idea except there are no flights available."

"What about the Riviera? I always thought that would be romantic for a honeymoon."

"Too crowded this time of year."

"Antarctica. That would certainly be different."

"Too cold."

"Italy! Rome, Venice, Florence."

"Exchange rate unacceptable. We could never get enough Liras for our few dollars. Besides, I don't think the Parthenon is open yet."

"Where then?"

"I thought that I would take you some place truly romantic where we could be alone and not be disturbed by anyone. The services are simple but the scenery is beautiful. It would be a real back to nature experience. Fresh water, fresh air . . ."

"Very funny. Well, I guess at least we won't have to worry about packing or jet lag or speaking the language and at least it's not Mooselookmeguntic Lake. But I think that we should do something special."

"Like what?"

"I don't know."

They lay in silence for a few minutes each imagining their own honeymoon knowing that it would never be possible. Madaline continued, "You know, I always thought that I would have graduated from college and started my career before getting married and having babies. I really miss school. I wonder how Ellyn is doing. I wonder if they gave her a new roommate. I wonder if they ever figured out where, I mean when, we went. Do you mind being married to someone who isn't a college graduate?"

"How could I? You're the smartest girl in town." Steve kissed his wife and climbed out of bed.

Steve preferred using the upstairs hall bathroom. It was more comfortable and spacious than the powder room off the hallway on the first floor. He grabbed a bucket of water and headed up the stairs through the canvas tarp. There was a biting chill in the air. As Steve gingerly sat on the toilet, he decided that he would have to make do (or make do-do, he joked to himself) with the downstairs facilities until spring.

When he was finished, he poured most of the bucket of water into the toilet to flush it clean. He used the remaining water to wash his face and brush his teeth.

He found Madaline still languishing in bed. He warned her that she might want to dress warmly and use the downstairs bathroom.

Steve pounced on Madaline and they wrestled until Madaline broke free. Steve made the bed and cleaned up their living quarters while Madaline had her turn in the bathroom. As Steve was picking up their clothes off the floor, he heard his name, and the voice did not sound happy.

Steve found Madaline in the hallway holding her nose and contorting her face in disgust. Steve's stomach nearly turned as the putrid smell reached his olfactory senses. In the bathroom, the toilet was gurgling and churning as it poured colored water with raw feces onto the rich gray carpeting. There was nothing they could do to stop the flow. After a few minutes it slowed and then stopped. The frozen ground must have prevented the pipes from draining and the toilet had backed up. The stained water had flowed out into the hall and the nauseating smell was permeating the house.

"Some honeymoon, Steve!"

*   *   *

Several hours later, the newlyweds had scooped up most of the solid matter and had mopped up as much of the liquid as they could extract from the carpet. They no longer noticed the smell, though neither of them had been able to eat a thing all day.

Steve found some carpet deodorizer. He read the directions. It said to "sprinkle liberally on the soiled area." He dumped the entire container on the carpet and watched as the white powder was soaked into the carpet fibers. He read on, "Allow to absorb odors for several minutes and then vacuum thoroughly." Oops. The only vacuum cleaner was electric. Even the Dustbuster was useless. They would have to pull the carpet and hope that the smell had not soaked through to the wood beneath.

As Steve dragged the last section of damp carpet into the back yard, he felt something cold land on his face. It was beginning to snow.

CHAPTER TWENTY-SEVEN

The days passed and blended into each other. They lost track of whether it was a Tuesday or a Saturday, and it really did not matter. There were no classes to attend, no doctor's appointments to miss, and no television shows to vary in schedule. Sometimes on a vacation, it is fun to lose track of the time or what day of the week it is, but there is always a built in clock in the back of the mind noting how many days are left until the real world comes crashing back. This was not a vacation, and the real world was constantly crashing around them. Strenuous days were spent foraging for food, restocking water and wood supplies, and trying to keep their home intact. A flurry of physical activity during the day would help limit to nighttime the persistent nagging worries that haunted them both. How would they survive the winter? What would childbirth be like? How could they feed another mouth and protect the child from the ever-present dangers in the wild? What if one of them got very sick and needed a doctor? What will happen when Steve runs out of his pills for his Hemopalpacemia? How will they cope when they run out of gasoline and bullets and batteries? As the days approached their shortest, Steve and Madaline had many hours of darkness to ponder their situation. Their sleeping hours were interspersed with frequent horrifying nightmares. The first pale light of dawn was a welcome friend to the two survivors of yet another night.

Sometimes their days were filled with horrors that exceeded even their worst nightmares. These events provided new material to occupy their minds during the dark hours of anxiety, sleep, and fear. They had no haven where they could truly feel safe. November passed and there was no feeling of Thanksgiving. After all, the Pilgrims had not even been born yet.

One day while filling the buckets, Madaline slipped into the brisk waters of the stream. She screamed for help, but there was no one to hear her cries. She was able to get herself back to shore and drag herself onto the rocks. The sun was vacationing behind thick layers of clouds, and the winds from the northwest cut right through her soaked clothing. Madaline began to shiver within seconds of landing in the water. She knew that she had to get warm as quickly as possible. She had to get home, now. She began to run until her breath gave out. She continued at a frenzied walk, stumbling and picking herself up again.

Steve was in the yard splitting logs when she appeared over the horizon. He wondered where the wheelbarrow and the water were. Then he noticed how her arms hung limply at her side and her walking was stiff and uncoordinated. He ran to meet her. She fell into his arms and began to cry.

"What happened? Are you all right? You're freezing. Let's get you inside by the fire."

Madaline managed to say, "I lost one of the buckets. Now we only have two." Her body was shaking so hard, Steve could not tell if it was from her crying or from the cold. Steve was so worried about her and the baby, and all she could talk about was the damn bucket.

After that, with only a feeble protest from Madaline, Steve assumed all responsibility for collecting water. Madaline would try to stay as close to home as possible until the baby was born and the weather improved. Madaline had enjoyed her walks, but the baby was beginning to take a toll on her strength. She needed to eat more. She needed to stay warm. She needed her mommy.

*   *   *

Steve retrieved the wheelbarrow and the other buckets the next morning. At least they did not have to worry about anyone stealing them. He finished filling the two buckets and hurried home glad that the stream was not even further away.

Nearly two full weeks passed before Steve returned to the stream for more water. The day was even colder than usual so Steve bundled up in his down jacket and his leather gloves and wool ski cap. As Madaline saw him heading off with the wheelbarrow, she regretted never having bought him the Harvard scarf. She hoped that he would be warm enough. She shivered as she stood by the door, cognizant of the heat from the fire behind her, yet feeling the frigid grasp of the stream as it pulled her into its murky depths.

By the time Steve got near the stream, his feet were aching from the cold. His nose was running and he did not have any Kleenex so he wiped his nose with the back of his sleeve. The residue caked and froze on his upper lip. It had been so easy growing up to take clean, fresh, running tap water for granted. If they ever moved, he could definitely see the advantages of water front property even if flood insurance was unavailable.

Steve blinked. The familiar sight of the stream was dishearteningly altered. A glassy sheet of ice extended from both shores trying to reach its counterpart somewhere near the middle. A dark jagged section of flowing water was visible in between. Unlike a marriage, the colder it got, the more likely the two sides would become as one. Soon, they would be denied one of the basic necessities of life. Steve cursed himself for once saying that winter was his favorite season.

The dirt near the shoreline was frozen solid making a misplaced step potentially treacherous. Steve was unsure how to get close enough to the water without falling in. In this weather, that unintentional swim could be fatal. He found some medium size rocks nearby. He tossed one grapefruit-sized rock onto the ice near the shore. A dark white mark appeared where the rock struck, but it was otherwise unfazed. The rock settled on the top of the ice a few feet away. He threw another rock out closer to the center. The ice shattered and the rock disappeared beneath the gloomy surface. Steve could see from the surviving edges that the ice was still quite thin near the center. He would need to break the ice as close to shore as possible so that the neighboring ice would be strong enough to support his weight.

He would need to hurry because it had started to snow. He began a barrage of the largest rocks he could find and lift. Most of the rocks were too small to do any good and many of the larger rocks were frozen into the ground. Through persistence, he was able to carve out a large indentation in the ice bringing the exposed water closer to shore. He then felt secure enough to slide carefully out from the solid ground onto the frozen shelf with one bucket at a time. He stayed on his hands and knees to try to disperse his weight as much as possible. He had collected some other jars and bottles to compensate for the lost bucket. These vessels were smaller and more tedious to fill. Steve was aware of how much time was passing because the snow was beginning to blanket the shore and cover the wheelbarrow and its contents. Moreover, he was getting colder by the minute and would have to head home very soon.

As he neared the edge with the last two jars, he heard a loud wrenching cracking noise. He felt part of the ice below him give way. He flung himself backwards as a section of ice broke away from its anchoring and drifted off towards the center. The two jars floated momentarily in the water next to the miniature iceberg before filling with water and disappearing below the surface. Steve heard another cracking noise ripping through the ice. He was on his back and unable to move quickly so he froze. He lay as still as possible. He thought of Madaline and his unborn baby waiting for him to return. The noise stopped. The ice was still holding, but he was afraid to move. The snow was falling more heavily now and was landing and melting on his upturned face. His left foot felt cold and wet. He tried to shift slowly away from the edge. As he pressed down with both of his feet, he felt the left foot sinking without resistance. It was in the water. He pulled it out as quickly as he could and tried to drain some of the water out of his shoe. Some of it ran up his leg and sent shivers down his back. Inch by inch he started to shift along the ice until he could lower his left leg back onto solid ice. He continued slowly toward the shore, sensitive to any small noises indicating a weakening of the viability of his platform. Moments later, he hugged terra firma reminiscent of hijacked passengers kissing the ground upon release. He wondered if his near disaster would make Madaline more nervous or make her feel that she had not been such a klutz after all.

The wheelbarrow was barely recognizable beneath its blanket of fresh snow. Steve realized that if he had known it was going to snow, he could have saved the trip by collecting and melting snow to get water. He would have to design a collection system for snow as well as rain. The easiest thing would be to funnel all of the gutters into a giant water trough. That sure would save a lot of wheelbarrow miles.

Steve noticed how wet his gloves were when he grabbed onto the wheelbarrow handles. It was a mixture of sweat, melted snow and overflow from the stream onto the ice that he had been desperately gripping. He also felt his soggy left sock though the sensation was becoming less precise as his foot grew numb to the cold. He would have to hurry.

As Steve left the shelter of the woods, he became confused. Everything looked different. The snow was so heavy it was almost blinding. The storm had caused the skies to darken prematurely and his familiar landmarks were all neutralized in white camouflage. He started in a direction that looked familiar and seemed logical, but then the terrain altered and Steve knew he had made a wrong turn. He changed course heading further south. Or was it west?

Steve stopped, released the wheelbarrow handles and wiped the snow off his cheeks and out of his eyebrows. The snow in his eyebrows was melting and running down across his eyes blurring his vision further.

Steve thought he saw the house. He turned in its direction. As he got nearer, he saw that it was only an irregularity in the hill's contour. He turned back to get his bearings off the hills behind him, but the whirling snow hid them from view.

He could not panic. He had to maintain control and think. All he could think about was panicking. His throat grew tight. He imagined Madaline's lips. His throat relaxed. He trudged on.

It never occurred to Steve to abandon the wheelbarrow. The heavy load was slowing his progress, but he was not about to be defeated in his single chore of the day. Steve saw a giant "Y" in front of his eyes. He could not figure out what it was. Then he realized that he was only imagining it. The "Y" was a giant divining rod. He cursed the image. He was not looking for water. He wanted to get away from the water. Then he realized that the wheelbarrow also had a "Y" shape. He held onto the two handles and was following the front wheel. Perhaps the wheelbarrow would lead him home. It had been there many times and would not be thrown off by a little snow.

Steve began to limp. His left foot was beginning to hurt even though it did not feel as cold as his right foot. The pain brought him back to his senses. The wheelbarrow was not a horse. It was not alive. It could not lead him home. He had to do that himself.

The sky grew darker and Steve began to lose hope. He was getting so tired. Maybe he would just lie down for a little while and rest before continuing on. He saw a giant tree ahead. He could get some shelter under the tree.

The tree was coming closer. He could see the soft ground underneath. He would not rest for long. The branches were so broad, they would give good shelter. There, he saw it again. Below one of the branches a light flickered. He headed toward the light. Suddenly the front wheel of the wheelbarrow dropped in front of him and some of the water in the buckets sloshed into the wheelbarrow. Steve stumbled down the same drop. He knew where he was. He had just left the Carlsons' yard and had gone down the curb into the street. He was home.

*   *   *

Madaline carefully trickled more hot water into the dishpan where Steve's left foot was soaking. Much of the skin was still a pasty white, but some darker color was returning to the upper part of the foot.

Madaline had used a metal bookend, the first thing she could grab, to chip the ice away from Steve's shoelaces in order to get his foot out of its frozen prison. The bookend was shaped like the Eiffel Tower, a souvenir from the Harris' trip to France when Steve was 14. She had filled the dishpan with water that had been sitting near the fire. Steve screamed. The warm water shot excruciating pain through every nerve fiber in Steve's foot. It felt like his foot had been immersed in molten lava, as best as one can imagine.

Madaline had emptied the dishpan back into the plastic Clorox bottles near the fireplace. She fought her way outside through the storm door that was buffeted by the wind and nearly yanked off its hinges. She seized one of the buckets from the wheelbarrow that Steve had abandoned in the yard. She had to shatter the thin layer of ice on top to get to the cold water below. Steve stuck his foot in the cold water with only a slight grimace. Once Steve's foot had acclimated to the colder water, Madaline began the process of adjusting the water up to body temperature by slowly adding hot water and occasionally ladling out the excess before it overflowed.

As her body worked to help Steve's foot, her mind was paralyzed, transfixed on the thought of having to amputate Steve's frost bitten foot. She was sure she would faint if she had to saw off his foot, and she was sure that he would die from bleeding to death. That would leave her alone to have her baby and to try to raise him or her, neither of which she believed she could do without Steve's help. She was jolted out of her trance when Steve said, "I can feel my toes. Look, they're wiggling."

Madaline fixed Steve some warm soup and tucked him in bed. She wrapped two extra blankets around him, ignoring his protests of being too warm. She would protect him. They would have to protect each other.

CHAPTER TWENTY-EIGHT

The days and nights grew colder as December crept by. Madaline was beginning to wonder whether they were approaching a new ice age. She could not recall such a cold winter. She did remember that it had snowed incomparably more when she had been little, with snowdrifts often looming over her head. Steve had wisely pointed out that her size at the time may have contributed to the perceived relative abundance of the snow.

The constant chill in their bones could also be attributed to the greater exposure to the elements. The fireplace provided their main source of heat. Except for the family room and to some extent the kitchen, the bulk of the house was unheated. Every time the door was opened to get more wood or to go outside for any reason, including to relieve the bladder or the bowels, a blast of arctic air swept through the room. At other times, the room would grow unbearably stuffy as the fire and their pumping lungs jointly consumed the oxygen. Madaline remembered the homeless men and women she had met at the shelter who spent most of their days and many nights exposed to the ravages of the weather. In some ways, their suffering must have felt more extreme because it was juxtaposed with those in their temperature controlled Mercedes and heated homes.

Christmas was a non-event. Even if they had known which day was the 25th, they would not have celebrated. After all, Christmas was a holiday to celebrate the birth of Christ. Six long centuries would have to pass before the manger in Bethlehem would even be built. Furthermore, Steve and Madaline did not feel much like celebrating anything. One morning, Madaline discovered blood between her legs. She panicked that she might be losing the baby. The bleeding stopped, but a depression settled over the parents-to-be. They felt helpless to save their child if anything should go wrong.

Madaline was growing larger and having trouble fitting into her clothes comfortably. Winter felt like it was never going to end. They were getting cabin fever and were getting on each other's nerves. Boredom was their constant companion. Steve decided that they should have a party. They would make silly hats and play games and have a big feast. Little did he know that the party would cause two deaths and nearly kill him as well.

*   *   *

Madaline decided on the menu. She would make a venison stroganoff of sorts. She would marinate thin slices of the smoked deer in a red vinegar sauce. Using a bottle of ranch salad dressing, she would add canned tomatoes and sauté the venison before spooning the sauce and the meat over a bed of fettuccini noodles.

She would use the last cake mix for dessert. It was fudge marble cake. There was also a container of milk chocolate icing. As she read the directions, her heart sank. The cake mix called for 2 eggs and a half-cup of vegetable oil. She had used up the last of the vegetable oil and they had not had eggs for months. She was determined to make this party work. Besides, she had an intense craving for chocolate cake. In the back of one of the shelves over the sink was an unopened jar of mayonnaise. She had avoided using it in the fall because the label read, "After opening, must be refrigerated." She made an executive decision that now was as good a time as any to open it because she needed it for the cake, and the cold weather would keep the mayonnaise from spoiling until they used the rest up. Since mayonnaise contains eggs and oil, the missing ingredients, it just might work.

It did. Or at least it smelled and looked like it did. Madaline had wrapped the two cake pans in aluminum foil and suspended them in the fireplace with a steel rack. One of the edges got a bit burned, but other than that, they looked fine when then dropped onto the cooling racks. Madaline had wanted to surprise Steve, but it was impossible to do anything without the other person knowing. Even if Steve had not seen what she was doing in the kitchen, he would have smelled the cake as it cooked and cooled. After she iced the cake, she put it on display, proud of her work, and proud that her will power had dominated her cravings and the cake was still in one piece.

Steve put on his coat and hat and selected a sharp knife from the kitchen knife block. He would trim a prime piece off the deer's flank and Madaline would turn it into a very special meal. His mouth watered.

The wind had died and it was a quiet evening. The most audible noise was Steve's feet crunching across the crusty snow. Steve imagined that he heard trucks on the highway in the distance. It was only a breeze periodically gusting through the trees by the stream. The thin layer of fresh snow that covered the older hard snow beneath absorbed most of the other nocturnal noises of nature. Steve had marveled at how the snow stayed so white. He recalled how in Philadelphia and even in Cambridge, the snow turned various shades of brown and gray within hours of falling. Here, nature itself was the only source of pollution to affect the luster of the snow. It provided a blueprint of the sundry and various activities taking place both day and night. Animal droppings of diverse sizes and patches of yellow corresponded with the pattern of foot prints meandering across the countryside divulging the comings and goings of the neighborhood's residents. The neat thing about footprints is that they prove the maker has been there after it has gone. After all, a footprint is not visible while the foot still resides within its confines.

Steve did not have the flashlight, but the three quarter moon shown brightly. He did not stop until he had already passed over them. He had been thinking about the cake and the venison and was not really watching where he walked. The size of the footprints, however, registered in his subconscious as noteworthy. When their existence reached his conscious state, he realized they were extraordinary, perhaps dangerous. He turned around to examine the trail that had intersected his path. He had never seen prints like them before. They reminded him a little of prints from a large dog. He would have to show Madaline.

In the converted work-shed/smoke-room, Steve selected one of the hind flanks from which to amputate their dinner. He had trouble seeing in the shed, so he wedged one of his gloves in the crack of the door to keep it open and allow some of the moonlight to glow inside. He started to cut at the meat, but nothing happened. The knife was sharp but the flesh was frozen solid. He would have to take the whole flank into the house and try to defrost part of it by the fire. He should have thought of that before. Now their feast would be delayed for hours. Steve extricated the flank from the hook that suspended it off the ground. The frozen meat was deceivingly heavy. He hoisted it onto his left shoulder and bent over to retrieve his glove with the bare hand that was carrying the knife.

As Steve walked back toward the house, he paused again to examine the large tracks. He was surprised to see a second set of prints running parallel to the first. He was amazed that he had missed them the first time. These prints appeared even larger than the others.

It all happened so fast. Steve heard a single ferocious growl inches from his left ear as the flank of venison jammed into his shoulder throwing him face first onto the ground. The venison was ripped out of his grasp. He heard the noise again, this time not as close and with an eerie guttural harmony. He was certain that there were more than one. As he recovered from the face plant, he rolled onto his back careful not to stab himself with the knife that he still clutched in his right hand. About twenty feet beyond the end of his feet he saw them fighting over the meat. They snarled at each other baring their fangs and maneuvering around the cervine trophy at their feet. Steve had only ever seen a wolf before at the Philadelphia Zoo. These were different somehow. They were larger and their fur was much thicker. Their fangs also appeared longer and sharper, but that may have been Steve situational bias.

Then Steve heard another guttural rumble. This growl came from the shadows of the house to his right. Standing poised in the darkness, the third wolf strained its hind legs as if ready to pounce. Steve could see the green light reflecting off its eyes. The rest of its savage mass was a blur. Just before the wolf attacked, Steve heard the door open and Madaline's voice call out, "Steve, are you all right?"

The attack was swift and smooth. Steve was an easy target, unable to move quickly from his horizontal position. His only protection was the steel blade that had failed on the frozen deer. Steve raised his left arm in defense and the jaws of the wolf closed down. The fangs ripped through the material of his coat and his shirt. He could feel his arm being crushed in the vice-like grip. The pain was intense and yet it felt like it was happening to someone else. He felt removed from the slow motion scene as if he were watching a movie. His right arm and the knife were pinned under the weight of the carnivorous creature. Steve concentrated his mind on controlling every muscle that had been developed from years of rowing and more recently from chopping wood and hauling water. He arched his back and flung the bulk of the wolf off of his right arm. The knife was free. In a feverish frenzy, he swung the knife around in an arch toward the side of the wolf's neck. He felt the knife penetrate. He pulled it out and stabbed again and again. The sensation was orgasmic. As the grip on his arm loosened, the pain flooded back to him. In a last effort, he was able to shove the wolf off of him onto the snow by his side. Even in the dark, the amoeba-like splotches of blood in the snow were visible.

In spite of his strained breathing and the ringing in his ears, he was able to hear Madaline's voice again. It said, "Watch out!" Out of the right corner of his eye, he could see Madaline standing in the lit doorway of the family room holding the gun from Yuki. She was aiming it at him! Steve turned his head just in time to see one of the other wolves bounding toward him from the left. The wolf leapt. A shot rang out. Steve held his breath and covered his face. A peaceful sensation penetrated his body. He was not afraid of death. He welcomed its rescue.

Steve felt the wolf land on him but he did not feel the sting of his fangs or his claws. He only felt its weight. He did not move. Neither did the wolf. Another loud bang shattered the heavy silence. It evolved into a staccato yelping noise that faded into silence.

After a minute, the world stopped spinning. He began to think rational thoughts again. There was no denying the pain in his left forearm, and he was aware that he was getting cold. He also thought that he heard another voice, one that was not his own. He opened his eyes. He saw Madaline standing over him, wearing nothing but a shirt and blue jeans, struggling to pull the body of the dead wolf off of his chest. She still held the gun in one hand and was peering frantically about. Finally the wolf gave way and Steve was freed of its burden. His breaths no longer took such grave effort. Madaline helped him to his feet and guided him back into the house. She was speaking to him, but the words made no sense. He stared back at her trying to understand.

Madaline got him settled on a chair near the fire. She carefully removed his coat and shirt, peeling the tattered remains of both away from his blood-coated skin. With some warm water and antiseptic, she began to clean his wounds. There were only four punctures where the teeth broke the skin. His clothing had provided some minimal protection. Around the puncture marks and in five other places, dark bruises had already begun to form. There was a viscous fluid coating parts of the arm near the wounds. Madaline rubbed some between her fingers trying to ascertain its origin. It was clear and slimy. She raised her fingers to her nose. There was a distinct rancid odor that reminded her of rotten hamburger. She realized what it must be. She quickly wiped off her fingers on the towel and bathed Steve's arm to clean off the repulsive goo. It was the wolf's saliva.

Two of the punctures were quite deep and Madaline had trouble getting the bleeding to stop. She applied a loose tourniquet above the elbow to slow the bleeding. She fed him the last of his little white Hemopalpacemia pills.

Madaline, who had fainted when she was given her first influenza shot as a child, was proud of her emerging nursing skills. Nevertheless, she dreaded any further serious injuries without the pills, and she prayed that her baby would not suffer from the same disease. In this world of rough edges, it was all too easy to shed blood.

After she finished attending to Steve and he drifted off to sleep, Madaline noticed that she was shaking. She wrapped herself up in a blanket and sat near the fire. Even after she warmed up, she kept shaking. She felt so lonely and scared. She did not like having to be the strong one.

Later on, she remembered the meat. She put on her coat and a pair of Mrs. Harris' snow boots and took the flashlight. She saw that the two bodies of the wolves remained where they had left them. The wolf that she had wounded was nowhere to be seen. Neither was the venison. She saw the marks in the snow where something had dragged it off. She wondered what could have been strong enough to move so much weight. She decided that she did not want to know. Shining the flashlight in all directions, she mustered up her courage and headed for the smoke house. She found a nice piece of frozen carcass and dragged it back to the house. She was not going to let anything spoil her special dinner.

*   *   *

The meat was slow to thaw. It had been in a deep freeze for several weeks. Madaline kept the flank away from the direct heat of the fire because she did not want the outer layers to start to cook while the insides were still frozen. Madaline resigned herself to the fact that their special dinner would have to wait until the next day. By then, the meat would be ready to cook and Steve should be feeling much better, with a ravenous appetite from skipping dinner. Madaline fixed herself a light supper of soup and crackers. She sent her thanks through the millennia to Steve's mother who had been such a prolific grocery shopper. Then she settled in next to Steve and made herself cozy for a long winter's night.

The next morning, Madaline awoke to Steve's moans. He was sweating profusely and tossing about. She felt his forehead with the back of her hand. He was running a high grade fever. She soaked a towel in cold water and laid it across his brow. He did not awaken, but his movements eased. She removed the bandaging from his forearm to check the status. Everything was much more defined. The bruises had darkened to a deep purple with grayish blue borders. The puncture marks looked like small drains in the center of a dark cesspool. The skin adjacent to the punctures was pasty white, the color of death. Three of the punctures were smooth ovals while the fourth was a jagged tear. Madaline could see the dried blood near the fourth hole and was thankful that it had clotted. She cut off some fresh gauze that she had found in the master bedroom medicine closet and reapplied the bandaging. Once the tape was securely attached, she gently stroked Steve's face until his eyes opened. He looked so stunned and scared when he awoke. Madaline wept inside for him. She wanted to hug him and make it all better. Instead, she held his head upright and handed him a small glass of water. She stuck two aspirins in his mouth and told him to drink. She could not find a thermometer, so she did not know his temperature, but she did not want to take any chances. The aspirin would help keep his temperature down and make him feel more comfortable. As Steve settled back and drifted off to sleep again, Madaline decided that their dinner could wait another day. With their natural cooling system, none of the food would spoil. The cake might not taste as fresh, but it would still be good. She tried not to think about the cake too much, but it was hard. Her cravings were getting stronger. Oh, the sacrifices she had to make for her man.

As Madaline sat in the easy chair trying to think of anything but the cake, she felt some indigestion in her stomach. Then it happened again. This time she was sure of it. The baby had kicked! There was something alive inside of her. Her face lit up in a huge smile. But then she frowned. She felt that pain in her tooth again. It made her whole jaw ache. She opened the door and scooped up some fresh snow. The cool moisture as it melted in her mouth helped ease the pain. She was too happy to worry about a little pain.

* * *

Steve recovered and their dinner was a great success. The mayonnaise cake was even better than they could have hoped. Everything seemed to be going pretty well. Except for Madaline's tooth.

Weeks passed. Some days were okay, but other days the pain was intolerable and growing worse. Madaline tried to chew only on the left side of her mouth. If the food was too hot or too cold, sharp pains shot right through her tooth on a direct short connect to her brain. Soon the melting snow no longer provided relief, only additional unpleasant spine tingling sensations. Madaline could feel that her jaw was swelling, and soon it was visible to Steve as well. The tooth would have to go.

Steve remembered when he was a child, barely able to look his father's belly button in the eye, and one of his teeth had come loose. He had fidgeted with it for a day, wiggling it back and forth, and it was driving him nuts. Besides, he had heard about the Tooth Fairy and he wanted his fair compensation for this suffering. His best friend, Paul, had already lost two teeth and had a dollar to show for it. His mother agreed to let Paul come over to play and to see his loose tooth. When Paul arrived, they went straight to Steve's room. Steve told Paul his plan. He wanted to yank his tooth out so that he could put it under his pillow that night. Steve had gotten some thread from his mother's sewing drawer. They tied a primitive noose for his tooth and tied the other end to the doorknob. Steve sat in a chair and braced himself. Paul's job was to slam the door. Just as Paul started to swing the door closed, Steve had second thoughts. He chickened out and screamed, "Wait!" It was too late. The door hit the frame and his bloody tooth hit the floor. It was still attached to the blue thread. Near the tooth, the thread looked purple. When his mother heard the screams, the one before the door closed and the one after it slammed shut, she rushed to his room. Steve mustered the most stoic face a five year old could and said everything was fine. He resisted the urge to cry because Paul was there. The next morning, two shiny quarters had replaced the tooth under his pillow. His mother had seen what she needed to see.

Madaline's tooth was a different story. It was not loose. There was no gap between the tooth and the gum where a thread could be tied. In fact, the gum was so swollen that the lower part of the tooth was becoming obscured. Steve replayed some of the scenes from his favorite westerns in his head. He knew what he had to do.

Madaline was curled on the sofa reading the "DOR-ENZ" volume of the encyclopedia. They had decided to save the novels and other reading material for later. They needed to know as much practical information as possible. Madaline started with the first volume and Steve with the last. They would try to read cover to cover omitting the history and biographical sections. They figured that these had limited application except when concerning inventors. One night at dinner, they both agreed that they wished they had spent more time in their youths reading the encyclopedia. It was a wealth of information.

While Madaline was reading, Steve got the Yellow Pages from the kitchen and one of the obsolete phones from the closet. He carried the phone book and the phone to the desk where the phone used to sit before it was relegated to deep storage. He opened to the section for "Dentists." He picked up the phone and dialed seven numbers. Madaline looked at him in shock and suspended amusement. After a moment, Steve began to carry on a one-sided conversation, "Hello, may I speak to Doctor Rosenquist please?" Pause. "Thank you." Longer pause. "Hello, Doctor. I have a problem that I hope you can help me with. We appear to have an impacted molar or an infracted bicuspid or a depressed canine, I'm not sure which. Anyway, to tell the tooth, it's got to go." Steve sought and found the upturned tips of Madaline's mouth. "No, it's not constipated. What I mean is we need to remove the little fellow. What should we do?" Steve nodded his head, occasionally saying, "Uh huh," and pretending to take copious notes. He continued, "No, we don't have a jack hammer." Pause. "Yes, I believe we do have a crow bar." Pause. "Anesthesia you say. I think we are plumb out of Novocain. We may have some Solarcaine or perhaps a branch of sugar cane." Pause. "Thank you Doctor, you have been very helpful." Pause. "Address for the bill? Don't trouble yourselves. I have your address. The check will be in the mail. Good day." Steve replaced the phone in the cradle. Madaline looked amused and worried. She had good reason to feel worried. Then she saw the pliers.

*　　*　　*

"The tooth has to go. The tooth has to go. If it stays, it will only get worse." Steve kept repeating these words to himself trying to buck up his courage. He was certain that in some ways, he would feel as much pain as Madaline, and she was going to feel a lot of pain. There was no anesthesia, not even a shot of whiskey to dull her senses. The act would be torturous, the residual pain, agonizing, but eventually, it would get better, not worse.

Madaline lay down on the sofa with a pillow under her head and another under her knees. Steve found a stuffed dog that his mother had saved from his childhood. He gave it to Madaline so that she would have something cuddly to squeeze when the pain became overwhelming. He propped the flashlight on a pillow as close to Madaline's mouth as he could get it without interfering with his movements. He looked into her eyes. She looked so scared. She did not ask any questions, just blindly did as she was told.

Steve took a deep breath and said, "I love you very much, Lin." Madaline smiled. It was a sweet smile, and Steve could sense her love. Steve basked in the beauty of her smile. It had been one of the first things he noticed about her. He tried not to think how what he was about to do would permanently mar her beauty. He knew that true beauty emanated from the soul; nevertheless, he would miss her perfect mouth. He imagined kissing her with a huge gap in her teeth. Her face altered into the form of a witch. Witches always had one tooth missing in the front. His mind was playing terrible tricks on him. He had to stop thinking so much. He had to do this. He had to do this.

His kissed Madaline on the lips and told her to close her eyes. He pressed the sides of her mouth to get her to open wide. He located the offending tooth. He wanted to be sure that he had the right tooth, God forbid. He had gotten a number of different pliers from the toolbox. He had needle nose pliers, vice grip pliers, and the normal kind of pliers in two sizes. He decided to use the needle nose pliers. He started to reach into her mouth with the pliers when he realized that he should really sterilize them. "No, it was not a delaying tactic," he told himself. He needed to think about possible infection. Steve boiled some water on the fire and dunked the pliers. He used another pair of pliers to pull them out of the steaming water. He dried them carefully with a clean towel. Now he was ready.

Madaline was still lying on sofa, silent in her own thoughts. Her hands rested protectively on her belly, cradling the infant inside. She looked helplessly at Steve, opened her mouth and closed her eyes once again.

It was hard to get a good grip on the tooth. There were no flat surfaces, especially on the back. Steve was also having trouble seeing. With the pliers and his hand in the way, he could not get a good view of the tooth. "How do dentists do this?," he muttered in silent frustration.

When he had a decent grip, he bit his lip and twisted the pliers hard. The pliers slipped off the tooth and came free of Madaline's mouth. The subsequent scream and tears wrenched Steve's heart. He knew that it was not his fault, but he felt responsible for her pain. He wanted to change places with her though he knew he could not. If he had been able to switch, would he have felt the same? He wondered.

Ice! That would help. He hurried outside and broke some icicles off the overhang from the roof. He inserted a section of ice inside her lip, and another on the inside of the tooth. He held it there until Madaline stopped whimpering. He could feel the concurrent pain and deadening as the feeling left his fingers where they held the ice. When these pieces melted, he added two more sections. As least this would numb part of the abuse.

Steve sterilized the vice grip pliers as he had done with the others. Maybe these would hold better. They had to.

He adjusted the tension on the pliers and snapped them into place. His luck appeared to be changing. They held tight. Steve climbed on to the sofa with one knee on either side of Madaline, careful not to put any pressure on her mid section. He needed to get as much leverage as possible. This tooth was not going to leave its roots without a good fight. Steve fought back the nausea that was rising from his stomach. He closed his eyes and wrenched the pliers with all of his might.

He heard screaming. It was his own. He looked down at Madaline and she looked dead. She had fainted. Blood was oozing out of the right edge of her mouth. The pliers were still in his hands and they were still attached to the inside of Madaline's head. "Damn, damn, damn, damn, damn." Steve felt like a broken record. Then he stopped. He felt it again. The pliers felt loose. He reached inside Madaline's mouth with his finger. There was blood everywhere. The pliers were still securely attached to the tooth. But, the tooth had come loose. Encouraged, Steve gave another good yank and the tooth ripped free. He raised the bloody pliers in the light and examined his trophy. He was bathed in sweat. His head was spinning.

It was done. The tooth was out. He remarked out loud, though there was no one to hear him, "How can something so small cause so much suffering?"

He used more ice to ease the bleeding. He cleaned up the blood as best he could and he lovingly washed Madaline's face. Madaline revived what seemed like hours later. Her consciousness was short lived. The pain was still too much for her to bear. Fortunately, the human body had its own way of protecting from pain. Madaline relapsed into a restless unconsciousness.

After several days, Madaline was able to eat solids again without too much complaining. Steve had gotten quite adept at mashing her food. Madaline found it uncomfortable to smile, and her vanity prevented her from unwittingly doing so. Even with her mouth closed, she felt ugly. She was certain that part of her lip was sinking into the gap where her tooth had been, thereby distorting her face. Steve's reassurances did little to comfort her. The only thing that eased her self-consciousness was the passage of time. Time was their friend and their enemy.

CHAPTER TWENTY-NINE

The days passed and they waited. They waited for the weather to warm and they waited for Madaline's belly to grow. This was their main focus as there was not even any grass to watch growing. They were happy that the days were growing longer. Amusing themselves was difficult, especially during the nighttime hours when they were not ready to sleep. Without light, they had to rely on their minds and their bodies for entertainment. As Madaline's pregnancy advanced, she became more uncomfortable with lovemaking, so they had to rely more and more on their minds to pass the hours. They played word games such as, "I went on a trip and I took an atomic apple, a big belly, a corrected calendar, a delicious deer, etc." and "Ghost" where each player would give a letter in turn, spelling a word, but trying not to complete a word.

They also spent hours trying out names for the new baby. They had to focus equally on girls' and boys' names. Steve wanted to name the baby after a relative and Madaline wanted to use a biblical name. They easily ruled out "Moon Beam" and "Chastity." They did not want to be trendy. After all, all of the kids in his or her class would have the same name anyway. Each night, they would settle on two names only to trash them the next day. If they named him after Steve's father, he might get called, "Silly Billy" or "Bill the Pill" or even worse, "Wilbur" with a talking horse accent. Or if they named her "Sarah," they might hear the likes of, "Is Sarah doctor in the house?" They realized the ludicrousness of these discussions, but they persisted nevertheless. Thank heaven the sun was setting later each day.

The snow melted and the grass began to grow. The neighborhood was filled with small wildlife, such as birds and chipmunks, which had been absent during the colder months. Everything seemed to be going just great.

"Madaline, Madaline. I've got good news. You remember the old expression, 'Nothing is certain in life except death and taxes'? Well, it's probably sometime in April and we don't have to pay any taxes! No taxation without representation. I never met a tax I didn't like. Tacks should be for holding down carpeting not for robbing hard working people. Withholding, social security, property, federal, state, local, excise, earned income, passive, windfall profits, value added, sales, regressive, progressive, and my all time favorite, retro-active. They're all gone. They don't exist. We can keep one hundred percent of our earnings. What earnings, you say. Earnings, schmearnings, at least there are no taxes."

"You're certainly in a good mood, Steve." Madaline was sitting on the sofa busily knitting. She had pulled a knitted blanket apart and was using the wool to make a baby blanket, some booties, a little cap and a miniature sweater. She had never done much knitting before, so it was trial and error, mostly error. "Let me feel your forehead. Yes, I think I have your diagnosis. You've got Spring fever. Don't worry. It's treatable. I prescribe one dose of summer and it will certainly go away."

"Well, I think you're right. Spring is my favorite season. It is such a romantic time. The flowers are blooming and the birds are singing and it's not so damn cold. Remember, we started officially going out in the spring."

"That seems like so long ago." Madaline turned her attention back to her knitting as she pictured their first spring together in Cambridge. "Knowing what you know now, what would you have done differently?"

"I would have asked you out the minute I met you."

"That very sweet, honey. But I meant, what would you have done differently to impact the world?"

"What do you mean?"

"I don't know. Like, would you have studied medicine to try to find a cure for cancer? Or would you have gone into politics and tried to accomplish world peace?"

"Those are both very worthwhile goals, but I think that the likelihood of either would have been quite slim. But, hey, we have world peace and there doesn't seem to be any cancer floating around, so I guess it worked for now. Let's try not to fight. This world isn't ready for a cold war or even a frying pan war or the war of six stitches. How's the baby doing?"

"I think we'll have to start the world soccer league. This little guy won't stop kicking. Last night, it felt like he was having a fight with himself. He kept lashing out in all different directions."

"How come every time you are complaining about something to do with the baby, suddenly it becomes a 'he'?"

"Well it makes sense doesn't it?"

"You're right." Steve decided to drop the subject, because there was nothing to be gained and Madaline was getting in one of her moods where her logic did not necessarily correspond with Steve's. "You asked me what I would change. On a more practical level, I wish that I had learned more about things, like how to build a clock or how to grow wheat or how to make a generator. There are so many things that we could really use. My mind is cluttered with such useless trivia as quantum mechanics and calculus and French. And the worst of all is history. I guess we should rename it, "future." We can teach our kids about the future. Imagine if Harvard had offered a class on the future. We could have studied about things that had not happened yet. Who'd believe it? I guess fact sometimes is stranger than fiction." Steve paused in deep thought. "You asked what I would have done differently. I wonder what we can do NOW to make a difference. We have the ability to shape the future. We could warn FDR about Pearl Harbor. We could advise JFK about the hazards of convertibles in the hot Texas sun. We could tell Lincoln to avoid thespians." Steve's voice changed as his enthusiasm lapsed into sorrow. "I could keep Foster from joining W or at least off the roof, and I could keep my parents away from the IAPA Meeting."

"Steve, there's nothing we can do about that. We can't change history. Otherwise it wouldn't be history. If things had happened differently, we would know about it. It would have already happened, that is, it would have happened before we ended up back here."

"Maybe we can change things. Maybe there are millions of parallel worlds. Why can't things be different? Think of a room with a mirror on each wall. In one mirror, you see the reflection of the other which shows the image of the first and so on to infinity. Or take a video picture of the television showing the live image from the video camera. Theoretically these images should all be the same to infinity, but eventually they change. There are imperfections in the mirror or dust on the camera lens. These distortions get magnified over time and mutations appear. Eventually the original image may be just a set of dots with no resemblance to the original image. Maybe time does the same thing. Time can have no beginning and ending, so maybe it just keeps repeating itself. Maybe it is cyclical and each time it just changes slightly. We learned about the big bang theory. After the world finishes expanding, it will contract again, eventually leading to another big bang. As it is contracting, does time reverse itself? When the next big bang occurs, the sequence of events will be entirely different. There is no way that things could exactly replicate themselves. I believe that time is more like a yo-yo. It can't be one straight infinite continuum. That would make no sense. Things have to be able to change. We have to try."

"What are you suggesting?"

"I don't know. Maybe we could make a time capsule. We can preserve our warnings for future generations. It's worth a try. Please, Madaline. We have to try."

Madaline put down her knitting. "Okay, dear. What do we do?"

Madaline and Steve spent the next three days preparing the time capsule. They tore key pages of history out of the encyclopedia. They wrote pages of notes about wars and assassinations and diseases. They decided that plastic would outlast metal and since they had a large Tupperware container, this would also be much easier than trying to weld a metal safe. Madaline put some rice in the Tupperware time capsule. She hoped that this might absorb any moisture and help preserve the pages. The last thing they put in was a letter from each of them to their respective parents. This was the hardest thing for them to write. They found that words were not adequate to express their feelings. How can anything replace the warmth of a hug or a kiss? At least this was something. It helped them to face their feelings and their fears and their loneliness. It helped them to close out a major chapter in each of their lives.

The three days went quickly. They both liked having a project. It gave them a sense of purpose. The potential impact of any of this information on the future was overwhelming. What if Kennedy lived? What if the US never entered World War II? What if the AIDS epidemic were stopped early on in central Africa? The time capsule took on a life of its own. They felt reverent as they sealed and burped the container. They covered it with a tarp and buried it on the top of a nearby hill. They marked the site with a large rock on which they engraved with a hammer and chisel a large downward pointing arrow. When they were done, they felt exhilarated. They were very impressed with what they had done. They hoped that it would make a difference. Just in case, they decided to teach their children all that they had written and ask that they pass these stories down through the generations. Madaline had always enjoyed the game, "Whisper down the lane" as a child and wondered what the final messages might be.

Steve and Madaline would never know that the human who found the time capsule spoke no English. Even if he did, he would not have been able to glean any message from the dust that covered the bottom of the plastic vessel.

*   *   *

Spring was bursting out all over. The winter had been harsh on many of the man-made objects unaccustomed to such relentless cold. The macadam of both the driveway and the transported segment of Willow Lane bulged and separated. Large clumps of grass and assorted weeds appeared in the gaps. Healthy rains soon turned the once neatly trimmed yard into a veritable outback. The treasured remains of the gas supply could not be sacrificed for the lawnmower. It did not seem to matter. Steve did not expect the neighbors to complain.

The gas grill fire had burned much of what had been stored in the garage, but Steve still kept some miscellaneous garden tools and other equipment in the open air space. He had to be extra cautious when getting them because a raccoon family had moved in and the mother could be overly protective. Steve had seen enough fangs for one year.

The tire on the over-used wheelbarrow went flat and could not be repaired. Steve managed to fashion a wooden wheel to replace the other. This worked well except it had a rougher ride so more water tended to spill on the return trips.

The greatest loss to date was a large section of the roof that was blown off during an unusually heavy rain storm. Steve nailed a canvas tarp over most of the damaged section. Nevertheless, water continued to make its way into the interior of the house causing the ceilings in his parents' bedroom and later in the living room below to collapse. Steve was glad that his parents could not see what had become of the house that they had struggled to finance and maintain for so many years.

Steve and Madaline gave up trying to relocate the bats to the outside. The upstairs belonged to them. Since they no longer used the indoor plumbing, the tarp across the stairwell remained in place except when they needed something unusual from the attic or a closet.

With the warmer weather, they spent more and more time outside. Some of the smells inside ripened as the warm weather gave them a boost. Steve had no idea how to flush out the backed up plumbing and so they grew accustomed to the ever-present stench. Steve dug a pit several hundred feet from the house. Using logs and mud and a few recycled boards, he built a small outhouse over the pit. He painted a half-moon on the door. Madaline liked that final touch. She spent more and more time staring at the inside of the door with the half-moon painted on the outside. In the corner, next to the door, was a very elaborate spider web. She watched each day as the spider added more rows to his web and collected its victims. She wondered why spiders always seemed to live alone. How did spiders have babies? And how did baby spiders keep from falling between the threads? Everything she saw in nature reminded her of babies. If all went as planned, she should be having her baby within the next few weeks. She could hardly wait. It was so exciting. She was so scared.

One morning as Madaline closed the door to the outhouse, the roof collapsed. Steve heard the noise and his heart stopped. When he turned to look, he saw Madaline standing outside, both hands resting on her belly, surveying the damage.

Steve ran to her, the partially skinned body of a woodchuck still in one hand. "Lin, are you all right?"

"I guess that last deposit I made was just too much for the old girl. I'm glad I was heading out instead of in."

"I'm so sorry. I never was very good at building things. I thought I had plenty of nails in there. I guess my design was flawed, or else the wood was rotten. I was so scared when I heard that noise. If you had been in there . . ." Steve was unable to say the rest.

"I'm fine. Don't worry, nothing happened. I think I'll let you clean up, however. I need to go lie down for a while. I guess the excitement did kind of get to me. Be sure to wash your hands when you're done."

"Yes, mother." Steve's voice sounded mildly sarcastic, but in his heart he was pleased that Madaline would make such a good mother. He did not mind if she practiced a little on him. He, too, was getting excited. He was really looking forward to being a father. He only wished that his parents knew that they were going to be grandparents. They were always so busy, but this would mean a lot to them.

As Steve began to remove the damaged portion of the outhouse in disgust, he received encouragement from an unexpected source. Inside the outhouse, the resident spider was already hard at work repairing the damage to his web. If the spider could do it, so could Steve, only this time he would do it better. He had to. Someday soon, the outhouse would have a new customer.

CHAPTER
THIRTY

The last few weeks of Madaline's pregnancy seemed interminable. Her back became a serious problem. She had constant pains in her lower back and zinging spasms that shot up the left side of her spinal cord. She needed Steve's help with everything, even getting up off the seat after using the outhouse. She was very embarrassed to ask for Steve's help with this, but one time she got stuck. She tried calling for Steve but he was out of earshot. She finally managed to get up by rocking herself forwards and backwards. Her back got strained even worse in the process, so after that, she did not hesitate to ask Steve to stand by.

She was amazed how much she ate. Nothing tasted that good, but she always wanted more. Their reserves of food were dwindling, so the selection became more and more limited. No pickles and ice-cream for this poor expecting mother.

One evening, Madaline stood in front of the mirror in the living room. She had wanted to use the mirror in the master bedroom, but climbing the stairs was out of the question. She had taken her shirt off and was examining the vast expanse of her belly. She did not recognize herself in the reflection. Steve saw her there and came in and stood next to her, admiring the progress. He thought she looked beautiful. She thought she looked abominable. Steve took off his shirt and inflated him tummy as far as he could. Madaline had teased him that he looked pregnant when he did that. Now that he modeled his inflated belly next to the real thing, it was hardly convincing. Steve did not say anything, but he could not remember other pregnant women looking so large. He assumed that it was because he had never seen a pregnant woman au natural before.

Madaline spent the last week mostly in bed. Her feet and ankles were painfully swollen and her back was degenerating further. She was desperate to having her baby because she could not imagine that child birth could be any worse than this stage of being pregnant. She even had to ask for Steve's help to roll to her other side. It had been a long time since she had slept in her favorite position, on her stomach.

Steve tried to make her as comfortable as possible. He gave her feet massages every evening before going to sleep. He rested his head gently on the mound of her belly and listened to the myriad of sounds within. He never tired of feeling the small feet kicking. Madaline, on the other hand, was not as endeared to this sensation. She could not escape the kicking by simply removing her hand from her belly.

Madaline napped constantly during the day because she did not sleep well at night. It seemed obvious that her little baby did not tell time well and was unaware of customary sleeping protocol.

They did not know what day of the week it was let alone what day of the month, so they decided that they would set their child's birthday as June 30th, or the day the corn stalks reached one foot in height. Madaline would experiment and find some way of making a cake in order to celebrate this special birthday every year. She would have plenty of time for that. Now she needed to focus on having her baby. She and Steve both read as much as they could find in the encyclopedia. Steve searched through all of the other books in addition looking for something helpful. There was not much. His parents had had the advantage of a doctor and a hospital and their parents and friends for advice. Steve and Madaline were completely on their own.

Steve was asleep when he felt something tugging at his arm. It was Madaline. Her water had broken. The next nineteen hours lasted an eternity and yet were over in a blurred flash. They knew to time the contractions, but they were not sure why. There was no hospital to rush to when the contractions grew closer. Steve jerry-rigged stirrups to elevate Madaline's feet. He used the backs of two chairs and attached two padded belts to support the ankles. He got clean sheets, boiled some water and sharpened a knife to cut the umbilical cord. He was not sure what the boiled water was for, but they always told someone to boil water in the movies, so he did not want to be caught short in case some mysterious need arose. If nothing else, he could use the water once it had cooled to clean the baby and Madaline.

The activity helped keep Steve from getting too nervous. Madaline tried to rest as much as possible to conserve her energy. The contractions which were coming closer together and getting more intense made resting difficult. Some of her muscles already felt like her jaw muscles used to after having her mouth hyper-extended by the dental hygienist at her semi-annual cleanings.

The day started off cool, but as the afternoon advanced, the air in the house grew stagnant and heavy with humidity. Steve tried to keep Madaline comfortable with damp cloths. He felt like a Roman slave standing over her fanning her with a magazine.

It was still light outside when the screaming started. Steve felt helpless. He tried not to let Madaline know how scared he was. He kept saying, "Everything is going to be just fine." He hoped that he was not lying to her.

As the sun began to set, Steve's energy began to wane. He had been awake with Madaline since the middle of the previous night. He berated himself for feeling tired. Madaline was the one doing all of the hard work.

Shortly after 9:00 o'clock, Madaline let out a prolonged yell. She started breathing very rapidly. Between her legs, Steve could see the small head beginning to crown. She was having the baby. Steve shouted, "Okay now, push. Give it all you've got." They were not sure how to time the pushing with the contractions. Somehow, in spite of all their ignorance, the baby began to emerge, slowly at first, and then with a final push, it slid all the way out, dragging its umbilical cord and lots of slimy tissue and fluid with it. Steve eased it out from between Madaline's legs and placed it on a clean white towel. He was flooded with emotions. He could see that it was a boy. He had had a son. Madaline had given birth to a boy. But he looked so ugly, all mashed and contorted. No, he was the most beautiful baby he had ever seen. He was a father. He was so proud. Madaline was so wonderful.

Steve cleaned the baby as best he could and place him in Madaline's arms. The miniature lungs announced to the world that he would be a force to be reckoned with. With a quick slash of the knife, Steve severed the umbilical cord. Their son was now on his own, a living, breathing human being.

Madaline looked exhausted. She tried to relax, swimming in the joys of parenthood. But the contractions continued. They were even more painful than before. Madaline was too tired to even scream. Why was she still having contractions? Was she going to die? She wanted to enjoy her baby, and now this.

For some reason, Steve looked between her legs again. He thought that his eyes deceived him. There was another small head trying to burst into the world. Madaline did not believe him, but she pushed anyway. Whatever it was, she wanted to get it out so she could rest. Steve took back their son and laid him carefully on the floor in a blanket. He wanted to hold him so badly, but he had to help Madaline.

This time it took longer. Madaline was too tired to push as hard, but finally, the second baby, another boy, was born to Madaline and Steve Harris. He was smaller than the first and darker in color, almost purple. He did not cry like his brother had. Suddenly Steve panicked. "Babies are supposed to cry, aren't they?" he thought to himself, afraid to alarm Madaline. He had to do something. He picked his second son up by the legs. He had seen that done on television. He spanked him gently but firmly. Still the only crying was from his older brother. Steve put him done and thought fast. There was a thin film across his face. Steve wiped it away with a towel. He spanked him again and this time the baby cried, quietly at first and then with more energy as his lungs filled with air. Steve could hardly breathe himself he was so excited, distraught, tired, proud, scared and happy. Tears streamed down his cheeks. He finished cleaning the newest born and placed him next to Madaline. He gathered the first baby off the floor and held him tightly. Then he put him near his mother as well. Madaline was too tired to do anything besides hold them and kiss them each once. Soon she was asleep, a peaceful smile painted on her face.

Steve sat down in the chair, overcome with fatigue. Inside, he was jumping for joy. He could not believe it. God had blessed them with two healthy children. Twins!

*   *   *

Steve and Madaline loved being parents, except for one thing—Diapers! They had cut up some blankets and made plastic pants from garbage bags, but it seemed like they were always running out of clean diapers. Madaline was in charge of nursing, so Steve was appointed head laundry man. As Steve made the regular trek to the stream with a wheelbarrow full of odoriferous diapers, he wished that he were able to nurse the babies instead. No matter how hard he scrubbed the diapers on the rocks, he was never able to get out all of the residue. Gradually the diapers turned a dingy shade of brown.

Steve was careful to collect their drinking water upstream from where he did the laundry. The environmentalist in him would berate himself for polluting the stream, but he could figure out no other feasible alternatives.

Naming their sons proved to be more difficult than they could have anticipated. They continued their nightly debates over different names. A week after the boys had been born; they still referred to them as the "Bigger One" and the "Smaller One." They were fraternal twins, so they did not look exactly the same, but their differing sizes were the most distinguishing features.

Finally, Madaline put her foot down. "We are going to decide once and for all on names for these children tonight. It doesn't really matter what we name them. The important thing is that they have names. You name the Bigger One and I'll name the Smaller One. We're each allowed one veto if we can't stand the name. Agreed?"

"Fine. I have mine picked. I want to name him after my two grandfathers. My mother's father was Calvin and my father's father was Clayton. How does Calvin Clayton Harris sound?"

"I don't know. Calvin is kind of a strange name. It reminds me a little of Alvin, one of the Chipmunks."

"Well, if you don't like it, you can use your one and only veto, but then you're stuck with whatever I decide."

"Okay, you win. Calvin Clayton it is."

"And what about your name for the Smaller One?"

Madaline had decided weeks ago on her favorite name, but she was afraid that Steve would not like it. She decided to take a risk and invoke the rules of the game. "I think I'll name him after one of Noah's sons, Ham. And for a middle name, Lot, for the son of Haran. I think that those are nice biblical names."

"Ham Lot Harris. You've got to be kidding." Madaline did not respond. She maintained her best poker face. "I think that I have to use my veto. I'm only doing this with the kid's best interests at heart. I'm sorry."

"That's okay, dear. In that case, we'll name him Abraham Luke Harris."

After hearing Ham Lot, Abraham Luke sounded wonderful to Steve. "That sounds just fine. If he doesn't like the name Abraham, he can go by Luke. So, Calvin and Abraham it is. Now that wasn't so hard, was it?"

CHAPTER
THIRTY-ONE

Ten more winters came and went. Steve learned how to till the fields and became an accomplished hunter. Madaline spent half of this time pregnant and most of the rest of the time nursing. Six more healthy children were born to Steve and Madaline during this decade. They named them Thomas, Joan, Jennifer, Elizabeth, Robert and Fiona.

Sadly, their fourth child died within minutes of being born. She was premature and her lungs had never fully developed. While Madaline held Thomas, and Calvin and Abraham played nearby, Steve dug a grave and they buried their first daughter. Madaline read from the Bible and wept as she said a prayer. Steve choked back his tears but was unable to speak. Finally he said, "Since it is my turn to name our child, I would like to name this baby Hope. We will always have Hope in our hearts. May God keep and protect her and give us strength to carry on without her." Madaline started to hum a hymn as Steve covered the small body with dirt. She only managed a few notes before grief overcame her. The service continued in silence except for the occasional squeals from the twins.

Ten years had been hard on the house. Most of the paint had peeled and some of the wood had rotted. The cinderblock frame for the lab and the brick facing on the house were the only parts that remained unaltered. Steve had patched other parts of the house as best he could. With the growing family, they needed to expand their winter quarters beyond the family room and the kitchen. The easiest space to insulate was the dining room. Steve built bunk beds along two of the walls. The living room became the play area. With the second fireplace, they were able to heat this area as well. Consequently, it meant that Steve had to prepare twice as much firewood before each winter. As the nearby trees were felled, this task became more and more onerous. The wheelbarrow was rusting through and Steve was anxious about what he would do to transport the wood so far once the wheelbarrow had disintegrated.

Calvin and Abraham were good workers. Even Thomas and Joan would sometimes accompany Steve to the stream for water or more firewood. The older kids enjoyed working in the gardens. Steve was happy to have their help because he hated gardening. He also hated doing laundry, so he appreciated Abraham's and Joan's help with this. One time when Steve nearly bled to death from a close encounter with a black bear protecting her cub, the kids assumed all of his chores. They were quick studies and eager to learn.

Calvin and Thomas especially enjoyed hunting. They would sometimes come home with dead squirrels and birds, victims of their slingshots. Calvin also loved to fish. Abraham would often go with his twin to the stream and sit on the bank and read while Calvin fished. Abraham loved the rippling noise of the water as it flowed over the rocks.

Madaline and Steve frequently were amazed at how different the twins were. Abraham never did catch up to Calvin in size. While Madaline had good luck teaching all of her children how to read and do math, Calvin had the most trouble concentrating and learning. He seemed as smart as the other children but he usually stared out the window instead of paying attention. The only time he seemed to pay close attention was when Steve or Madaline was teaching them something about science. Calvin liked building things and exploring new places. Abraham preferred to explore new places and different times through reading.

For their tenth birthday, Madaline and Steve gave Calvin a new fishing rod. Steve had fashioned the rod from an oak sapling and had shaped several nails to create a triple pronged hook. Calvin was delighted. Abraham received a book on the presidents of the United States and a new writing pad. When Abraham had heard that there was a president named after him, he became obsessed with the notion of becoming president one day. He even designed a cabinet appointing each of his siblings to different cabinet posts. If they did something to annoy him, he would demote them to an aide or if they really made him mad, he would assign them to state government posts. This angered the other kids even though they did not understand what it meant. From the spark in Abraham's eyes, they knew that it must be something bad. Abraham would often come into the house covered with dirt and bruises after an attack from Calvin or even some of the younger kids. He was good at teasing, but he was not good at defending himself or fighting back.

After the twins had finished eating the wheat cake that Madaline had made for their birthday, Calvin invited Abraham to go to the stream with him to try out the new fishing rod. It was a sunny day and Abraham had his new book to read, so he thought that would be fun. Madaline and Steve kissed them goodbye and wished them a happy birthday. Madaline told them to be back by dinnertime. She promised that she would fix a special fish dinner if Calvin caught anything.

On the way to the stream, Calvin kept kicking stones at Abraham and trying to trip him. Finally, Abraham turned on Calvin in anger. Calvin flinched because he thought his smaller brother was actually going to hit him. Instead, Abraham shouted, "You are hereby removed from the cabinet. I make you an under-secretary to the minister of foreign affairs for the state of Wallacesylvania." Calvin hit Abraham. Abraham fled and yelled back, "And I revoke your parking privileges." Calvin tried to chase Abraham, but Abraham was faster. His rapid legs had saved him many times in the past from the wrath of his bigger twin.

When Calvin got to his normal fishing spot, Abraham was already there reading his book. Calvin left him alone, but said just loud enough for Abraham to hear, "You're a spastic weenie."

Abraham looked up from his book, anger lining his eyes. "You're the spastic weenie, bear behind breath. And you can call me 'Mr. President.'"

Calvin looked at Abraham. He had made himself a nametag that said, "President Abe Lincoln." Abraham stuck his tongue out at Calvin.

"Whatever you say, Mrs. President."

"Take that back, you ignorant toadstool." Abraham threw a stick at Calvin. It missed and splashed in the water beyond.

Calvin put down his fishing rod and climbed the rock to Abraham's perch. He grabbed the nametag off of Abraham's chest and tore it into three pieces. He then yanked the book out of Abraham's hands and leapt back down to the water's edge. Calvin held the book out over the water threatening to drop it in. Abraham scrambled down the rock to rescue his birthday gift. Just as he got to Calvin, he tripped and unintentionally kicked Calvin's fishing rod into the water. Calvin watched as the rod disappeared into the dark running water. Calvin let out a piercing war cry and spun around with the book smacking Abraham squarely in the head. The impact knocked Abraham off his feet into the water where his head hit a rock. Calvin looked, stunned by what had happened. He studied Abraham's body as it lay face down in the water. He made no move to help his brother. Abraham's legs were swept slowly away from the shore and then the current caught his body and it began to drift downstream. Calvin stayed where he was. He knew that he should do something, but a small voice inside his head said, "Let him go. He's nothing but trouble. He always gets half of whatever is rightfully yours. Let him go. It was an accident. Mom and Dad will understand."

Soon Abraham's body disappeared from sight. Calvin looked down at his hands. He still held Abraham's book on the presidents. Without further thought, he threw the book into the water and watched it sink. "So long, Mr. President." Calvin sat down on the rock. He had to think. He needed to get his story straight before telling his parents what had happened to Abraham.

*　　*　　*

Thomas and Joan were helping Steve weed and water the cornfield. Calvin ran the last few hundred feet to the house. He wanted to make his concern seem real. Madaline was nursing Fiona on the front steps. She saw Calvin appear over the rise.

"Mom, Mom, it's Abraham."

Madaline shouted toward the field, "Steve, come quick. Something's happened to Abraham." Calvin stopped near his mother on the steps, looking wet and slightly winded. "What happened, honey? Where's Abraham?"

"He fell in the stream. I couldn't get him out. It was terrible. I tried to save him. I lost my new fishing rod trying to help him."

Madaline was beginning to panic as Calvin was talking. Steve came running from the field. "Calvin, tell me what happened?"

"A giant snake bit Abraham while he was reading. He tried to get away from the snake. Abraham jumped in the water to get away from the snake, but the snake followed him. I saw him trying to beat the snake to get it to leave him alone. I jumped in to help him and the snake tried to get me. I was able to get away from the snake, but by the time I looked back for Abraham, he had disappeared. I think he must have drowned. I think that the snake bite must have killed him."

Steve grabbed Calvin by the arm and dragged him toward the stream. "Come with me Calvin. Show me where this happened. Maybe we can find your brother." Steve did not know how much to believe. Calvin had a wild imagination and would often tell unbelievable tales. Nevertheless, he wanted to be sure Abraham was all right. Madaline handed Fiona to Tommy and told the other kids to wait in the house. She ran after Steve and Calvin. She did not want to believe Calvin, but she could not help the tears that began to pour down her face.

Calvin led them back to the stream. There was no sign of Abraham. Steve and Madaline shouted his name. Calvin did, too. Steve wandered around looking for clues. He could see footprints near the water, but there was nothing too unusual. He saw something lodged on a rock a short ways downstream. He walked through the undergrowth along the banks to get a closer look. It was Calvin's fishing pole. Steve began to get worried. This corroborated Calvin's story so far. Maybe something had happened to Abraham.

Back near the rock, Madaline found two pieces of torn paper. There was writing on them. It looked like Abraham's penmanship. One read, "INCOLN." The other read, "ABE L." Madaline screamed. She knew the story of Cain and Abel. She feared the worst. How could her son, her first born, be a murderer? She refused to believe it.

When Steve saw the pieces of paper, he looked somberly at Madaline. When they asked Calvin how the paper got there and why it was torn, Calvin appeared caught in a lie. He hesitated and then said that the snake must have ripped it. Madaline and Steve were horrified to think that the creature that had torn the paper had most likely been the same to cause Abraham's death. But they did not think it was a giant snake.

Darkness forced them to give up the search. When they got back to the house, the other children were all crying. They had never before been left alone for so long.

Calvin stuck firmly to his story. He got angry when they kept questioning him. They never did find Abraham or his body. They were left not only with great sadness but also the evil suspicion that the death had not been an accident. They could not have felt more anguish. Steve and Madaline forbid any of the other children to go fishing with Calvin alone. They said that the water was too dangerous. In their hearts they dreaded that their oldest son was the true source of the danger. That night in bed, when she could stop crying, Madaline whispered to Steve, "If we can't keep our own children from killing each other, how can we ever guarantee world peace? If the Bible speaks the truth, then the entire world will descend from our family. How can this evil be stopped? How can we keep from destroying ourselves?"

Happy birthday, Calvin. Happy birthday, Abraham.

CHAPTER
THIRTY-TWO

Madaline and Steve and their children went on to invent and reinvent many things. Their greatest frustration was in knowing the benefits of something but not having all of the components necessary to make it. Even something as basic and simple as paper eluded them. Gradually many of the supplies that they found in closets and drawers throughout the house were used up and they had to learn to cope without them. Sometimes when they took one step forward, they slid back two steps in the interim.

One day, Madaline was lying in a vine hammock cradling her newest granddaughter in her arms. In the yard, Elizabeth and Fiona were minding their nephews and nieces. Steve came out of the house with a hollowed out gourd carrying some water for Madaline. He attracted her attention when he shouted, "Yubba dubba do!"

Madaline surveyed the scene in the backyard and smiled. Half of the children were wearing tattered cloth hand-me-downs. The others were wearing pants and shirts made from different animal skins. Even their toys seemed primitive. There were no battery-operated, noise-generating, mind-numbing toys in sight. The stone and wooden toys were all user-propelled.

Everyone had chores to do, but there was plenty of time for the younger children to play. Madaline and Steve felt that it was important for the kids to have a real childhood free from the worries and concerns that dominate the minds of responsible adults.

They treasured these times for their children and grandchildren because in some ways they felt that they had been cheated out of part of their childhoods. They had not planned on growing up so quickly.

Birth control devices were not high on their list of necessary inventions. Having kids was a lot of work, but the alternative was inconceivable. Steve and Madaline had five more children. Each of their children had at least four children except for their youngest daughter who was unable to conceive. Within two generations, there were scores of Harris' swarming all over Harrisburg. After one more generation, there were hundreds.

Madaline and Steve discussed sex openly with their offspring. They did not want any shame associated with a function that was mandatory to perpetuate their species. Inbreeding was a grave concern, but there were no alternatives. Four of their grandchildren had physical disabilities of varying severity. Madaline continued to teach the children and was sad to see some of her grandchildren having great difficulty grasping new concepts. Some of her younger children proved to be excellent teachers and Madaline recruited them to help with the slower learners.

By the time the first great grandchild was born, the Harris family had outgrown the original homestead. New homes began to dot the countryside as the second generation began to spread out. The homes were generally one-room log cabins with a stone fireplace and a large water storage compartment.

It seemed like a new great grandchild was being born every week. In one week, shortly after a very heavy snowstorm, the first great great-grandchild, Geoffrey, was born and two days later Steve and Madaline's 63rd grandchild, Christian, was born (okay, so his parents were a bit progressive for their time). As they were growing up, Geoff loved to introduce his great uncle who was two days younger and two inches shorter than he was.

Madaline gave up trying to send birthday rocks, a clever innovation in a paperless society. She had trouble even keeping track of the names. She was so confused, yet she was so happy. She was always willing to baby-sit. Looking back to when she had been in college, she could not have imagined herself one day being perfectly content, rocking her great great-granddaughter in her arms.

No matter how many good things happen in life, it seems that something bad always has to happen to overshadow the rest.

*   *   *

One of their older grandchildren, Guede, had recently built a new cabin near the stream. He and his family were sleeping soundly one hot summer night. The coals in the outdoor grill area from the evening meal had not been properly covered and a breeze blew some dried grass onto the coals. They ignited and spread to the dried grass surrounding the grill. The flames swept quickly toward the cabin and soon engulfed the outside walls. The only one to fully awaken from the smoke was the baby, and the others ignored his howling. The next day, Guede's uncle found the charred remains of the cabin covering the unrecognizable bodies of the entire family. The bones of the baby were found outside of his crib. He must have climbed over the sides, but died before he could crawl to his parents' bed to arouse them.

Robert, Steve and Madaline's fourth oldest son, had captured and domesticated some goats. He had bred them and had a large flock that he used for milk and meat. After the fire, Robert gave a goat to each household. The goat was to be tied near the front door to act as an alarm for fire or other danger such as large predators. This failed miserably. After a while, most of the goats were kept in pens far away from the houses. There had been too many false alarms.

*   *   *

Bad things always seem to happen in threes. The following week, two of Joan's grandchildren left the house to collect berries and go fishing. They were cousins and were both ten years old. They had not returned by dinnertime. A futile search that evening was terminated by darkness. The next day, the search continued as hundreds of aunts and uncles and cousins scoured the countryside. They never found any traces. Madaline and Steve could not help but think of Abraham. That night, the other parents all tucked their children in extra tight and gave them an additional hug and kiss. Life is so precious and yet so fragile.

The third incident nearly killed the patriarch of the family. Steve's activities had become somewhat curtailed due to a bad back, but he still insisted on making the long journey to the stream to collect water for his household. Sometimes several grandchildren or great grandchildren would go along with him and sometimes he would go alone.

Two days after Joan's grandchildren had disappeared; Madaline was in the remains of the family room sewing together some black cloth to make a funeral shroud for her great grandsons. Joan's daughters, Sarah and Lisa, did not want to acknowledge that their children were dead. They wanted to keep on looking and hoping. Madaline, however, firmly believed that it was important to have some closure. They would hold a simple service and pray that God look over them wherever they might be.

As Madaline was sewing, there were women working in the kitchen and children playing at her feet. She recognized some of them but she did not know their names. She knew all 64 of her grandchildren, but she could only name a few of the nearly four hundred great grandchildren who occasionally came to visit. She reckoned that there also were probably a couple hundred great great-grandchildren crawling and running around the homes of Harrisburg.

As she was adding some finishing stitches, she heard a great commotion in the yard. The women in the kitchen and some of the children rushed out to investigate. Madaline followed.

The sight that greeted her eyes nearly took her breath away. Three of her grandsons were carrying Steve and they were all covered with blood. She had no doubt that it was all Steve's blood. One of the grandsons, she could not remember his name just then, gave a sketchy report. His son had found Steve in the woods being mauled by a large brown bear. The boy had managed to lure the bear away from Steve using himself as bait. He knew the woods well and had headed straight for the thickest underbrush where the bear's passage was severely hindered. The youngster made it safely back to his house where he got help for Steve. He was unharmed except for a lot of scratches. He was proud that he had saved his great grandfather, but he was mortified that he had wet his pants in the process.

Madaline examined Steve's wounds. Several of the gashes were quite deep. She needed to stop the bleeding. Steve was already looking anemic. With the help of some of the women who had been in the kitchen, Madaline made thick mudpacks. She applied these compresses to each of the wounds and covered them with damp cloths. If she could stop the bleeding, she would worry about infection later.

The bloodied grandsons carried Steve into the house and tried to make him comfortable on the sofa in the family room. Two of the legs of the sofa had broken and Steve had removed the other two, so the sofa now sat on the floor. This was fortunate because Steve rolled off the sofa several times that night as he tossed about with a rising fever. The next day, Madaline started to prepare herself for the death of her husband. They had been through so much together. Madaline could hardly believe that he would be taken from her in this manner. She started saying her prayers. Later that night, his fever broke and he began to accept liquids. It was several weeks before Steve had the strength to do more than hobble outside and sit in the shade. Eventually he regained his strength, but somehow after that he looked older to Madaline. The next time she looked in a mirror, she realized that she, too, looked much older. Nevertheless, in spite of her hair that was mostly white, she still looked beautiful. Ever since they had run out of shampoo many years ago, she had worn her hair short. Fidgeting with her hair in front of the cracked mirror, she made a decision. She was going to grow her hair long again. Steve would like that, she assured herself.

EPILOGUE

Many more winters passed and many more babies shed their first tears as they entered this cold, hard world. Madaline and Steve could hardly have been happier. They were frustrated that they were increasing unable to do many things themselves, but they were pleased that so many of their offspring competed to provide assistance.

They had moved into a new home nearer to the stream. The second floor of their house had submitted to the ravages of the weather and the years and had collapsed. This had destroyed the ground floor in the process. Some of the materials had been used in building their new house. Two great grandsons had moved the entire chimney and fireplace from the family room brick by brick and had reassembled it on the end of the new house. Steve liked the new house because it was on a hill and had a wonderful view. He enjoyed sitting on the front porch with Madaline talking about their lives. He could talk about the same thing night after night and never get bored. Steve was obsessed with the concepts of time and space. He still believed that if his parents could master time travel, so could he. Madaline would smile and endure. After all of these years, she was still in love.

Steve could still walk, but only with assistance. One of their granddaughters had fixed them a delicious eggplant parmesan-of-sorts dinner. After sipping their warm herbal after-dinner drink, Steve asked Madaline if she would like to take a stroll. Madaline still took many walks herself and was delighted that her husband was feeling well enough to come along. They wandered slowly up the slope behind the house. Madaline held Steve's arm and he held his two canes. At the top of the incline, they stopped to rest. Steve stared deeply into Madaline's eyes.

"I married the most beautiful girl in the world."

"No, you married the oldest girl in the world."

"Well, I always knew the value of a good antique." Madaline playfully slapped his arm. "You look so lovely with your hair hanging down your back. When we get back to the house, maybe you can do your imitation of Lady Godiva for me." Again, Madaline brushed his arm with a gentle swing.

"I love you so much."

"I love you, too, Lin. More than you can imagine. I remember telling you not to come with me back in time. I thought it would be too dangerous. I have often thought what it would have been like without you. I am glad that you were so brave and foolish."

"I can't imagine a life without you in it, either. I must admit that things did not turn out as I had originally anticipated. I think that I will never get over my craving for chocolate. Maybe someday soon, one of our offspring who inherited my sweet tooth will invent a good facsimile. Then my life would be fulfilled."

The sun was getting lower in the sky. Suddenly two foxes ran past them apparently unperturbed by the human obstacles. Steve and Madaline were equally startled and Steve grabbed for Madaline's arm to support himself and to comfort her. They looked in the direction in which the foxes had disappeared. They could not locate the foxes, but their eyes, nevertheless, met a marvelous sight. They saw two elephants lumbering across the field on the far side of the stream. They seemed so incongruous. Their faith in their vision was further tested when they saw two tigers and a pair of penguins ambling along together. Steve rubbed his eyes. Madaline blinked. Then they heard thunder.

"Madaline, honey, do you see what I see?" Madaline nodded affirmatively. "I suppose that this is what happens when Alzheimer's disease sets in. I hope that you did not catch it from me."

"Steve, darling, we had better head back to the house."

"That's a good idea, my love. It looks like rain."

www.ingramcontent.com/pod-product-compliance
Lightning Source LLC
Chambersburg PA
CBHW021510240626
47154CB00002B/570